An Admission of Weakness

by

Erik Walter

An Admission of Weakness

Books by this Author:

Loving Johnny
The Music Professor
No Regrets
The Man Next Door
Just My Luck
Never Again
The Gallery
The Inheritance
The Storm
A Home for Stewart
Logan and Buddy's Story
The Reunion
To Slay a Dragon
Journey Back to Green Grove
An Extraordinary Ordinary Man
The Fortune Teller
The Songbird Sang
The Chosen Ones
Always Yours
The Kidnapping
The Founding of Green Grove
The Crop Duster
The Impostor
An Admission of Weakness

An Admission of Weakness

Foreword

The Butterfields are a family with secrets. Naomi is a devoted mother and wife, but she has a secret life about which her husband knows nothing. Katie, the eldest daughter, has a secret love. Camilla, the younger daughter, has fallen for a man intended for someone else. Justin wants a career of his own, but his father has different plans for his life. Ruby, the grandmother, is hiding something from her family as well.
Blair, the oldest son, has perhaps the biggest secrets of all.

Robbie Lee is from an underprivileged family in Mississippi. He reveals his secret in a very public manner and is forced to flee for his life.

It turns out it's not so simple to be honest with the people they care about; it's easier to lie, at least until it isn't.
Can these people overcome the obstacles they've created for themselves and open their hearts to true love?

Only time will tell...

An Admission of Weakness

"My father always told me
that what's wrong with lying
is that it's an admission
of weakness.
If you're the strongest,
you can afford to tell
the truth.
— K. J. Parker

Above all, don't lie to yourself. The man who
lies to himself and listens to his own lie comes
to a point that he cannot distinguish the truth
within him…and having no respect, he ceases
to love.
— Fyodor Dostoevsky

An Admission of Weakness

CHAPTER ONE

"You got ten seconds to git outa my house and off my property!" Otis Lee shouted angrily while he clumsily brandished an ancient double-barreled shotgun.

"Put the gun down, Otis!" his wife Flora exclaimed. "You know you ain't gonna shoot him."

"The hell I ain't!" he yelled.

The forty year old woman attempted to wrestle the weapon from her husband's hands, but he shoved her aside impatiently and resumed aiming it at his eldest son.

"If you want to shoot me, Pa," Robbie did his best to appear unafraid, "go ahead. The best thing for this family would be if your worthless ass sits in jail for the rest of your life."

He glanced at his four wide-eyed sisters. They ranged from ages seven to fourteen and were horrified by the scene unfolding in front of them. His sixteen year old brother Rhett had disappeared before the confrontation began.

Robert Eustace Lee, or Robbie as he was known, was the oldest Lee child at eighteen. He was named after his father's hero, Civil War General Robert E. Lee, as well as his mother's great-grandfather. Their tiny village of Toadback, Mississippi was named for Grandpa

An Admission of Weakness

Eustace's uncanny ability to catch toads in the local swamp after dark.

The town consisted of a dilapidated restaurant called The Muddy Pig, so named for its signature dish, a sort of pork/gravy/potato concoction. The Pig, as it was locally known, was owned by a pair of bachelor twin brothers named Elmer and Delmer. It featured a pool table and bar and was the favored hangout for the local men after work.

Besides the restaurant, there was also a two room post office, a Southern Baptist church, a decaying general store filled with mostly outdated grocery items, and a few dozen houses badly in need of paint.

The streets were unpaved and often muddy and rutted, and weeds grew tall and abundantly in vacant lots and on the street corners. The only sidewalk in town extended from the post office and church to the restaurant, and a single pole light lit up the business district.

Most of the town's citizens worked at the meat-packing business located just west of town. Its greedy owners enjoyed a luxurious lifestyle while barely paying a living wage to their two hundred employees.

Otis worked in the fly-infested facility as a janitor and handyman. He made homemade whiskey on the side with his brother Cletus to pay the bills. Unfortunately, he and Cletus drank more moonshine than they sold.

An Admission of Weakness

Meanwhile, Flora was employed as a cook/waitress at the restaurant. She worked ten hours a day, six days a week, and spent her days off sleeping. She had been a pretty, idealistic young woman when she married Otis. Years of hard work had made her face careworn, her hands roughened, and her shoulders stooped.

In spite of being employed, the Lees struggled to pay their bills and put food on the table. The only vehicle they owned was a decrepit, thirty year old Ford pickup. Otis drove it to work every day, leaving Flora to walk to the restaurant.

The Lee family lived in a weathered, ramshackle house by the side of a dirt road on the northern edge of the village. It was little more than a shack with two bedrooms, one for Otis and Flora and one for the four girls. Robbie and his sixteen year old brother Rhett shared the worn sofa bed's wafer-thin mattress. The children attended a rundown school in a nearby town. It had a surprisingly good curriculum, thanks to its few dedicated teachers. Robbie worked hard at his studies and was at the top of his class. It was his plan to go to college, and he knew the only way that would happen is if he got a full scholarship. When he wasn't studying, he spent his time helping his siblings with their homework, getting them ready for school each morning,

An Admission of Weakness

cooking their supper, and washing their clothes. He did the grocery shopping and maintained the house and lawn as best he could.

He did his chores willingly and without complaint because he knew if he didn't take care of things, no one would. His siblings were counting on him for the love and discipline they didn't get from their indifferent parents. It wasn't that their mother was unkind; she was too tired to show them any attention, good or bad, but she knew Robbie had the household under control.

Otis, on the other hand, was usually brusque and impatient with the children, especially Robbie. It almost seemed he held a grudge against the youth, although Robbie had no idea why. He tried to stay under the radar when his father was around.

Thankfully, Otis and Cletus spent most evenings in the tumbledown shed out back where they made their illegal whiskey. Toadback's sole police officer was one of their best customers, so they didn't worry about being shut down by the authorities.

It was thanks to Robbie that his sisters were excelling at their schoolwork. He knew that an education was crucial if any of them wanted to get out of Toadback. He couldn't bear the thought of his brother and sisters spending their lives working at the meatpacking plant, so he made sure every day to remind them that the sky was the limit as far as their futures went. As for himself, he was determined to get as far from Toadback as possible. He was going to get his degree in business, and then he planned to become the CEO of some big corporation in any state that wasn't in the South.

He was young, but he had seen enough of the ignorance and right-wing conservatism that plagued the southern states from Texas to Florida. His father was a far-right extremist who believed every American should be white, heterosexual, and Christian. He had had numerous arguments with him on the subject that always led to shouting matches. His mother would be forced to intervene. Unfortunately, she always sided with her husband to keep the peace. Robbie merely wanted him to understand that everyone deserved equal rights regardless of their gender, sexual orientation, skin color, or religious beliefs. It was pointless, he knew, but he had to keep trying.

There were few people more racist or homophobic than his father, although everyone of his acquaintance was bigoted. For his own safety, he had kept his sexuality a secret. No one knew he was gay, not even Rhett, who was his closest friend in the world. He trusted him to keep his secret, but the boy had enough with which to deal without adding to his problems.

An Admission of Weakness

Aside from coping with distant parents and extreme poverty, Rhett was also dyslexic, had a speech impediment, and was born with a weak leg for which he was forced to wear a brace. He struggled with his schoolwork, so Robbie spent a lot of extra time with him to make sure he made it through his classes.

Rhett looked like the rest of the Lee children. He was blonde with blue eyes, and he had a bewitching smile. Unlike the others, however, he was too thin and somewhat frail. Robbie watched over him like a mother hen and worried that the boy might fall behind once he left for college.

It was only due to Robbie that his brother and sisters were capable of critical thinking. If left to their father and community, they would grow up as narrow-minded and bigoted as the adults in their lives. Robbie was careful to teach them that every person had value and deserved happiness. There was no place for hatred, he told them. It was better that he was indoctrinating them with love instead of the things taught to them by television or their local Baptist minister.

So what had led up to the confrontation with his father? It all started with the valedictorian speech at his commencement ceremony.

The event was to be held in the school's gymnasium on a hot, humid day. The dozen or

An Admission of Weakness

so fans blew the hot air around but did little to cool the huge room. Parents and families of the graduates sat in the uncomfortable folding chairs, sweating and waving hand-held fans in a futile attempt to alleviate the discomfort from the oppressive heat.
As the valedictorian, Robbie was expected to address the crowd. He was generally a confident, happy person, but he was nervous about giving this particular speech.

He stood in front of the cracked mirror in the Lee's tiny bathroom one evening and studied his reflection. Not so bad, he decided. Whisper soft, dirty-blonde hair, soulful eyes almost a royal blue, an ingenuous smile, and an athletic build from years of hard work. He maintained a short beard and mustache more out of convenience than anything.

An Admission of Weakness

His physical appearance was unimportant to him. He kept his teeth brushed and his body clean, but the appeal of designer clothes and stylish haircuts was lost on him. He had more important things to deal with, such as making sure Rhett and his sisters were safe and had every opportunity for a happy, prosperous future.

He was unaware of it, but his tousled hair and scruffy beard were quite attractive to the opposite sex. The girls at school flirted with him on a daily basis, but he seemed not to notice.

However, there was one particular boy who had caught his attention. His name was Aaron, and

An Admission of Weakness

Robbie thought he was beautiful. Of course, Aaron was presumably straight, so it didn't matter anyway.
It wasn't like he had time to be involved with anyone. He had more than he could handle as it was. Still, it was pleasurable to watch Aaron sit with his friends in the cafeteria or run up and down the football field.

But back to his speech. He had made the terrifying decision to use it as the vehicle in which he came out and stood up for himself and other gay students.
It was frightening because he was pretty sure he knew how people would react. He would be lucky if they didn't tar and feather him and run him out of town or even shoot him. Folks around Toadback liked their guns and thought gay people were an abomination that should be eradicated from the face of the earth.
Their community was made up of as many Black people as white, but as in the rest of American culture, the voice of the Caucasian population took precedence over everyone else. At any rate, he needed to stand up for the gay community – his community – especially since there was so much fear-mongering going on in the country at the present time.
Pushing everything else from his mind, he attempted to focus on his speech, and he felt he

An Admission of Weakness

finally nailed it after hours of writing and editing and re-editing.

"Can I wead it?" Rhett asked as he leaned over his shoulder and peered at the hand-written pages in front of his brother.

"No," Robbie hastily covered the paper on the corner desk in the living room. "It's, uh, not quite ready yet."

The rest of the family had gone to bed, leaving Robbie and Rhett alone for the night.

"Aw, come on," Rhett said. "Why not?"

"Look, things are going to change around here," Robbie said uneasily. "I'm probably not going to be very popular with people after graduation."

"Why not? Evwyone likes you," Rhett frowned.

"There's something I have to do, and I don't expect people are going to be happy about it," Robbie said.

"What does this have to do with your speech?"

Robbie studied him for a minute and sighed resignedly.

"I guess you're going to find out anyway," he said. "Just promise to keep an open mind."

"Isn't that what you've always taught us?" Rhett grinned.

He sat down on the sofa bed and began to read. It took him longer because of his dyslexia. As he expected, shared experiences with Robbie's fellow students were recounted, favorite

An Admission of Weakness

teachers thanked, and hopes for the future expressed. Many of the stories were humorous, and all shared one major theme: the past shouldn't dictate the future. History was merely a springboard for what was to come.

At one point, Rhett's eyes opened wide, and Robbie watched him warily.

"Awe you saying what I think you awe saying?" Rhett looked up at him.

"Probably," Robbie said tentatively.

"Holy cwap," Rhett whistled. He resumed reading to the end and set the pages down.

"Awe you sure you want to wead this in fwont of evwyone?"

"I have to," Robbie said.

"Well, you were wight when you said people won't like it," Rhett said.

"I only care what you think," Robbie said.

"I think you awe vehwy bwave," Rhett said. "But why didn't you ever tell me?"

"We've had a few other things to focus on," Robbie said dryly. "Besides, it didn't feel right to talk about it."

"It's not like I didn't alweady know," Rhett said.

"You knew?" Robbie frowned. "How?"

"You don't spend your whole life with your best fwiend and not know a thing or two about him," Rhett grinned. "I've seen how you look at Aawon Pwuitt. And all the girls at school

An Admission of Weakness

awe cwazy about you, but you never notice them at all."

"So it doesn't bother you?"

"Does it bother you that I have a gimpy leg and don't talk wight?" Rhett shrugged.

"That's not quite the same thing," Robbie pointed out. "And you talk just fine."

"It's part of who I am just like being gay is pawt of who you awe," Rhett said. "You could have told me so you weren't so alone. You shoulda known I wouldn't judge you."

"I know," Robbie grinned sheepishly. His expression sobered. "Just so you know, everyone else will. Ma and Pa aren't going to be happy about this."

"So what else is new?" Rhett chuckled.

"I may be forced to go away," Robbie said. "You'll be in charge of the girls, getting their meals and helping with homework."

"I know," Rhett nodded unhappily. "I always knew this day was coming. I'm weally going to miss you, but you can't stay here. It won't be safe."

"I wish I could take all of you with me," Robbie said, referring to his siblings.

"I wish you could too," Rhett said. "You're the only fwiend I have. Makes me alweady feel kind of lonely."

"I'm going to miss you too," Robbie said. "But we'll find a way to keep in touch somehow."

An Admission of Weakness

"How? I'll never get out of here," Rhett said hopelessly. "I'm too dumb to get a scholarship; no one is going to give me a fwee wide."
"You are not dumb," Robbie said sternly. He knew all too well how the other school kids teased and bullied his brother. He had had to step in on more than one occasion. "And you will get out of here, even if I have to come down here and pack your bags myself. I promise this is not all there is for you, or for the girls either."

The time for Robbie's speech had come at last. He smiled at the crowd and opened with a humorous story about his first day of high school, and in no time, the audience was eating out of his hand. After all, he was well liked in the community, as Rhett had said. He was sweet natured, funny, and cute, and people were naturally drawn to him.
It wasn't until he shared his final thoughts that things began to turn against him.

I want to leave you with these final words. Like many of my fellow classmates, I have great dreams for the future, both for myself and my brother and sisters. And one thing I've learned here, thanks to some of the great teachers I mentioned earlier, is to face life honestly and always do the right thing. Don't be afraid of the consequences of your actions if you're

An Admission of Weakness

doing what you know to be right. If it is, things will always work out.
So I want to face my future honestly, and that means being honest with the people in my life. And if my being truthful with you helps someone listening to me now, then it will be worth it.

He took a deep breath and continued.

Every one of us is special, and it is our diversity that makes us great. Some of us are scholars, athletes, musicians, or artists; Black, white, Latino, Asian, Native American. We're carpenters, secretaries, teachers, farmers, and every other occupation you can think of. Each of us is unique, but we're also the same. We're all part of one race: the human race. You have been my community for the past eighteen years, but there's another community I've been a part of, not by choice, but by design. Simply being part of that community is no longer enough without actually acknowledging it. It makes it seem as though I'm ashamed of it, and nothing could be further from the truth. Some of the people in my community are the best people on the planet. So while I'm like many of you, I'm also different. I expect there are some in this gymnasium right now who are different in the same way I am, and I want them to know they are not alone.

An Admission of Weakness

There is a national organization called The Trevor Project that does some very important work for LGBTQIA+ youth. You may not be aware of this, but LGBTQIA+ young people are at greater risk of suicide than their straight counterparts.

He looked up and noticed an immediate difference in his audience. Their individual expressions had changed from smiles to uncomfortable frowns. Determinedly, he went on.

If there are any young people listening now who are struggling with their sexuality, I beseech you to contact The Trevor Project, because if you're like me, you feel alone most of the time.

You see, I'm part of the LGBTQIA+ community myself. It wasn't something I chose, nor was I groomed by anyone to be this way. It's simply the way some people are. It has nothing to do with good and evil, as many would have you believe. It is merely a part of nature. What you need to understand is that none of us, gay or straight, have any say in determining our sexuality.

So let these words inspire you to open your mind and allow people to be themselves without judgment. They're going to be who they are anyway, and the more loving and accepting we can be of those that are different, the more

An Admission of Weakness

unified and stronger we become as a community.
Thank you.

There was a smattering of applause, but many in the audience got up to leave before he even finished speaking. A few people shook his hand, but most of them avoided him as he made his way to the parking lot. He noticed Aaron and his friends in the crowd scowling and whispering to one another. He looked for his family, but the only person waiting for him was Rhett.
"They left ahead of time so they didn't have to talk to anyone," Rhett said. "Pa was plenty mad."
The two brothers walked apprehensively to the rusty truck. Along the way, they were bombarded with jeers and curses from classmates and adults alike, but Robbie ignored them, and he wouldn't let Rhett react either. They climbed into the back of the truck with their sisters and rode home in silence.
When they arrived at the rundown house, Otis parked in the weedy drive, and he and his wife walked inside without a word to their children. The six young people followed behind, but Rhett pulled Robbie aside.
"I'll be along," he said in a low voice. "There's something I've got to do."
With that, he limped away.

An Admission of Weakness

Robbie couldn't blame him. It was probably better if none of the children were present for what he knew was going to be an ugly encounter. With a resigned sigh, he walked up the sagging back steps and into the kitchen.

An Admission of Weakness

CHAPTER TWO

Robbie faced his father with as much bravado as he could muster.

"You want to shoot me, Pa?" he said. "Go ahead. The best thing for this family is if your pathetic ass rots in jail for the rest of your life." He glanced at his terrified sisters.

"Go on to your room, girls," he attempted to sound calm. "I'll handle this."

"No," Vaneeta, the fourteen year old moved to stand next to her brother and defiantly face their father. "If he shoots you, he has to shoot me too."

"Me too," the three younger girls echoed. They surrounded their oldest brother. Even if they didn't fully understand what was going on, they knew to whom they owed their allegiance. Robbie took care of them and loved them, whereas their father did nothing but complain about how much they were costing him. Their brother taught them lessons about love and acceptance, while their father got drunk and gossiped about everyone they knew.

"Girls, go to your room," Flora said. "Robert, I think you'd better do as your father says."

"You're siding with him?" Robbie said incredulously. "He's standing there with a loaded shotgun threatening to shoot me."

"I'm tryin' to keep you from dyin' in this kitchen," his mother said.

An Admission of Weakness

Something in her voice made him look more closely at her. Her eyes didn't appear angry, merely careworn and defeated. Jeez, he hadn't really considered how hard her life must have always been. For the first time, he felt an inkling of sympathy for her.

"I'm going," he turned back to his father. "You'll never see me again, because once I leave here, I'm never coming back."

"Good!" his father sneered. "I don't want no goddammed faggot a'livin' under my roof."

"I'm going to make something of myself, no thanks to you," Robbie ignored him. "And when I do, I'm going to make sure Rhett and Vaneeta and the little ones have the lives they deserve. You sure haven't given us a decent life."

"Git out!" his father turned the shotgun toward a blank wall and fired, peppering the wood, plaster, and siding with enough shot to blast a jagged hole the size of a watermelon in it. The girls and their mother screamed, and Vaneeta shoved Robbie out the kitchen door.

"Run!" she cried before turning and wrestling the gun from her father. The other girls and their mother joined her and finally succeeded in taking the firearm from him. He shoved them aside and picked up a baseball bat by the back door.

Robbie staggered and nearly fell on the uneven ground. He righted himself just in time to see

An Admission of Weakness

Uncle Cletus's '74 Chevy Nova skid to a stop with Rhett behind the wheel.

"Get in!" he yelled over the noise of the un-muffled engine. "Hurwy."

Robbie took one look at the kitchen door, where his father was emerging with the bat in his hands, before jumping in the passenger seat. Without waiting for him to close the door, Rhett hit the gas, and the car spun its tires and sped away into the sultry gathering dusk.

"Sowwy I disappeared," Rhett said. "I thought you might need a quick getaway."

"The asshole shot a hole in the side of the house with that old shotgun of his," Robbie said.

Rhett's eyes widened, and he whistled at this news. Robbie frowned when he noticed the road they were on.

"Where are we going?"

"To the twain station. You're taking the twain to Illinois," Rhett grinned. "I packed up your things before gwaduation and stuck them in the car."

Robbie turned and was astonished to see two garbage bags and two suitcases held together with duct tape in the backseat.

"H-how did you –?" he sputtered.

"I knew he'd do something stupid," Rhett said, "so I borwowed Uncle Cletus's car and had it weady."

He handed his brother an envelope.

An Admission of Weakness

"What's this?" Robbie frowned.
"It's money for a twain ticket," Rhett said. "There's enough to get you by for a few days."
"Where'd you get this?"
"The girls and I pooled what we had," Rhett shrugged. "Ma even contwibuted some."
"You're kidding," Robbie couldn't believe his ears.
"She's been saving back money for you to take to school this fall. When she heard what we were doing, she put her money with ours and told me to keep it safe."
"Do you think she knew…?"
"I don't know," Rhett pondered this. "Maybe."
"I feel bad about taking your savings," Robbie said. "It's not right all of you giving your money to me."
"Did I ask for your opinion?" Rhett grinned mischievously. "Just shut up and say thanks."
"Thanks," Robbie said. "I'll pay you all back, I swear."
"Don't you see?" Rhett said. "If you make good, then that means there's hope for the rest of us."
"I'll make good, and as soon as I do, I'm coming back for the rest of you. I promise I'm not leaving you behind."
"I know," Rhett said. "You're going to be a big success. There's no doubt about it."

An Admission of Weakness

Robbie arrived in Champaign-Urbana, Illinois late the next evening. He took a cab from the train station to a motel near the university and checked into a room. He was exhausted after the long trip and needed a hot shower and a good night's sleep before facing his future.

An Admission of Weakness

CHAPTER THREE

While Robbie was staring down the barrel of a loaded shotgun, Blair Butterfield was facing a challenge of his own. The eighteen year old had graduated that very day from Green Grove High School in Green Grove, Illinois.

Green Grove was a pleasant town of ten thousand people located amid the rolling hills of north central Illinois. It was surrounded by the rich, black farmland for which the state was known. The corn and bean fields were a bright, healthy green at this time of year.
The lawns of Green Grove were a velvety verdant hue as well. The idyllic town was filled with neighborhoods of neatly maintained homes, many with colorful flower gardens and white picket fences.
The busy downtown consisted of a four block stretch of two and three-story brick buildings, most adorned with green and white striped awnings. There were businesses ranging from a butcher shop to a sewing boutique, an art gallery to a law office, as well as men's and women's clothing stores, a cobbler shop, diner, bakery, hardware store, and many other enterprises. Shoppers would stop on the sidewalks and visit with neighbors and friends between large flower pots of purple petunias, yellow marigolds, and trailing ivy.

An Admission of Weakness

The town also featured several parks, automobile and farm machinery dealerships, and numerous restaurants. There was a small but active hospital as well. Old-fashioned street lamps and brick paved streets provided a quaint atmosphere.

Green Grove's school system was regarded as second to none in the state. The curriculum was progressive and interesting, but also strict and challenging. Bullying was taken seriously and considered a zero-tolerance offense.

One unusual aspect of Green Grove was that it was quite integrated for a town its size, especially in the Midwest. The citizenry was fairly evenly distributed between white and Black, with a smattering of Latino, Native American, and Asian people included in the population too.

The community was founded in 1880 by John Goodfellow on the principle that all people are equal regardless of skin color, gender, sexuality, religious beliefs, disability, and so on. That ideal had been challenged on occasion but was still prevalent today.

Blair was a handsome young Black man with a perfect smile, twinkling brown eyes, and a muscular physique. He was six feet, one inch tall and weighed two hundred ten pounds. His brown complexion was flawless, and his short hair was coal black.

An Admission of Weakness

He had been quite popular in high school thanks to his athletic prowess as well as his genial personality. It was difficult for him at times living down the fact that his father, Dr. Carter Butterfield, was the superintendent of schools for the district. Dr. Butterfield insisted that his four children receive no special treatment because of him. The teachers and staff took him at his word because he was an intimidating man with a way of making people do what he wanted.

Since middle school, Blair had dated one of his classmates, a lovely dark-complected girl named Danielle Morgan. Her parents lived in Chicago, about an hour and a half to the east. They were quite affluent and could have easily

An Admission of Weakness

sent her to a private school in the city, but with their busy social life, her mother preferred having her out from underfoot. Therefore, she insisted Danielle attend classes in Green Grove from sixth grade on. She arranged for the girl to stay with her husband's father, retired Army Captain Charles Morgan. The seventy year old man lived in a modest bungalow on the east side of Green Grove. He was a lifelong military man who moved from Butler Army Base in Springfield when he and his wife retired. Sadly, his wife of forty years had passed away, leaving him with only his granddaughter for company.

Blair was smart and did well with his studies, but they weren't his main focus. He was more interested in Danielle, working out, and football. He had earned the position of star quarterback because of his strong, quick throwing arm and fleetness of foot. It was due to him that the Green Grove team had won the playoffs for the past two years.

Because of his talent on the football field, he was fortunate enough to win a full scholarship to the University of Illinois in Urbana. His father was thrilled beyond words that his son was going to play for the Fighting Illini and that it was going to cost him very little.

Blair was looking forward to getting out from under his father's constant watch. He loved his dad, but Carter was a stern man with old-

An Admission of Weakness

fashioned ideals. Like most teens, Blair yearned for freedom and the chance to be his own person.

Overall, life was good. He was popular with his classmates, had loving parents, a comfortable home in which to live, and a beautiful girlfriend. What more could he want?

It turns out, he wanted out of his relationship with Danielle. She was beautiful, it was true, but she was also vain and spoiled. She could be demanding and selfish too.

Besides, he wanted the chance to meet other people. This was the time to sow his wild oats, and he didn't want to miss out.

Blair's parents threw him a big party the evening of his graduation. Friends, most of the football team, neighbors, teachers, the mayor and her husband, as well as other local dignitaries attended.

As it was winding down, he decided it was now or never. He straddled the wide balustrade surrounding the verandah behind the six-bedroom, Tudor style house while he and Danielle kissed voraciously. She unzipped his pants and fondled his privates in an effort to make him hard.

"Stop," he broke the kiss and stuffed his erect penis back into his underwear. "Someone will see."

"So? It wouldn't be the first time," she giggled.

An Admission of Weakness

"Why don't we just talk for a while?" he suggested.

"Let's go up to your room instead," she pulled him by the hand.

"Not while everyone is still here," Blair said. "Mama would be upset if I spoiled her nice party."

Danielle pouted and turned to lean back in his arms.

"Fine, although this is nothing like the parties Mother and Daddy hold. Those are really spectacular."

"I'll bet," Blair said. "When was the last time you saw your folks?"

"It hasn't been that long," she said evasively. The truth was it had been a year since her parents last visited Green Grove. "They're very busy, you know, what with Mother's business and all their social events."

"I never understood why they sent you here," Blair frowned. "There must be plenty of good schools in Chicago."

"Mother thinks Green Grove is the best school in the state," Danielle said. She sat up straight and turned to glare at him. "What are you implying?"

"Nothing," he said hastily.

"Mother wanted me to have the best, and that meant coming here," she said heatedly.

"Besides, Grandpa needed me. He's all alone, you know."

An Admission of Weakness

"I'm sure he's glad you're here. Of course, you'll be leaving soon for school."
"I don't leave for Dartmouth for another two and a half months."
"Speaking of college," he said tentatively, "there's something I want to talk to you about."
"You want me to go to the U of I with you," she smiled knowingly. "I want that too, baby, but you know I can't; Mother insists I attend an Ivy League school."
"I know," he said. "You're going to be a thousand miles away at Dartmouth while I'm at the U of I for the next four years."
"So?" she chuckled. "That just means you'll be really glad to see me at Thanksgiving."
"I might not come home for the holidays," he said tentatively.
"I'll make it worth your while," she grinned impishly and reached back to put her hand down his pants.
"My point is, we're both going to be busy with classes and activities and stuff. Football's going to take up a lot of my time."
"If you can't come home at Thanksgiving, I'll just come to Urbana," she said. "You can't expect me to wait until Christmas to see you."
"That's what I'm saying. Do we really want to do the long distance thing for the next four years?"
"What are you saying?" she scowled. "Don't you want us to be together?"

An Admission of Weakness

"Yes, of course I do," he lied. "But we've dated since sixth grade. We're going to be meeting all kinds of new people, so maybe we shouldn't put all our eggs in one basket."

"That's a horrid thing to say! You want to date other people, don't you?"

"Everyone says long distance is hard to do," Blair said. "I think we should keep our options open. Like, if you meet someone at Dartmouth, you should feel free to go out with them if you want."

"What you mean is that you want to sleep around," she said coldly. "Don't think you're fooling anyone with this nonsense."

"It's not nonsense," he said. "I'm trying to be practical. We've never dated anyone but each other. Wouldn't it be healthy to explore other relationships so we know this is the one we want?"

"If you want to break up, just say it," she snapped. "I'm a big girl. I can take it."

"You know I care about you," he began.

"Don't give me that bullshit!" she said angrily. "I know when I'm being dumped."

"It's not like that."

"That's exactly what it is! You're just too cowardly to say it."

"Fine," his temper flared. "We're breaking up. Are you happy now?"

"I hate you!" she slapped him across the face, burst into tears, and ran into the house.

An Admission of Weakness

"Dammit," he sighed and rubbed his stinging cheek.
That hadn't gone as well as he hoped. Knowing Danielle as he did, this likely wasn't over yet.

"What the hell is wrong with you?" Carter Butterfield shouted while he paced up and down the modern kitchen.
"Nothing is wrong with me," Blair said defensively.
"Then why did you break up with Danielle? She's the best thing that could have happened to you. Her family's got money. Real money. Your future would have been set."
"I didn't break up with her," Blair said. "I just said I thought we should see other people now that we're going off to college."
"You don't drop a perfect girl like Danielle and hope you'll meet someone better," Carter said, exasperated.
"She's hardly perfect," Blair snorted. "She can be a real bitch sometimes."
"Blair, dear, language," his mother said mildly.

Forty-nine year old Naomi Butterfield was an elegant, dark-skinned woman. Her hair, clothes, makeup, and jewelry were always impeccable. She was a stay-at-home mom at the insistence of her husband. She had been content to be a full-time homemaker and mother when her children were small. But now that they were

An Admission of Weakness

grown, she longed for something to fill her days other than cooking and cleaning and making sure her two sons were keeping up with their homework. Her two daughters, Katie and Camilla, were out on their own, so there were just the two teenage boys Blair and Justin, her husband Carter, and her mother Ruby to see to. Many years ago, her grandmother taught her to sew, and she had become quite skilled since then. It was something she enjoyed, and her handiwork was displayed throughout her magnificent home: pillows, quilts, curtains, not to mention the clothes she had made.

She often daydreamed about making a career out of it. There was a new fashion designer in town, a talented young man who was just starting out, and she ached to join him in creating the fabulous gowns she had seen at his very first fashion show, held right here at the art gallery downtown.

She tentatively broached the subject to her husband, and he immediately said an emphatic no. A wife and mother belonged in the home, he said. If a woman was single, he had no problem with her having a career to earn a living. However, he believed that once a woman committed to marriage and motherhood, the choice was made.

Besides, he told her, how would it look to the community if the school superintendent's wife worked outside the home? They would think he

An Admission of Weakness

wasn't taking care of his family, and he would appear less of a man.
Resignedly, she agreed and dropped the subject. After all, she reasoned, she had a fulfilling life with four beautiful children, a devoted husband, loving mother, a lovely home in which most could only dream of living, and her social groups. She had some dear friends: Dr. Lee's wife Olivia, the bank president's wife Edith Johnson, and Chief Warner's wife. She should be satisfied with that.

"Sorry, Mama," Blair apologized for swearing and then turned back to his father. "This is my life. If I don't think she's the right girl for me, I should be able to make that decision."
"You're far too young to decide something so important for yourself," his father brushed his words aside. "I'm your father, and I know what's best for you. You are going to keep seeing Danielle, major in business, and then someday take over her parents' corporation."
"Just because you're head of the entire school system doesn't mean you're infallible."
"Son, I'm trying to keep you on the right path," Carter said patiently. "That's a father's job. Your mother agrees with me."
"Mama?"
"I don't think there's any question that your father wants what's best for you," Naomi said carefully.

An Admission of Weakness

"Do you want me to marry a girl I don't love?" Blair demanded.

"Of course not," she began. "But –"

"You see," Carter said triumphantly. "Your mother knows that Danielle is the girl for you."

"I think the boy knows his own mind," a voice called from the kitchen door.

The three of them turned to the newcomer.

"Quit badgering the boy," Ruby said.

Ruby was Naomi's seventy year old mother. Like her daughter, she was elegant in appearance, but unlike Naomi, she wasn't about to let any man tell her what to do. She often told her daughter to stand up to Carter, but her words fell on deaf ears.

"With all due respect," Carter frowned. "I don't need your advice on raising my family."

"Sure you do," Ruby said. "You're just too damn stubborn to admit it."

"Mama, please let Carter handle this," Naomi said.

"Why, so he can force Blair into a life he doesn't want?"

"That's not what I'm doing at all," Carter said.

"That's exactly what you're doing," Ruby said. "It's what you always do."

"Mama," Naomi said, mildly reproachful.

"Well, somebody needs to set him straight," Ruby said. "You won't do it, so I'm going to." She turned to her son-in-law.

An Admission of Weakness

"You can't keep running your children's lives for them. They're smart enough to handle things for themselves."

"Thanks, Gran," Blair grinned and kissed her cheek.

"I never liked Danielle anyway," she winked at him. "Too uppity for my taste. That grandfather of hers has spoiled her terribly."

"Ruby, why don't you go up to your room and take a nap?" Carter snapped.

"Why don't you?" Ruby retorted. "We could all use a few minutes of peace."

"Surely there's a pill up there that will put you to sleep."

"All I need to sleep is listen to you talk for five minutes," she said.

"Naomi, would you please control your mother," Carter gestured to the older woman.

"Mama –" Naomi began.

"Stop Mama-ing me," Ruby frowned. "You're Blair's mother. Tell him what you genuinely think, not just what Carter wants you to."

"Look, Dad," Blair said. "I'm doing everything you want: I'm going to the U of I, I'm playing football, and I'm studying business like you told me to. Let me handle my love life by myself. Okay?"

"Fine," Carter shrugged. "Do as you like. Obviously, what I think doesn't matter around here. I'll never tell you what to do again."

An Admission of Weakness

"Oh brother," Grandma Ruby rolled her eyes. "You sound like a pouty little boy who isn't getting his way. Fifty years old, and my students are more mature than you are." She was referring to the second grade class where she volunteered as a teacher's assistant.

Ruby Michaelson had been a teacher herself until retiring a few years ago. One of the great joys of her life was connecting with young people, and throughout her career, she had taught every level from elementary school to undergraduate.

As a young woman, her husband had run off with a dental hygienist while Naomi was still in diapers, and Ruby was forced to raise her daughter by herself. Being a strong woman, she was determined not to be a victim. So instead of feeling sorry for herself, she put herself through college and even went on to receive her master's degree. All the while, she put her daughter's welfare first.

When Naomi turned eighteen, Ruby made sure she got a college education. So Naomi attended the University of Illinois, and that's where she met Carter.

Carter was originally from Green Grove and planned to return there after graduation. He and Naomi received their degrees, and Carter took a job as the Green Grove High science teacher.

An Admission of Weakness

Naomi, in an uncharacteristically bold move, insisted that her mother join them. After all, her mother had sacrificed so much and worked hard to be both mother and father to her. She felt it was her turn to give back to the woman she loved and admired more than any other person in the world. Since they were young and newly married, Carter gave in to her, and Ruby moved north to the small town with them. Although Naomi received a Bachelor of Science in Communication degree, she never worked outside the home in spite of encouragement by her mother. She became pregnant right away and was content to raise her family while her husband was the breadwinner.

Carter fumed and headed for his study while Naomi, Ruby, and Blair cleaned up the dirty dishes and trash left over from the party. Once the house was in order, Blair went up to the bedroom he shared with his sixteen year old brother Justin.

An Admission of Weakness

CHAPTER FOUR

Justin Butterfield, like many teenagers, alternated between being cocky, surly, cheerful, self-conscious, clumsy, lazy, energetic, and endearing. He irritatingly questioned everyone about everything except for his father, whom he had long ago placed on a pedestal.

It was his father's wish that he become a doctor, so though Justin had no desire to be part of the medical field, he agreed to study medicine.

His own ambition was to be a personal trainer and run his own gym. Building his physique had worked out well for his brother, and he was determined to follow in his footsteps; he would be on the football team and date the prettiest girl in school.

Unfortunately, he accepted at face value many of his father's more conservative ideals. For instance, he believed it was a woman's duty to become a wife and raise a family, the man was the head of the household, and being gay was a choice, to name a few. He believed in civil rights for people of color, but not so much for anyone else.

"You is a real dick, you know dat, bro?" Justin said when Blair entered their room.

He was lying on his bed, twirling a basketball and staring up at the ceiling.

An Admission of Weakness

"Takes one to know one," Blair began to undress for bed. "And it's you are, not you is. Talk like a normal person."

"I heard you break up with Danielle while she had your dick out," Justin said. "Talk about a stupid thing to do."

"I didn't break up with her, and you need to stop eavesdropping on other people's conversations," Blair scowled.

"Why? No one in this family tells me nothin'. If I didn't eavesdrop, I'd never know what's going on."

"Danielle and I are none of your business. And if you can't talk right, don't talk at all."

"Why would you break up with the hottest girl in Green Grove right after she got you hard? That doesn't make no sense."

"Any sense," Blair corrected him. "And it doesn't have to make sense to you because it's none of your business."

"Didn't you like fuckin' her?" Justin ignored him.

"That's none of your business."

"Aw, come on," Justin pleaded. "Please tell me."

"It was fine," Blair said. "I just don't think she's the one. I want to see what else is out there."

"You should do like Dad said," Justin advised. "He knows about these things better than you do."

An Admission of Weakness

"At least I know more than you," Blair retorted.
"So tell me what it's like to have sex," Justin said.
"It's okay, I guess," Blair shrugged. "It's not as good as everyone says it is."
"Maybe you're doing it wrong."
"I'm not doing it wrong," Blair said dryly. "I mean, it feels good and all. I just don't see what the hype is all about."
"Maybe there's something wrong with you," Justin said. "Do you have erectile dysfunction?"
"Listen, Dr. Freud, I don't need advice on sex from a punk kid."
"I knew it; you can't stay hard when you're fucking," Justin said knowingly. "That's harsh, man."
"I stay hard," Blair said indignantly. "I'm a teenager; I'm always hard."
"Me too," Justin said frustratedly. "I wish I was old enough to fuck a girl instead of jerking off."
"Well, you're not, so just drop it," Blair said.
"The legal age in Europe is sixteen," Justin said.
"Fine. Go to Europe and have sex," Blair said. He brushed his teeth, peed, and then climbed into his twin bed.
"Good night," he said.

An Admission of Weakness

"I still think there's something wrong with you," Justin said. "Danielle's too fuckin' hot to be the problem."
"Will you shut up, for Christ's sake!"
Blair turned out the bedside light and turned away from his annoying little brother.

For hours that night, Blair tossed and turned as sleep eluded him. His brother's words echoed in his brain. Maybe he was right; perhaps there was something wrong with him, and it was worrisome.
From all he had learned from movies and his friends, sex was supposed to be this incredible, life-altering, earthshaking thing that everyone craved.
But was it really? After all, he had done it a few dozen times with Danielle, and he agreed that the end result was worth the effort. But he could jerk off by himself and get the same effect, so what was the point of being with someone?
The guys at school described sex like it was the greatest thing on earth. Surely they couldn't all be wrong about it, could they? And when they saw a pretty girl, or even talked about one, they all got excited. All except him, that is. He must be missing something.
When asked, he told his friends that sex with Danielle was amazing, but that wasn't true. He felt like he was merely going through the

An Admission of Weakness

motions to get to a climax. Danielle seemed to think it was fantastic, so he figured the reason he wasn't more enthusiastic about it was because she wasn't the right girl for him.
But what if that wasn't it? What if there was truly something wrong with him? Getting hard wasn't an issue, but then again, guys his age could get an erection without consciously thinking about anything. Jeez, he could be daydreaming about something as innocuous as his last football game and become aroused. Come to think of it, every time he thought about his teammates, or the locker room, or being tackled by another guy on the gridiron, he got a hard on. But that was just natural, he told himself. After all, half the guys in the locker room got erections while they snapped towels and horsed around with each other. It didn't mean anything; it was just the nature of the beast.
He should have tried harder when fucking Danielle. She was one of the prettiest girls in town, and she obviously enjoyed their time together more than he did. Perhaps he was too focused on football or his studies and should have given her all his attention.

Three hours downstate from Green Grove, the Registrar at the University of Illinois sympathized with Robbie Lee's situation and kindly made arrangements for him to move into

An Admission of Weakness

his dorm room early. It was little more than a closet big enough for a twin bed, a dresser, and a small desk and chair. That didn't matter to Robbie. It was clean and private, and after all, he only needed it for sleep and studying.

His advisor found him a summer job as a waiter at one of the campus's food emporiums. It wasn't exactly his dream job, but he was grateful for the income.

When he wasn't working, Robbie spent his time reading ahead in the textbooks for his upcoming business classes. He did some exploring of the campus, but he felt uncharacteristically shy in this intimidating new environment, so he stayed in his dorm room for the most part.

While he waited tables, he encountered a number of fellow students who were taking summer classes. To his astonishment, several of these people were openly gay.

He knew openly gay people existed, of course, but this was the first time he had met any in real life. The few gay people he knew back home were firmly ensconced in their closets for their own safety.

For the first time in his life, he was able to truly be himself, and the freedom made him giddy with joy. He didn't have to watch how he walked or talked or worry about how he was perceived by other people. Not that he cared before, but it had been too dangerous to live

An Admission of Weakness

openly in a homophobic society that would gladly have unalived him. His own father was the perfect example of that.

By the time the fall semester began, Robbie had made several friends. With his good looks and cheerful personality, he was quite popular with the other students. They took him to parties and clubs, and he soon fell in love with dancing. He had never had the opportunity to dance back home, and he found that he was surprisingly good at it.

One of his friends, a young man named Grant, saw how well he moved on the dance floor and encouraged him to try out for cheerleading. Grant was a cheerleader and offered to coach him, and Robbie eagerly agreed. After all, these were his college years, his time to try new things, to push out of his comfort zone and blossom into the man he was to become.

He spent the next several months practicing and learning, and by the next spring, he was ready for the tryouts.

Along with practicing to be a cheerleader and spending time with his new friends, Robbie also studied hard. He was determined to be the best student he could be to make his brother and sisters proud.

Shortly after the fall semester began, Robbie walked down the hall to his dorm room. It had

An Admission of Weakness

been a long day, and he had lots of studying to do before bedtime.
Standing in front of his door was a group of eight or ten athletic looking Black men. They were laughing and shoving each other good naturedly, clearly partying with the occupant of the room across the hall from Robbie.

Robbie had seen the man fleetingly when he moved in but had not had the opportunity to introduce himself. His initial impression was that the man was exceedingly handsome, muscular and fit, with a beautiful smile. However, he came across as rather superficial and arrogant. Fortunately, Robbie was smart enough to know first impressions could be wrong, so he kept an open mind. He nodded and smiled at him a few times in the hallway, but the guy was either engrossed in his phone or was with someone and ignored him.
He learned from his dorm-mates that the man's name was Blair, he was from northern Illinois, an elementary education major, and he was at the university to play football.
He had learned as a boy to avoid jocks because, in his experience, they were usually bullies. He wasn't necessarily their target because he was athletic and they didn't suspect he was gay. But he had intervened in enough situations involving Rhett and others to know who the worst bullies were.

An Admission of Weakness

But now that he and his fellow students were adults, he assumed such childish behavior was a thing of the past. So he didn't anticipate any trouble when he approached the rowdy group of teenagers.

"Hey, guys," he smiled as he tried to maneuver his way through the throng to his door. "Excuse me."

Someone playfully shoved someone else, who bumped against Robbie and knocked him off-balance. His books fell to the floor.

"Hey, watch it!" the assailant addressed Robbie with annoyance.

Normally, Robbie had no problem letting accidents like this go, but something in the tone of voice being used immediately put his back up.

"Don't you mean 'I'm sorry'?" he frowned.

"Why should I say I'm sorry?" the man said.

"Because you bumped into me," Robbie said.

"Chill, little guy," the tallest and broadest man chuckled and hooked a muscular arm around his neck. "It was just an accident."

"I know it was an accident," Robbie said. "But I'm not going to apologize for something that wasn't my fault."

He glared at the man who had bumped into him and blinked with surprise. It was Blair, the guy who lived across the hall, the same one who

An Admission of Weakness

had ignored him on at least two occasions so far.

Blair, not wanting to appear weak in front of his teammates, scowled at him.

"So you're saying it was my fault?"

"I'm saying that if you bump into someone, say you're sorry and make sure they're all right."

"I only bumped into you because you were in the way," Blair said.

"I was trying to get in my room."

"So go in your room and stop bothering us," Blair said impatiently.

"I'm going," Robbie headed into his room, but before he closed his door, he heard someone utter one more word.

"Faggot."

Robbie set his books on his desk and stepped back into the hall.

"What did you say?"

The men eyed one another uncomfortably but didn't speak.

"So what?" Robbie glared at each of them in turn. "You're brave enough to say it behind my back but not to my face? I thought big, bad football players were tougher than that."

"Hey!" one man said sharply. "You need to go in your room so you don't find out how bad we can be."

"So ten dumb jocks are threatening to beat up one guy, is that it? Why don't you save your energy for the next game?"

An Admission of Weakness

The big guy laughed at that.
"You're either really stupid, or you got a mighty big set of balls on you," he grinned.
"Well, I'm not stupid," Robbie couldn't help but smile too.
The others laughed except for Blair.
"Okay, we won't call you faggot and you don't call us dumb," the first man said. He extended his huge hand for a dap handshake. "Deal, blondie?"
"I'm not crazy about blondie either," Robbie shook his hand and then bumped fists with him. "The name's Robbie."
"Cool, man," his new acquaintance chuckled. "I'm Andres."
It turned out that Andres was the captain of the football team. He and his friends shook hands with Robbie, but Blair held back.
"This is Blair," Andres said. "He's sorry for calling you a faggot."
"No I'm not," Blair said. "Just look at him; you can tell that's what he is."
"Well, if he's going to call me a faggot, I get to call him a dumb jock," Robbie said.
"Come on," Blair scowled while his friends laughed uproariously. "Let's get the fuck outa here."
"See ya later, guys," Robbie called after them and then added mischievously, "Bye, DJ."
"Who's DJ?" Andres looked puzzled.
"He is," Robbie pointed at Blair.

An Admission of Weakness

"What the hell are you talking about?" Blair frowned.
"Don't worry, you'll figure it out eventually," Robbie grinned. He stepped into his room and shut the door.

That first meeting set the tune for Blair and Robbie's relationship for the entirety of their freshman year. They tended to avoid each other whenever possible, but when they did encounter each other, Blair always rewarded Robbie's sunny smile with a scowl and a flip of the bird.
"Faggot."
"DJ," Robbie would always chuckle in response.

Robbie kept in touch with Rhett through a couple of cheap Android cell phones he found for sale on a campus bulletin board. One of his friends showed him how to set them up, and he sent one to his brother. It was tricky as to whether he would even get it, but his mother took in the mail that day, and she made sure he received it.
Rhett's classmates were adept with phone technology like most teens, and one of them showed him how to use the device.
"Wobbie?" he said cautiously after tapping the call button. "Is that you?"

An Admission of Weakness

"Can you believe it?" Robbie exclaimed. "We can talk to each other whenever we want."
"I just can't let Pa find out about it," Rhett said.
"Keep it on silent," Robbie advised.
"I will," Rhett said. "So tell me about school."
The two talked for an hour that first day, each unwilling to hang up. They shared everything that had happened in their lives since Robbie left for school. Rhett assured him that their sisters were doing well, and Robbie told him about hopefully becoming a cheerleader.
"Maybe I'll see you on TV sometime," Rhett said eagerly. "How cool would that be?"
"It would be very cool," Robbie agreed. He added hesitantly, "Has Dad asked about me?"
"We're not allowed to mention your name," Rhett said. "He tells people you're dead."
"Figures," Robbie said bitterly. "The bastard."
"Who cares what he thinks," Rhett snorted. "I can't wait to see you at Chwistmas. We can catch up then."
"Rhett, you know I can't come back there," Robbie said uncomfortably.
"But I miss you," Rhett protested. "When will I get to see you?"
"I don't know," Robbie admitted. "Maybe you can come visit me here sometime."
"I'll never be able to afford that," Rhett said.
"I'll save some money back and buy you a train ticket."
"You need that money to live," Rhett said.

An Admission of Weakness

"I also need my brother," Robbie said. "I can live without pizza if it means I get to see you."

Blair drove home for the Christmas holiday. His parents, Grandma Ruby, and Justin had driven down to the campus every other weekend for the home football games, but their visits were uncomfortable because his father still hadn't forgiven him for breaking up with Danielle.

Dr. Carter Butterfield was descended from a long line of slaves owned by a particularly ruthless plantation owner in Mississippi. The horrific tales of slave life had been handed down from generation to generation ever since. For the past five years, he had made it his life's mission to gather and catalog those stories. He had done countless hours of research in an effort to learn as much as possible about his heritage. His plan was to compile those stories into a book for future generations of his family. His family had suffered horrors that most people could never understand, but after reading through his family's history, his eyes had been opened. The hell that his ancestors endured was proof of the white man's inhumanity and the Black man's courage and endurance. Systemic racism still flourished in the United States, and even though it wasn't in the form of slavery, not much had changed in

An Admission of Weakness

four hundred years. In fact, it seemed as if the progress they had made as a people was being forced backward now.

That was why he returned to Green Grove when he married Naomi. Somehow, the ignorance and bigotry of the rest of the world had bypassed the town. People here respected one another; skin color, gender, sexual orientation, and religion didn't matter to them. Everyone was treated with dignity, and they lived side by side without conflict.

Occasionally, an outsider would try to stir things up, but it never lasted because Green Grove's citizens knew better than to allow anyone to disrupt their peace. John Goodfellow, the town's founder, insisted that Green Grove's schools teach facts, even when those truths were uncomfortable to learn. That still held true today.

Carter wanted his children brought up in such an environment. He didn't want them to be afraid to walk down the street, fearful of their white neighbors and police officers. He wanted them to know they could become anything they wanted, even though he chose their career options himself.

His parents had raised him to believe in his abilities and intelligence, and that led him into the field of education. His father was a professor before his passing; Carter saw the

An Admission of Weakness

difference he made in the lives of many young people.
As a result he, too, wanted to influence young people to become doctors and lawyers and politicians.
Because of his family's roots in slavery, it was not surprising that Carter held a grudge against the white culture in the United States and Europe. From his perspective, the white man was guilty of most of the world's greatest atrocities: slavery, genocide of Native Americans and Jews, imperialism/colonialism, most wars, the Crusades, the Inquisition, and the list went on. Naturally, he realized that not every white person was evil, but as a whole, their governments were. They feared people of color and were desperate to keep them under their thumbs. It was an ongoing practice in the USA, even though the ones propagating it were the very ones who insisted that racism did not exist.
Carter was proud of his family, proud of his ancestry, and proud to be Black. He was quite liberal in some ways but unexpectedly conservative in others. The wife belonged in the home, the man was the head of the household, and marriage should be between one man and one woman. It was the way he was raised, he argued, and what was good enough for his parents was good enough for

An Admission of Weakness

him. He chose not to see the irony of that statement.

He didn't pretend to understand homosexuality. If one could choose to be gay, he reasoned, they could choose to be straight. So why would anyone blatantly opt to make their lives more difficult? It seemed obvious that it went against nature as well as God's will, and that made it a sin.

Perhaps it was the stubbornness that was bred into his ancestors to survive slavery and oppression that had made him inflexible when it came to some liberal ideas. Politically, he was quite liberal; he believed in civil rights and equality for everyone except for gay people.

An Admission of Weakness

CHAPTER FIVE

Blair walked in the back door of his parents' house carrying a laundry bag containing a month's worth of dirty clothes.
"Mama, I'm home," he called out while he carelessly dumped the bag on the laundry room floor. "I brought home some laundry I thought you could do for me."
He headed to the kitchen, where his mother and sisters were preparing supper.
"Mama's not your personal slave, you know," Camilla reminded him.
"Don't let Dad hear you say the 's' word," Katie teased. "He'll give us a two hour lecture on the subject."

Camilla Butterfield was two years older than Blair. She was an attractive young woman who preferred to wear clothing that reflected her Senegalese heritage. Her usual garb was a richly colored boubou, a wide, light, comfortable garment. Like her mother, she had a gift when it came to sewing, so most of her clothes were handmade.
Camilla was a free-spirited artist who had painted the walls of her bedroom with a mural of Black heroes such as Dr. Martin Luther King, President Barack and Michelle Obama, Rosa Parks, Maya Angelou, John Lewis, Langston Hughes, Sojourner Truth, as well as

An Admission of Weakness

some of her favorite Black actors like Vanessa Williams, Beyoncé, and Denzel Washington. She had spent the past two years with the Peace Corps in Senegal as a Youth Development Officer, a job she relished. With her generous and outgoing personality, it was a good fit for her. She cared little for material possessions and preferred making the world a better place by helping people.

After high school, her father arranged for her to attend law school, but she merely patted his hand and explained that she had no desire to be part of such a profession. He threatened and cajoled, but he found it was useless to argue with her because she refused to understand his desire to see her succeed.

"I'll be fine, Dad," she said with her gentle smile. "Just worry about getting your book published."

As for Katie, she was two years older than Camilla. She had attended Yale University and earned her Master of Science in Nursing degree. It was her father's desire that she become a medical doctor, but he finally acquiesced when she promised to get her doctorate in nursing. After her graduation, she accepted a position as head of nursing at a large hospital in Los Angeles. It wasn't the job she would have preferred, but it was what her father wanted, so she tried to make the best of it.

An Admission of Weakness

She and Camilla were alike in that they were both outgoing, giving people. Katie preferred the clinical side of her profession; that was where she felt she could make the most difference.

Like her mother and grandmother, she was tall, sophisticated, and charming. She was strong and independent as well except for where her father was concerned.

Sometimes she would scold herself for giving in to her father's wishes regarding her career. After all, it was her life, not her father's. For Katie had a secret that no one was aware of except for Blair. She knew her father would never accept it, so she kept it quiet.

"It's good to have you home," Ruby gave her grandson a hug and kiss on the cheek. "My goodness, I think you're even taller than when you left for school."

"I'm a growing boy," he grinned. "So when's supper? I'm starved."

"Go get washed up," his mother smiled indulgently. "And tell your brother to do the same. Supper's almost ready."

"Camilla, are you glad to be home from Africa?" Blair asked.

"I'm glad to be wherever I happen to be."

"He's asking if you missed us," Justin said.

"Of course I did. You know I love you all."

An Admission of Weakness

"We love you too," Naomi smiled. "We're glad you're home."

"What are your plans now that you're done with the Peace Corps?" Carter asked. "It's not too late to go to law school. All I have to do to get you in to the U of I this semester is make a call."

"I thought I might volunteer at the school like Gran," Camilla said. "Or become a nursing assistant at the hospital."

"Camilla, if you want to help people, become a doctor or lawyer," her father said.

"You make it sound like being a doctor is better than being a nurse," Katie frowned.

"Of course it is," Carter said. "That's why I tried to convince you to go to medical school."

"I didn't want to go to medical school," Katie said, exasperated. "Do we really need to go through that again?"

"Of course not," Ruby said firmly. "Blair, tell us about dorm life. Have you made some good friends?"

"Mostly just from the team," Blair shrugged. "There are some good guys in the dorm, but the guy across the hall is a jerk."

"Why do you say that?" Carter asked.

"For one thing, he's queer, and he calls me a dumb jock whenever he sees me. I can't stand him. He's all blonde and buff and thinks he's hot stuff. He couldn't be any whiter if he tried."

An Admission of Weakness

"You're not a dumb jock," Naomi reassured him. "All my children are smart."
"Except for Justin," Blair teased.
"I'm smart," Justin said indignantly. "I'm going to be a doctor, you know."
"That's a scary thought," Katie grinned. "Can you imagine him as a doctor?"
"Blair, how are your business classes going?" Naomi changed the subject.
"They're fine," Blair shrugged and avoided her eye. He glanced surreptitiously at Katie. "We're learning about, uh, accounts payable and receivable."
The truth was that, in spite of his father's wishes, Blair had decided on education as his major with a minor in drama. So far he hadn't told his family except for Katie.
"Maybe you should take some education classes," Katie suggested.
"Don't be ridiculous," their father said. "Your focus should be on becoming the head of a large corporation such as Morgan Enterprises. That's where the money is."
"Being a teacher isn't ridiculous. You're an educator, and so was Gran," Blair pointed out.
"And now she lives with us," Carter said.
"If you're implying that I can't afford to live on my own, why don't we compare bank accounts?" Ruby said.
"If you have so much money, why don't you stop living off of –?" Carter said.

An Admission of Weakness

"Carter," Naomi said sharply. "This is Mama's home. She is living with us because we want her here."
Ruby smiled sweetly at Carter, who merely glared at her and took a bite of his salad.
"I'm just saying there's nothing wrong with being a teacher," Blair said.
"I think you'd be a great teacher," Camilla said.
"He's majoring in business, and that's the end of it," Carter said firmly.

"You're going to have to tell him eventually," Katie said.
"How can I tell him?" Blair said glumly. "You heard him at supper."
The two were sitting on the bed in her bedroom.
"So you're just going to wait until graduation and let him find out then?"
"If I tell him now, he'll make me switch majors."
"He's going to kill you, you know," Katie said.
"I know," Blair groaned and flopped back on the mattress. "God, why doesn't he ever listen?"
"He thinks he knows what's best for us," Katie shrugged.
"You're going to have to tell him about you-know-who," Blair said.
"He'll disown me," she snorted. "Right after he's done killing you."

An Admission of Weakness

"Then do something about it," Blair said. "He'd have no choice but to accept it."
"I'm not ready yet," she said.
"When are you going to be ready?"
"I don't know. Maybe when you tell him you're an education/drama major."
"Okay, we'll both tell him our secrets at the same time," Blair grinned.
"I can see it now," she chuckled. "Mama will faint, and he'll have a heart attack."
"We'd better have the paramedics standing by," he laughed.

"Everyone, this is Michael," Carter introduced the smiling stranger to his family, who were sitting at the dining room table.
It was Christmas Eve, and the Butterfield house was festively decorated with garlands, bows, poinsettias, white lights, and three Christmas trees. Nat King Cole's smooth voice sang Christmas carols in the background.
"Hello, Michael," Naomi shook his hand before turning to her husband questioningly.
"I invited Michael to dinner," Carter said.
"Didn't I tell you?
"It must have slipped your mind," Naomi said dryly. "I'll get another place setting."
"I'll get it, Mama," Camilla said. "Michael, you can sit next to me."
"Actually, Justin, you move next to Camilla and let Michael sit beside Katie," Carter said.

An Admission of Weakness

Once they were all seated, Carter spoke up again.

"Michael, this is Katie, the one I was telling you about."

"It's nice to meet you," Michael smiled. "You're a nurse, aren't you?"

"She's the head of nursing at Los Angeles Osteopathic Hospital," Carter said. "Katie, Michael is a med student at the U of I."

"I thought you looked familiar," Blair said.

"Oh yeah, I've seen you," Michael grinned. "You're in my Intro to Drama class."

"Drama?" Carter frowned at his son. "You're taking a drama class?"

"It's, uh, an elective," Blair said uncomfortably. "I thought it sounded easy so I could focus on my business classes."

"It's actually fun," Michael said. "Your son is very good at it." He turned to Blair. "I didn't realize you were a business major. For some reason, I thought you were in education."

"You concentrate on the important classes," Carter said sternly. "I'm not putting you through college to become an actor."

He shuddered at the thought of one of his children involved in the sordid world of acting.

"I don't think there's anything wrong with acting as a hobby," Naomi said tentatively. "We have an excellent theater group here in town."

An Admission of Weakness

"Asher Reardon is an actor, and he's worth almost two hundred million dollars," Justin chimed in.

"Eat your dinner," Carter frowned.

"Asher Reardon's gay too," Michael commented.

Everyone stopped eating and looked up at him.

"What do you mean 'too'?" Justin asked. "Are you queer?"

"No," Michael glanced uncertainly at Blair's frowning face. "I, uh, don't know why I said too. I just meant he's gay and so is his husband."

"His husband would have to be, I imagine," Ruby chuckled.

"Two men marrying is unnatural," Carter scowled.

"It's sick," Justin added.

"Totally sick," Blair agreed.

"What does it matter to you three how other people live their lives?" Ruby demanded. "If two people fall in love and find happiness, who are you to judge them?"

"It goes against God's will," Carter said.

"Oh please," Ruby said. "Don't get me started on God's will."

"Enough," Carter said severely. "Katie, I think you and Michael have a lot in common. He wants to live in the city too."

"Actually, I prefer a small town like Green Grove to Los Angeles," Katie said.

An Admission of Weakness

"No you don't," Carter said. "So, Michael, tell Katie about school. She's going to get her doctorate in nursing, you know."
"Someday," Katie said evasively. "Being a nurse is what I always wanted to be. I just don't know why I had to go to Yale to become one."
"Er, med school is grueling," Michael said hesitantly. "Sometimes I think it will never end, but I keep plugging away at it."
"Anything worth doing is worth doing well," Carter glanced sternly around the table. "All of you remember that."

Michael said a hasty goodbye after dinner. Carter closed the front doors and turned angrily to his daughter.
"You made absolutely no effort with Michael."
"What was I supposed to do?" she demanded. "Run off with him and elope?"
"Of course not."
"I wasn't interested in him," she said. "I'm sure he's very nice, but he's not for me."
"He's perfect for you," her father said.
"Let the girl alone," Ruby interjected. "She knows her own mind."
"Thank you, Gran," Katie said gratefully.
"Go wash a dish or something, Florence," Carter said.
"I liked him," Camilla said hesitantly. "I could see myself dating someone like him."

An Admission of Weakness

"You're not his type," Carter brushed her aside impatiently.
"How do you know what his type is?" Katie said. "And how do you even know him?"
"It doesn't matter," Carter said. "I'll call him later and smooth things over."
"Fine," Katie said. "I hope the two of you will be very happy together."

Blair felt a growing restlessness when he returned to school in January. Football was going well, he enjoyed his education classes, and he was having fun with his friends. He'd even had sexual encounters with one woman after another, sometimes two at a time. Perhaps that was the problem, he mused. The sex always felt good, but as soon he climaxed, the experience felt hollow to him. It was exciting to be with women other than Danielle, but to be honest, he'd just as soon jerk off and spend time with his teammates than go on a date.
The guy across the hall was still bugging him. Every time his friends were hanging out in his room, the damn faggot would stop by to say hi, or some of the guys would spend time over in his room.
"Why don't you stay the fuck away, Blondie?" he groused one day. "Me and my friends don't want you around."
The two were standing in Robbie's dorm room.

An Admission of Weakness

"Then why do they come over to visit all the time?"

"I know what you're doing, you know. It's what you gay guys do. You pretend to be friendly and try to convert straight guys."

"Well, you caught me," Robbie said. "That was my goal all along."

"I knew it," Blair said.

"The truth is, I'm in love with you, DJ," Robbie said dramatically, a hand to his heart. "I just haven't had the courage to tell you yet."

Without warning, Blair slugged him and towered over him when he fell to the floor.

"Don't ever say that again!" he shouted furiously.

"It was just a joke, man," Robbie worked his sore jaw.

"It wasn't funny."

"Actually, I think it's hysterical," Robbie got to his feet. "The idea of anyone falling in love with a knuckle-dragger like you is laughable."

"Bullshit," Blair said. "Plenty of girls want me."

"Not to help them with their homework, that's for sure," Robbie said.

"What's that supposed to mean?"

"It means you're a dumb jock like I said. The only reason you're here is to play football. That's all you are: football, hanging out and acting tough, high-fiving your buddies and having belching and farting contests."

An Admission of Weakness

"Fags like you don't know shit about what straight guys do."
"I know toxic masculinity when I see it," Robbie snorted. "Like punching someone instead of talking. You're as pathetic as they come."
"And you're as faggy as they come," Blair snapped.
"I'd rather be faggy than like you," Robbie said. "Faggy people have a heart. We know what it's like to be bullied by hateful people like you."
"You don't know me at all," Blair said.
"Sure I do. You're a super macho guy who acts tough to hide your insecurities, and you think every woman and gay guy wants you just because you're handsome. You're afraid to have an honest emotion, and your tiny brain is in your little dick."
"You think I'm handsome?" Blair said
"Oh my god," Robbie groaned.
"So you think I'm handsome, but you don't want me?" Blair said. "Please."
"You just proved my point," Robbie said. "You want everyone to want you, but you get mad if it's a gay guy."
"Just stay away from me and my friends from now on," Blair said heatedly.

Blair and Andres and their friends sat on the bleachers on the basketball court and watched

An Admission of Weakness

the cheerleading tryouts in April. Most of the guys went on and on about what they'd like to do to the pretty women while Blair sat silently observing.

"You could have any one of them," Andres nudged him with his elbow. "Why aren't you down there showing them your moves, Casanova?"

"I don't want just one of them," Blair grinned. "I want all of them. And I'll have them too."

His smile faded when the women left the court and the men ran out onto the shiny wood floor.

"Holy fuck," he scowled. "Look who's down there."

Andres followed his gaze and grinned.

"Robbie," he said. "He's trying out. Good for him."

"I told you he was a faggot," Blair muttered.

"So what if he is," Andres shrugged. "He's a nice guy. He's funny."

"He's not so nice," Blair said. "He tried to come on to me a few weeks ago, and I slugged him."

"You did what?!"

"He told me he wanted me, and I slugged him," Blair repeated.

"Dammit!" Andres said angrily. "I don't care what he said to you. You can't get into any fights. I can't afford for you to get thrown off the team. And you can't afford to lose your scholarship."

An Admission of Weakness

"It was just one time," Blair said. "I told him to stay away from us."

"If he becomes a cheerleader, he'll be around us a lot," Andres said.

"I gotta put a stop to this," Blair abruptly stood up and made his way down to the floor.

An Admission of Weakness

CHAPTER SIX

Robbie pounded on Blair's door across the hall. "DJ!" he shouted.
To be honest, he had called Blair DJ for so long that he couldn't remember his real name. At the moment, he was so angry that he didn't care what it was.
Blair opened the door and glared at him.
"What the fuck do you want?"
"Did you tell the coach to keep me off the team?" Robbie demanded.
"So what if I did?" Blair folded his arms. "What are you gonna do about it?"
Robbie shoved him and simultaneously locked a heel behind his ankle, sending Blair to the floor on his back. It was a tactic he had learned from his brutish cousins back in Mississippi. Blair blinked up at him with astonishment, but he swiftly got to his feet with his fists at the ready.
"Man, you're gonna be sorry you did that," he seethed, humiliated that this gay white boy had gotten the better of him so easily. Thank god none of his friends were around to see it.
"Oh yeah?" Robbie smirked. "Why don't we see what Andres has to say about it?"
"So you're a snitch besides being a fuckin' fag," Blair scowled.
"I didn't snitch the last time, did I?" Robbie said. "But I know what getting in a fight could

An Admission of Weakness

cost you, so maybe I'll go to Andres or even Coach Wilkensen this time."

"I still ought to punch you out," Blair said.

"Go for it," Robbie said defiantly.

Blair thought better of it and dropped his fists.

"Why do you care if I'm a cheerleader or not?" Robbie demanded.

"I told you I don't want you around me and my friends."

"Wow," Robbie shook his head disgustedly. "You would ruin something I've worked really hard for just for the sake of your fragile male ego? You're even more pathetic than I thought."

"No, you're pathetic, Blondie!" Blair spat. "You just want to be a cheerleader so you can see me and my buddies naked."

"I don't need to see your tiny dick to get my thrills, asshole," Robbie retorted. "And just so you know, the coach didn't listen to you. I made the team."

He turned to go but couldn't resist one last comment.

"See you in the locker room," he chuckled and returned to his own room.

"Fuck!" Blair fumed.

By now, Robbie's schedule was brutally rigorous: a full class load, cheerleading, working part time, studying, and spending time with his multitude of friends. He barely found

An Admission of Weakness

time to sleep, but he didn't care because he was having the time of his life.

He was out of the closet, and it felt wonderful! No one cared that he was gay except for the idiot jock across the hall from him. Many of his new friends were gay, and he was finally loved and accepted for who he truly was.

He made a point to avoid Blair as much as possible, not because he was afraid of him, but because he didn't want negative energy in his life. God knows he had been surrounded by it all of his life, and he was not having it again.

Blair spent the summer at home in Green Grove. Camilla was working as a CNA at the hospital, a job she thoroughly enjoyed. Justin was out most of the time with his friends, and Grandma Ruby tutored several students at the request of her son-in-law. Carter went to the office every day and worked on his book in his free time.

Blair found a summer job at the enormous recycling plant west of the downtown, although he spent a couple of weeks sleeping late and catching up with friends. Now that he was no longer tied to Danielle, he looked up several female classmates and fucked them to try to satisfy his libido.

That left Naomi alone much of the time. She kept up the house, cooked meals for whoever was home at the time, and did the shopping.

An Admission of Weakness

One day while she was downtown, she passed by the last shop on the east end of the four block stretch. This was where W. H. Abernathy – aka Billy or Snake – designed and sewed his fabulous gowns. At the moment, there were three stunning evening gowns on mannequins in the windows. The door opened while she paused to admire them, and a voice addressed her.

"Naomi, it's so nice to see you," June Shaw smiled.

June and her husband Lawrence owned the local Cadillac dealership, and June was the foremost seamstress in town. She worked at Worthen's, an upscale women's clothing store two blocks away.

"Hello, June. How are you?"

"Tired," June chuckled. "That's why I'm glad I ran into you."

"Excuse me?" Naomi looked confused.

"I just meant I've been burning the candle at both ends lately," June explained. "Between working here and at Worthen's, it's more than I can handle. The demand for an Abernathy gown has skyrocketed; we've got orders coming in every day from all over the country."

"I can see why," Naomi said. "I saw the show at the Gallery, and his dresses are absolutely breathtaking."

"How would you like to be part of his next show?"

An Admission of Weakness

"You mean walk down the runway?" Naomi frowned.

"That, and actually helping make the dresses," June said. "You're an excellent seamstress, and I think you would be a huge asset to us here."

"You want me to work here?" Naomi placed a hand to her breast. "Oh my."

"Just think of it," June said. "You could help create something beautiful for women all around the world."

"It sounds fabulous," Naomi said hesitantly. "But Carter would never –"

"Don't say no right now," June interrupted her. "Think about it. There's no one I'd rather work with."

"How many hours would you need someone?" Naomi asked tentatively.

"As many hours as you want," June said. "You could work full time as far as I'm concerned.

"Oh no, I don't think –"

"Or even a few hours a day," June said. "With Justin nearly grown, I thought you might have some free time on your hands."

"I do spend a lot of time alone," Naomi admitted. "The children have their own things, Carter is always working on his book, and Mama is tutoring full time these days."

"So come help me here," June said. "You'd really be doing me a favor. And Snake is so great to work with. He'd let you have any dress you want for whatever it costs to make it."

An Admission of Weakness

"Oh my," Naomi breathed. "I'd love that."
"And you have the perfect figure for any of these," June gestured to the dresses in the windows. "Think how marvelous you'd look at the Christmas Ball or walking down the runway at Snake's next show."
Naomi imagined Carter's reaction if she told him she was working as a seamstress.
"I won't have you working," he would say. "You have plenty right here to keep you busy: your family, this house, and your husband. What would people say if I let you take a job sewing other people's clothes?"
Her expression hardened. Dammit, she had a right to do this if she wanted to!
"You know what?" she said to June. "I'll do it. How would it be if I worked from ten to two?"
"That would be marvelous," June hugged her enthusiastically. "Oh, I can't tell you how happy this makes me."
"Could we keep this between us for now?" Naomi said hesitantly.
"Whatever you want," June smiled. "Can you start tomorrow?"
"I'll be here," Naomi smiled back.

"He kept coming over to my room whenever the guys and I were hanging out," Blair complained at the dinner table that night.
"Mama, this roast is delicious," Camilla said. "Did you do something different?"

An Admission of Weakness

"And now he's a freaking cheerleader so he can hang around the team," Blair added.
"That's 'cause he's a fag," Justin said.
"Justin," Naomi scolded him. "Language."
"What does it matter if he's gay or not?" Camilla asked. "Is he a nice person?"
"Not to me," Blair frowned. "People seem to like him, though."
"It sounds like he has a crush on someone on the team," Carter said disapprovingly. "Those people try to convert unsuspecting victims. You should keep away from him."
"That's what I'm saying," Blair said. "I'm trying to stay away from him, but he keeps finding ways to be around all the time."
"Dad, gay people don't convert straight people," Camilla chuckled. "Where'd you get an idea like that?"
"You're too naïve," Carter said dismissively.
"No, you're just homophobic," Camilla said, unruffled. "You know lots of gay people. Why would you believe something so ludicrous about them?"
"People are gay by choice," Carter said stubbornly. "The only way they can propagate their lifestyle is to make others turn too."
"No one is gay by choice," Camilla said. "A person's sexuality is simply part of who they are. It can't be changed."
"Camilla, you have no idea what you're talking about," Carter said. "Blair is young and

An Admission of Weakness

inexperienced. He's away from home for the first time. He's a prime target for someone like this cheerleader."

"Why don't we change the subject?" Naomi spoke up. "There are surely more pleasant topics to discuss."

Carter told them about some new research he was doing on the Butterfield family, and they discussed that for a while.

"I'm thinking of taking some sewing lessons," Naomi said during a lapse in the conversation.

"That's nice, dear," Carter said absently.

"Why do you need lessons?" Justin asked. "You're already really good at it."

"There's always room for improvement," Naomi said. "June Shaw has offered to teach me a few things, and I would like to do it."

"I don't see a problem as long as it doesn't interfere with your household duties," Carter said.

"She's not a maid, you know," Camilla said.

"When have I ever let anything interfere with you or the children?" Naomi demanded heatedly.

"I'm just saying," Carter wiped his mouth with his napkin and scooted his chair back. "I've got some work to do. I'll be in my study."

He left the room.

"You should make roasts like this all the time, Mama," Blair stood up and threw his napkin

An Admission of Weakness

down. "I'm meeting the guys to shoot some hoops."

"I'm coming too," Justin said.

"And I have a date to get ready for," Camilla said. "Do you want me to help clear the table?"

"No," Naomi said. "Go get ready for your date. I'll take care of the table."

"You're the best," Camilla kissed her cheek and hurried upstairs, leaving her mother sitting alone.

Naomi gazed around the empty room and sighed heavily. Finally, she brushed a tear away and resignedly began to stack the dirty dishes to carry to the kitchen.

"An embellished pashmina?" Snake said. "That's just what it needs. Good thinking, Naomi."

Snake, aka Billy, was a twenty-six year old, long-haired, tattooed ex-biker/thug from Chicago. He was hardly the sort one would expect to be a fashion designer. He and June's son had fallen in love after Snake arrived in town.

June grinned and patted her on the shoulder. She knew she had done the right thing bringing Naomi into the business. Besides her sewing skills, Naomi also had a good eye when it came to fashion. She was always impeccably dressed whenever she attended school or city functions.

An Admission of Weakness

Naomi flushed with pleasure at the compliments. She was amazed that an artist as gifted as Snake would listen to her suggestions. He and June had already raved about her sewing in the past week.

The work that Naomi did at home – cooking cleaning, sewing, caring for her family and home – went largely unnoticed by her children or husband. It wasn't that they were ungrateful; they simply took her for granted.

It seemed to Naomi that people rarely noticed her. She blended into the background at social gatherings, and there were many times she would start to speak only to be drowned out by someone else.

So when a handsome, talented young designer and an expert seamstress noticed her work, it was a huge boost to her ego.

It wasn't that she didn't know her worth. Her mother had instilled that into her from her earliest memories. However, over time her husband had overshadowed her with his domineering personality and loud voice. Her mother encouraged her to stand up and make herself heard, but after years in a subservient role, she was accustomed to being in the background.

Snake's words today had awakened something in her, a sense of pride she had almost forgotten. Being part of a team like this took her back to her college days when she was

An Admission of Weakness

young and carefree. It felt liberating, and she couldn't help but smile and hum a tune while she worked.

"I miss you," Katie said into the phone at her Los Angeles apartment.
"I miss you too," Dillon said.
"One day soon we'll be together for good, I promise," Katie said.
"You know, I'm starting to think that's not true. It's been years, and we're no closer to being together than we were at the beginning."
"These things take time," Katie said. "You know how Dad is."
"Why do you insist on living your life for him?"
"I'm not," Katie frowned. "You don't understand."
"You're right. I don't understand," Dillon agreed. "You're working a job you don't like, in a town you don't like, and you're keeping us apart simply to keep your father happy."
"I'm not trying to keep us apart," Katie insisted.
"Are you sure about that? You care more about what your father thinks than me."
"He just has to be approached carefully," Katie said.
"I don't see what he has against me anyway."
"It isn't you he doesn't like," she said cautiously.

An Admission of Weakness

"It's because I'm not a rich doctor," he said dryly. "The only thing that matters to him is that you marry someone wealthy."
"He's from a different era," Katie explained.
"Look, Katie, I love you," Dillon said. "But I'm not going to wait forever. Either you tell him about us, or I'm done."
"I'll tell him soon," she promised. "The next time I come home."
"If you don't, I will," Dillon said grimly.

Dillon Talbot and Katie had been classmates all through school. The two started dating when they were thirteen years old and eventually fell in love.
Dillon was a gawky teenager. He was what most people called a nerd in high school, the sort of guy who took his studies seriously and wore a pocket protector and thick glasses. The first time Katie brought him home, her father hadn't bothered to hide his disdain.
"Your folks own the Talbot Saddler Company," Carter frowned.
"Yes, sir," sixteen year old Dillon fidgeted nervously. "It was the first Black owned business in town."
"That's a nice enough little business, I suppose," Carter said grudgingly.
"It's not so little," Dillon said. "We offer –"

An Admission of Weakness

"So what are your plans after graduation, young man?" Carter interrupted him. "Do you want to be a doctor? A lawyer?"

"Actually, I'm planning to join Mom and Dad in the business," Dillon said. "I'm very interested in developing the Internet sales side. And I like working the ranch too."

"Do your parents still raise those beautiful horses?" Naomi asked.

"Yes, ma'am," Dillon smiled with pleasure. "Our Clydesdale line dates clear back to Scotland. My family was one of the first ones in this part of the country to have one."

"Sounds like an expensive waste of time to me," Carter frowned.

Dillon's more recent family history dated back to the founding of Green Grove when they owned the original blacksmith/farrier business as well as the first stable. An ancestor of Dillon's had been forced to flee Tennessee after their house was burned by the Ku Klux Klan. He settled his family in Green Grove and served on the first town council.

Eventually, the family acquired land on the northwestern outskirts of town. There they raised the enormous horses on their two hundred acre ranch. Eventually, they began offering horse boarding, training, and riding lessons. Dillon was especially fond of the horses and spent as much time with the

An Admission of Weakness

Clydesdales, Arabians, Thoroughbreds, and Quarter Horses as possible.

The site of the original blacksmith shop was on the west end of the downtown, between the hardware store and the police station. It had eventually become the Talbot Saddler Company and now employed two hundred people. It appeared deceptively small from the street but was actually an enormous Morton Building. The building's charming facade resembled an old-west storefront with wagon wheels, hitching posts, rocking chairs, and watering troughs.

Besides crafting high quality saddles and bridles, the business also made leather cowboy and work boots, belts, purses, wallets, leashes and dog collars, and more. Dillon's parents Clint and Marci worked mostly in development of new products while they oversaw their dedicated staff.

They sold products to businesses all over the country, and with their newly developed website, they had more business than they could handle.

"The ranch is quite profitable," Dillon frowned. "It doesn't cost money; it makes money."

"It's a lovely property," Naomi said. "I enjoy driving by there when we go to the club."

An Admission of Weakness

She was referring to the Indian Trails Country Club, which was located across the highway to the west of the Talbot ranch.

"But think of the difference you could make in the world as a doctor or lawyer," Carter said. "We need more Black professionals."

"I think we need more Black owned businesses," Dillon said.

"But what kind of future does a business like yours have?"

"Dad, Dillon and his parents don't have to justify their business to you," Katie said with annoyance.

"Katie, go do your homework," Carter scowled. "Dillon, I'll show you out."

An Admission of Weakness

CHAPTER SEVEN

The second time Dillon encountered Katie's parents was after the graduation ceremony held on the back lawn of the Green Grove High School.

In the two years since he was introduced to the Butterfield family, Dillon developed his physique and exchanged the thick glasses for contacts. Gone were the pocket protector and frumpy clothes, and in their place was a fashionable wardrobe. He had become a confident and attractive young man.

Katie ran over to where Dillon and his family were standing. She leaped into his arms and squeezed him. Carter and Naomi followed her with the rest of the Butterfield family in tow.

"Clint, Marci," Carter shook their hands grimly.

"Marci, it's so nice to see you," Naomi smiled warmly. "Hello, Clint."

"Naomi. You're both looking well," Clint grinned. "Ruby, it's good to see you."

"Katie, I hope you're coming to Dillon's party this evening," Marci said.

"Katie's having her own party," Carter said.

"It's just the family," Katie said. "I'll have time to run out to the ranch later."

"Dillon, congratulations on being salutatorian," Ruby hugged him. "I'm so proud of you."

An Admission of Weakness

"And Katie, it's a real honor to be valedictorian," Marci said. "You should feel very proud."

"She's been accepted at Yale," Naomi put a parental arm around her daughter. "She's worked hard to get there."

"What school are you going to, Dillon?" Carter asked.

"I'm studying business and computer science at Rolling Hills," Dillon said.

He was referring to the highly regarded community college located east of town. It had been built shortly after the town was founded.

"I see," Carter frowned. "And then?"

"I'm going to work for Mom and Dad," Dillon said.

"But surely you're going to a proper college," Carter said.

"Rolling Hills is an excellent school," Ruby said. "I taught there for years."

"But how is he going to make anything of himself without a college education?" Carter demanded.

"A college education obviously didn't make you any smarter," Ruby said.

"Mama," Naomi shook her head.

"Well, we'd better get going," Marci said with a strained smile. "We have to finish getting ready for the party. Katie, I hope we'll see you later."

An Admission of Weakness

"I'll be there," Katie said. "See you later, Dillon."
After the Talbot family headed to their car, Katie turned on her father angrily.
"Did you have to do that?"
"Do what?" Carter said.
"He knows what he did," Ruby said dryly. "He just doesn't see anything wrong with it."
"You embarrassed Dillon and me!" Katie snapped. "I'm surprised his parents still want me to come to his party."
"The boy has no motivation," Carter said firmly. "I want you to break up with him."
"Carter, she loves him," Naomi said.
"Nonsense," Carter said. "She's far too young to know anything about love."
"I wasn't much older than Katie when I fell in love with you," Naomi reminded him.
"That was different," Carter said. "You were more mature than Katie."
"So now you're saying I'm immature?" Katie said indignantly.
"Compared to your mother at your age? Yes, I am," Carter said.
"Mama," Katie turned to her mother. "I won't be home for supper. If Dad wants to apologize, I'll be at Dillon's."
"Your mother made your favorite meal," Carter said. "You're coming home with us."
Katie responded by hugging her mother and grandmother and then walking toward the

An Admission of Weakness

parking lot without a backward glance. The others turned back to Carter.
"What?" he said innocently.
"Dad, you just don't get it," Camilla sighed.
"I do get it," Carter scowled. "And she is not going to marry that boy. I won't have it."

Robbie worked fulltime and took an additional six credit hours of classes that summer. He talked to his brother at least once a week, and the two made plans for Rhett to come for a visit over the following Christmas break.
His class schedule that fall was tight with little free time to be had. He got a job in the university bookstore on the weekends to earn money for Rhett's train ticket.
The best part of the semester was cheerleading. The men and women on the team were very nice, and many of the women made their attraction to him known. He started casually dating a fellow cheerleader, an attractive, dark-headed young man named Devon who was very sweet.
Devon often stayed over because evening and nighttime were the only times Robbie was available to him. Not surprisingly, Robbie had never had a boyfriend before, and he was understandably anxious about his first sexual experience. Fortunately, Devon was gentle and guided him through it so that it was a pleasurable experience for both of them.

An Admission of Weakness

"Is that your faggot boyfriend?" Blair taunted one morning after Devon left for classes.
He leaned against Robbie's room's doorjamb with his arms folded.
"No, that's my straight boyfriend," Robbie replied while he made his bed. "I haven't told him about my faggot boyfriend yet. Do you think he'll be upset?"
"How can you have a straight boyfriend?" Blair asked skeptically.
"Oh my god," Robbie rolled his eyes. "The same way you have a lesbian girlfriend."
"I don't have a lesbian girlfriend," Blair frowned.
"Exactly," Robbie chuckled.
"You're not making any sense," Blair shook his head.
"Why do you care about my love life?" Robbie asked.
"Because it grosses me out knowing what the two of you are doing a few feet away from me."
"You can join us if you want. That way you wouldn't miss out on any of the action."
"You're sick," Blair scowled and turned to go.
"I don't think about your sex life," Robbie stopped him. "Why do you fantasize about mine?"
"I-I don't fantasize about it," Blair sputtered. "I just know what you're doing, and I don't like it."

An Admission of Weakness

"How do you know what gay guys do in bed?"
"Everyone knows, and it's disgusting."
"If you've never tried it, how do you know it's disgusting?"
"I ought to punch you again!" Blair growled and balled his hands into fists.
"If you don't like what I have to say, don't come over here," Robbie said. "It's not like I invited you."
"Fuck you," Blair gave him the finger and returned to his room.

The snow hit central and northern Illinois hard in December that year. One Saturday, Robbie and his friends built a fort and snowman out of snow outside the dorm. When some of the football players walked by, Robbie mischievously through a snowball at Andres, the team captain.
"Okay, Blondie," Andres grinned and stooped to make a snowball. "You're a dead man."
Robbie ducked behind the snow barricade just as the snowball flew over his head. He threw another one, and it struck another team member. In no time, there was a full-blown war being waged between the two sides. People laughed and ducked and tried to cram snow down the shirts and pants of their opponents. It was all great fun until Blair hurled a snowball directly at Robbie's face from close range. He was known for his throwing arm, so there was a

An Admission of Weakness

great deal of momentum behind it. The force of the impact landed Robbie on his back.
He shook his head to clear his brain, and his friends helped him sit up dazedly in the snow. Once he regained his senses, anger took over. He gathered snow in his hand and approached Blair with a steely look in his blue eyes.
"You son of a bitch," he said. "You did that on purpose."
"Sure I did," Blair smirked. "What are you going to do about it?"
Robbie unexpectedly smashed the snowball into his face. Blair coughed and sputtered to clear the cold water from his windpipe. In a fit of fury, he lunged for Robbie and knocked him onto his back once again. He straddled him and used his fist to hit him twice before Andres and the other guys were able to pull him away.
Robbie lay still on the ground, and Devon tried to wake him.
"I'm calling 911," somebody hastily pulled a phone from their pocket. "Don't move him."
"Cover him with our coats," another person said.
Robbie's friends surrounded him while Andres dragged Blair away.
"That's it," he jabbed a finger in Blair's chest. "You're sitting out the next game!"
"You don't have the authority to do that," Blair said scornfully.

An Admission of Weakness

"You try anything like this again, and I'll see to it you're off the team," Andres said coldly. "This is your final warning."

"He started it," Blair protested.

"No, he didn't," Devon snapped and shoved Blair. "You did. We all saw it. I'm going to report you. This was a hate crime."

"Yeah!" the others gathered around angrily.

"Devon, guys, let me take care of this," Andres held them back. "Trust me; he's not going to get away with it."

Robbie sat up at that moment with the help of his friends.

"Don't move," Devon said. "You might have a concussion."

"See," Blair said. "He's fine."

"You'd better hope he is," Andres said. "If the coach finds out you sent a student to the ER, you'll be lucky if you don't get kicked out of school."

After spending four hours at a nearby Emergency Department, Robbie was released and sent back to his dorm room with instructions to rest for forty-eight hours. Devon wanted to stay the night with him, but Robbie sent him away so he could sleep. He had a slight headache and wanted to be alone. The nerve of that bastard to hit him! Was he really so homophobic that he would risk his football scholarship?

An Admission of Weakness

Just before ten o'clock that evening, there came a knock on his door.
"I'm asleep," he called out.
He was usually a social, gregarious person, but tonight he felt irritated with people in general.
"No, you're not," Blair said.
"Get away from my door or I'll call Campus Security."
"I just want to talk," Blair said. "I won't hit you."
"Why the hell would I want to talk to you?" Robbie said. "I'm calling downstairs."
"Fine, I'll go," Blair said. "Jeez. I just wanted to see if you're okay."
Robbie responded by throwing a shoe at the door.

The next day, Andres knocked on Robbie's open door.
"Robbie?" he called.
"Come on in," Robbie grinned. He was sitting cross-legged on his bed with a pile of textbooks and a laptop in front of him.
"Aren't you supposed to be taking it easy?"
"That's why I'm not at work," Robbie said. "I decided to use the time to study for finals this week."
"How are you?"
"My jaw's a little sore," Robbie said.
"Holy shit, your face is all bruised," Andres whistled and sat down in the desk chair.

An Admission of Weakness

"Thanks to your jackass friend," Robbie said.
"He is a jackass sometimes," Andres agreed.
"So I guess you'll be going home for break."
"That's not really an option," Robbie said.
"Why not?"
Robbie explained about coming out in his speech and how his father had shot a hole in the side of the house right before he left for Urbana.
"I'm sorry," Andres said sympathetically.
"It's okay," Robbie said. "The good thing is that my brother Rhett is coming to visit me."
"You two get along well?"
"He's my best friend. I've always had to watch out for him. I think that's why we're so close."
"Why did you have to watch out for him?"
Robbie told him about Rhett's disabilities and his sweet, vulnerable nature.
"He's the kindest person I've ever known," he added. "I'm lucky to have him."

"You've got to be shitting me!" Blair said angrily. "I'm not doing it."
"What the fuck did you just say to me?" Coach Wilkensen growled.
"I mean, isn't there something else I could do?" Blair hastily amended his words.
"Not if you want to stay on the team and keep your scholarship."
"But –"

An Admission of Weakness

"I'm done with this conversation, Butterfield," the coach said. "Take it or leave it."
"You don't even know this guy," Blair said. "Who told you…?"
Even as he asked the question, he knew the answer: Andres.

"Why would you do this to me?" Blair yelled. "I thought we were friends."
"We are friends," Andres said calmly.
"Friends don't ruin their friend's Christmas holiday by making them chauffeur some fag around town," Blair snapped.
"Look on the bright side," Andres chuckled. "You get to stay on the football team."
"I was already on the team," Blair said irritably. "Why did you have to stick your fucking nose into my business?"
"Why are you so homophobic?" Andres countered.
"Why do you like gay people so much?" Blair said.
"Because I don't care who they sleep with."
"Why do they choose to be that way when they don't have to?"
"Choose to be?" Andres frowned. "You mean like you chose to be Black?"
"It's not the same thing."
"Bro, people don't choose their sexuality," Andres said.

An Admission of Weakness

"Sure they do," Blair said. "Everyone has those feelings, but that doesn't mean you have to act on them."

"What feelings?" Andres looked puzzled.

"You know," Blair said. "Where you're physically attracted to someone of the same sex. You don't do anything about it because you know it's wrong."

"Oh," Andres nodded slowly. "Like how you're physically attracted to Robbie, but you don't do anything with him because it would be wrong."

"Exactly," Blair said. "So you know what I'm talking about."

"No, bro, I really don't," Andres said. "I don't have those feelings toward guys."

"Yes, you do," Blair frowned. "Everyone does."

"No they don't. Straight people aren't physically attracted to the same sex. That's why we're straight."

It was Blair's turn to look confused.

"Straight men have no desire to have sex with other men," Andres said.

"You can't tell me you wouldn't sleep with Robbie if he'd let you," Blair said.

"No way," Andres said. "So you're attracted to Robbie? I mean, the way you are to girls?"

"Of course not," Blair pshawed the idea. "I'm as straight as they come."

"Are you sure? Because it's cool if you're not."

An Admission of Weakness

"I'm not gay, bro!" Blair said sharply. "I like women."
"'Cause I can see that Robbie is good-looking," Andres said. "All the girls think he's hot."
"He's a pussy," Blair scowled. "I don't like pussies."
Hmm, Andres mused, there may be truth to that statement, just not the kind that Blair meant.

Classes ended on Friday, and Rhett arrived on Saturday afternoon. Blair drove Robbie to the train station, complaining under his breath the entire time.
"If you're going to be a jerk about this, you might as well go on home and let your family put up with you," Robbie said disgustedly.
"How would you like it if your whole Christmas break was ruined because of the faggot across the hall?" Blair snapped.
"Are you talking about me or you?" Robbie grinned.
"Shut the fuck up."
"I didn't ruin your holiday," Robbie said. "That's between you and your coach. Look, I don't want you to not see your family on Christmas. So once you take us back to the dorm, you're off the hook. You can go on home."
"Why don't you go home for Christmas?" Blair frowned. "Why is your brother coming here?"

An Admission of Weakness

"My dad threatened to kill me the last time I was home," Robbie said dryly. "Going home isn't really an option."

"He didn't really do that, did he?" Blair said.

"Yeah, he kinda did," Robbie said.

The two walked into the station and checked the train schedule. Rhett was due to arrive any minute.

When the train stopped, passengers began to alight, and Robbie searched the crowd anxiously. Making a trip of this kind by himself was a first for Rhett, and he was worried that it might prove too much for him.

At last, his brother stepped awkwardly from the train with a backpack strapped to his back. He looked around uncertainly and smiled with relief when he saw Robbie.

Robbie ran over and swept him into his arms. The two squeezed each other as if they never wanted to let go. Finally, Robbie stepped back and held him at arm's length.

"You've grown," he said. "You're almost as tall as me."

"I'm five foot ten now," Rhett grinned proudly.

"You look great," Robbie told him.

"And you look fantastic," Rhett said.

He glanced curiously at Blair.

"How was the trip?" Robbie asked. "Did you have any trouble?"

"Evwyone was weally nice," Rhett said. He hugged him again. "I'm so happy to see you."

An Admission of Weakness

"Me too," Robbie smiled happily.

Blair stood back and watched the touching reunion. He was surprised to see that Blondie's brother was too thin, couldn't pronounce his 'r's, and had a distinct limp. His clothes were shabby and ill-fitting, and his sneakers were practically threadbare. His backpack was held together with duct tape.
Come to think of it, Robbie's clothes, shoes, laptop, and phone were all old and in pretty poor condition, but he hadn't paid attention to that until now. The man was so nice looking and cheerful that everything else about him faded into the background. And he had the greatest ass he'd ever seen as well.
Obviously, Robbie came from a poor family. And based on his and Rhett's accents, they were raised somewhere in the south.

"Rhett, this is DJ," Robbie introduced them. "This is my brother Rhett."
"The name's Blair," Blair said stiffly.
"Oh yeah," Robbie grinned. "I forgot."
"It nice to meet you," Rhett smiled and shook Blair's hand. "You guys awe fwiends?"
"Not at all," Blair said wryly.
"Are you hungry?" Robbie ignored him. "We can get a pizza or go to the cafeteria."
"I'm kinda tired," Rhett said.

An Admission of Weakness

"Then we'll get a pizza delivered and let you rest," Robbie said solicitously.
"Don't spend money on me," Rhett said.
"You've spent enough alweady just getting me here."
"We can afford a pizza," Robbie grinned. "And we have to celebrate you being here. After we have pizza, I'll treat you to some ice cream."
He put an arm around Rhett's shoulders and guided him to Blair's car.

Robbie knocked on Blair's door after retrieving the pizzas from the front desk downstairs.
"You're welcome to join us," he said. "I got extra."
"You think that's going to make up for me missing Christmas with my family?" Blair said sourly.
"I told you you're off the hook," Robbie said. "Go home."
"I can't," Blair said. "Coach says I have to stick it out."
"You want me to talk to him?" Robbie offered.
"I think you've done enough already."
"Okay, I just thought you might not like being alone," Robbie shrugged. "Suit yourself."
Rhett limped into the hall.
"Come have some pizza," he said. "It's the least we can do since you dwove us."

An Admission of Weakness

Blair's heart melted when he looked in Rhett's ingenuous blue eyes. There was no guile there, only sincerity and kindness.
"I guess I could eat a couple of pieces," he said reluctantly.

An Admission of Weakness

CHAPTER EIGHT

The three sat down in Robbie's room, Rhett and Robbie on the bed and Blair on the desk chair.

"You play football?" Rhett asked between bites of the delicious pizza.

"Yeah," Blair said briefly.

"What number awe you?"

"Seven."

"That's a lucky number," Rhett said. "I'm pwetty good at volleyball."

"Isn't that kind of hard with your –?" Blair broke off abruptly.

"I can't wun, but I'm good at hitting the ball," Rhett didn't take offense.

"What's wrong with your leg?"

"It's a congenital thing," Robbie answered.

"I'm sorry," Blair said awkwardly.

"It's okay," Rhett said. "It only bothers other people, not me."

"So are you a fag too?" Blair asked.

"Hey!" Robbie said heatedly. "You don't have the right to ask him that. What if he didn't know I was gay? You would have just outed me."

"I don't mind if he asks," Rhett said. "I like girls. They just don't like me because I don't talk wight and have the limp."

"So you're not attracted to men at all?" Blair frowned.

An Admission of Weakness

"No," Rhett said. "What about you?"
"What about me?"
"Do you like guys or girls?"
"He's one hundred percent breeder," Robbie said dryly. "He has a different woman in his room every night. Sometimes two women."
"Speaking of that, where's your boyfriend tonight?" Blair asked.
"He went home for the holidays," Robbie said.
"You didn't tell me you have a boyfwiend," Rhett nudged his brother.
"It's just a friends with benefits kind of thing," Robbie said. "He's a fellow cheerleader."
"I can hear the two of them going at it practically every night," Blair said.
"I have to do something to drown out the noise coming from your room," Robbie said. "That last one was a real screamer. Or was that you?"
"At least I don't take it up the ass," Blair retorted.
"You don't know what you're missing," Robbie grinned. "I could show you if you want."
He and Rhett chuckled while Blair stood up and threw his pizza down.
"Keep your fucking dick to yourself," he snapped. "And never imply that I'm gay again."
"Blair's a little sensitive when it comes to his masculinity," Robbie explained. "He has TDS."
"What's TDS?" Rhett frowned.

An Admission of Weakness

"Tiny dick syndrome," Robbie couldn't help but burst out laughing, and his brother joined him.

"Fuck you guys," Blair scowled. "My dick's bigger than both of yours put together."

Something about that statement struck Robbie as especially funny, and he rolled on the floor, unable to control his laughter. Blair stormed from the room and slammed the door behind him.

"Can you look out for Rhett for a few hours?" Robbie asked Blair one morning. "I got called into work."

Blair was wearing only a pair of tight boxers, and Robbie couldn't help but gulp at the sight of his muscular chest and arms, lean abdomen, and thick thighs.

"I wouldn't know what to do with him," Blair yawned and stretched. "Find another baby-sitter."

"Forget it," Robbie turned away. "I should have known better than to ask you."

"Fine," Blair said with a much put-upon sigh. "What do I have to do?"

"Just make sure he doesn't get lost and no one bothers him. He's not used to big cities."

"Urbana is hardly a big city," Blair snorted.

"It is to him," Robbie said. "Take him to get something to eat. I gave him some money."

"Fine," Blair rolled his eyes and sighed again.

An Admission of Weakness

"And be nice to him," Robbie said sternly. "If I hear you've said anything mean, I'll take you out like I did before."
"That was pure luck," Blair frowned. "You'll never have the chance to do that again."
With one unexpected shove and a quick move of his foot, Robbie toppled Blair to the floor as he had done before.
"What was that you said?" he stood over him. "Now be nice to him or else."

"So do you want breakfast or what?" Blair asked sullenly after knocking on Robbie's door.
"Can we go to Le Peep?" Rhett said eagerly. "Wobbie says it's weally good."
"Fine," Blair sighed.

"Doesn't it bother you to have a gay brother?" Blair asked while they ate their omelets.
"No," Rhett said. "Why would it?"
"You don't think there's anything wrong with it?"
"It's just pawt of who he is," Rhett said. "Why? Do you think there's something wong with it?"
"It goes against nature."
"It's pawt of nature," Rhett disagreed. "Why else would there be gay whinocewoses and penguins and stuff?"
"You don't think it's a choice?"

An Admission of Weakness

"Is being Black a choice?" Rhett asked. "Is being stwaight a choice? When did you choose to be those things?"
"I didn't," Blair said uneasily.
This conversation was becoming a little too real, so he changed the subject.
"What do the doctors say about your leg? Can't they do something about it?"
"I only ever saw one doctor about it when I was little," Rhett said. "He said nothing could be done."
"What about exercises or a brace?"
"I have a bwace, but it doesn't fit me anymore," Rhett said.
"You know, the university has a whole team of physical therapists," Blair said. "Why don't we go talk to them? They might have some suggestions for you."

Blair and Rhett drove to the athletic department, where Blair introduced Rhett to a couple of therapists who worked with the university's sports teams. They had helped him once when he pulled a muscle during a game. Rhett explained to them what his childhood doctor told his family when he was four years old.
"Isn't there something he could do to make his leg stronger?" Blair asked.
He and Rhett spent the entire morning in the department, and Rhett met with more

An Admission of Weakness

therapists, nurses, and even a doctor. By the time they headed back to the dorm, after thanking the staff repeatedly, Rhett had a new brace and pages of exercise instructions to follow.

"I can't believe they gave me this bwace," he said happily.

He was already standing straighter and walking with more confidence. Having a quality brace that actually fit him made all the difference.

"It was an old one they had lying around," Blair said.

"I don't care," Rhett smiled. "It's new to me."

Blair couldn't help but smile too. Rhett was a very sweet soul who was grateful for any bit of kindness shown him. He had probably seen a lot of bullying and ugly behavior in his lifetime.

"What's your family like?" Blair asked over lunch in the cafeteria.

Rhett talked about his parents and sisters, their impoverished existence, his father's cruelty, and about his best friend Robbie.

"Did your father really threaten to kill him?" Blair asked skeptically.

"He shot a hole in the side of the house," Rhett said.

"Why?"

An Admission of Weakness

Rhett told him about Robbie's valedictorian speech and the backlash the family had experienced from the community since then.
"It was stupid to say anything," Blair said. "He should have kept his mouth shut."
"It wasn't stupid," Rhett said indignantly. "It was bwave."
"But why did he have to broadcast it to the world? His sex life is nobody's business."
"He wasn't talking about sex. Evwyone thinks being gay is all about sex."
"Isn't it?"
"He was talking about gay kids that need to be loved and accepted for who they awe just like evwyone else."
"Are you sure you're not queer?"
"You don't have to be gay to understand what it's like. Since he came out, three kids have told me they're gay. They're too afwaid to tell anyone else because their parents would kick them out.
"They said Wobbie let them know they weren't the only one. He gave them hope for the future."
"If you say so," Blair shrugged.

The two young men returned to the dorm.
"Can I see your woom?" Rhett asked.
"It looks like your brother's," Blair said. "But you can see it if you want."

An Admission of Weakness

He opened the door to his room, and Rhett stepped inside and looked around.
"That's Langston Hughes," he pointed to a poster on the wall.
"Yes, it is," Blair said, surprised.
"'Hold fast to your dweams, for without them life is a bwoken winged bird that cannot fly.'"
"How'd you know he said that?"
"He's one of Wobbie's hewos," Rhett said. "He wote that quote on the living woom wall so he could see it evwy day. He taught it to all of us."
Wow, Blair thought, a white southerner who was actually capable of critical thinking. He knew he was stereotyping, but he believed most white people were racist at least to some degree.
"He was gay," Rhett interrupted his thoughts.
"Who was?"
"Langston Hughes."
"No, he wasn't," Blair frowned.
"Yes, he was," Rhett said and pointed to a collage of pictures. "So were Bayard Wustin, Mawsha Johnson, and James Baldwin. There were lots of Black gay people who made a diffewence. Alvin Ailey, Audwe Lorde, Bawbwa Jordan, Won Oden."
"How does a white boy from Mississippi know all that?"
"Wobbie," Rhett shrugged. "He taught us that Black history and gay history are American history, and we should know about them."

An Admission of Weakness

"I thought all white southerners were racist," Blair said bluntly.

"We're not all ignowant wednecks," Rhett said dryly. "You of all people should know not to steweotype."

"Why me of all people?" Blair frowned.

"You're a Black football player," Rhett said. "People might assume you're like Herschel Walker: dumb, violent, with a bunch of kids he never waised, barely able to put two words together."

"I'm nothing like that idiot," Blair said heatedly.

"I know. But you get my point."

"I get it."

"So don't lump all us southerners together," Rhett said. "Some of us awe okay."

Blair watched Robbie from across the hall. Their doors were open, and he could see Robbie and Rhett talking and laughing together.

Apparently there was more to this guy than just being gay. He had a brain too. Not to mention he was kind of adorable. He couldn't get his perfect ass out of his mind. God, and those blue eyes…

Oh fuck. He shouldn't be having those kinds of thoughts. He should keep his attractions focused strictly on women.

An Admission of Weakness

Damn it, was Robbie's gayness rubbing off on him, as his father predicted might happen? Or were Andres and Rhett right, and being gay wasn't a choice? Did that mean these thoughts and feelings he was having were born into him? Did it mean he was gay because he was attracted to men, Robbie in particular?
He had always assumed everyone felt attraction for their own sex, but Andres said that wasn't true. So what did these feelings mean?
One way to find out, he decided. He was excited and terrified to put his theory to the test, but he knew he needed to know.
He walked across the hall. Robbie was wearing a torn pair of running shorts and an old Obama tee shirt, revealing his hairy legs.
"Hey, Blair," Rhett grinned up at him.
"Hey, bro," Blair smiled back.
"Thank you for what you did for him today," Robbie said.
"All I did was take him to eat," Blair shrugged.
"I mean taking him to the athletic department and getting his new brace. I never would have thought of that."
"We had fun," Rhett grinned. "He showed me all awound the athletic depawtment and his woom. He's a nice guy."
"No, he isn't," Robbie said. "Don't let this act of his fool you."
"Rhett said you're a nice guy too," Blair said. "If that's true, you've kept it well hidden."

An Admission of Weakness

"You're both nice guys," Rhett said. "You should be fwiends."
"I'm not friends with fags," Blair said.
"And I'm not friends with homophobic pricks," Robbie retorted.
Blair changed the subject.
"Do that one cheer for me."
"Cool!" Rhett cried. "I wanna see a cheer."
"Do a cheer? Why?"
"I, uh, want to show my girlfriend," Blair lied.
"If you have a girlfriend, why do you sleep with half the campus?"
"I don't sleep with half the campus," Blair rolled his eyes.
"What's it like having sex with girls?" Rhett asked eagerly. "I'll bet it's fantastic."
"Rhett, you're too young to ask those kinds of questions," his brother scolded him
"I'm seventeen," Rhett said.
"Sex isn't all it's cracked up to be," Blair shrugged. "I do it because it feels good to cum, but jerking off is just as good."
"Weally?" Rhett looked disappointed. "I thought it would be better."
"Trust me," Robbie said wryly. "Sex is great whether it's gay or straight. He just doesn't know what he's doing."
"I do too," Blair said indignantly.
"That's even worse," Robbie chuckled. "You must be lousy at it if you know what you're doing and it still isn't good."

An Admission of Weakness

"The last one didn't scream for nothing, you know," Blair said.
"She was probably trying to get away."
"Forget it," Blair turned away, exasperated.
"What cheer did you want to see?" Robbie called after him.
Blair turned back.
"The one where you swivel your hips and talk about taking the ball back."
"Oh, the one to 'About Damn Time'," Robbie nodded.
He pulled up the song on his phone, and the music filled the room. He waited for his cue and then performed the cheer as best he could in the cramped room while Blair filmed it. Blair instantly felt his manhood began to swell at the sight of the blonde-haired man dancing and jumping to the music. God, he was so attractive. He was muscular and lean, and he had a hairy chest and legs. One thing that turned Blair on more than anything else was a hairy man.
When the cheer ended, Robbie turned the music off and caught his breath.
"That was fantastic," Rhett said enthusiastically.
"It was okay, I guess," Blair shrugged.
"I wish I looked like you or Blair," Rhett said wistfully.
"You look great just as you are," Blair said, not wanting Rhett to feel bad about himself. God

An Admission of Weakness

knows, the kid had enough issues with which to cope.
"I do?" Rhett looked surprised.
"Sure," Blair said. He added snidely, "And you're way nicer than your brother."
"And I'm way nicer than you," Robbie said.
"So what does that make you?"
"Shut up."
"Blair's good-looking," Rhett said. "You two would make a great couple if Blair was gay."
"But I'm not," Blair said quickly.
"You said that awfully fast," Robbie smirked. "Are you trying to convince us or yourself?"
"I'm not gay no matter how much you want me to be," Blair said.
"Who said I want you to be gay?" Robbie frowned.
"You'd go to bed with me in a heartbeat if I'd let you," Blair snorted.
"So you've thought about going to bed with me," Robbie grinned impishly. "Good to know."
Rhett watched the interaction between the two men with interest. Now that he knew Robbie was gay, it was obvious to him. And he had a sneaking suspicion about Blair as well; the way he watched Robbie dance was a giveaway.
"I'm hungwy for pizza," Rhett said unexpectedly. "Stay and have some with us."
"He's too afraid I'll ravage him," Robbie chuckled.

An Admission of Weakness

"I'm not afraid of anything," Blair scowled. "Order the pizza, and it'll be my treat. But I'm only staying because of Rhett. He's a good guy, unlike you."

"You are such a sweet talker," Robbie laughed and squished Blair's cheeks together.

"Cut it out," Blair brushed his hand away with annoyance.

Damn, the mere touch of Robbie's hand was enough to send a charge shooting straight to his groin. His manhood immediately came alive and began to swell. He'd had no trouble getting hard with all the women he'd been with, but no bolt of lightning had ever struck him with any of them. As much as he didn't want to admit it, that had to mean something.

When the pizza arrived, the three of them sat down in Robbie's room to eat it.

"What kind of girls do you like?" Rhett asked.

"All kinds, I guess," Blair said vaguely.

"They all have big boobs," Robbie chuckled.

"You must be a boob man."

"What's your girlfriend like?"

"Does she know you sleep with every woman you meet?" Robbie asked.

"Actually, we kind of broke up," Blair said.

"You just said you wanted a video of me to show her," Robbie frowned.

I think I see what's going on, Rhett thought.

"Is she pwetty?" he asked.

An Admission of Weakness

"Are her boobs bigger than her brain?" Robbie grinned.
"She's the prettiest girl in Green Grove," Blair ignored him.
"Where's Gween Gwove?"
"It's about three hours north of here."
"What's it like?"
"It's the nicest town in Illinois," Blair said.
"Why did you break up with your girlfriend?" Robbie asked.
"She's going to Dartmouth, and I didn't want to do long distance."
"Did you love her?"
"I don't know," Blair said. "Maybe."
"So you might get back together," Rhett said.
"We might," Blair said without conviction. "I'm only nineteen. I think I should play the field a little."
"You've certainly been doing that," Robbie said dryly. "Both literally and figuratively."
"So I like sex," Blair said. "Why do you care what I do?"
"I don't," Robbie said.
"Sex must be better than you said if you do it all the time," Rhett said.
"He's just trying to get it right for once," Robbie chuckled.
"Why don't you like gay people?" Rhett asked.
"I just don't, that's all," Blair shrugged.
"I'll bet your dad is homophobic."
"Why do you say that?"

An Admission of Weakness

"You had to learn it somewhere," Rhett said. "Most people learn it at home."

"I didn't learn it. It's natural to hate gay people."

"Whoa!" Robbie frowned. "That's harsh."

"No one is born hating," Rhett snorted. "Hate is learned. Believe me, I've seen enough to last me a lifetime."

"Look, I'm tolerant enough to sit here and eat pizza with one," Blair said. "Isn't that enough?"

Rhett smiled inwardly because he was pretty sure he was eating pizza with two.

"Yes, your mind is amazingly open," Robbie grinned.

"Are you judging me?"

"Sort of," Robbie chuckled.

Blair shoved him good-naturedly, and Robbie responded in kind. Rhett watched with amusement as the two began wrestling. Blair managed to force Robbie onto his back. The physical contact made him hard, but he didn't care. This felt good, and he didn't want to stop. He straddled Robbie and grinned down at him.

"You really thought you could beat me?"

Robbie reached up and tickled him, and Blair rolled onto his side and curled up defensively.

"If I knew that's all it took, I'd have done that sooner," Robbie laughed.

"You guys awe too much," Rhett joined his brother in laughter.

An Admission of Weakness

"Are you laughing at us?" Robbie frowned and turned to Blair. "We should get even."
"No!" Rhett said hastily.
He tried to move away, but the other two were too quick for him. They all tickled each other and laughed until they had to gasp for breath.

An Admission of Weakness

CHAPTER NINE

Blair drove Robbie and Rhett to the train station a few days later.
"I'm gonna miss you," Rhett said unhappily.
"Me too," Robbie hugged and squeezed him hard. "But I'll send you another ticket next summer so you can visit again."
"At least I got to see where you live and meet Blair." He whispered into Robbie's ear, "I think he likes you."
"Nah, but he definitely likes you," Robbie grinned. "How could he not?"
"How could I not what?" Blair frowned.
"Like Rhett," Robbie said.
"I do like Rhett," Blair said. "I like him a lot."
"Me too," Rhett reached over and embraced him. "Look after Wobbie for me."
"He doesn't need anyone to look after him."
"Please?"
"Okay, sure," Blair acquiesced.
"And pwomise you'll be his fwiend."
"I don't think that's going to happen," Blair said uneasily.
"Pwomise me," Rhett squeezed him harder.
"I'll try," Blair said.
"The train's boarding, boys," the porter said as he passed by.
"Here's fifty dollars for the trip," Robbie pressed some bills into Rhett's hand. "Tell Ma and the girls merry Christmas."

An Admission of Weakness

"I will," Rhett said.

The two brothers hugged again.

"Call me when you get home," Robbie said emotionally. "And call if you have any trouble."

"Here's my number," Blair handed a slip of paper to Rhett. "If you can't get hold of Robbie, call me."

"Thanks," Rhett said.

"Why are you doing something nice?" Robbie said suspiciously.

"I'm always nice," Blair said.

"You're never nice."

"Thanks for all you did for me, and for buying me bweakfast and lunch and pizza and stuff."

"You're welcome," Blair grinned. "I had fun. You're a great guy even if you are related to him."

He gestured rudely to Robbie, but he winked at Rhett so he would know there was no malice behind it.

"He's a great guy *because* he's related to me," Robbie said. "I'll bet your parents wish they could say the same thing about you."

"I won't be here to wefewee," Rhett reminded them. "So you guys have to get along on your own."

"I'm gonna miss him," Blair said after the train pulled away. "He's a sweet kid."

An Admission of Weakness

"Yes, he is. Thank you for all you did for him, and for giving him your phone number. I think that meant a lot to him."

"I didn't do anything," Blair said. "I wish I could have done more." An idea occurred to him. "Dammit, I should have gotten him a Fighting Illini shirt or something to take back with him."

"You being his friend meant everything to him. He's so used to being bullied by jocks, having a handsome college football player as a friend was a big ego boost for him."

"Handsome?" Blair frowned.

"Don't worry," Robbie said. "I'm not coming on to you. Your fragile masculinity is safe."

"Don't start that bullshit again," Blair scowled.

"I take it back," Robbie said. "You're not handsome at all. In fact, I didn't want to say anything before, but you're kinda hideous. I hope that doesn't hurt your feelings, but at least now you know how I really feel."

"You're awful cocky for someone who's dating a fag like Devon."

The two walked to the car.

"What's wrong with Devon?" Robbie frowned.

"He's a priss-ass," Blair shrugged. "And he's not that good of a cheerleader. He looks like he's got a small dick."

"At least he knows how to use it," Robbie grinned.

An Admission of Weakness

Blair put him in a headlock and thumped the top of his head before Robbie could pull away.
"Did you just give me a nuggie?"
"Be glad that's all I did," Blair chuckled.
"Come on, loser, I'll buy you a burger."
"I'm not a loser."
"You date a loser, you're a loser," Blair said firmly.

Blair awoke with a start during the night and sat bolt upright. He wiped the sweat from his brow and took some deep breaths to calm himself.
His dream was coming back to him:

It had seemed so vivid. He was at home in Green Grove, and he had just brushed his teeth. He came out of his bathroom and was startled to see Robbie in his bed, smiling enticingly at him.
"Come to bed," Robbie patted the mattress next to him.
"What the fuck are you doing here?" Blair quickly shut the bedroom door to the hall before turning back to his unexpected guest.
"You invited me," Robbie frowned.
"No, I didn't. You've got to go. If my dad sees you in my bed, he'll kill you. And probably me too."
"He knows you're gay, right?" Robbie said.

An Admission of Weakness

"Uh, sure he does," Blair lied. He thought a moment. "Wait, I'm not gay."

"Of course you are," Robbie said. "Rhett told me so. He wouldn't lie."

"Rhett said I'm gay?"

"He said you got hard when we were wrestling. That means you're gay."

"No, it doesn't. Just because I'm attracted to you doesn't mean I'm gay too."

"Of course it does," Robbie chuckled. "Straight guys don't get hard-ons with other guys unless they're gay."

"Everyone has those feelings," Blair said desperately even as his dick swelled.

"No, they don't."

"But I'm straight. I have sex with women all the time."

"You fantasize about me, don't you?" Robbie said.

"Sometimes," Blair said weakly.

"You think about what it would be like to kiss me and hold me, what my lips would feel like on your body, how fantastic it would feel to fuck me."

"That doesn't prove anything," Blair insisted.

"You said yourself you don't like having sex with women," Robbie reminded him. "You fantasize about guys while you're with them just to have an orgasm."

"How did you know that?"

An Admission of Weakness

"I know you, Blair," Robbie said. "You've tried to be straight all your life, but it's not who you really are. That's why you act homophobic. You're afraid someone will find out your secret.

"Come out of the closet already," he went on. "Get in bed, and I'll show you your true self. The only way to be happy is to be who you really are."

"I-I can't," Blair began to sweat. His manhood was harder than it had ever been. "My dad would kill me."

Robbie arose and walked across the room toward him, completely nude. His body was as breathtaking as Blair had imagined. He wanted nothing more than to take him in his arms and kiss him and to take his beautiful manhood into his mouth.

"I want to be with you," Robbie kissed him gently and caressed his cheek. "Don't you want to be with me?"

"I do, more than I've ever wanted anything," Blair breathed. He blinked and took a step back. "But I'm supposed to be straight. Everyone is expecting me to be straight. If I ever acted on these feelings, I don't know what my dad would do. Your dad tried to kill you; my dad might do the same thing."

"Your dad is an educated man," Robbie said. "He would never resort to violence."

An Admission of Weakness

The bedroom door banged open just then, and Blair's dad burst into the room.
"What the hell's going on here?" he demanded.
"Your son is gay," Robbie said.
"No, I'm not!" Blair exclaimed. "He doesn't know what he's talking about."
"I knew it. I knew there was something wrong with you. How dare you bring this, this homosexual into my house," Carter scowled and pulled a pistol from his belt. He aimed it at Robbie, but suddenly it morphed into a shotgun, and before Blair could stop him, he fired it. Robbie grimaced with pain before vaporizing into thin air.
"*No!*" Blair cried with an outstretched hand. But it was too late; Robbie was gone. Carter turned the shotgun on Blair, and just as he pulled the trigger, Blair awoke with a shout!

God, he panted, what a nightmare! It took him a moment to realize where he was, and another several minutes to calm himself.
Eventually he picked up his phone and speed-dialed Andres.
"Hey, bro," Andres said sleepily. "What's going on?"
"I had a nightmare, and I need to talk to someone about it."
"Do you know what time it is?" Andres yawned.

An Admission of Weakness

"I'm sorry," Blair looked at the digital clock by the bed. "Go back to sleep. I'll talk to you tomorrow."

"No, I'm awake," Andres said. "Go ahead. Tell me about your nightmare."

Blair hesitated. How much should he confide in Andres? He knew he was his friend, and he trusted him, but just how far could that trust go?

"Talk, man," Andres prodded.

"Okay, but this was just a dream. It's not how I really feel or anything."

"Okay."

"Okay, so I was at home in my bedroom," Blair began. "And...and Robbie was there."

"What was he doing?"

"He was...uh, he was in my bed."

"That's wild, brother," Andres said. "Were you in bed with him?"

"I was in the bathroom."

"What was he doing?"

"He was just laying there. He said I needed to be my real self, and his brother Rhett said the same thing."

"His brother was there too?"

"No, that was earlier," Blair said impatiently. "And then my dad came in, and he aimed a gun at Robbie, and...and he shot him."

"Holy fuck," Andres said. "Why would he do that?"

An Admission of Weakness

"Robbie told him...he told him I was a fag. I told my dad it wasn't true, but he shot him anyway. And then he turned the gun on me, and that's when I woke up."

"Jeez, that's one hell of a dream," Andres said. "What do you think it means?"

"I don't know. What do you think it means?"

"I'd tell you, but you'd probably get mad at me," Andres said.

"I won't get mad," Blair said.

"I think it might mean you're gay and you're attracted to Robbie," Andres said bluntly.

"I'm not gay."

"Was Robbie wearing clothes?"

"No, he was, uh, naked," Blair said reluctantly.

"Bro, I think you're gay," Andres said. "Or at the very least, you're questioning your sexuality."

"I'm almost twenty years old, and I've slept with lots of women. How can I be questioning my sexuality?"

"I don't know. Maybe it's something you've repressed all these years, and now it's trying to come out," Andres suggested.

"Is that possible?" Blair asked uncertainly.

"Man, I'm not a psychologist," Andres said. "I think you need to ask yourself some tough questions and be honest with yourself."

"What if it turns out I'm a fag?"

"Have you ever been with a guy?" Andres asked.

An Admission of Weakness

"No, of course not," Blair said.
"But you want to be with Robbie?"
"I think so."
"Were you hard in your dream?"
"Yes," Blair admitted reluctantly.
"Do you like having sex with women?"
"I like getting off," Blair said uncertainly.
"Maybe you should try being with Robbie and see if it's something you really like."
"What if I like it more than being with a woman?"
"I'll still be your friend," Andres assured him. "Nothing's gonna change. None of the guys need to know if you don't want them to."

Blair thanked him and ended the call. He had some hard thinking to do.
Was he attracted to women? Kinda sorta. That was what he was supposed to be, wasn't it?
Was he attracted to guys? If he was honest with himself, yes, he probably was. He liked their muscles, their hairy bodies, their masculinity, their asses, their dicks. He found himself growing hard even now.
Was he attracted to Robbie? Most definitely. Robbie was beautiful, inside and out. He was sweet, kind, funny, outgoing, and cheerful, while at the same time masculine and strong. He had those beautiful blue eyes, the dirty-blonde, spiky hair, the hairy chest and legs, and the lithe, muscular physique.

An Admission of Weakness

Blair suddenly felt a longing inside that he had never known before. He had felt something akin to it when he was around Andres and some of the guys, but this was much stronger.

The next morning, Blair knocked on Robbie's door.
"I want to decorate my room for Christmas," he said.
"Why not just go home?" Robbie said. "I'll tell the coach you've fulfilled your duty to me."
"I think I'll stick around," Blair said. "I already told the family I won't be there for Christmas."
"So why are you telling me you want to decorate for Christmas?" Robbie frowned.
"Go with me to buy some decorations. I'm no good at that kind of thing."
"You think I am because I'm gay?"
"Well, yeah. Aren't you?"
"Actually, I am," Robbie admitted.

Blair and Robbie carried their armloads of decorations to the dorm and set about adorning Blair's room with a small tree, lights, garlands, and poinsettias. Robbie put some Christmas music on his phone to play in the background.
"It looks fantastic," Blair said.
"I told you we bought too much," Robbie said.
"No, we didn't," Blair grinned. "Your room is next."

An Admission of Weakness

They put up the remaining decorations across the hall until Robbie's room was as Christmassy as Blair's.
"It looks like Santa Claus exploded in here," Robbie joked. "But I love it. It's starting to really feel like Christmas."
"How about we go out for dinner for Christmas Eve?" Blair suggested.
"Okay, what's going on?" Robbie asked suspiciously. "Why are you being nice to me?"
"Who else am I going to spend Christmas with around here?" Blair said. "I'm kind of stuck with you, so we might as well make the best of it."
"I get all goosepimply when you talk sweet like that," Robbie grinned.
"Fine," Blair shrugged. "Spend Christmas alone if you want. Makes no difference to me."
"No, I'll spend Christmas with you," Robbie said. "You're better than nothing."
"Gee thanks," Blair chuckled.

On Christmas Eve, Blair and Robbie dined at Biaggi's, an Italian restaurant on South Neil Street.
"You know, if people keep seeing you hanging out with a gay guy, they might think you're gay too," Robbie said.
"Let them think what they want," Blair shrugged.

An Admission of Weakness

"Okay, who are you, and what have you done with DJ Butterfield?"
"I didn't know you knew my last name," Blair looked surprised.
"I know things about you," Robbie said.
"How?"
"From Andres and the guys," Robbie said. "And I looked up the town you're from. Your dad is the superintendent of schools, and you have two sisters and a brother. You live on Washington Street."
"What, you don't know my blood type?" Blair said dryly.
"O positive," Robbie said.
"How the fuck did you know that?" Blair frowned.
"I didn't," Robbie chuckled. "O positive is the most common blood type, so I took a chance."
"Oh," Blair looked relieved. "I know all about your family too. Your dad is a custodian, your mother's a waitress, your oldest sister's name is Vaneeta, and you're from Toadback, Mississippi."
"You learned all that from spending time with Rhett. Now what's my last name?"
"Goldstein?"
"Close," Robbie laughed. "It's Lee."
"Wait, your name is Robbie Lee? What's your middle name? Don't tell me it's Edward."
"It's Eustace. Robert Eustace Lee."

An Admission of Weakness

"Robert E. Lee? You've got to be fucking kidding me!"

"Afraid not."

"There's no way I can live across the hall from a fag whose name is the same as the commander of the Confederate Army."

"I didn't choose my name, you know," Robbie said.

"I can just hear my dad," Blair groaned. "He's got a real thing about the Civil War and the South. Our ancestors were slaves."

"Well, just for the record, I was all for slavery and secession from the Union, but I've changed my mind since then."

"You think this is funny?" Blair said. "You can never meet my family when they're here for games. My dad would go ballistic."

"He doesn't like gay white guys from Mississippi named after the man who commanded the southern army in defense of slavery?" Robbie said. "That seems odd."

"You joke, but he really doesn't. I suppose Rhett's middle name is Butler," Blair said sarcastically.

"It is," Robbie chuckled.

"You're shitting me," Blair said.

"It's true," Robbie laughed harder. "*Gone with the Wind* is my mom's favorite movie."

"Holy fuck," Blair laughed until the two were doubled over with mirth.

An Admission of Weakness

CHAPTER TEN

Robbie and Blair stayed up late on Christmas Eve. They lazed about on Blair's bed and talked and laughed for hours.

"Jeez, it's almost two in the morning," Robbie yawned at last. "I should go to bed."

"You don't have to go yet," Blair said.

"I do if you don't want me to fall asleep in your bed," Robbie said.

"Let's keep talking," Blair said.

He shivered and unfolded a soft fleece throw. Before Robbie could react, Blair sat down next to him and covered them both with the blanket.

"Are we having a sleepover?" Robbie asked hesitantly.

"Chill, man. It's just a blanket," Blair said.

"I'm not going to fuck you."

"Are you sure?" Robbie chuckled. "This is pink camouflage."

"It was a gift from my sister Camilla," Blair grinned. "She has unique taste."

"I think I'd like her," Robbie said. "Tell me about the rest of your family."

The two continued to talk while they snuggled ever closer under the blanket. Robbie tingled with excitement at being this close to the man he had desired intensely from the first day they met.

Meanwhile, Blair tried to keep from hyperventilating and his pulse from racing

An Admission of Weakness

while he carried on his half of their casual conversation. It wasn't easy for him because he was beginning to realize the full extent of his desire for the man cuddled up against him. This went beyond anything he had ever felt for a woman.

Perhaps that explained why sex wasn't very satisfying. Maybe it would be better with a man. The problem was, he didn't know exactly what sex between two men entailed.

Eventually, as their weariness grew, the conversation ebbed, and the two dropped off to asleep. When Blair awoke a little later, he looked over and studied Robbie's serene face. He had such long lashes, full lips, and sexy eyebrows, and his hair was downy blonde and soft to touch when it had no product in it. Quietly, he stood and pulled his Henley shirt over his head and stripped off his jeans. He was wearing a pair of snug white briefs that left little to the imagination.

He carefully laid the sleeping man down and climbed into bed to spoon him from behind. Tentatively, he placed an arm around him, kissed his shoulder, and closed his eyes.

God, if his family could see him now, lying here nearly naked with his arm around a fag. His dad and Justin would flip out, Grandma Ruby and Camilla would say it's no big deal, but he was unsure about Katie and his mother. Andres would be cool, but his other teammates

An Admission of Weakness

could be quite homophobic and insensitive. Friends back in Green Grove would be surprised, but they would be supportive.

But what did all of this mean? Suppose Robbie and he had sex, was he ready to admit he was gay? Bisexual? Merely experimenting? Could he handle an intimate relationship with a man? Should he give up on women, or should he try harder with them? Or maybe he should just place them on a back burner for now.

Robbie pushed against him and rolled onto his back. Their faces were an inch apart, and Blair threw caution to the winds and kissed him. He was trembling with desire and trepidation.

Holy fuck, his lips were soft. Oh yeah, this felt right. His penis was rock hard as he leaned in and kissed him harder. Robbie's eyes fluttered open and he grinned sleepily.

"Hey," he whispered.

"Hey," Blair smiled.

Robbie suddenly remembered where they were and jumped off the bed.

"What the hell are you doing?" he demanded.

"I'm sorry," Blair said. "But –"

"You were kissing me," Robbie said. "Why would you do that?"

"I know I shouldn't have, but I wanted to see what it felt like."

"I don't understand," Robbie frowned. "You're straight, and you hate fags."

"I do hate fags," Blair said.

An Admission of Weakness

"So what are we doing?"
"I don't know. But maybe I don't hate you as much as other fags."
"Am I supposed to say thank you?"
"No. I'm just saying, I'm starting to think you might be right about that whole toxic masculinity thing."
"Meaning...?"
"I'm not sure," Blair said carefully, "but I may not be as straight as I thought."
"Not as straight?"
"Look, this is all new to me," Blair struggled with his words. "I'm not sure of anything right now. All my life I thought I was one thing, and now suddenly I'm finding I might have been wrong. Ever since I met you...I don't know, I guess you've made me question some things."
"I have? How?"
"Just by being you," Blair said. "I keep thinking about you, picturing you cheering or standing up to me when I gave you a hard time."
"I didn't have any choice," Robbie said.
"You could have avoided me and the guys, but you didn't. I tried to intimidate you, but it didn't work. You weren't afraid, and you were so nice all the time. And then Rhett came here, and he said some things that made me think too."
"He has a way of doing that to people," Robbie said.

An Admission of Weakness

"Anyway, I had a dream where you confronted me at home in Green Grove."

"You had a dream about me?" Robbie said, surprised.

"It was a nightmare, actually. You were in my bed naked, and –"

"Whoa, whoa, whoa," Robbie became a little more awake. "You dreamed I was naked and in your bed. Holy shit!"

"Anyway –"

"Give me a sec," Robbie held up a hand to stop him. "I want to digest that for a minute."

"Will you shut up and let me talk? This is serious."

"You're telling me," Robbie whistled.

"Forget it," Blair rolled his eyes and turned away.

"I'm sorry," Robbie said. "I'm just having a hard time picturing you dreaming about me naked. You're the most homophobic person I know."

"Anyway," Blair said, exasperated. "You told me it was time to come out of the closet, and then my dad came in, and he…he got really angry."

"Jeez," Robbie said with a sense of wonder. "This is the last thing I ever expected to hear from you."

"I've always known something was wrong," Blair said. "I don't react to women like my friends do. Every guy in school wanted

An Admission of Weakness

Danielle, but I couldn't get excited about her, and I really tried."

"But you had sex with her?"

"We fucked all the time, but I was just doing what was expected of me," Blair shrugged. "It was okay, but I never felt satisfied even after I shot my load. She has a really great body, big tits and a tight pussy…"

"That's enough details," Robbie grimaced. "I get the picture."

"My point is, I never questioned my sexuality. Until now, that is."

"Have you ever done anything with a guy?"

"No. Have you ever done it with a girl?"

"No way," Robbie wrinkled his nose. "Gross."

"It's not so bad," Blair said. "Anyway, while Rhett was here, I realized I liked you a whole lot more than I thought."

"Why?"

"I don't know," Blair said. "At first, I thought you were a jerk who was trying to make the whole world gay, but then I got to know you. You were a lot nicer than I thought, and I pictured you and me…doing things."

"What kinds of things?"

"The kinds of things people do when they're attracted to each other."

"So all of this is because you're attracted to me?" Robbie said incredulously. "How is that possible?"

An Admission of Weakness

"I thought because I was having those feelings, everyone else did too, but Andres and Rhett said they don't. I was taught that being gay was a choice, and you chose to be gay while I chose to be straight."
"You know that's not true, right?" Robbie frowned.
"I'm not sure," Blair said. "All I know is that I get hard every time I'm around you. When I saw you in my dream, I thought you were beautiful."
"Thanks, but I might not live up to your expectations in real life."
"You already have," Blair said.
Robbie noticed for the first time that Blair was nearly nude.
"You took your clothes off," he said.
"I thought maybe we could…you know," Blair said.
"I don't think that's such a good idea."
"Why not?"
"You're obviously confused, and I don't think jumping into bed with the first guy you see is the way to figure it out."
"Don't you want to be with me?" Blair said.
"That's beside the point," Robbie said. "Do you even know what guys do in bed?"
"I know some," Blair said. "I thought you could show me."
"You don't even like me."

An Admission of Weakness

"Okay, here's what I say: we do this, and if I hate it, we can go back to hating each other."
"I don't know about you, but I like it to mean something when I have sex," Robbie said.
"How many guys have you been with?"
"Two," Robbie said. "How many women have you been with?"
"I don't know," Blair shrugged. "A few dozen or so. But I've never been with a man, so you're two up on me.
"Look, you said yourself we're not even friends, so it's not like we're going to ruin a friendship or anything."
"You're not going to freak out in the middle of things and beat me up, are you?"
"Not unless you're really bad at it," Blair teased.
"You're the one who needs to worry about being bad at it," Robbie said.
He thought for a moment and then disrobed.
"Well, here's the real thing, like it or not," he turned in a circle with his arms spread.
"I like it," Blair said and hastily removed his underwear.
The two stood in front of each other, and Blair was trembling.
"Are you sure you want to do this?" Robbie asked. "Because I don't want to push you into anything."
"To be honest," Blair gulped, "I'm scared to death, but I'm as ready as I'll ever be."

An Admission of Weakness

"You don't need to be scared," Robbie smiled. "We can do as much or as little as you want. Just promise me that you won't wake up tomorrow with regrets and never speak to me again."

"Can we just do this?" Blair said tremulously. "I'm about to lose my nerve."

Robbie stepped up and kissed him hard and passionately. He guided him back to the bed and pushed him down.

For the next two hours, the men made love to one another. It was clumsy and awkward, and elbows and knees ended up in places they didn't belong. But it didn't matter to them because it was intense and passionate.

"Holy fuck," Blair muttered when Robbie went down on his nine inch manhood. "This is insane."

"Do you want me to stop?" Robbie frowned.

"God no," Blair put his hands on Robbie's head and pushed him back down onto his dick.

Robbie sucked on him and pulled on his balls while he fingered his virgin ass. Blair uttered other phrases such as "Oh my god", "Nothing has ever felt like this before" "You're incredible".

He moaned and groaned and cried out and shouted when Robbie sucked on his nipples and his armpits and his ass. He eagerly imitated Robbie's actions, and when at last he inserted

An Admission of Weakness

his manhood into Robbie, he felt a thrill such as he had never experienced.

"Oh god," he groaned as he held Robbie's ankles in his hands. "This is so much better than a pussy."

"Thanks?" Robbie gasped.

Blair was so intense and innocent and endearing, that Robbie unwittingly opened his heart to him that night. It was the first time he had allowed any man in emotionally this way, but it seemed he couldn't help it. He and Blair were having more than sex, and though he knew it was unlikely, he hoped Blair felt the same way.

Blair awoke early on Christmas morning. When Robbie finally yawned and stretched, he found himself alone in Blair's twin-size bed. He glanced around, and his heart sank. Blair was nowhere to be seen.

Oh god, Blair had flaked out on him as he feared. The guy found he didn't like gay sex and was now going to avoid him for the rest of their college careers.

Dammit, he knew going to bed with someone still in denial about his sexuality was a mistake, but he had foolishly decided to risk it. And now his exposed heart was vulnerable to wounding. He sat up on the side of the bed and rubbed his tired eyes. He jumped when the door opened

An Admission of Weakness

unexpectedly, and Blair appeared carrying a box of donuts.

"Damn, I thought I'd get back before you woke up."

"Where'd you go?"

"To get donuts from that place you like," Blair said. "Remember last night you said you could really go for some? I wanted to surprise you."

"So you didn't –" Robbie stopped himself.

"Didn't what?"

"Uh, nothing," Robbie smiled. "That was really nice of you."

Blair handed him the donuts and quickly undressed. He climbed onto the bed behind Robbie and pulled him back to sit between his legs.

"How do you feel this morning?" he asked.

"I'm great," Robbie took a bite of a glazed donut and relaxed into Blair's arms. "More importantly, how are you?"

"I'm fantastic," Blair grinned. "Last night was unbelievable. Didn't you think so?"

"I did," Robbie nodded.

"I had no idea sex could be like that. It was a totally different experience from being with a woman. I want to do it again and again, and I want to try other things too."

"With me or with other guys?" Robbie asked hesitantly. "Or with girls again?"

An Admission of Weakness

"What do you mean?" Blair frowned. "Why would I do it with a woman? I've already been there, done that."

"Sooo...does that mean you want to meet other guys or...?"

"Do you not want to date me?" Blair said. "I thought last night meant something to you."

"It did," Robbie said hastily. "It absolutely did. But I'm your first. I thought you might want to play the field like you were saying the other day."

"I'm not saying I'm ready to adopt a kid with you, but I'd like us to date and see where this thing goes." He added diffidently, "I like you, Robbie. We've known each other for a year and a half, and I feel like we're developing a real connection. I thought you felt it too."

"I do," Robbie said. "It's just that you said you wanted me to show you what to do, so I thought this was more of an experiment to you."

"So the cocky gay guy with the smart mouth has insecurities," Blair grinned.

"Yes, he does," Robbie said. "And the dumb jock has some real depth to him. Who knew?"

"I'll show you some depth," Blair took the donut from him and put it back in the box. With little effort, he pushed Robbie aside and lay down on top of him. He kissed him passionately before enthusiastically taking his manhood into his mouth.

An Admission of Weakness

God, why had he never done this before? Robbie's body was so much more beautiful than Danielle's: the hair, the muscles, the masculine smell, the ass – he couldn't get enough of rimming it.

When he began fucking Robbie's perfect ass, he was forced to stop frequently to keep from cumming too soon. He positioned Robbie on his back, against the wall, on his knees, over the side of the bed, and a dozen more positions. The two made love into the afternoon before napping in one another's arms.

"I have something to tell you," Blair said into the phone later that day.

"Merry Christmas to you too," Katie said dryly. "I can't believe you're not here."

"Sorry. Merry Christmas," he said sheepishly. "How are things at home?"

"Dad tried to fix me up with another guy at dinner last night," she said.

"You know, why not tell him about you and Dillon?" Blair said. "What's the worst that could happen? He gets mad for a while? He'll have to welcome Dillon into the family when you guys get married."

"Why don't you tell him you're an education major with a drama minor?" she said. "What's the worst that could happen? He gets mad for a while and then disowns you?"

An Admission of Weakness

"Okay, I get the point," he said. "So who was the guy?"
"Some doctor friend of Dad's from Rockford."
"You didn't like him?"
"He seemed nice," she shrugged indifferently. "It doesn't matter because I'm in love with Dillon."
"How long can you string Dillon along?" he asked. "Isn't he going to get tired of things the way they are sooner or later?"
"He's already tired of it," she said. "I tried to tell Dad and Mama about him this morning, but Dad was upset that I didn't give Ted a fair chance last night. You can't talk to him when he's angry."
"I know," Blair said. "But listen, I need to tell you something important."
"You've met someone," she said knowingly. "I knew it. Just don't tell Dad because he's still not over you breaking up with Danielle."
"I didn't break up with her," he said. "I just thought we should see other people since we're going to be a thousand miles apart for four years."
"I for one am glad she's gone," Katie said. "She was too spoiled. You deserve someone nice."
"I've met someone nice," he said hesitantly.
"I thought so," she grinned. "I could hear it in your voice. It sounds lighter and happier."
"Really?" he smiled.

An Admission of Weakness

"So tell me about her," Katie said impatiently. "I just hope she's Black. You know how Dad feels about white people."
"Will you just be quiet and let me talk?" he said uncomfortably.
"Fine. Talk."
"Okay. So it's another student. A cheerleader."
"An education major?"
"A business major," he said.
"At least Dad will like that," Katie said. "Maybe it will make it easier to tell him you're studying education instead of business."
"I don't think there's going to be anything easy about this," he said dryly.
"So what's her name?"
"It's, uh, Robbie," he said tentatively.
"That's cute. Short for Roberta. Where's she from?"
"A little town in Mississippi."
"Oh, a southern girl, huh," she mused. "Is she pretty?"
"Very," he said.
"So what's the problem? Are you worried that Dad will be upset you're giving up on Danielle? Because that's a given."
"A little, but there's more to it."
"Like what?"
He hesitated. This was the big moment, telling a member of the family that he had suddenly discovered he was into men. And to make things worse, he had fallen for a white guy.

An Admission of Weakness

"What?" she prodded.
"Okay, before I tell you, I want you to remember that I'm still the same person. I haven't changed."
"Okay."
"In the past year or so, I've started realizing why it didn't work out with Danielle or any other girl."
"Oh my god," she breathed. "Are you saying what I think you're saying?"
"I'm saying that I've had feelings all my life that I didn't understand until recently. See, the person I've met –"
"Is a man? Oh my god. You're gay? How have you not told me this before?"
"I didn't know I was gay," he tried to explain. "And I might not actually be gay. But I met Robbie, and I realized why I never enjoyed being with a woman. He's the most beautiful person I've ever known."
"Oh my god."
"Will you stop saying oh my god? I'm already freaked out enough."
"Can you imagine Dad's reaction to this? You should tell him you're an education major at the same time. He won't care about that when he hears you're gay."
"I don't plan on telling him any time soon."
"How long have you known this Robbie person?" she asked suspiciously. "Are you sure he isn't influencing you?"

An Admission of Weakness

"We met freshman year. He lives across the hall from me. And I don't think a person is gay by influence."
"But you're kind of naïve, and this is your first time away from home. Maybe he's confused you because you haven't met the right woman yet."
"I'm not that naïve."
"Is it serious?"
"It is as far as I'm concerned," he said.
"Have you done it yet? Is he your first?" she asked hesitantly.
"Yes and yes."
"Don't you think you should date some more women, maybe play the field for a while? That's what college is for."
"I think I'm done dating women for now," he said. "And as far as dating other guys, I'll never find anyone better than Robbie. He's perfect."
"No one is perfect," she said.
"I know that," he said patiently. "But he's the nicest, sweetest, strongest, bravest person I know."
"But he's your first. I think you should get out there and see what else is available."
"I've found the one I want."
"You can't know that," she said. "Seriously, you should play the field, men and women."
"You found your guy in middle school," he reminded her. "He was your first, so what's wrong with Robbie being mine?"

An Admission of Weakness

"It's different with guys," she said.
"How do you know?"
"I don't, I guess," she said. "I just want you to be sure."
"Jeez, I'm not marrying him. We're just dating."
"So who are his people? Grandma knows people from Mississippi."
"His last name is Lee," he said, anticipating the worst.
"Robert Lee?" she chuckled. "What's his middle name? Edward?"
"Actually, it's Eustace."
"Oh my god!" she cried. "A Black, gay southerner named Robert E. Lee? You can never introduce him to Dad unless he changes his name."
"He's, uh, not Black," Blair said uncomfortably.
"So he's Latino? Asian? Native American?"
"He's, um, white," Blair said.
"Please tell me you're joking. A gay white boy from Mississippi whose name is Robert E. Lee? Oh my god. Are you trying to kill Dad?"
"I can't help who I fall in love with," Blair said.
"You just started dating."
"I've known him a year and a half," Blair said. "And I've met some of his family. His brother Rhett. He's a real sweet kid with a speech impediment and a bad leg."

An Admission of Weakness

"Do they at least have money like Danielle's parents?"
"They're dirt poor. Robbie is only able to go to college because he got an all inclusive scholarship."
She started laughing.
"What's so fucking funny?" he scowled.
"I'm sorry, but it just keeps getting better. You're dating Robert E. Lee, a gay, white, impoverished boy from Mississippi. I can just see Dad's face when you tell him."
"I'll be sure and have plenty of witnesses around so he doesn't kill me," he said dryly. He hesitated apprehensively. "Are you upset about this, Katie?"
"Of course not," she said. "I'm just surprised. All that matters to me is that you're happy."
"I wish Dad would react that way," he said bitterly. "No one can ever tell him anything."
"At least you'll always have me on your side," she said. "And Camilla and Gran. And Mama too."
"Mama will go along with Dad," he snorted. "She doesn't think anything he doesn't tell her to."
"And Justin thinks everything Dad says is the gospel truth," she added.
"That's three to three," he said grimly.
"Just tell Robbie to wear his running shoes when he's introduced to the family," she joked.

An Admission of Weakness

"I'll try to distract Dad long enough to give him a head start."

"Ha-ha, very funny," he said.

An Admission of Weakness

CHAPTER ELEVEN

Blair ended the call with Katie and walked over to Robbie's room. It was dark outside, and the room seemed full of the Christmas spirit with all the cheerful decorations.
"How's your family?" Robbie looked up from his textbook when the door opened.
"They're good," Blair said.
"How'd they take it when you told them about me?"
"Surprisingly well," Blair said.
"It didn't ruin their Christmas?"
"Not at all."
"I feel bad for keeping you here," Robbie said.
"You didn't keep me here; I did. Did you talk to Rhett?"
"I did, and the girls too," Robbie grinned. "Ma was at work, so I didn't get to talk to her."
"They're all good?"
Robbie nodded and pulled a green and gold wrapped package from underneath the bed.
"What's this?" Blair frowned.
"Merry Christmas," Robbie said happily.
"Why'd you go and do that, bro?"
"It's nothing special," Robbie shrugged.
Blair sat down on the floor beside Robbie and ripped the paper off. Inside the box was a 5x7 photograph of Blair, Robbie, and Rhett at the train station. It was in a cheap plastic frame that Robbie had found at the dollar store.

An Admission of Weakness

"Are you kidding?" Blair smiled with pleasure. "This is great. I'll be right back."
He got up and left the room, only to return a moment later with a University of Illinois gift bag in hand.
"Here," he grinned.
Eagerly, Robbie pulled a bunch of tissue paper and an officially licensed orange and navy Fighting Illini hoodie from the bag.
"Cool!" he cried delightedly.
"I got a tee shirt for Rhett and each of your sisters too," Blair said. "Do you think they'll like them?"
"You bastard," Robbie said.
"Why? What'd I do?"
"You've spent the last year and a half hiding what a nice guy you are," Robbie grinned. "Here I was falling for a guy I thought was a total jerk."
"You fell for me a year and a half ago?" Blair looked surprised.
"I tried not to, believe me," Robbie chuckled. "Now I'm glad I did, but you made me work for it. That's why I called you a bastard."
"I guess that's no worse than DJ, Blondie," Blair grinned.

"This is a lot to take in," Andres shook his head dazedly. "You and Robbie are a couple. I can't believe you actually did it."

An Admission of Weakness

"It doesn't change anything," Blair said hastily. "I'm still the same guy."
"I know," Andres grinned. "Relax."
"I'd rather no one else knew," Blair said.
"That you're gay or that you and Robbie are a couple?"
"We're not necessarily a couple," Blair said. "And I'm still not sure I'm gay."
Andres picked up the picture from Blair's desk and examined it.
"Who's the skinny kid with you and Robbie?"
"That's Rhett, Robbie's brother. Can't you see the family resemblance?"
"Nah," Andres chuckled. "All white people look alike to me."

Naomi sewed the final ivory bead on the gown's bodice and stepped back.
"It's perfect, Naomi," Snake smiled as he walked around the mannequin. "You've really outdone yourself."
"Thank you, Mr. Abernathy," she said demurely.
"Please call me Snake or Billy. Otherwise, I'm going to have to call you Mrs. Butterfield."
"Okay, Billy," she grinned.
"June and I were talking," he glanced over at his partner, who nodded subtlety. "We were wondering how you would feel about heading up the new line of bridal gowns."
"Me?" Naomi said, taken aback.

An Admission of Weakness

"You have an amazing eye," June said.
"Would I still make the gowns?"
"Yes, but you'd also collaborate with Snake."
"You're already an asset to the company," Snake said. "But I'd like you to consult on the wedding gowns before they go on the website, the same way June does on the evening gowns. We have thirty orders for the two bridal gowns I've already designed. With things getting so busy, I need your help."
"Please say you'll do it," June said.
"I-I'll have to talk to Carter," Naomi said tentatively.
"Talk to whoever you want as long as you say yes," Snake grinned.

Naomi thought about Snake's offer while she scraped food scraps into the disposal. She was beyond flattered that he and June thought so highly of her work. Their offer was a dream come true, but what should she do about it? Obviously, Carter wouldn't approve. He still didn't know she was working outside the house, and he would be livid to learn that she had deceived him.
Yet this was something she would very much like to do. Imagine her actually having a say in the design of an original gown.
"Mama, where are my jeans?" Justin yelled down the staircase and interrupted her reverie.

An Admission of Weakness

"Which ones?" Naomi stopped what she was doing and walked to the bottom of the stairs.
"The ones with all the holes," he shouted.
"They aren't fit to wear in public," she frowned.
"That's the whole point," he rolled his eyes. "God, you are so provincial sometimes."
"I don't want you wearing them," Naomi said.
"Where are they?"
"They're in your bottom dresser drawer."
"Jeez," she heard him say as he returned to his room.
She sighed and returned to the kitchen to load the dishwasher.
"Mama, I can't find my new paint brush," Camilla said as she entered the room. "And is my laundry done?"
"Your boubous are on the dryer, and the rest is already put away in your room," Naomi said. "I haven't seen your new brush. Isn't it with the others?"
"If it was, I wouldn't be looking for it," Camilla said. "Can you help me find it?"
Mother and daughter examined Camilla's bedroom, and sure enough, the brush in question was in a box mixed in with older brushes.
"Oh, here it is," Camilla chuckled. "I looked right at it and didn't see it."
She kissed her mother on the cheek and turned to her newest painting of James Baldwin.

An Admission of Weakness

"Naomi, why isn't my newspaper on my desk?" Carter walked into the room.
"I'm sorry, dear," Naomi said. "I haven't had a chance to get it from the front porch."
Carter sighed in a put-upon way and headed down the stairs.
"Carter?" she called after him.
"Yes?" he paused on the landing.
"Why don't we go see a movie?" she suggested. "There's a new Asher Reardon movie playing at the Victoria."
The Victoria was the freshly renovated art-deco theater located at the east end of the downtown, and Asher Reardon was the most famous movie star on the planet. He had recently married a young farmer from east of Green Grove, and the town had adopted him as one of their own since that time.
"Not tonight," Carter said. "After I read the paper, I have some old letters to go over for the book."
He walked on without a backward glance and disappeared into his study. Naomi sighed and looked into her mother's room.
"What are you doing tonight, Mama?" she asked.
"Some of the girls and I are taking in the movie at the Victoria," Ruby donned an earring while examining her reflection in the cheval mirror. "If I was ten years younger or Asher Reardon

An Admission of Weakness

was ten years older, I'd steal him away from that young man he married."

"Mama," Naomi chided her.

"Okay, twenty and twenty," Ruby shrugged. She noticed her daughter's expression and turned to her.

"Do you want to come with us?"

"No, you and your friends have fun," Naomi said.

"I suppose Carter's working on that damn book of his," Ruby said grimly.

"It's important to him," Naomi said.

"And you aren't?"

"I don't know," Naomi sighed. "Am I important to anyone anymore?"

"You're the most important thing in the world to me," Ruby walked over and embraced her. "Why don't you and I go to the movie together?"

"No thanks," Naomi smiled thinly. "Go have fun with your friends. I think I'll catch up on some reading."

Ruby watched her enter her bedroom across the hall and scowled. She finished preparing for her evening and, without knocking, threw open the door to Carter's study.

"Hey!" he said sharply. "Have you never heard of knocking?"

"Have you forgotten you have a wife?" she retorted.

"What the devil are you talking about?"

An Admission of Weakness

"Why are you sitting in here alone?" she demanded. "Go spend time with Naomi."
"She was going to a movie or something," Carter said vaguely. "Besides, I have work to do."
"Is this damn book more important to you than she is?"
"Of course not."
"Then talk to her. She's unhappy."
"Naomi's unhappy?" he looked concerned. "She's never said anything to me."
"Perhaps she did, but you were too busy rifling through those dusty old papers of yours."
"Has she said something to you?" he asked.
"No, of course not," Ruby said. "You know she would never complain about anything if her life depended on it. You and the children come first for her."
"If she hasn't said she's unhappy, how do you know she is?"
"A mother knows these things."
"Oh for heaven's sake," he waved her away. "Go polish your broom or cast a spell on someone. Perhaps there's a coven convening somewhere."
"I'm warning you, Carter," she said seriously. "Take care of Naomi, or you might lose her."

After she left his study, Carter walked up the stairs to the bedroom he shared with his wife.

An Admission of Weakness

He found her sitting in a rocking chair with a book in her hands.
"Naomi, are you okay?" he asked abruptly.
"Yes," she looked up with surprise. "Why do you ask?"
"No reason," he rolled his eyes and closed the door.
Damn his mother-in-law! Making a mountain out of a molehill and wasting his time when he was busy.

"I'm in," Naomi told Snake and June. "Just keep it between us. I don't want it getting back to Carter."
Not that he would notice whether she was home or not, as long as his meals were on the table, that is.
"Wonderful!" June and Snake cried simultaneously.
"In that case," Snake smiled. "Let me show you the newest design I've been working on."
He led her over to a drafting board in the corner and pulled a second stool up beside his.
She listened happily while he described his inspiration for this particular dress.
"Have you considered a veil?" she asked.
"I think a veil sends the wrong message, like the woman is to be modest and obedient. This dress is geared more to a young, contemporary woman."

An Admission of Weakness

"I know," she said. "But I'm not talking about wearing it over the face. And think how a veil could bring some older women to consider a more modern take on the traditional."
She made a few rough sketches to show him what she meant, and he nodded thoughtfully. "I like it. Let's give it a try."

Flora Lee eyed Rhett's University of Illinois shirt and the others Blair had sent.
"Robbie sent you these?"
"His fwiend Blair did," Rhett grinned ecstatically. "He's the one I told you about. The football player."
"Why is he sending you expensive gifts?" she asked suspiciously.
"He's my fwiend," Rhett said. "He wanted to do something nice for us."
He handed her a small gift-wrapped box.
"What's this?" she frowned.
"It's for you," Rhett said. "Fwom Blair."
"Why would he send me something?"
"Because I told him all about you and the girls."
"He sounds like some rich Yankee," she said disapprovingly. "I don't need his pity."
"Ma, the war is over," he rolled his eyes. "And this isn't about pity. It's about him being a fwiend of Wobbie's and mine who just wanted to give us each a Chwistmas pwesent."

An Admission of Weakness

Warily, she opened the package and studied the bottle of perfume.

"Oh, this is much too nice for someone like me."

"Why would you say something like that?" he frowned. "You're as good as anyone else."

A smile spread slowly across her face, and she dabbed some of the aromatic liquid behind her ears.

"No one's bought me a present in twenty years," she said. "This makes me feel like a girl again."

Her careworn face relaxed and looked twenty years younger for just a moment. But then her good sense returned, and her expression hardened.

"I'm too old for such nonsense," she said. "Just pour it down the drain."

"No," he said firmly. "You know you like it, so you're going to wear it. Who deserves it more than you? Blair obviously wanted to make your life a little nicer. So enjoy it."

"I got a modeling job," Blair said excitedly one evening in February.

Since Christmas, he and Robbie had spent every free moment together. They couldn't seem to get enough of each other physically, and Robbie opened his heart even more to him. A romantic relationship with a man was new to

An Admission of Weakness

both of them, so there was much they had to learn about themselves as well as each other. As for Blair, he was happier than he had ever been. He was surprised at how quickly his feelings for Robbie were developing. The man was everything he could have ever asked for, and he liked himself better than he ever had before when he was with him.

"Seriously?" Robbie said. "That's amazing." He chuckled at the look on Blair's face.

"I don't mean it like that. It's fantastic. You've definitely got the body for it."

"That's better," Blair seemed mollified. "Actually, it's not just me; this modeling agency from New York is doing a photo book of college athletes from the Midwest. They picked me and Andres and a couple of the other guys."

"What do you have to do?"

"I don't know," Blair shrugged. "All I know is I'll be traveling on weekends for location shots."

"Weekends?" Robbie frowned. "That's the only time we get to see each other."

"We see each other practically every night."

"To sleep and have sex," Robbie said. "Weekends are our time to really talk and be together."

"We're talking right now," Blair chuckled.

"Maybe I could come with you?" Robbie suggested.

An Admission of Weakness

"I'll be too busy with the rep and the photographers. Besides, don't you have to work?"

"I can take a few days off," Robbie said. With his busy schedule of classes, studying, cheerleading, and working a part-time job, he could use some time off, especially if it meant spending more time with his boyfriend.

"No, you can't," Blair frowned. "You're saving money for Rhett and your sisters."

"But you and I don't do anything except stay in my room and order in."

"You know why that is," Blair said. "No one can know about us. I have a reputation to maintain."

"I know. You want everyone to think you're a tough, macho breeder," Robbie said. "But is that more important to you than our relationship?"

"I don't want anyone knowing about us," Blair said stubbornly.

"Andres knows," Robbie reminded him. "Your family knows."

"That's diffcrent. Andres is my best friend, and my family is three hours away."

"But wouldn't you like to be out? Think how free we could be. We could go to restaurants and shows and games together. I want the whole world to know that Blair Butterfield is my boyfriend."

"Since when am I your boyfriend?"

An Admission of Weakness

"Aren't you?" Robbie said, surprised.
"Why do we have to label it? Why can't we be two guys hanging out and having sex?"
"So this is a friends with benefits thing to you?"
"It sounds like you want to call the Black guy your boyfriend so you can show me off like a prized bull," Blair scowled.
"That's not what I mean, and you know it. I just thought we were both invested in this relationship."
"Have you thought about my scholarship?" Blair said. "If Coach Wilkensen finds out I'm gay, he might kick me off the team or something."
"You and I both know that's not true."
"Look, this modeling thing could be good for me," Blair said. "Who knows? It might lead to a professional modeling career."
"But you want to be a teacher."
"Do you know what teachers make?" Blair snorted. "I could make ten times that in modeling."
"I didn't know you cared about the money," Robbie said.
"I'm used to nice things," Blair said. "I won't be able to afford anything on a teacher's salary."
"But you said you want to make a difference –"
"I don't want to be poor," Blair said.

An Admission of Weakness

"Fine. I want you to do whatever makes you happy."
"The rep recommended that I get some tattoos," Blair opened his laptop and pulled up information on the Internet. "She said I need to look edgier, more dangerous."
"I think you look fine the way you are," Robbie said.
But Blair was focused on his research and didn't hear him.

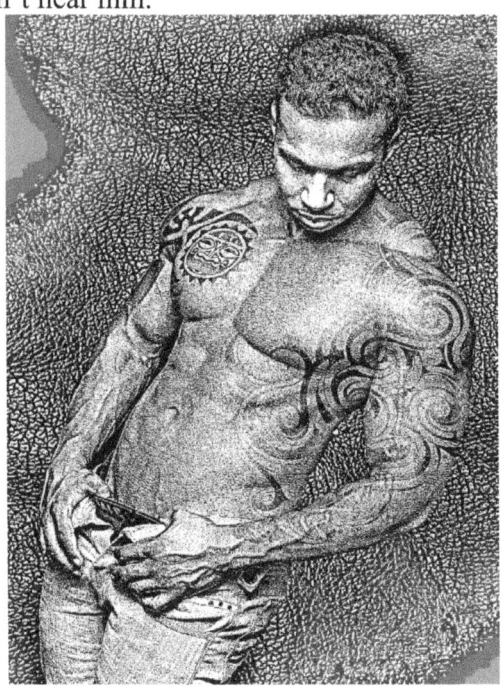

Over the next week, Blair acquired a number of tattoos on his arms, shoulders, and torso with

An Admission of Weakness

the rep's money and supervision. Robbie couldn't deny that they were very sexy and added a certain fierceness to Blair's physique. They seemed to affect his character as well; he acted tougher and more arrogant. He began spending more time at the gym and working out more intensely. His already deep voice became sultrier, and he reveled in the attention from his female admirers.

An Admission of Weakness

CHAPTER TWELVE

One evening, Blair and Robbie sat together on Blair's bed. Robbie told him about his day and something Rhett had said while Blair texted Andres and other people.
"Did you hear what I said?" Robbie asked.
"Uh, yeah," Blair nodded absently. "One of the photographers wants to do a shoot in my room."
"Can you put the phone down for a while? This is the first time I've seen you in days."
Another text came in, and Blair laughed and nodded while he responded.
"Chad is so funny," he said.
Someone texted him, and he turned the screen away from Robbie as he wrote back.
It wasn't ideal, Robbie thought ruefully, but at least they were together.
"Blair?"
But Blair didn't hear him. He seemed completely caught up in the whole modeling thing. The rep who was handling the development of the photo book was an attractive, young, blonde-haired woman with large breasts who wore miniskirts and low cut blouses.
"Why is she around you all the time?" Robbie frowned with displeasure.
"It's her job," Blair said. "Me and the guys have to spend time with her."

An Admission of Weakness

"In your dorm room?" Robbie said dryly. "I think she's after more than pictures."
"She's not like that and neither are Fred and Chad."
"I don't trust them either," Robbie said. "Two gay guys who take pictures of you and Andres practically naked."
"How'd you know we were naked?"
"You let them take nude pictures of you?!" Robbie said, outraged.
"I always have something covering my dick," Blair said. "I can't let them take completely nude pics; I'd get in trouble with the university."
"I don't like this," Robbie scowled. "I don't trust these people."
"Are you jealous?" Blair grinned.
"No," Robbie lied.
"You have to trust me," Blair tousled Robbie's hair. "You're making something out of nothing."
The door suddenly burst open, and three of Blair's teammates entered the room.
"Hey, brother," one of them, a young man nicknamed Slick said. "You and that Tiffany were sure getting cozy in the bathroom –"
Blair immediately shoved Robbie away.
"Don't sit so close, man," he frowned.
"What's going on here?" Slick glanced at each of them suspiciously.
"What do you mean?" Blair stood up guiltily.

An Admission of Weakness

"You said you didn't like Blondie, and now we find him practically sitting in your lap? What the fuck, bro?"
"We weren't sitting together," Blair snorted derisively. "You think I'd sit that close to a fag on purpose?"
"I don't know. Would you? Are you a fag or something?"
"Of course not," Blair scowled and turned to Robbie. "Get this through your head, bro. I'm not fucking gay, so keep your distance."
"You need to go, Blondie," Slick said grimly. "I thought you were cool, but now we find you hitting on my bro here. I ought to fuckin' punch you out."
Robbie was too stunned to say anything in his defense. He glanced at Blair with disbelief, but Blair moved over to stand with his friends. Swallowing with difficulty, Robbie picked up his textbook and left the room.

"Sorry about that," Blair said at three o'clock in the morning when he climbed into bed with Robbie.
"What are you doing?" Robbie frowned.
"The guys and I went out for pizza and then to a club," Blair settled onto the narrow bed with an arm around Robbie. "It was wild."
"I'm glad you had fun," Robbie said sarcastically.
"I did," Blair chuckled. "Tiff went with us."

An Admission of Weakness

"Her name is Tiff?"

"It's actually Tiffany," Blair said. "But she asked me to call her Tiff."

"Well, isn't that sweet."

"She is sweet," Blair said. "And pretty too. She wants to be my agent."

"Your agent?"

"She says I have a huge future in modeling."

"What does that mean? Does she have other modeling jobs lined up for you?"

"I think so," Blair said. "She's getting the contracts made up for me to sign. Isn't that cool?"

"Are you sure this is what you want?" Robbie asked.

"Why wouldn't it be?"

"Are you sure you can trust her?"

"Not this again," Blair frowned. "Just because she's attracted to me, you don't trust her. That's not cool, bro."

"So why don't you crawl in bed with her, bro?" Robbie elbowed him roughly off the bed onto the floor.

"Hey!" Blair scowled. "What the fuck?"

"That's what I'm saying to you!" Robbie said angrily. "What the fuck was that you did in your room with Slick and the guys?"

"I said I'm sorry," Blair got to his feet. "What more do you want?"

"I want a boyfriend," Robbie said heatedly. "What I don't want is to be your dirty little

An Admission of Weakness

secret that you treat like shit every time your friends are around."
"I don't do that."
"That's exactly what you did last night!" Robbie shouted.
"And I've apologized for it," Blair said.
"And that makes it okay? I don't think so. I need to be your boyfriend no matter who's around."
"We've been through this," Blair said impatiently. "You know how I feel about you calling me your boyfriend. I'm not discussing it again."
"Then call Tiff and spend the night with her. At least you wouldn't have to hide her when the guys stop by."
"This is ridiculous," Blair said, annoyed. "You know, I think I will call her. If I'm going to be with someone who acts like a woman, it might as well be a woman!"
With that, he touched his phone's screen a few times.
"Hey, Tiff," he said as he stormed from the room. "Are you still up? I'm coming over."

Robbie didn't see Blair for a few weeks after that except to witness him go into his room with Tiffany a few times.
He was obviously sleeping with her, based on the moans and yells coming from Blair's dorm room. So it was back to having sex with

An Admission of Weakness

women again; apparently, Blair had just been experimenting with him after all.
Well, that was fine. Blair could do what he wanted without him because he wasn't going to live a life in the closet just to please a guy. Unfortunately for him, that guy just happened to be the one he was in love with.

"God, you're such an animal," Tiffany cried while Blair pounded her pussy ruthlessly on his bed.
Her words encouraged him to fuck even harder until she was practically screaming with pleasure. He purposely left his door open so Robbie would be sure to see them.
"Your dick is so big."
"Holy fuck, you feel good," he gasped and leaned down to suck her nipples.
It was true, it was pleasurable making love to this beautiful woman, but it didn't compare to his times with Robbie. Still, he wasn't going to make the same mistake he had made with Danielle, so he forced himself to make his best effort. He kissed, sucked, and licked every part of her body for an hour before finally inserting himself into her vagina.
After a half hour, he finally climaxed, shouting and groaning and writhing with pleasure. Part of it was true pleasure, and part of it was so that Robbie would hear him.

An Admission of Weakness

Damn him, Robbie scowled! Blair was already cocky without all the added attention from Tiffany and lots of other women. Now he was insufferable.
Their relationship clearly wasn't meant to be. Blair loved his ego and his macho reputation more than Robbie, so what was the point?
He closed his eyes to clear his mind. He didn't have time to dwell on this; he was too busy with midterms and the rest of his obligations. His classes had to be his focus now.

Blair spent all of his free time with Tiffany and the two photographers. They showered him with compliments on his body, laughed at his jokes, and bought him presents, including lots of new clothes, jewelry, and a Rolex watch. They took him out to expensive restaurants and introduced him to top executives from the publishing company producing the photo book. Sometimes Fred and/or Chad spent the night with him, but it was usually Tiffany. She managed to convince him he was actually straight with a few gay tendencies, which made sense to him. He still didn't enjoy sex with women like he did with Robbie, but being straight would solve a lot of his problems, not the least of which was his feelings for Robbie. There was also his father to consider, because there was no way he would ever approve of a gay son, especially one with a white southern

An Admission of Weakness

boyfriend. With a woman, he could potentially have a family someday, something he couldn't have with Robbie.

Once he was married to a woman, he would be able to forget about Robbie once and for all, according to Tiffany. She was purposely distancing him from Robbie and his other friends in an effort to make him more dependent on her. However, it was so gradual that he didn't notice what was happening.

Blair groaned around Chad's manhood when Fred's rigid dick slid into his ass. His own penis was embedded deeply in Tiffany's vagina. By pivoting his hips, he was able to fuck her while simultaneously being fucked himself. With Chad facefucking him too, he was in sensory overload heaven, and he was determined to enjoy it.

After Chad and Fred climaxed a little later, Blair continued fucking Tiffany.

"You're sure you're on the pill?" he panted.

"Would it be so bad to have a baby with me?" she kissed his face and neck while she bounced up and down on him.

"No, of course not," he said hesitantly.

"You said your dad wants grandchildren," she reminded him. "And think how beautiful our babies will be."

"They will be beautiful," he agreed.

An Admission of Weakness

"Once we're married, I want to have a dozen children with you."

"When we're married?"

She leaned over and pulled a small box from her purse, careful not to let him slip out of her. "I was going to do this later, but here," she said.

Blair opened the velvet-covered box, and his jaw dropped. Inside was a glittering diamond men's wedding band.

"Blair Butterfield," she slid up and down on him while Chad and Fred licked his cock when she was at its apex. "Will you marry me?"

"Seriously?"

"I love you," she said. "We belong together."

"But what about –?"

"You're not gay," she said.

"How do you know?" he asked.

"Trust me," Fred said. "You're just one of those guys who can literally fuck anything."

Blair held her waist and forced her to bounce up and down harder on his dick while Chad sucked his nipples and Fred kissed him.

"Oh fuck," he panted. "Yes, I will marry you."

"Wobbie?" Rhett said into the phone.

"Hey, little brother," Robbie grinned. "How are you?"

"I'm good," Rhett said. "What's wrong?"

"Nothing," Robbie said, surprised.

"Something's wong. Tell me what it is."

An Admission of Weakness

"I'm fine," Robbie assured him.

"Is it Blair?"

"No, of course not. He's fine. Did you all get the gifts he sent?"

"Yes," Rhett said. "Ma liked the perfume. She wears it evwy day."

"He bought her perfume?" Robbie said. "He didn't tell me that."

"The girls love their shirts. Be sure and tell Blair."

"I will," Robbie promised.

"I've started working at the westauwant as a busboy after school," Rhett said proudly. "I can buy my own ticket to come see you this summer."

"That's great," Robbie said. "I can't wait to see you. It'll be nice to see a friendly face."

Something was obviously going on with Robbie, Rhett decided. It wasn't so much what he was saying as the tone of his voice.

"Did you and Blair bweak up?" he frowned.

"Don't be silly. It's just hard to find time to be together. I'm so busy with everything, and he's doing some modeling for a photo book."

"Wow, that's impwessive," Rhett grinned. "Now I can say my bwother's boyfwiend is a college football player and a model."

"Yep, you can definitely say that."

An Admission of Weakness

"Bro, you're gonna marry her?" Andres said with disbelief. "You've known her eight weeks."

"She wants to marry me," Blair said. "I could see myself falling in love with her."

"She just wants you to sign her contracts," Andres said. "That's all she's after. Once she has that, things will change."

"I've already signed the contracts," Blair said.

"Did you read them before you signed?"

"I didn't have to," Blair said. "I trust her. She loves me. She said so."

"She loves your dick," Andres said bluntly.

"It's more than that."

"What about Robbie? You told me you were in love with him."

"I can't be with him and have a modeling career."

"And that's more important to you than he is?" Andres whistled. "That's cold, bro."

"He didn't understand, and neither do you."

"Oh, I understand," Andres said. "You're as shallow as hell. All you want is attention, and you don't care where it comes from. You'd rather get rich and have Tiffany stroke your ego than something real with Robbie.

"Well, I got news for you. Money isn't real. It's not going to make you happy like Robbie will."

"It turns out I'm not gay after all," Blair said. "Tiff says I'm straight."

An Admission of Weakness

"You're letting someone else tell you who you are? The only reason you can do it with a woman is because you think about Robbie when you do it. And it's what you learned as a teenager, so you're used to it."
"I'm starting to really like it," Blair lied. "Tiff is terrific in bed. She'll make a good wife. She's pretty and smart and successful."
"Robbie is pretty and smart and successful," Andres said. "And he's got something Tiffany will never have."
"A dick?"
"No," Andres said pointedly. "Your heart."

"Mama, I need to tell you something," Naomi closed her mother's bedroom door.
"It's about time," Ruby sat up against the headboard.
"What do you mean?" Naomi frowned.
"I know about you working at Abernathy's."
"How'd you find out?"
"I'm your mother," Ruby chuckled. "I know everything."
"Carter can't find out," Naomi said.
"I think you should tell him," Ruby said. "Let him know you have a mind and a will of your own."
"He'd be furious."
"If his masculinity is too fragile to handle a strong woman, let him blow a gasket. It'd do him good, and me too," Ruby grinned. "I'm

An Admission of Weakness

tired of him strutting around here like he's the cock of the walk."

"He is the head of the household," Naomi pointed out.

"No, he's not!" Ruby said impatiently. "The two of you are partners. He's not your boss; he's your husband. You have as much say around here as he does."

"That's not how Carter sees it."

"Then educate him," Ruby said. "He's a smart man. Once you explain things to him, maybe he'll treat you like an equal instead of a servant."

"Mama."

"Anyway, tell me about the job."

"Oh, Mama, it's wonderful," Naomi said. "Billy and June are so kind, and they listen to my ideas. They like them too. I've already been promoted to consultant over the wedding gown division."

"That's marvelous," Ruby said. "And just look at you. This is the first time I've seen you excited about anything in years."

"It is exciting," Naomi admitted. "For the first time, I feel like I'm part of something."

"You're part of this family," Ruby reminded her.

"But I'm not needed anymore," Naomi said. "The children are grown, Carter has his book, and you have a job and friends that keep you

An Admission of Weakness

busy. All I have is this house. I'm merely a maid in my own home."

"You are much more than that," Ruby said. "It's easy for the children to take you for granted because they know you'll always be there for them. The same with Carter. But they love you and couldn't survive without you. Neither could I."

"Thanks, Mama."

Naomi sat down beside her, and the two women talked for an hour about the gowns Naomi had sewn as well as the ones for which she was acting as an advisor.

An Admission of Weakness

CHAPTER THIRTEEN

Katie drove her rental car to the Talbot Ranch northwest of Green Grove. She hadn't told her family or Dillon she was coming home because she wanted to surprise them.

The impressive two-story log main house came into view as she drove along the winding driveway. It was a large building with lots of windows, vaulted ceilings, slate and white pine floors, and an open staircase. It was rustic in a sophisticated, elegant sort of way. Clint and Marci, Dillon's parents, had furnished it with expensive, tasteful, traditional furniture. The kitchen was state-of-the-art, and there was a polished oak grand piano in the living room. The floor plan was open, giving the place an airy, relaxed feel.

The second house on the property was a much more modest log cabin with front and back porches, two bedrooms, and a loft overlooking the living room, kitchen, and dining room. It was furnished in a similar manner as the main house.

The barn and the stables were also built of logs to tie in with the two houses. There was even a thirty foot log windmill. The lawns, trees, shrubs, and flowers were neatly maintained, as were the pastures, paddocks, and fences.

What a lovely place, Katie smiled. She pictured herself living here someday with Dillon. She

An Admission of Weakness

would get a job at the local hospital, and the two of them would raise a family.

Her destination today was the smaller house, where Dillon lived. She drove past the main house and parked the car. As she alit from the vehicle, a voice called to her.

"Katie?" Dillon called from a nearby corral. He was working with Strike, one of the younger Clydesdale horses. Strike was a massive steed, standing just over six feet at the shoulder, and he weighed about two thousand pounds. Fortunately, he was as gentle as a kitten, although he had a stubborn streak as well.

"What are you doing here?" he frowned.

"I wanted to see you," she smiled. "Strike's looking good."

Dillon vaulted over the fence and swept her up in his arms. He spun her around before setting her down and kissing her.

"God I've missed you," he said.

"Me too."

"Hey, Joe," he called to someone in the distance. "Take over with Strike, will you?"

"Sure thing, Boss," Joe hollered back.

Dillon took Katie by the hand and pulled her into his cabin. After an energetic hour in the bedroom, the two sat down on the living room sectional for a glass of wine.

"What made you decide to fly to Illinois?" Dillon asked.

An Admission of Weakness

"I had some time off, and I missed you so much," she said. "And I had an idea about Dad."

"We tell him the truth?"

"And risk a murder-suicide? I don't think so."

"He can only murder us if he can catch us," Dillon grinned. "I say we hide the guns, tell him, and then run like hell."

"Then it would just be a suicide," she said.

"I can live with that," he shrugged.

"Dillon, be serious."

"That wasn't serious enough for you?"

"What if I say I ran into you at the gas station or something, and you mention you remember Mama's cooking. That will give me an excuse to invite you over. We can pretend to catch up on old times, and Dad can get to know you better."

"Or we could just tell him the truth," he said wryly.

"Or," she said, "– and this might be better yet – we throw Blair under the bus and tell Dad he's studying elementary education and drama."

"We can't do that to your brother."

"Believe me, he has a bigger secret than that," she said. "If we ease Dad into the smaller secret, it might make it easier for all of us."

"What's the bigger secret?" Dillon frowned. "That he's gay?"

"You knew?"

An Admission of Weakness

"No, but I suspected it," Dillon said. "He never dated anyone but Danielle since middle school, and she was a bitch. Sure, she was pretty, but the only reason a guy would stay with her is if he needed a beard."
"Every guy in his class wanted to be with her," Katie reminded him.
"Because they were teenage boys thinking with their dicks," Dillon said.
"So what do you think of my plan?"
"We can't rat Blair out, but I suppose we could try the first idea," he said reluctantly.
"Good," she grinned. "Be at the house at six. I'll tell Mama you're coming."

"So, Dillon, how is business?" Ruby asked their guest.
"The saddler business is doing very well," he said.
"You look different from the last time you were here," Justin said. "You must work out."
"I do," Dillon chuckled. "I'm still a nerd, but I don't look as much like one now."
"You're very handsome, dear," Naomi smiled.
"Thank you, Mrs. Butterfield."
"So you're still selling shoes and belts to a couple of stores," Carter frowned. "How profitable can your parents' business be?"
"We sell much more than shoes and belts," Dillon said patiently. "We design a wide variety of leather goods from boots to jackets to

An Admission of Weakness

saddles right here in town, and we sell to stores all over the world."

"But there are thousands of shoemakers to compete with," Carter argued. "Surely the market is saturated."

"Not for high-quality goods at reasonable prices," Dillon said.

"The ranch is doing well?" Naomi intervened. "All those lovely horses?"

"They're doing quite well, thanks," Dillon grinned. "You should come out and visit sometime. We have a beautiful colt named Spike I'm working with."

"I will," Naomi smiled. "It'd be nice to see your mother again. I haven't visited with her in a while."

"Stop by the downtown store," Dillon suggested. "She and Dad are there Monday through Friday."

"They leave those expensive horses to be cared for by hired hands?" Carter said. "That seems risky."

"If you consider me a hired hand, then it's not at all risky. I help with the Saddler, but I mostly care for the ranch and the horses. We have a few hired hands, but I prefer to do most of the work myself."

"The place looks beautiful," Ruby said.

"So you can't afford enough hands to handle the ranch?" Carter said.

An Admission of Weakness

"We can afford all the hands we need, Dr. Butterfield. You know, first you think we have too many hired hands, and now you're worried we don't have enough. Excuse me, but which is it?"

"I'm just saying it takes a special kind of person to manage a business successfully."

"What makes you think I'm not that kind of person?" Dillon said heatedly.

"I remember your grades in elementary school," Carter said. "Mostly B's and C's. A few D's as well."

"Well, I was the salutatorian of our high school class, just a few points behind Katie!" Dillon snapped.

"Don't raise your voice to me," Carter said sternly.

"I'm not a student anymore," Dillon said. "And I'll talk to you with respect when you can do the same to me."

"Respect must be earned," Carter said.

"Dad," Katie frowned. "Stop it."

"And respect goes both ways. I see no need to earn the respect of someone I don't respect," Dillon said coldly.

"How dare you! I will not be spoken to in such a manner in my own home!" Carter said indignantly.

"Carter, be quiet!" Ruby said. "You have no right to be rude to our guest."

An Admission of Weakness

"He's not my guest. I didn't invite him here," Carter scowled. "He invited himself."
"Dad, that's enough!"
"It is enough," Dillon wiped his mouth and pushed his chair back. "I'm out of here."
"Dillon, please don't go, dear," Naomi said.
"I'm sorry, Mrs. Butterfield, but I can't stay in the same house with him. He's as big an asshole as he was ten years ago."
"Why, I-I never!" Carter sputtered.
Dillon and Katie left the house, Justin continued eating, and Ruby turned angrily on her son-in-law.
"How dare you treat him like that!" she glared at him. "Don't you know better than to be rude to a guest in your home? And he's a friend of Katie's. Do you have any idea how much you embarrassed her?"
"I don't like that kid."
"I don't care if you like him or not!" Ruby snapped. "You made a fool of yourself, and I'm embarrassed for you."
She threw down her napkin and stormed from the room.
"Carter, how could you?" Naomi eyed him reproachfully. "He's a nice boy. He didn't deserve to be attacked like that."
"I don't want him getting the idea that he's good enough for Katie," Carter said firmly. "He's not welcome in this family."

An Admission of Weakness

"He may not be a doctor or lawyer, but he's good enough for Katie if she says he is."

"Thank god she's living in California," Carter said. "Too far away for him to get any ideas about her again."

"But remember how fond they were of each other in high school," Naomi said. "They were so sweet together."

"What's that got to do with anything?" he asked impatiently.

"We don't always get to choose who we fall in love with, Carter," Naomi said before silently leaving the room.

"Dad, can I talk to you?" Justin knocked on the study door.

"Of course," Carter removed his reading glasses and tossed them onto the desk in front of him. "I always have time for you. What's on your mind?"

"I was wondering why you don't like Dillon," Justin said hesitantly.

"He's unambitious," Carter said. "No college education, no plans to better himself, not willing to explore the world and see what's out there."

"But maybe he's satisfied with his life the way it is," Justin frowned. "Maybe he doesn't need to explore the world."

"He's lazy," Carter said. "Your sister has worked too hard to become the success she is to

An Admission of Weakness

spend her life supporting a shiftless lay-about who is too indolent to earn his own living."
"He must be making some money," Justin said. "His folks drive BMWs, and he has a new pickup truck. They pay twenty-five dollars an hour to start at the Saddler."
"They're probably drowning in debt."
"Did you know they sent two of their Clydesdales to pull the grand marshal in the last Rose Bowl Parade?"

An Admission of Weakness

"Is that supposed to impress me?" Carter snorted.

"I think it's impressive," Justin said. "It has to be a huge honor to be asked to the Rose Bowl Parade. Dillon's doing something right."

"I suppose even he can't do everything wrong," Carter acknowledged reluctantly.

"And Talbot Saddler has over two hundred employees. The company Web page is amazing. Dillon's sister designed it. That sounds successful to me."

"Clint and Marci got lucky," Carter said dismissively.

"Don't you think you're being too hard on them?" Justin said.

"Are you questioning my judgment?" his father frowned.

"I just think Dillon's a nice guy," Justin shrugged. "He's always happy every time I see him."

"He may be nice and happy and all that nonsense, but that isn't the same as successful."

"Are you happy?" Justin asked.

"What kind of a question is that?" Carter snapped. "Of course I'm happy."

"Why?"

"Why?" Carter appeared confused. "I have a successful family, a top notch education, an excellent job, and a lovely home. What more could I want?"

An Admission of Weakness

"Are you and Mama still in love?"
"Justin, where is this line of questioning coming from?"
"Well, you're always at work or working on your book. Mama spends a lot of time alone."
"Nonsense. Of course I love your mother, and she loves me."
"I'm glad," Justin said. "I've been kinda worried about it."
"Well, you don't need to worry," Carter said in a fatherly voice. "The Butterfield family is doing just fine."

"That's it, Katie," Dillon paced angrily next to his ruby-red Chevrolet pickup. "That's the last time I try to talk to your father."
"I know you're upset," she said. "I'm angry too. Let him cool down for a while and then we'll try something else."
"No," he said firmly. "We either tell him the truth, or we call it quits."
"You don't mean that," she looked horrified.
"I do mean it," he said. "The only way he's ever going to treat me right is if we're married and he no longer has any say over you."
"He has no say over me now," she frowned.
"Do you hear yourself?" he said incredulously. "A second ago you were trying to come up with another idea to make him come around, which is never going to happen, by the way."

An Admission of Weakness

"So you just want to give up?" she said. "Pretend like we don't love each other and start seeing other people?"

"What other choice do we have?" he said. "I love you, and I want to spend my life with you. But are you prepared to live with the fact that he'll never accept me as part of your family?" When she didn't answer right away, he went on.

"So I guess that's my answer," he said. "Your dad is clearly the one running things in this relationship. You do whatever he says and to hell with what I want."

"That's not true," she said.

"Sweetheart, I love you, but it is true, and you need to face up to that. So I suggest you go back to California and that job that you only took because he insisted on it."

His eyes filled with tears as he stepped up on the porch of the cabin.

"We need to take a break from each other for a while."

"You don't mean that," she wiped the moisture from her cheeks. "I love you. I'll go talk to him."

"Don't you see? We can't be in a three-way relationship with him. I need this to be between you and me." He choked back a sob. "But as long as you think you have to have his approval, you and I can never be."

An Admission of Weakness

He walked into the house and closed the door, leaving her lost and broken.

Camilla knocked on Katie's bedroom door. Naomi had kept the room and its contents just as she left it when she moved to California.
"Katie, it's me."
"Go away," Katie said tearfully.
Camilla opened the door hesitantly and peered inside the dark room. She sat down beside her sister on the bed and turned on the bedside lamp.
"I'm sorry about Dillon," she rubbed her shoulder soothingly.
"How did you know?"
"It was pretty obvious after I heard what Dad did at supper," Camilla said dryly. "You brought Dillon here to try to get Dad to change his mind. Why didn't you tell me about the two of you?"
"It doesn't matter now," Katie dried her eyes and sat up. "He ended things."
"No, he didn't," Camilla chuckled. "He just wants you to forget Dad and do what's right for you. And that means quitting your job, moving back to Green Grove, and marrying Dillon."
"You can't possibly know any of this unless you spoke to Dillon."
"You're more transparent than you think," Camilla said. "I knew when you were in high

An Admission of Weakness

school that you and Dillon were meant for one another. He worships the ground you walk on."
"Not anymore," Katie said sadly.
"Of course he does," Camilla said. "He's known you for fifteen years; he knows your good qualities as well as your bad. He's known all along how difficult Dad is, and he still stuck it out. That's how much he loves you. I guess the question is how much do you love him?"
"I don't like most men," Katie said. "Straight men are usually after one thing, but Dillon has always been different. He sees me as a partner, someone to build a life with, not just a sex object."
"He's one in a million," Camilla agreed. "I wish I could find someone like him."
"You will," Katie said. "If it's your heart's true desire, the universe will find a way to make it happen."
"That's what Mama always told us," Camilla smiled. "Do you really believe it?"
"I do," Katie sighed dejectedly. "The universe did it for me, but I screwed it up."
"It's not too late to fix the situation," Ruby said from the doorway.
"I don't know, Gran," Katie reached out for her, and Ruby sat down and enfolded her in her arms.
"Camilla's right," Ruby said. "Dillon loves you."

An Admission of Weakness

"Did everyone know about us all this time?" Katie frowned.

"Camilla and your mother and I knew," Ruby said.

"And Blair," Katie added. "I told him."

"The point is, you and Dillon love one another," Ruby said. "Stop listening to your father."

"Why does everyone think I only do what Dad wants?"

"Because you do," Ruby said.

"But he only wants what's best for me," Katie said.

"Bullshit," Ruby snorted.

"Gran!" Camilla looked scandalized.

"Your father wants what's best for him," Ruby said. "Not that he doesn't love all of you very much. He's a good man, but he thinks that what's best for everyone is what's best for him."

"So what do I do about this?"

"You put Dillon first," Camilla said.

"No, you put you first and Dillon second," Ruby corrected her. "Never put a man first."

"I don't understand what Dad has against Dillon," Camilla said.

"Your father believes that in this country, Black people have to work extra hard to succeed. That's how he was raised, and he isn't wrong. We are always at a disadvantage. No matter whether we like to believe it or not, the

An Admission of Weakness

color of our skin is always going to work against us because we live in a straight, white, Christian male dominated society. They want to keep the power, but they don't want to take responsibility for the problems they cause by holding people of color, women, and gay people back."

"What's that got to do with Dillon?" Katie said. "He's successful, his parents are successful."

"Yes, they are," Ruby agreed. "But in your father's eyes, a person has to have an advanced degree and work in a high profile profession like doctor or lawyer. He thinks Black people should settle for nothing less."

"Success can only be measured in happiness," Camilla said.

"Dillon's always happy," Katie said. "Except for tonight."

"Let him cool off," Ruby advised. "Give him time to realize what losing you would mean. He'll run to your side, I guarantee."

She turned to her other granddaughter.

"And as for you," she smiled. "You are going to find the person who is a perfect fit for you. He may not be who you have pictured, so you have to keep an open mind. Trust me, he's going to find you, and he will be amazing."

"You sound like Mama," Katie said.

"Who do you think taught her?" Ruby chuckled.

"Thanks, Gran," Camilla hugged her. "I love you."
"I love you both very much," Ruby said. "And that will never change."

An Admission of Weakness

CHAPTER FOURTEEN

Blair continued spending time with Tiffany and her photographers. They kept him constantly occupied so that he was completely separated from Andres and the rest of his friends. Tiffany convinced him that she was the key to his brilliant future as a model. With all the adulation from her and his peers, Robbie was all but forgotten. Sometimes he passed him in the hall but never acknowledged him.

Blair traveled with Tiffany and Fred and Chad and posed for dozens of photo shoots before the end of the semester. He fucked her nearly every night, and he endeavored to put forth his best effort when they were intimate. It helped that she was an enthusiastic partner and told him he was an incredible lover.

Occasionally Tiff would allow Fred and Chad to join them, but she made sure Blair focused on her, although she did permit him to fuck them once in a while. If he had been honest with himself, he would have admitted that he preferred being with them over Tiffany. Unfortunately, the brief stint of introspection and self-honesty he had experienced with Robbie was over thanks to Tiffany's carefully organized efforts. She recognized his need for attention, so she made sure he received lots of adoration from dozens of men and women who practically worshiped at his feet. In no time,

An Admission of Weakness

she could manipulate him as easily as a trained seal.

"I want to do a shower shot," Fred, the attractive, forty-five year old photographer, said.
"The coach said I can't do nudity," Blair said.
"It will be tasteful," Chad assured him. "Just some side shots. We won't show anything you don't want us to show."
"Although we should," Fred grinned. "Your dick is spectacular. You could have a huge career as a porn star. I'd even do it with you."
"Thanks," Blair flushed with pleasure at the compliment. "I think I'll stick to modeling."
"Why not do both? I know a guy who can set you up. We're talking really big money."
"How big?"
"You'd be driving a Mercedes in a matter of weeks."
"Seriously?" Blair said. "What would I have to do?"
"Whatever you want, baby," Fred grinned and kissed him. "Just imagine making a living having sex with as many women and men as you want."
"The really kinky stuff pays the best," Chad said. "I'd do that with you."
"What's considered kinky?" Blair asked curiously.

An Admission of Weakness

"Leather, watersports, cock and ball torture, bondage, discipline, you name it."
"I've always been curious about stuff like that," Blair said thoughtfully.
"You need a porn name," Fred said.
"Something like Dick Savage or Butch Dickinson."
"Dick Savage has a nice ring to it," Blair said.
"Great. I'll take care of everything," Fred grinned. "With that body and dick, you're going to be a huge star."
Blair considered this while Fred kissed him again. In less than five minutes, he was taking turns fucking first Chad and then Fred.

Once the shoot was organized at a local gym, Blair stripped off his clothes and donned a robe. Tiffany walked into the shower room and sized the environment up. There were a dozen men and women setting up equipment and arranging things just so. Two men set up a leather sex sling while others leaned a heavy wooden St. Andrew's cross against a wall.
"Where's Ollie?" she demanded.
"I'm here," a rough looking man carrying a suitcase stepped into the shower room and removed all of his clothes. He had a long ponytail, several scars, and multiple tattoos. The other people undressed as well, much to Blair's surprise.

An Admission of Weakness

"Okay, here's what I want: close-ups of his chest, dick, ass, and armpits," Tiffany said.

"Whoa," Blair held up his hands. "No dick or ass shots."

"Oh right, sweetie," Tiffany waved away his concerns and winked at Ollie. "Of course not."

"Why are you wearing a robe, and why's everyone getting naked?" Blair asked. "This is just another photo shoot, right?"

"Of course. I'm going to join you for the pictures," she grinned. "Ollie works better if everyone's naked. Chad, Fred, what are you waiting for?"

She removed her robe while Chad and Fred swiftly disrobed.

"You're all going to be in the pictures with me?"

"That's right," Fred said. "These are going to be action shots, so pretend that Tiffany's a hooker, and the two of you have just finished having sex. That's why you're taking a shower together."

"What will you two be doing?"

"We'll just be in the background," Chad said vaguely. "You know, to give the pictures a little depth."

"Are those movie cameras?" Blair frowned at the objects in Ollie's and another man's hands.

"We're using them to take stills from," Ollie said. "Your job is to fuck her while we take some lighting shots."

An Admission of Weakness

"Isn't this whole thing a little too suggestive?" Blair said warily. "The coach will never go for it."

"I already talked to the coach, and he's fine with it," Tiffany said while she slid his robe from his shoulders.

"I feel like something's going on," Blair said hesitantly.

"Nothing's going on," Tiffany assured him.

"We need you hard," Fred said.

"Why?" Blair said.

"You can't fuck her if you're not hard," Ollie said.

"You give off a different energy when you're fucking, sugar," Tiffany explained. "It comes across in the pictures."

"I guess that makes sense," Blair nodded. "So this is just to take still shots from?"

"Absolutely," Tiffany kissed him. She began kissing him ardently while Chad knelt down and blew him.

Before Blair knew it, his manhood was in the man's mouth while Fred rimmed his ass. Blair's length grew hard, and he surrendered himself to his baser instincts. After all, these people were experts in the photography business, so they knew what they were talking about. Besides, Tiff had his best interests at heart; the two of them were going to be married in another few weeks, after all.

An Admission of Weakness

He hadn't told his family about the wedding. His father was going to be furious with him that he was marrying a white woman instead of Danielle, and he decided he wanted to enjoy a few weeks of wedded bliss before bringing Tiffany home.

After a minute, Tiffany lay down on the sling. "Okay, Blair, put your dick in slowly," Ollie moved close with his camera. "We want to enjoy every inch. Brenda, it needs to hurt." Tiffany cried out in exaggerated pain as Blair inserted his dick into her body.
"Ahh, fuck yeah," Ollie grinned as he filmed a close up of Blair's thick appendage sinking deeply into her while his associates filmed their bodies and faces.
"All the way in."
In his sex-addled mind, Blair pictured himself with Robbie and began to power fuck her.
"Hey, slow down and enjoy it," Fred gradually inserted himself into Blair's ass. "I want you to fuck yourself on me while you fuck Tiff."
"Oh yeah," Blair groaned with pleasure.
"Tiff, lean up so he can suck your tits," Fred said.
Fred, Chad, and Tiffany changed positions three times over the next forty-five minutes, and Blair allowed himself to suck and kiss their various body parts until he couldn't hold back an orgasm any longer. He shot his load into

An Admission of Weakness

Tiffany while Fred and Chad tried to keep him going, but he pulled away from the three of them when his brain cleared from its orgasmic fog.

"Do all these people have to be here for this?" he frowned. "I'm not used to performing in front of a crowd."

"You just did for forty-five minutes," Ollie lowered the video camera and grinned. "And we recorded every second of it."

"That wasn't long enough, Ollie," Tiffany said. Suddenly gone was the dainty, feminine voice Blair was used to; now it sounded hard as nails. "We need at least sixty minutes raw footage for this first scene."

"Get him hard again, and then we'll go on," Ollie said. "I want Tina on the sling with Chad, Fred on the cross, and me and Brenda on the bench this time. Blair will take turns with all of us. Then I'll pair up with Blair while Brenda takes on Fred and Chad."

"Hold on," Blair said. "You're telling me this is all just to get stills of me for the photo book?"

"Don't be so naïve, kid," Ollie smirked while a Goth-looking woman blew him. "God, you're really as stupid as Brenda said."

"Who the hell is Brenda?"

"Just calm down, darling," Tiffany embraced him and tried to kiss him.

Blair pushed her to arm's length and held her there.

An Admission of Weakness

"You did all of this just so I'd do porn with you?" he said incredulously.
"This is what you agreed to, remember?" Fred said. "I told you I was going to set it up for us."
"That's right," Chad said. "I was there."
"I know, but I didn't realize we were serious."
"Didn't you read your contract?" Ollie said. "It's all in there. You agreed to fuck whoever and whatever we tell you to: guys, women, sheep, you name it."
"You signed the contract, Blair," Tiffany caressed his privates to get him hard again. "It was all right there in black and white."
"But I didn't understand!" he cried. "I never would have signed the damn thing if I'd known about this."
"I'm sorry," Tiffany said. "I should have made it clearer to you."
"You all have been using me and lying to me," Blair said.
"Surely you don't believe that I would ever lie to you," she looked wounded.
He slapped her hand away and snatched up his clothes.
"You did lie to me," he hastily dressed. He was so irate that he was close to tears. "You said this was all for a photo book."
Tiffany took his hand and kissed it and said in her most ultra-feminine voice, "Sweetie, I didn't tell you about this because I didn't think it mattered. I thought you'd be pleased."

An Admission of Weakness

"Bullshit," he wrenched his hand away. "You tricked me into doing this. Do you even love me?"

"Honey, of course I do," she said. "Why else would I be marrying you?"

"I'm not sure anymore," he said grimly.

"Look, when you told Fred you wanted to do porn," she said, "I thought this was something we could do together."

"You made it very clear that this is what you wanted to do," Fred added.

"I thought we were just talking," Blair said.

"Then why did you sign the contract?"

"Look, sweetie, we can't just stand around and talk about this. Ollie's doing this as a favor to us," Tiffany said.

"How is this a favor?" Blair demanded.

"He's the best in the business," she said. "He only works with the top stars, but I convinced him you were going to be his next big sensation."

"You really think I could be a star?"

"Absolutely," Ollie said sincerely. "You've got what it takes."

"Why all the secrecy then? Why not let me be part of planning this whole thing?"

"You have no experience with porn," Tiffany said. "Besides, you're the star; you don't need to worry about the technical aspects."

"So Chad and Fred and all these other people signed the same contract?"

An Admission of Weakness

"That's right," Tiffany said. "But you get top billing."
"Look, you and Tiffany are getting married. Don't you want to make her happy?"
"Of course I do," Blair said. He turned to Tiffany. "You really want to marry me? It isn't just so I'd do porn with you?"
"Of course not," she kissed him and rubbed his hand on her groin. "I love you, baby."
"But I don't think I want to do this for a living," he said. "Why can't I go back to being a model?"
"Oh for Christ's sake!" Fred snapped. "You were never going to be a model. This whole thing was to get you and those other Midwestern rubes to sign the fucking contract."
"And you did," Chad said. "And you're going to be a huge star once Ollie does his magical editing. You're going to make all of us rich."
"I knew it!" Blair scowled and removed his fingers from her vagina. "You're full of shit. This whole thing is about money."
"Fine," Tiffany dropped the voice and the act and put her robe on. "Ollie and I brought you into it because you've got the body and the dick and you're willing to fuck men and women."
"I should have known," Blair said bitterly. "You don't love me at all, do you?"
"Of course not," she snorted. "You're a dumb jock who's lousy at sex."

An Admission of Weakness

"What about Andres and the other guys? Did they go along with this?"

"You were the only one stupid and arrogant enough to fall for it," Ollie chuckled.

"Well, I'm smart enough to walk away from it," Blair headed for the door.

"You can try," Tiffany said. "But we have a contract, remember?"

"But I didn't understand what you were making me do."

"We have two witnesses who watched you sign," Tiffany said. "The same two who you were having sex with on camera. You looked plenty willing when you were pounding their asses."

"Enough of this," Ollie said impatiently. He turned to Tiffany. "After the next scene, I think he and I should take turns fucking you and Tina. You can go down on Craig. The different skin tones will complement each other."

"That would look great," she agreed.

"That will be enough for today, and then we'll switch it up tomorrow," Ollie said. "I'll write up a script tonight."

"I'm not doing any of that," Blair said firmly. "Contract or no contract. Sue me if you want, I don't care."

"Then expect to hear from our lawyers," Tiffany said coldly.

"Now let's not get unpleasant about this," Ollie said. He spoke in an almost fatherly tone.

An Admission of Weakness

"Blair, I understand your situation. You think having sex for money is beneath you, and you feel that we've been dishonest with you."
"That's right."
"And you don't care about all the money you'd be making?"
"No, I don't," Blair said.
"Not even the fact that you could probably retire a wealthy man in about ten years?"
"Not even that," Blair insisted.
"Well, that's too bad," Ollie said. "Because if you don't fulfill your contract, I will have to go to the university and tell them what you've been doing." He held up the camera. "I have all the proof I need right here."
"And once he does that, you can say goodbye to your scholarship and your degree," Tiffany added.
"You can't do that!" Blair cried.
"We can, and we will," Tiffany said. "Now let's get the next scene ready. By the way, tomorrow we'll shoot in your dorm room. I'm anxious to use a strap-on to fuck you while the other three girls have their way with you."
"No!" Blair said indignantly.
"You don't have a choice, man," Ollie said. "Now get those clothes off, and let's get back to work."
He reached over and unfastened Blair's jeans. Reluctantly, Blair disrobed and joined Tina and Chad at the sling.

An Admission of Weakness

"I need your help," Andres said.
"For what?" Robbie looked up from his desk and grinned. "That calculus is kicking your butt, isn't it?"
"It's Blair."
"Then I can't help you," Robbie's smile faded. "Get his entourage to lend a hand. Of course, they've been lending a lot more than that all semester. There were a dozen or more women up here the other day. All worshiping the great and mighty Blair Butterfield."
"He's in trouble," Andres said.
"Like I said, he's got his precious Tiff to help him," Robbie said bitterly. "From what I hear every night, they fuck so often, I'm surprised she's not pregnant."
"That's all over," Andres said.
"Aw, she dumped him already, poor baby? And you want me to help him get over a broken heart?" Robbie said sarcastically. "Sorry, I'm still trying to get over the one he gave me, so I don't have time to help anyone else."
"Listen, I'm the first one to agree with you that he's an idiot," Andres said.
"And arrogant and selfish and stupid and narcissistic and –" Robbie started counting off on his fingers.
"Okay, I get it, you're angry, and you have every right to be. I don't know why you ever fell for him in the first place."

An Admission of Weakness

"We all do stupid things, I guess," Robbie said grimly.

"Look, none of that matters now," Andres said impatiently. "He's got himself into some serious trouble."

"What kind of trouble?"

"The kind that could lose him his scholarship and get him kicked out of school."

Andres went on to explain Blair's predicament.

"It serves him right," Robbie said callously.

"Yes, it does," Andres agreed. "But he's my friend, so I don't want to see his life ruined because of his stupidity. And I don't think you do either."

"I suppose not," Robbie said reluctantly. "But why come to me?"

"You're the smartest person I know," Andres said. "And I think you still love him, even if he is a moron."

"I can't stand the sight of him," Robbie snorted. He sighed resignedly. "But I'll help in any way I can."

"Do you have a copy of this contract?" Robbie asked briskly.

"No," Blair stared down at his hands.

"That figures," Robbie muttered.

"What's that supposed to mean?" Blair scowled.

"It means you're a worthless piece of shit!" Robbie snapped.

An Admission of Weakness

"Let's play nice," Andres said. He turned to Blair. "Can you get a copy of it?"
"I've asked repeatedly, but they keep saying I don't need to see it."
"We need to know what it says," Robbie said. "Maybe they're making all of this up."
"Can they really go to the university?" Andres asked.
"I suppose they could," Robbie said. "That's why we need to know exactly what the contract says."
He thought for a moment.
"How many videos have you made?"
"Ten so far," Blair admitted reluctantly.
"All with her?" Robbie wrinkled his nose distastefully.
"Not all of them," Blair said uncomfortably. "Some were with Fred and Chad, and one with Ollie."
"No one else?"
"Well, there were six other guys and four other wom–"
"Never mind," Robbie held up a hand. "I don't want to know."
"Look, I know I screwed up," Blair said sourly. "You don't have to sit there and judge me."
"Yes I do, you fucking prick!" Robbie shouted angrily. "Because you're a fucking idiot, and you treated me like shit. You think everyone wants you because you're so hot, you arrogant sonofabitch, and then you have the nerve to ask

An Admission of Weakness

for help when you've single-handedly done everything possible to ruin your life! You wouldn't be in this mess if you weren't a self-absorbed narcissist who thinks the world revolves around you."

"I didn't ask for your help, asshole!" Blair retorted.

"Fine," Robbie stood up to leave. "Good luck with your career in porn. I hope you make lots of money and get to sleep with every woman between here and Texas. I hope you end up with a dozen kids with a dozen different women. It would serve you right!"

"That's enough!" Andres slammed his hand down on the desk. "Robbie, sit down. You promised to help him, and I'm not letting you go back on your word."

"Whatever," Robbie rolled his eyes, but he sat back down. "When are you making your next video?"

"Tonight at seven," Blair said sullenly.

"Where?"

"In that half-burned warehouse next to the Interstate. Why?" Blair said belligerently. "You want to come watch?"

"Fuck you!" Robbie glowered. "You can get yourself out of this mess by yourself because I'm out."

"Robbie," Andres said.

"Do you have any idea how much you hurt me?" Robbie went on emotionally. "I have to

An Admission of Weakness

hear you and that bitch having sex right across the hall practically every night. And if it's not her, then it's those guys or god knows who else. You don't care who you sleep with, and you sure as hell don't care about my feelings. You always cared more about your image than me.

"I loved you," Robbie's voice broke, "and I was nothing to you but a hole to use when you were horny. You threw that love in the garbage for your reputation and some big modeling career. Well, I hope it was worth it."

His eyes filled with tears.

"I'm outa here."

Blair turned to Andres.

"So now what?"

"Is that all you've got to say?" Andres asked disgustedly. "He just poured his heart out to you, and you sat there and said nothing."

"What could I say?" Blair said. "He was right about everything. I hurt him badly, and I don't have any excuses to offer."

"Why don't you try – oh, I don't know – apologizing? What about telling him you love him?"

"What's the point? He obviously doesn't love me anymore."

"Man, you are one dumb motherfucker," Andres shook his head in disbelief. "He wouldn't be so upset if he didn't care about

An Admission of Weakness

you. And you acted like he meant nothing to you at all."

"I really am sorry how I treated him," Blair said. "I'm sorry I screwed it all up. He deserves better than me."

"That's the fucking truth," Andres said. He sighed. "Let me think about what to do now."

An Admission of Weakness

CHAPTER FIFTEEN

"Okay, hold it there," Ollie said as he adjusted the lighting for the next video.

Blair paused with his dick halfway in Tina's vagina. He was wearing only a leather harness across his muscular chest. Tiffany, Chad and Fred, and a dozen other nude men and women were standing off to the side. Tiffany looked up when Robbie walked into the half-demolished metal building.

"Who are you?" she scowled before she recognized him. "Oh, you're that kid that lives across the hall from Blair, the one he says is obsessed with him."

"Yeah, that's me, the guy who's obsessed with Blair," Robbie tried to keep the bitterness out of his voice. "I heard him talking about his new career, and I thought maybe I'd try out for it too."

Tiffany walked around him and studied him up and down. He avoided looking at her naked body.

"The face isn't great, but it'll do, I guess," she said. "The body's so-so. Let me see your dick."

With great reluctance, Robbie steeled himself and dropped his pants. Tiffany nodded approvingly, and he quickly covered himself.

"Are you bi?" she asked.

"No, strictly gay," he said hesitantly.

An Admission of Weakness

"Pity," she shrugged. "Oh well, we have some pills to take care of that."
She called to one of the men standing nearby. "Ken, get over here and get him hard."
Ken dropped to his knees and eagerly took Robbie's length into his mouth. He was very good at sucking dick, and Robbie's manhood rose to full attention under his ministrations.
"Okay, that's enough," Tiffany said. "Let's see you in action. Take off your clothes."
While Blair finished his scene, Robbie undressed, and she examined his entire body, even hefting his balls in her hand and spreading his hairy ass cheeks apart.
"You look better naked. So you think Blair's hot, am I right?" she said. "Let me see you make out with him."
"I'd rather do it with Ken here," Robbie said.
"Blair," she ignored him. "Get over here."
Blair used a towel to wipe the sweat from his forehead after he pulled out of Tina. He threw his used condom onto a pile of discarded rubbers and noticed Robbie's naked presence with astonishment.
"What are you doing here?"
"I want to be a porn star," Robbie shrugged. "I figure if you can do it, anyone can."
"I'm serious," Blair frowned. "Why are you here?"
"Don't worry; I won't steal the spotlight from you, your highness."

An Admission of Weakness

"Okay, I like this antagonism you two have going," Tiffany said. "Hey, Ollie, let's try these guys out together. He's got a great hairy ass for those close-ups you were talking about."
"Isn't there anyone else I could do it with?" Robbie asked.
"Why? You afraid you can't handle my big dick," Blair taunted him.
"That little thing?" Robbie snorted. "The way I remember it, it wasn't worth my time. Besides, it's how you use what you've got that counts, and you don't have a fucking clue."
"Okay, shut up," Tiffany said, becoming annoyed. "You, what's your name?"
"Eddie."
"Let him fuck you."
"I don't know where his dick's been," Robbie said.
"He's clean," she said. "What, you think I'm going to let him fuck me if he wasn't?"
"His dick is ugly," Robbie said. "He's ugly."
"I am not!" Blair said indignantly.
"Ollie, come over and fuck Eddie," Tiffany said.
Ollie handed his camera to another man and walked around Robbie appraisingly.
"Nice," he nodded.
He slipped a condom on and without warning shoved his manhood into Robbie's ass. He fucked him standing while the others gathered around to watch. He placed an arm around

An Admission of Weakness

Robbie's chest to hold him in place while he nuzzled his earlobe.

"Let the camera see how much you like being fucked," he whispered.

He continued fucking him for several minutes and then finally pulled out.

"He's good," he said. "Let Blair try him out."

"Lay down on the bench and let him fuck you," Tiffany said.

Damn, Robbie thought, I hadn't counted on any of this. What the hell am I doing? I should leave now while I have the chance.

"Lay down," Blair pointed to the bench.

"Fine," Robbie gritted his teeth. "But this is the last time you ever get to touch me. You got it?"

"Trust me, I wouldn't be touching you now if I didn't have to," Blair said coldly.

"You're a fucking prick," Robbie assumed the position with his legs in the air. "I should have let you get kicked out of school."

Blair's dick was already hard at the sight of Robbie's naked body, and he donned a condom before inserting himself into Robbie's ass, just as he had done dozens of times before.

"Act like you like it," Blair hissed down at him while he held his ankles.

"I hate it," Robbie groaned. "And I hate you."

"Fine," Blair said dismissively. "See if I care."

He was careful not to show how much those words hurt. Instead, he closed his eyes and

An Admission of Weakness

savored the feeling of being in Robbie's ass once again. God, it felt good.

As for Robbie, he tried to focus on the bright lights and cameras moving around them, anything to take his mind off the man inside him.

After twenty minutes, Ollie stopped them. "Okay, Eddie, take this pill and rest for a few minutes."

Five minutes later, Robbie's manhood was painfully hard, and he was to find that it would stay that way for the next three and a half hours.

"Brenda, you and Ken get in there," Ollie said. "John, I want Eddie to blow you while Ken fucks him. Let's see how much he can take. Brenda, I want him to fuck you for ten minutes. Tina, you Ginny and Scott be ready to jump in. Eddie, I need to see a lot of enthusiasm. Got it?"

"Sure," Robbie said.

Oh god, he panicked, what had he done? He'd only been with a couple of guys his whole life, and now he was in the middle of an orgy, for god's sake! How could he get out of this now? Finally, he decided his only choice was to grit his teeth and act like he liked it.

Ken and John began their scene with Robbie, and then Tiffany lowered herself onto his hard manhood.

An Admission of Weakness

"Eddie, you've never had a pussy as tight as hers," Ollie said. "Let me hear you."

"Oh fuck yeah," Robbie gulped. "You're going to make me shoot my load with that tight pussy." After ten minutes, another woman took her place while Robbie was forced to go down on yet another woman. Eventually, Ollie called in more men and women until Robbie was being gangbanged in every possible way by every man and woman in the room. He was on his feet, lying down, squatting, tied to a St. Andrew's cross, in a sling, on top of people, under them, sitting on them, behind them, and more. He nursed on nipples, pussies, and cocks, rimmed asses, inserted fingers, and even swallowed Blair's piss. He did whatever Ollie and Tiffany directed him to do with as much passion as he could muster.

Blair watched with disbelief and then displeasure while his companions took turns with Robbie, some of them twice. Robbie seemed to be thoroughly enjoying himself no matter who he was with or what he was doing. He went down on Tiffany and the other women and then fucked them like it was the greatest thing in the world.

Blair felt a surge of jealousy course through him, and he recognized the irony of that. After all he had done, he had no right to be jealous, but he couldn't help feeling possessive.

An Admission of Weakness

Fine, he admitted reluctantly, whether he was gay or straight, he did indeed love Robbie, although he had no right to. And obviously Robbie hated his guts.
So why was Robbie here? Was he serious about becoming a porn star? The very idea was comical; sweet, innocent Robbie involved in the sordid pornography business? And yet, there he was doing things he never would have believed Robbie could do, including swallowing his urine with a lot of gusto.

At midnight, five hours later, Robbie's ass, mouth, nipples, and dick were tender, and he longed to take a dozen hot showers to try to wash the shame and guilt off of him. He had been with every man and woman in the room doing things he never even imagined before. Gingerly, he donned his underwear and then the rest of his clothes.
"You did great, kid," Ollie put an arm around Robbie's shoulders. "You look good on film too. I see you potentially becoming a real star. I'm willing to offer you a contract if you're serious."
"I'm serious," Robbie assured him.
"There's just one thing. You got to be willing to move around," Ollie said. "We go where the talent is, and we're moving to Chicago next. You okay with that?"

An Admission of Weakness

"I don't know," Robbie frowned. "I'd have to quit school."
"But think of the money," Ollie said. "Depending on how many videos you do, a young buck like you could make five thousand dollars a day or more. All the sex you want while you get paid for it. The only thing you have to do is work out a few times a day to stay in shape. The rest of the time you're fucking and figuring out ways to spend all that money."
"It sounds tempting," Robbie said. "What kind of contract would I have to sign?"
"I just happen to have one right here," Ollie grinned. "You don't need to read it; it just says you have to be eighteen. I would never steer you wrong, I promise."
"I'd still like to look through it before I sign," Robbie said. "Is this the same contract you gave Blair?"
"It's the standard agreement," Ollie nodded.
"Will I have to work with him?" Robbie asked.
"Sure," Ollie said. "You'll work with whoever we tell you to."
"I don't think I could stay hard all day," Robbie frowned.
"You had no problem tonight after you took one of Tiffany's special pills. They'll make you hard no matter what," Ollie chuckled. "The FDA doesn't need to know our business, now do they?"
"No, I guess not."

An Admission of Weakness

Robbie looked meaningfully over at Blair, who was watching him suspiciously.
"What'd you say, Butterfield?" he said loudly. "You need to talk to Ollie?"
"Yeah, I do as a matter of fact," Blair said with annoyance. "Why does he get a contract already? Does he get the same money as me? Do I get top billing?"
"Go ahead and sign," Ollie said to Robbie. "I'll be right back."
Ollie and Blair walked off together while Robbie discreetly snapped a picture of the contract on his phone and then hid it in his pocket.
His eyes widened as he read. There were some seriously disturbing things in it. Basically, whoever signed this contract became a virtual slave to Ollie and Tiffany and could be forced to do some extremely nasty, illegal things.
He was no legal expert, but even he could see how ridiculous the terms were. No one in his right mind would sign it unless they had no standards whatsoever.
"Did you sign it?" Ollie returned and sat down.
"I'm good with everything except I think I should get top billing over Blair," Robbie said.
"That's no problem," Ollie said smoothly. "Whatever you want, Eddie baby."
"Okay then," Robbie grinned and took a deep breath. "I guess I'm in."

An Admission of Weakness

He picked up the pen and signed the contract. After Chad and Fred witnessed it, Ollie folded it and put it in his suitcase.
"Do I get a copy?" Robbie asked.
"You don't need one," Ollie put an arm around his shoulder again. "Old Uncle Ollie will always take care of you, I promise."

Robbie showed the contract to a friend of his named Benny who was studying to become a lawyer.
"There's no way this contract is legal," Benny said. "The only way someone would sign this is if this Ollie person failed to disclose the material facts or if he used undue influence on your friend. Also, there are at least five points in this contract that are unconscionable. That alone makes it null and void. Some of these items are definitely illegal. Who exactly are these people?"
Robbie told him what little he knew about Ollie and Tiffany.
"So she works for this publishing company?" Benny asked.
"As far as I know," Robbie nodded.
"Let me do some checking."
After a few days of research, Benny found some disturbing things on the Internet about Ollie and Tiffany, and he showed his findings and the contract to a local detective with whom he was acquainted. She did more research, and

An Admission of Weakness

it turned out the pair had been involved in a number of illegal enterprises from New York to Illinois.

"Their real names are Brenda and Oliver Branch. There are a dozen outstanding warrants for both of them," she said grimly to Robbie. "I've alerted the police."

"So what does that mean?" Robbie asked.

"It means you can tell your friend it's over; he has nothing to fear from this couple ever again."

"Brenda and Oliver Branch?"

"Mr. and Mrs.," she said. "They're scam artists, thieves, forgers, and the list goes on. The police have been looking for them for five years."

Robbie thanked the detective and Benny for their help. He was greatly relieved that Blair's scholarship and status as a student and football player was safe. Even if they weren't meant to be a couple, he still wanted only the best for his former lover.

He knocked on Blair's door.

"Who is it?" Blair snapped from his dorm room.

"It's Robbie."

"What do you want?"

"Will you open the door?"

A moment later, the door was thrust open, and Blair's scowling face stared out at him. He was wearing shorts and a tee shirt.

An Admission of Weakness

"What?" Blair said impatiently. "I'm busy."
"You know what?" Robbie said. "Never mind. Have fun making your next video."
"Blair, who is it?" a feminine voice asked from behind him.
"It's nobody," Robbie replied for Blair. He shook his head in disgust. "You are unbelievable. You can't get enough sex in your videos, so you're bringing women back to your room? What will Tiff have to say about you screwing someone on the side?"
"Will you shut up?" Blair hissed angrily.
"You shut up," Robbie said. "Fuck you."
With that, he returned to his room.

A few hours later, Blair knocked on Robbie's door.
"Go away," Robbie said without opening the door.
"I want to talk to you."
"I don't have anything to say to you," Robbie said coldly.
"I talked to Andres," Blair said. "He told me that Tiffany and Ollie are in jail."
"Oh, too bad," Robbie said sarcastically. "Now you won't be able to fuck her every chance you get. And by the way, she's a married woman. Did Andres tell you that?"
"He told me everything. Will you open this goddamm door?"
"No."

An Admission of Weakness

"Look, the woman in my room is my sister Camilla."

There was no response because Robbie had put on his noise-canceling headphones and turned on his favorite soothing music.

"Robbie?"

Still no answer.

"Robbie!" Blair shouted and pounded on the door. "Robbie!"

After ten minutes, Blair finally gave up and returned to his room.

"And you say these people are in jail?" Coach Wilkensen said.

"Yes, sir," Blair said uneasily.

"What happened to the videos?"

"The detective said the cops confiscated everything," Andres said. "But it looks like most of them made it onto several porn websites."

"So this thing isn't over with?" the coach said.

"It is for me, sir," Blair said. "I'm out of it for good."

"How the hell did you allow yourself to get involved in this?" the coach asked angrily. "You know I could have you kicked out of school for this behavior."

"I know."

"Then why did you come to me with this?"

"I, uh, wanted you to understand that I know I made a serious mistake. I take full

An Admission of Weakness

responsibility, and I understand if you feel it necessary to remove me from the team," Blair gulped. "But I hope you won't, because my team and my education mean everything to me. I promise that nothing like this will ever happen again."

"Why didn't you tell me you were gay?" Coach Wilkensen asked.

"I didn't think it was important," Blair said. "I would never do anything inappropriate."

"You don't think making two dozen pornographic videos is inappropriate?" the coach said incredulously.

"Yes, of course I do," Blair said hastily. "I wish with all my heart that I could undo all of that. But all I can do is ask you to let me stay on the team."

"How can I believe you? The only reason you gave it up was because the people you were working with ended up in jail," the coach said. "If they hadn't, you'd still be doing it."

"But only because I didn't know how to get out of it," Blair said desperately. "I thought I was posing for pictures. But then they recorded me having sex and threatened to tell the university if I didn't do as they said."

"They were blackmailing him, Coach," Andres interjected. "He came to me to help him because he was desperate to get out of the whole mess, but he didn't know how."

"And it was Robbie Lee who turned them in?"

An Admission of Weakness

"Yes, sir," Andres nodded. "I went to him because he's the smartest person I know, and he managed to get a copy of the contract, and the police got involved from there."

"So this is going to become public knowledge?"

"The police said they'd keep everyone's names out of it," Blair said. "I didn't use my real name in the videos."

"Sir, it wasn't Blair's fault. I know he's pretty stupid sometimes, but he's a good guy. He doesn't deserve to be kicked off the team because of one mistake."

"I'd say making two dozen pornographic videos is equivalent to about a hundred mistakes," Coach Wilkensen said dryly.

He leaned back in his chair and regarded the two students on the other side of the desk while he rolled a pencil between his thumb and first finger. Finally, he sighed and sat up straight.

"Okay, here's what's going to happen. I ought to kick your ass from here to Chicago, but I'm going to refrain. You tell no one about any of this, and if anyone asks, you deny everything. As far as your status here at the university, you're still a student as long as there are no more infractions. Not even one. If I hear of anything at all, you'll be out. Do you understand me?"

"Yes, sir," Blair's throat tightened so that he could hardly swallow.

An Admission of Weakness

"You're going to suit up for every game next semester, but you're going to sit the away games out."
"But, sir –" Andres began.
"No, it's okay," Blair stopped him. "It's less than what I deserve."
"You're damn right it is," the coach snapped. "The only thing that's saving you is Andres standing up for you and Robbie Lee putting a stop to it."
He stood up and ran his hand through his hair. "Now get the hell out of my office," he said grimly. "And never speak of this again."

An Admission of Weakness

CHAPTER SIXTEEN

"Robbie won't speak to me," Blair dropped down heavily on his bed.
"I don't blame him," Andres sat down beside him. "I wouldn't either if I was him."
"I want to tell him I'm sorry."
"You're going to have to do more than that," Andres said. "Do you have any comprehension of what he did for you?"
"I know," Blair shrugged.
"He humiliated himself and risked his own college career for you, just so he could get a copy of the contract. He allowed himself to be gangbanged, and he even drank your piss, for Christ's sake. That's something he's going to have to live with the rest of his life."
"What about me and all the degrading things I had to do?"
"That was your own fault," Andres said. "You did it because you were too stupid to find a way out. He did it, not because he had to, but because he loves you. He sacrificed his dignity and his ass just so he could save you."
"He doesn't love me anymore," Blair said sadly.
"Do you love him?" Andres asked bluntly. "And be honest."
"It's not that simple," Blair began.

An Admission of Weakness

"For fuck's sake, do you love him or not?" Andres said impatiently. "But only say it if it's true. And look me in the eye when you say it."
Blair stared into his eyes uncomfortably.
"Okay," he said hesitantly. "I-I love him. He's the best thing that ever happened to me. I'd do anything to undo all the damage I've done."
"No, that's too easy," Andres shook his head. "If you want to undo the damage, stop making excuses and do it. Find a way to make amends. And then maybe you can win him back."

How could he possibly make amends after all he had done, Blair wondered? He had hurt Robbie too badly to just say he was sorry; he needed to do something more. He would have to think on it for a while.

Two days later, he slipped a piece of paper under Robbie's door and then returned to his room.

Robbie knocked on Blair's door that evening.
"Hey," Blair said warily.
"What is this?" Robbie held up the piece of paper that Blair had placed under his door.
"It's a deposit slip," Blair said.
"I know it's a deposit slip," Robbie said dryly. "Why show it to me?"
"It's the money I made from the photo shoot and the videos."

An Admission of Weakness

"Twenty-eight thousand, five hundred dollars?" Robbie said incredulously.
"I guess Ollie was expecting great things from those videos," Blair shrugged. He grinned tentatively. "Maybe if you'd waited a while before turning them in, you'd have had a big paycheck too."
"I didn't do any of that for the money," Robbie said indignantly.
"I know," Blair said hastily. "And I appreciate what you did for me. I know it wasn't easy for you."
"It looked easy enough for you," Robbie said.
"Well, I am a whore after all, at least according to you," Blair said.
"If the shoe fits," Robbie murmured.
"That's just great," Blair took a step back and started to close the door. "I'll see ya around."
"Wait," Robbie stopped the door with a hand. "What's this deposit slip all about?"
"Look at the name on the account."
Robbie took a closer look at the top of the slip. "This says Rhett Lee," he said, confused. "I don't understand."
"I thought the money should go to someone who actually deserved it," Blair shrugged. "I certainly don't after how I've behaved the last few months."
"You're giving this money to Rhett?"

An Admission of Weakness

"It might help with his schooling or something," Blair said. "I can't think of anyone more deserving than him."
"Hey, Blair," Camilla called out. "Let's get a pizza and stay in tonight."
"Of course you have a woman in your room," Robbie shook his head disgustedly.
He turned away, but Blair grasped his arm and forcefully pulled him into the room.
"Stop it," Robbie scowled and tried to free himself.
"Not until you meet Camilla," Blair said firmly.
"I don't want to meet another one of your girlfriends," Robbie said.
"Camilla, this is Robbie, the one I was telling you about," Blair said.
"Oh, Robbie," she rushed forward and hugged him enthusiastically. "I'm so glad to meet you!"
Robbie was too startled to do anything but hug her back.
"Robbie," Blair said dryly. "This is Camilla, my sister. I didn't get a chance to introduce you the other day after you jumped to conclusions."
"You're Camilla?" Robbie said. "Blair's told me all about you."
"He told me all about you too," she said. "Including what you did for him. You must really love him to go through all that."
"So you know about…?"

An Admission of Weakness

"He told me everything," she said. "That's why I'm here. He was beside himself over the whole mess, so I came down to see if I could help. Fortunately, you were already here to take care of things."

"I didn't do anything really," Robbie said.

"Yes, he did," Blair said. "I would have lost everything if it wasn't for him."

He and Robbie glanced awkwardly at one another, and Robbie backed toward the door.

"Well, you guys have a good time," he said awkwardly. "I'll see you later. Camilla, it was an honor meeting you."

"Stay for pizza," she said.

"I've got work to do," Robbie gestured over his shoulder. "Maybe some other time."

"You're welcome to stay," Blair said.

"No thanks," Robbie backed into the hall, bumping into the door jamb on the way. "I'll, uh, see you later. Maybe. Or maybe not. Whatever."

He turned and fled to his own room.

Naomi worked into the evening to finish up the hem of a particularly intricate wedding gown.

"Are you sure Carter won't mind you working so late?" June asked.

"Mama is making dinner for him and Justin, and Camilla is visiting Blair in Urbana," Naomi said. She added with some bitterness in her

An Admission of Weakness

voice, "Carter won't notice I'm not there anyway."

"I see. Do you want to talk about it?"

"There's nothing to talk about," Naomi shrugged.

"How's Justin doing in school?" June changed the subject. "He's a senior this year, isn't he?"

"He's doing well," Naomi said. "Mostly A's and B's, a few C's. He's quite good at football like Blair. I was hoping he'd qualify for an athletic scholarship. That was a godsend for Blair."

"He still wants to be a doctor?"

"He never wanted to be a doctor," Naomi said dryly. "Why can't I get this damn hem straight?"

June took her hands in hers.

"Let's take a break," she said gently. "My back is killing me."

She led Naomi to the break room, where the coffee and snacks were safely away from the clothes they were making. She poured them both a cup of coffee and sat down with her friend.

"Where's Billy tonight?" Naomi took a sip of the bracing liquid.

"He and Riley are spending a few days with his family in Chicago," June smiled fondly at the thought of her son and son-in-law. "Such lovely people."

An Admission of Weakness

"He and Riley are fortunate they found one another and that no one stood in their way." June felt there was more to come.

"Katie fell in love with Dillon Talbot in high school, you know," Naomi went on, half to herself.

"Clint and Marci have turned the Saddler into a major enterprise," June said. "And they have those magnificent horses. I don't know how they do it all."

"What about you?" Naomi said. "You have the dealership, Lawrence teaches karate, and you own all those properties. You're still sewing for Worthen's and now this. Aren't you overwhelmed?"

"Sometimes," June admitted. "Having you here takes a lot of pressure off."

"I'm glad."

"I didn't know Katie and Dillon were an item," June brought the conversation back around.

"Katie's loved him for years," Naomi nodded. "But she's in California, and he's here with the horses."

"I don't suppose he could give up the ranch," June said thoughtfully. "Why doesn't Katie move home? What better place to raise a family?"

"Carter won't hear of it," Naomi said.

"But if Katie and Dillon are in love, how does that concern Carter?"

An Admission of Weakness

"Everything concerns Carter," Naomi said. "The children don't make a move without his approval."

"I see."

"I shouldn't have said that," Naomi raised a hand to her mouth. "Obviously he loves his children very much."

"Of course he does," June agreed. "He wants what's best for them."

"It's just that sometimes he doesn't listen to what they want. Like Justin, for example. He doesn't want to be a doctor, and personally, I don't think he'd make a very good one."

"He can't tell Carter how he feels?"

"He's tried," Naomi said. "Carter doesn't understand."

"The same with Katie and Dillon, I take it."

"And Dillon is such a fine young man," Naomi said. "Katie would be lucky to marry him."

"I think she needs to tell her father how she feels and make him hear her."

"It wouldn't matter," Naomi sighed. "It's too ingrained now in the children to do as he says. Mama's the only one who isn't intimidated by him."

"Surely he doesn't want to intimidate his family," June said.

Naomi stood up abruptly.

"Let's get back to work, shall we?"

An Admission of Weakness

Carter was in bed when Naomi stepped into the bedroom.

"That was a good dinner tonight," he said as she passed through the bedroom to the bathroom. "You should make that dish more often."

"I'm glad you liked it," Naomi said sarcastically.

She donned her nightgown and sat down on the vanity bench to lotion her elbows, knees, and heels.

"Did you say you're playing some sort of card game tomorrow?" he said vaguely.

"That was Mama," Naomi frowned. "Did you even miss me at supper?"

"Miss you?" he turned to look at her. "Why would I have missed you?"

"I wasn't there, Carter," she said exasperatedly.

"Of course you were," he said. "We talked about playing tennis with the Coopers this weekend."

"And did I agree to it?"

"Of course you did. Mary Jo Cooper is one of your best friends."

"You are unbelievable," she put on her slippers and dressing gown.

"Why, thank you," Carter lay down and pulled the blankets up. He noticed her standing. "What are you doing?"

"I'm going to do a little sewing," she said stiffly.

An Admission of Weakness

"It's nearly eleven thirty," he frowned.
"I don't care!" she snapped. "I'm not tired."
With that, she left the room and closed the door sharply behind her. Carter shrugged and turned out the light.

"What are you doing up, Mama?" Justin closed the back door.
"Are you just getting home?"
"It's before midnight," he grinned and extracted a Coke from the refrigerator. "Where were you at supper?"
"At least you noticed I wasn't there," she muttered.
"Of course I noticed," he frowned and sat down at the kitchen table with her. "Don't tell me Dad didn't."
"Don't be silly," she patted his hand and attempted to smile.
"Has he always been like this?" Justin asked.
"What do you mean?"
"He's so wrapped up in his book, it's like nothing else exists," he said.
"He takes his family's history very seriously," she said.
"Doesn't that hurt your feelings?" he frowned.
"I'm fine, dear," she said. "Did you have fun with your friends tonight?"
"We played some basketball and then stopped in at Molly's."
Molly's was the popular downtown diner.

An Admission of Weakness

"Shirley always gives us extra fries," he grinned fondly at the image of the diner's owner giving them plates piled high with French fries.
"She's a lovely person," Naomi smiled.
"I think I'll hit the hay," he yawned and stood up. He leaned over and kissed her gently on the cheek. "Dad loves you, you know."
"And I love him," she nodded briefly. "Sleep well."

Blair packed his things in preparation of returning to Green Grove for the summer. It had been a week since he saw Robbie last, although he knocked on his door every morning and night.
Now that the whole mess with Tiffany and Ollie was straightened out, he was free to focus on his final exams. Truth be told, he had blown off his studies for much of the semester so he could soak up the admiration and hero-worship from those around him when he told them he was going to be a model.
God, what an idiot he had been! Andres and Robbie were right about everything. He was stupid, selfish, narcissistic, and vain, all the things they had accused him of. It would have served him right if he had ruined his whole life. And yet even after the horrible way he had treated Robbie, the man came through for him. He debased himself just to save the jerk who

An Admission of Weakness

had dumped him. To think what his selfishness had cost Robbie; it was unforgivable. So he didn't expect Robbie to come around.
After his last exam, Blair returned to his room. It was getting late, but he planned to drive the three hours home anyway. There was a note taped to his door. He removed it and entered the room to do one last walk-through before heading out. He paused to read it.

I never said thank you for the money you gave Rhett. It wasn't necessary, but I appreciate it, and I know he does too.
– Robbie

As he stood there with the door open, he saw Robbie unlock his door and steal quickly inside. He knocked on the door, but there was no response.
"Robbie, I saw you go in there," he said dryly.
Robbie opened the door enough to stick his head through.
"Oh, it's you," he said. He noticed the baggage behind him. "On your way out? Well, have a good summer."
He attempted to close the door only to have Blair block the opening with one of his size thirteens. Reluctantly, Robbie opened the door wider. He saw the paper in Blair's hand.
"Oh good, you got my note," he said. "I guess that says it all. Sooo...I've got some studying

to do. Be careful driving home. Oh, and it was nice meeting your sister."
"Will you look at me?" Blair said.
"I'd rather not," Robbie stared at the carpet.
"Why not?"
"You know why not," Robbie frowned. "You clearly don't feel the same, but it hurts me to even look at you, let alone to have you –"
He broke off suddenly and gulped.
"To have me what?"
"Look, if you're going to leave, just go, and stop torturing me," Robbie said. "I can't take much more."
"Robbie, I'm sorry I hurt you," Blair said.
"You were just being you, so I don't blame you anymore," Robbie said. "I knew who you were going in, and I should have known better than to get involved. So it's my own fault."
"Well, I forgive you," Blair attempted some levity. "Now let's move on."
"This is funny to you?" Robbie said with disbelief. "The daily agony I've gone through trying to get over you is humorous? I've done everything possible to avoid you, and I even bought special headphones so I didn't have to listen to you and all those people having sex. I've changed my schedule and stayed at the library as much as possible so I didn't have to be in my room any more than necessary.
"And you've spent the last three months laughing at my pain and walking around like a

An Admission of Weakness

peacock because everyone thinks you're the greatest thing on the planet, and they all want to sleep with you. And from what I heard coming from your room, most of them got their wish. You passed me in the hall and ignored me like I wasn't even there.

"My biggest mistake was thinking you loved me, but you never did. You were too narcissistic to love anyone other than yourself.

"But then Andres told me you were in trouble, and all I could think of is what I could do to help. Like a fool, I put my heart out there again and humiliated myself for you. I even went back and made more videos while the detective built her case."

"Are you done?"

"Am I done with you? Yes. Goodbye, Blair," Robbie said flatly and tried to shut his door once again.

Blair forced his way into the room and sat down on the bed. He glanced around and remembered painfully all the wonderful times they had shared here.

"You got to talk, and now it's my turn," he said. "So sit down and listen."

Robbie leaned his butt against the desk and crossed his arms while he stared at the floor.

"I will agree with you on everything you said except for one point," Blair said. "It's true I was a selfish, narcissistic prick. I was vain, and all the attention went straight to my head. I

An Admission of Weakness

treated a lot of people very badly, none more so than you.

"The worst of it all was that I knew what I was doing, but I couldn't seem to stop myself. No, that's not completely true. I didn't want to stop because I liked it. For the first time, I was really somebody.

"I've always had attention because of my looks and because I play football, but this was different. This was the big-time. A publishing company from New York City thought I had what it took to be in a book. And then Tiff – I mean Brenda – told me I would be a huge success as a model. I had all these ideas of grandeur floating through my head. I was going to be rich and famous and live in a mansion and drive a Mercedes. She knew just what to say to manipulate me, and I was stupid enough to believe everything she said. We were going to get married, so I assumed she meant all the nice things she was saying."

"Holy shit. You were going to marry her?" Robbie scowled.

"The point is, everything she said was a lie," Blair said.

"No, the point is that you were going to marry her," Robbie said heatedly. "Were you in love with her?"

"I thought I was, but I was wrong. And I didn't sleep with her nearly as much as you think."

An Admission of Weakness

"Please. I heard it for myself," Robbie said. "The fact that you thought you were in love with her, had sex with her, and were going to marry her just finished this whole thing for me."

"No, don't you see?" Blair said desperately. "Because of her, I realized that the only person I've ever loved was you."

"I think it means that you're too immature to know what love is," Robbie said. "If I hadn't stopped it, you'd be married to the skank by now."

"She was already married," Blair reminded him.

"But if she wasn't, you'd have married her or some other woman," Robbie said.

"Listen," Blair said impatiently. "You said I loved myself too much, and that's another point where you were wrong. I didn't love myself enough."

"Please, no one loves themselves more than you," Robbie snorted.

"You see, you don't know me as well as you think you do," Blair said.

"If I'm wrong, explain it to me," Robbie said.

"You'd have to know my dad," Blair said. "Nothing I've ever done has been good enough for him. I didn't bring home straight A's, I didn't mow straight lines in the grass. I didn't wash the car good enough, or make my bed right, or I didn't score enough touchdowns. I

An Admission of Weakness

wasn't strong enough or smart enough or talented enough.

"So I'm always trying to live up to this perfect standard that is totally impossible to achieve. And it's the same for Katie and Justin. Camilla somehow escaped it; she's just who she is.

"I've always known I have self-esteem issues, but I managed to fool everyone by acting cool and tough and confident. But I'm not confident, and that really came home to me when all of this porn business began. I had no idea how to get out of the mess I created for myself. If I'd just had a little self-confidence, I might have seen Tiff and Ollie for what they were, like Andres and the other guys did, and not let them suck me in.

"It all felt good, I admit, until it didn't. And then it was too late."

"You were feeling good when you were having sex with her and all the others," Robbie said accusingly. "You're just as confused now as you were when I met you."

"At the end, I couldn't even get it up unless she gave me one of Ollie's special pills. They made me hard enough to fuck anyone. How do you think we got through all those videos?"

"Please, I don't want to think about it," Robbie wrinkled his nose with distaste. "You still had sex with women, which is totally disgusting."

"And how many women did you have sex with in those videos?" Blair said.

An Admission of Weakness

"I was doing what I had to do," Robbie said.
"It sure looked like you loved every second of it," Blair said.
"Well, I didn't."
"Those pills of Ollie's make you horny enough to fuck anything and you don't care what you're doing. Don't you remember how tight Tina's pussy was, or how Ginny never shaved her –?"
"Stop! I don't want to think about it," Robbie shivered with displeasure. "My point is, you were going to actually marry her."
"Only because I thought I'd lost you," Blair tried to explain.
"You have lost me."
Blair chose to ignore that statement.
"And I pictured my dad and how happy he'd be to have a daughter-in-law, even a white one."
"I'll bet he was thrilled when you told him you dumped the white trash Mississippi boy," Robbie said sarcastically. "He's probably thinking of all the beautiful babies you and ol' Tiff were going to have."
"I never told him about her," Blair said evasively. "But are you hearing what I'm telling you?"
"Sure. You're sorry you were a jerk and did bad things and got caught and were nearly kicked out of school. I'm sorry too."
"I'm trying to apologize to you," Blair said.

An Admission of Weakness

"Oh, okay," Robbie said. He stretched out his right hand. "No hard feelings, pal. I'll see you around, bro. Now you'd better get on the road. I'm sure there are lots of girls back home just dying to fuck the great Blair Butterfield."

"Robbie, I love you!" Blair shouted. "I'm trying to tell you that I've never loved anyone else but you. I know I'm a simple-minded fool and an idiot and every other bad word you can think of, and I'm so sorry for what I put you through." His eyes filled with tears. "It kills me to think of what you've had to deal with the last three months. I'd give anything to go back and undo everything I did and take away all your pain. I'm sorry I tried to be straight and agreed to marry that horrible woman. I'm sorry I had sex with all those people. I'm sorry I let my ego get in the way of what we had, because you were the best thing that ever happened to me, and I want you back so much. I can't sleep, I can't eat without you. Nothing's any good without you.

"Ending up a porn star for the rest of my life wouldn't have been half as bad as losing you, because I love you more than anything in the world. You are sweet and kind and beautiful and almost perfect. I realize you could do way better than me, but if you'll take me back, I'll spend the rest of my life making it up to you and showing you how much I love you."

"So are you saying you're gay again?"

An Admission of Weakness

"I am done with women, I swear," Blair said. "I like dick. I like your dick and no one else's."
Robbie listened impassively. Finally, he spoke.
"So you want us to be a couple again?"
"More than anything."
"And you promise not to hurt me like this again?" Robbie said.
"I swear to fucking god I will never do anything to hurt you."
"Are you willing to sign an affidavit to that effect?" Robbie said with a straight face.
"I'll sign anything. Get a lawyer in here and draw up the papers," Blair said.
"Okay then," Robbie said.
"Okay then what?"
"You took the long way around, but you finally said what I needed to hear," Robbie said.
"So you'll take me back?" Blair stood up with hope in his eyes.
"You won't leave me for some sweet talking woman, even though you claim to be gay?" Robbie said.
"I'm done with women forever," Blair said.
"It's just as well, because apparently I'm not very good at it."
"So are you still attracted to women?"
"Not at all," Blair said. "I only acted that way because I thought I had to."
"So you're saying I can trust you?" Robbie said.

An Admission of Weakness

"I can't promise that I won't screw up," Blair said. "Neither of us is perfect. We just have to have faith in each other."

"I'd like to have faith in you," Robbie said. "But it's going to take some time. Everyone is entitled to one big mistake, and this was yours. Because I'm telling you right now, if you do anything like this again, I'll dump your ass quicker than you can say narcissist, and you'll never see me again."

"I promise I'll never make a mistake like this again," Blair said. "I just need you to tell me you still love me."

"Of course I still love you," Robbie said. "That doesn't mean I'll let you use me as a doormat."

Blair threw his arms around Robbie and picked him up off the floor. The room was too small to swing him around, but it didn't matter. Nothing mattered except that this beautiful person with whom he was in love loved him back.

An Admission of Weakness

CHAPTER SEVENTEEN

"Don't you have to get home?" Robbie said when Blair finally set him down.
"I'm not going anywhere tonight," Blair grinned lasciviously.
He leaned in to kiss him, but Robbie pulled back.
"Hang on a minute," he said.
"What?"
"Should we do this?"
"Why not?" Blair frowned.
"You're going to be gone all summer," Robbie said. "I'm not sure I'm ready to open myself to this and then have you disappear again. I didn't have you for the past three months, and I won't have you for the next three. What if you decide not to come back or you meet someone back home?"
"Do you not want to be with me?" Blair said. "Is this because I was with Tiff and those other women? I told you, that was all a big mistake."
"I know, but the thought of you with all those people really hurts. I was right here the whole time, and you chose to be with them. I think I need to work through my feelings about that."
"You haven't forgiven me, have you?" Blair stepped back.
"I just need time to process all of this," Robbie said. "You have to admit there's been a lot of shit to wade through since February."

An Admission of Weakness

"I know, but I don't want to leave things this way," Blair said. "Maybe I could find work here for the summer."
"It's okay," Robbie assured him. "Go work at the country club and then come visit sometime. I'll be right here."
"How'd you know about the country club?"
"Andres told me," Robbie said. "I asked him about you every now and then."
"You did?" Blair grinned.
"Of course I did," Robbie looked pained.
"God, I wish I hadn't stolen all this time from us," Blair took him in his arms again.
"Let's just start fresh," Robbie said. "We both know the truth of what happened, so there's no need to relive it. I want to learn from it and put it behind us once and for all."
"Me too," Blair said.
"Did you learn the lessons you needed to learn?"
"I did, I swear," Blair raised his hand in a boy scout's salute.
Robbie grinned and caressed his cheek. His smile faded to become a frown, and his eyes filled with tears.
"Give me time to put the past behind me," his throat tightened. "Go home and enjoy your summer."
"I can't believe I just got you back, and now I have to leave," Blair's eyes grew damp.

An Admission of Weakness

"Will you promise not to forget me over the summer?" Robbie sniffled.
"Are you kidding?" Blair dried his face. "How could I forget the man I love?"
"So you'll come visit me? Or I could come to Green Grove when I have a few days off."
"I'll come here," Blair said. "I don't think Dad's ready to hear that I'm back with my boyfriend."
"You never know. He might like me."
"Let me have the summer to get him used to the idea," Blair said.
"Camilla liked me," Robbie reminded him. "I'll bet the rest of your family will too."
"Are you sure you don't want to spend the night together?" Blair asked.
"Of course I do," Robbie said. "But I think it's too soon."
"Okay, but when I come back. You promise?" Blair said firmly.
Robbie nodded but didn't speak for fear of Blair seeing him cry.
"I, uh, I guess I should go," Blair said emotionally. "It's a three hour drive."
"Drive carefully," Robbie said. "Text me when you get there. And thank you again for what you did for Rhett. That was kind of amazing."
"It was nothing," Blair said.
The two men stared at each other for a long time. Finally, Blair gulped and put a hand up in a silent goodbye. Robbie merely nodded and

An Admission of Weakness

tried to smile, but his eyes showed the pain he was feeling.
Reluctantly, Blair backed away and then turned and left the room. When the door closed, Robbie dropped down onto the bed and cried. His tears were both joyful and sad, for he was happy beyond words to have Blair back, but it barely felt real because he was going to be without him for another three months.

Blair could barely see to drive as he headed west on Interstate 74 toward Bloomington. His tears blurred his vision, but it was impossible to stop them. His reunion with Robbie felt hollow since he had had to leave him immediately. Damn, the hours he had wasted, he thought regretfully. He had given his time and attention to people who only wanted to use and deceive him instead of to the people who loved him. Well, he was going to make it up to Robbie. The money for Rhett was merely a gesture, something to show Robbie that he was serious. He needed Robbie to believe that he truly loved him and to be able to trust him again.

"Where's Mama?" Blair asked when he sat down at the dining room table.
"She's busy," Grandma Ruby said. "I fixed dinner tonight."
"Ooh, spaghetti," Camilla grinned. "I love your spaghetti, Gran."

An Admission of Weakness

"Thank you," Ruby winked at her and set the salad bowl and garlic bread on the table. "Eat up. Justin, make sure you eat some salad."
Carter sat down at the table.
"Blair, it's good to have you home," he said.
"Thanks, Dad," Blair said.
"I take it you did well in your classes," his father said.
"More importantly, did you meet any nice girls?" Ruby asked.
"I, uh, did meet someone," Blair said awkwardly. "But it didn't work out."
"Was she as pretty as Danielle?" Justin grinned.
"On the outside maybe," Blair said. "But she turned out to be a liar and a bitch."
"Language," Carter said reprovingly.
"Yeah, but there were all those other women you told me about," Justin said. "Man, imagine all those tits and pus–"
"Justin!" Ruby said sharply.
"Blair made a really good friend instead," Camilla said.
"Andres?" Carter said. "Yes, we met him. He's gone to dinner with us on several occasions. Nice young man, studying to be a CPA."
"I was talking about another friend," Camilla said. "He lives across the hall."
"Not that southern boy you've talked about?" Carter frowned.
"The faggot?" Justin said disapprovingly.

An Admission of Weakness

"I thought he seemed very nice," Camilla said.
"That's not the sort of person you should be spending time with," Carter said. "White southerners are racists, and gay people are choosing to live in sin, that's all I'm saying."
"You can't stereotype people like that," Ruby frowned. "Not all southerners are racist. And the gay people I know are delightful."
"Southerners enslaved our ancestors for four hundred years," Carter asked pointedly.
"He's not racist in the least," Camilla said. "He's very sweet."
"Can we stop talking about him?" Blair said with annoyance. "What's Mama doing?"
Carter glanced around the table and noticed for the first time that his wife was absent.
"Where's your mother?" he asked Camilla.
"I don't know," she replied.
"Her sewing lesson ran long," Ruby said. She redirected the conversation. "Justin, graduation is next week. Are you excited?"
"I don't care about the ceremony," he shrugged. "I'm just glad to be done with school."
"You have college to look forward to, and then medical school," Carter said. "You're a long way from being done with school."
"Not everyone needs to go to college, you know," Ruby said.
"Maybe I could be something other than a doctor," Justin said hesitantly.

"Don't be ridiculous," Carter chuckled. "What else would you be?"

"I thought about starting up a gym," Justin watched his father warily. "The one here in town caters to young people with their machines and music. Older people feel uncomfortable going there. I thought I'd create one geared to people forty and older."

"That's a great idea," Ruby said. "People in town would be thrilled."

"There's an empty building next to Myra's Resale Shop," Justin said. "It's just right for a gym. It has all those windows across the front, and Neumann-Baum Park is across the street."

"Wow, Jus," Camilla smiled. "You've given this some thought."

"I love the idea," Blair said. "You should go for it, little brother."

"That's enough," Carter said sternly. "Justin is going to become a doctor. It's what we've talked about for years, and that's what he's doing. End of discussion."

"But, Dad –" Justin began.

"Blair, what were your grades this semester?" Carter ignored him. "All A's?"

"Not exactly," Blair said uncomfortably. "I got two B's and two C's."

"Those aren't the kind of grades that will get you a good job after graduation," Carter said severely. "You let this girl, whoever she was, distract you, didn't you? Damnation! What

An Admission of Weakness

have I told you about getting involved with anyone while you're in college?"
"That I shouldn't do it," Blair said. "I know, but I –"
"I'm very disappointed to hear this," Carter said.
"Of course you are," Blair murmured.
"What was that?" Carter looked up sharply.
"I was just saying the spaghetti is really good," Camilla piped up. "Great job, Gran."
There was a moment of silence while everyone focused on their food.
"You and Naomi got together in college," Ruby reminded her son-in-law.
"What's your point?" Carter asked testily.
"My point is that if Blair wants to get involved with some young woman at college, he should do it. She may be his perfect match."
"It was different back in my day," Carter said stubbornly.
"How?" Ruby said.
"Why don't you go in the kitchen where you be–?" he stopped himself in the nick of time.
"Why don't I do what?" she glared at him.
"Where is Naomi, dammit?" he scowled.
"That's what I thought," Ruby grinned with satisfaction.

"You've missed dinner three times this week," Carter scolded his wife.

An Admission of Weakness

"I'm sorry, dear," Naomi laid her dressing gown across the foot of the bed. "I guess I lost track of time."

"I don't like this," Carter said. "Your place is here making meals for your family."

"Mama made your dinner," Naomi said. "No one went without."

"Do you even care that Blair's home?"

"Of course I do," she said. "I just got caught up in my sewing, that's all."

"But it keeps happening, and I don't like it," Carter said.

"I said I'm sorry," she said patiently.

"And that excuses you ignoring your family?"

"I didn't ignore my family, Carter!" she began to lose her temper. "I like sewing, and there's nothing wrong with that. The family is fine, the house is fine, and you got your dinner. It's not like anyone notices whether I'm here or not anyway. I might as well be where someone appreciates me and cares about what I think!"

"Naomi!" Carter's eyes were wide. She had never spoken to him in such a manner in nearly thirty years of marriage. "You raised your voice to me."

"Because you never hear me any other way," she said. "This is the first time you've actually looked me in the eye in years."

"Don't be ridiculous."

"I'm not being ridiculous," she snapped. "It's the truth. The only way you notice me is if I'm not there to pour your coffee or put dinner on the table."

"That's simply not true," he said. "You're my wife. Of course I notice you."

"What did I say to you this morning at breakfast?" she asked.

"I don't remember word for word," he said.

"What was the gist of it?"

"It had something to do with the children," he said.

"No," she said. "I told you the Cadillac has a low tire."

"That's right," he nodded. "And I told you to have Justin put air in it for you."

"When did you kiss me last?" she went on.

"I kiss you every morning before I leave for work."

"And when else?"

"I can't be expected to remember every little thing, and I think I've had enough of this conversation."

He disappeared into the bathroom. When he came out, the bedroom was dark, and Naomi was lying on her side facing away from him.

"Is that building next to Myra's available to rent?" Ruby stopped by her grandson's bedroom.

Justin was lying on his stomach scrolling through his phone.

"Mr. Price wants to sell it," he looked up.

An Admission of Weakness

Randall Price was a multi-millionaire who owned much of the downtown. He had bought up buildings when their owners wanted to sell to make sure the downtown remained busy and cared for.
"You've talked to him already?"
"He came into Molly's one day when me and my friends were there," he said.
"Did you tell him what you wanted it for?" Ruby asked.
"No," he shrugged.
"Did he say how much he's asking for it?"
"No."
"Are you serious about this gym of yours?"
"I would be, but Dad will never let me do it."
"Forget your father for a moment," she said. "Are you serious about it?"
He pulled a loose-leaf binder from underneath the bed and handed it to her.
"What's this?"
"It's all my ideas and designs for the gym," he said. "Just in case I ever got the chance to make it real."
She leafed through the thick book with a sense of wonder.
"Justin, this is terrific," she smiled. "I had no idea."
"I never told anyone except Camilla," he said.
"I see. What do you know about running a business?"

An Admission of Weakness

"I took four years of business classes at school," he said. "I've worked at the local gym for the past two years. I'm not saying I know everything there is, but I have a reasonable grasp on the concept of making money.
"The only problem is, I don't have the startup cash unless Dad would let me have some of my college money."
"I know," she squeezed his arm. "But why don't we talk to Mr. Price anyway? He's a smart businessman. He might have some ideas."
"I guess it can't hurt just to talk," he shrugged.

The meeting with Randall Price took place a few days later at the building on North Market Street. He was a nice looking blonde haired man in his early fifties. After spending years in New York City making his fortune, he had returned to his hometown to marry his childhood sweetheart.
"Ruby, it's nice to meet you," Randall smiled and extended his hand. "I work with your son-in-law on the Gallery and hospital boards."
"Mr. Price," she shook his hand. "I think you know Justin."
"I met him a few weeks ago," Randall shook Justin's hand. "And please call me Randall."
"Justin has an idea he'd like to run by you regarding your building," Ruby said.

An Admission of Weakness

"I'm all ears," Randall pointed to three folding chairs in the otherwise empty building. "Why don't we sit down?"

Justin cleared his throat nervously and, with his grandmother's encouragement, showed Randall his binder and his ideas for the space. Both adults smiled at the young man's enthusiasm. They were impressed with his knowledge of the topic. Randall asked several questions and listened closely to Justin's answers.

"So what exactly are you asking of me?" Randall said.

"I was wondering if you'd consider renting the building," Justin said. "Maybe a rent to own kind of thing. I don't have any credit, but once the business is up and running, I'd have something to show the bank."

"I see," Randall said. "Look, I've got to go to New York to oversee the sale of my penthouse and deal with a few other matters. I may be gone for much of the summer. How soon were you planning to get things going if we're able to come to an agreement regarding your rent to own idea?"

"It's going to take some time to come up with the startup money," Justin said. "I'm supposed to start college in the fall, but I was planning to ask Dad for some of my college money. I'm afraid that's a long shot, though."

"What are you going to study?"

"Pre-med," Justin said.

An Admission of Weakness

"Excellent," Randall smiled. "My nephew is Dr Price."
"He's our doctor," Justin said. "He's nice."
"Have you always wanted to go into medicine?" Randall asked.
"To be honest, I don't want to," Justin said hesitantly. "That's what my dad wants, but I want to stay in Green Grove and open my own gym. It's what I've wanted to do ever since I started working out at the school gym as a kid."
"Your dad doesn't approve?"
"Carter has very strong ideas on every subject, even the ones that don't concern him," Ruby said wryly. "I'm sure you've learned that from your board meetings."
"So you're in no hurry then?"
"No, I guess not," Justin shrugged.
"Good," Randall said. "In that case, I'm going to tell Brad to put a hold on selling just yet." Brad Jameson was the town's leading realtor.
"I like what I'm hearing," he went on. "You have a solid plan here, one that I think could be quite profitable. Would you consider taking me on as a partner?"
"I guess so," Justin said.
"Then let me give this some more thought while you talk to your father, and I'll get back to you before the summer's over."
He said goodbye, and Ruby and Justin grinned and high-fived each other.

An Admission of Weakness

CHAPTER EIGHTEEN

"How's work going?" Blair asked.
"It's fine," Robbie grinned. "I've been training the new guy. He's a freshman."
"Is he a complete loser?" Blair chuckled.
"Actually, he's pretty great," Robbie laughed. "His name is Major, and he's one of your biggest fans. He was totally impressed when I told him Number Seven is my boyfriend."
There was silence on the other end of the call.
"What?" Robbie said.
"I'm still not comfortable with people there knowing I'm gay," Blair said.
"I think that ship has sailed," Robbie said wryly. "Everyone in the athletic department knows about the videos, so I imagine it's common knowledge by now."
"I suppose you're right," Blair relaxed a bit. "How's the country club job?"
"It's pure torture," Blair said. "I'm a lifeguard, so I'm sitting by the pool in my Speedos talking to my boyfriend on the phone."
"Sounds rough," Robbie agreed.
"Once a week I help maintain the greens."
"You maintain salads?"
"The golf greens, you moron," Blair burst out laughing.
"I'm from an underprivileged background, remember?" Robbie laughed. "The only kinds

An Admission of Weakness

of greens I know are the collard or dandelion variety."

"How's Rhett?"

"He's coming up over the fourth of July. You'll be here, right?"

"I'm not sure," Blair hesitated. "All the aunts and uncles and cousins are coming to town. Besides, I may have to work extra."

"That's okay," Robbie said. "He'll be disappointed, though."

"Me too," Blair said.

"You're still coming this weekend, right? I've got two days off."

"Actually, there's a wedding here at the club, and Emma asked if I could help in the kitchen," Blair said uneasily. "I couldn't very well tell her no. She's the one who got me this job."

"I thought we had this planned," Robbie frowned. "It's our first time together since February."

"I'm disappointed too," Blair said. "I just felt kind of obligated."

"I understand that," Robbie said. "My boss is an expert at guilting me into working extra."

"When are your next two days off in a row?" Blair asked.

"Not for another month," Robbie's smile faded. "But you don't have to wait for that. Just come down for the day or something. I miss you."

"I miss you too," Blair said.

An Admission of Weakness

"I'll even come up there," Robbie said. "Andres said I could borrow his car. Or maybe he'd come with. That'd be fun."
"No," Blair said sharply. "I mean, he's been here before, so it would probably be boring for him."
"Then I'll come alone," Robbie said. "I have next Thursday off. What about that?"
"I have to work next Thursday," Blair said. "So that won't work. But don't worry, I'll find a way to come down."
The two talked for a while longer until a youthful swimmer approached Blair with a question.
"I've got to go," Blair said. "Duty calls."
"I love you."
"I love you too," Blair smiled. "Talk to you tomorrow."

"Was that Blair?" Major asked eagerly.
"It was," Robbie grinned wistfully.
"What'd he say about me?" the big dark-skinned man asked.
"Nothing really," Robbie chuckled. "That was the first he'd heard of you."
"You didn't tell him I'm on the team," Major said.
"I didn't have a chance," Robbie said. "Don't worry. The first time he comes for a visit, I promise I'll introduce you. Say, what are you doing this weekend?"

An Admission of Weakness

"Nothing. Why?"
"Let's hang out," Robbie said. "I made reservations at Biaggi's, but he has to work. Let's go eat and then see a movie."
"It's a date," Major grinned and clapped him on the back, sending him sprawling.

"Dad, I need to talk to you about something," Justin said warily.
"Of course," Carter glanced up from his desk and frowned. "Does she need to be here?"
"I know I intimidate you, Carter, but try to keep your panties dry," Ruby said wryly as she sat down on the leather sofa.
"What is it, son?" Carter ignored her, as usual.
"You know how we were talking at dinner the other night?" Justin said uncomfortably.
"About what?"
"About starting a new gym in town," Justin said.
"In the old appliance store next to the Resale Shop," Ruby added.
"Who's doing that again?" Carter looked confused.
"Me, Dad. I would be doing it."
"That will be a little difficult to do while you're away at school," Carter chuckled.
"Well, that's the thing," Justin took a deep breath and looked to Grandma Ruby for support. She nodded at him. "I wouldn't be at college. I'd be here."

An Admission of Weakness

He cringed in anticipation of the explosion he knew was coming, and he wasn't disappointed.
"What the devil is going on here?" Carter demanded. "Is she trying to talk you into something?"
"You're the one doing that," Ruby said. "Why don't you listen to your son instead of always talking at him?"
"You are going to medical school!" Carter exclaimed angrily. "I will not listen to any more of this gym nonsense."
"It's not nonsense, Dad," Justin cried. "I have a solid business plan. Randall Price said so, and he's a millionaire, so he knows what he's talking about."
"He did say he liked the idea, Carter," Ruby said.
"What does Randall Price have to do with this?"
"He owns the building."
"What building?"
"The one next to the Resale Shop," Justin said.
"Take your head out of your ass and listen for once!" Ruby snapped. "This is something Justin wants to do. He has no interest in being a doctor. We spoke to Randall about renting or buying the building so that Justin can start his gym. What we want to know is if you'll give some – not all – of Justin's college money to him for startup cash."

An Admission of Weakness

"Are you out of your minds?! There is no way I'm going to let Justin throw his future away on a foolish idea. And shame on you for encouraging him. I've worked my whole adult life to make sure my children are successful, prosperous, and productive citizens, and they by-god will be!

"Go to your room," he said coldly to Justin. "And don't listen to your demented grandmother ever again."

Ruby nodded at Justin, who bolted from the room.

"How could you?" Carter seethed. "You want him to throw his future away like this, and for what?"

"I want him to be happy and healthy," she said. "That's all I want for any of my grandchildren." She stepped into his personal space and glared at him.

"And if you ever call me a name in front of another person again, especially one of my grandchildren, I'll reach one hand down your throat and the other up your ass until I can shake hands with myself in the middle!"

Katie didn't hear from Dillon for a few weeks. She longed to call him, but Ruby told her to wait.

"Men are dumb creatures," she said. "It takes them longer to figure things out. Eventually,

An Admission of Weakness

he'll realize that he loves you more than he hates your father, and he'll call."
One evening when Katie was at a restaurant with some of her girlfriends, her cell phone rang.
"It's him!" she squealed excitedly.
"Answer it! Answer it!" the others cried.
"Dillon?" she walked outside so she could hear. "How are you?"
"Miserable," he said.
"Why?"
"Because I'm not with you," he said. "And because I'm in love with the most wonderful woman in the world whose dad is a total dick."
"He absolutely is," she agreed. "Why can't he be like your parents?"
"It would sure make things a lot easier," he sighed. "Anyway, are you doing okay?"
"I'm all right, I guess," she said. "I've made a decision about all of this."
"I hope it's that you want to elope," he said. "Just tell me it's not that you want to break up."
"Of course not," she sounded horrified.
"Actually, it's neither."
"I'm listening."
"My lease is up in six months," she said. "I'm going to move home, if you'll have me."
"Are you fucking kidding me?!" he practically screamed. "Oh baby, I've waited to hear you say that for five years."

An Admission of Weakness

"I'm so relieved," she laughed nervously. "I was afraid you were calling to call things off."
"No way, babe."
"I thought I'd give notice at work in October, which will give them time to find a replacement. I've already spoken to the hospital there and asked them to keep me in mind for any nursing position they have open. I don't even care what it is, as long as it starts after the New Year."
"What about your dad?"
"We'll tell him together at Christmas when I come home. Blair, Camilla, and Grandma are on our side, and Justin will be too. I'm going to talk to Mama tomorrow, so it will be all of us against one."
"I don't want another confrontation," he frowned.
"It's my dad, so we probably don't have a choice in that regard," she said. "We'll do it as gently as possible, but he's going to have to accept you and me one way or another or else I'll be out of his life. He can't bully us any longer."
"Wow, who's this new tough-as-nails woman I'm talking to? Pretty damn sexy."
"I've been talking to the hospital psychologist," Katie chuckled. "Turns out that everything Gran has been saying all along was absolutely right."

An Admission of Weakness

"Is everything okay, dear?" Naomi said worriedly.
"Everything is great, Mama," Katie smiled. "I have some news for you, but you can't tell Dad."
"Did you and Dillon make up?"
"How'd you know?" Katie said with surprise.
"I'm your mother," Naomi smiled. "I knew when you were in college that you and he were still an item. He was so crazy about you."
"Why didn't you ever say anything?"
"I knew how your father felt, and I sensed you wanted to keep things secret," Naomi said. "I figured you'd tell me when you were ready."
"I love you, Mama," Katie said emotionally.
"I love you too," Naomi smiled. "Is that why you called?"
"Actually, there's more," Katie said. "My lease is up in December, and I'm planning to move home for good."
There was a moment of silence.
"Mama?"
"I'm here, dear," Naomi said tearfully. "You have no idea how happy it makes me to hear this."
"It makes me happy too," Katie chuckled through her own tears. "Now we just have to get Dad to accept Blair and his boyfriend, and then everything will be okay."
"Blair and his...what did you say?"

"Oh god," Katie covered her mouth in horror.
"I-I meant to say girlfriend. Girlfriend. I don't know what I was thinking."
"Are you telling me that Blair is gay?" Naomi sounded stunned. "Oh my god."
"No, Mama, it was just a…I meant to say…oh my god, he's going to kill me."
"Oh my god," Naomi repeated.
"Mama, listen to me," Katie said desperately. "He's not gay. He was just joking about it once, and I –"
"Blair is gay," Naomi said with wonder. "That makes so much sense."
"It does?"
"He was such a sweet, sensitive little boy, so different than Justin. Most of his friends were girls early on, and he loved to play with dolls. Then his friends were all the hyper-masculine football players. I saw how he looked at them; it was the same way you and Camilla did. And dating Danielle was the biggest clue."
"How was that a clue?"
"Let's face it. Danielle is not a nice person. The only reason sweet, naïve Blair would date someone like her was so no one would question his sexuality."
"I suppose."
"Oh my god," Naomi said again.
"Mama, there's nothing wrong with being gay," Katie said. "And you can't tell him that you know. He'll kill me."

An Admission of Weakness

"You didn't mean to tell," Naomi said. "And I'm not stupid; I have a college degree too, you know. I know there's nothing wrong with being gay. Still, I can't help but feel responsible."
"Why would you feel responsible?"
"Wait until you're a mother," Naomi said dryly. "Then you'll understand what I'm talking about. I just wish he'd told me."
"He will," Katie said. "He's just worried –"
"About his father," her mother finished. "He's right to be worried. Your father will not take this well."
"We'll have to work on him," Katie said.
"Oh my god," Naomi said suddenly. "You said Blair has a boyfriend?"
"Jeez," Katie groaned. "He's really going to kill me."
"Tell me about this boy," Naomi said. "Is he nice?"
"I haven't met him, but Camilla has," Katie said. "She said he's very sweet and totally adorable. His name is Robbie, he's from Mississippi, and he's a business major and a cheerleader. He lives across the hall from Blair. He and Andres are good friends from what I understand."
"Robbie," Naomi said thoughtfully. "That sounds sweet. What's his last name?"
"Lee."
"Robbie Lee," Naomi said. "Wait. Robert Lee? Please tell me some southern Black family

didn't name their son after a Confederate general?"
"It's Robert Eustace Lee," Katie said tentatively. "And he's not exactly Black."
"How is a person 'not exactly Black'?" Naomi frowned.
"You may want to sit down for this one," Katie said. "He's...white."
"So his parents are either exceptionally stupid or very racist," Naomi said.
"Don't those two things go hand in hand?" Katie said dryly. "From what Blair told me, they're the worst of the worst."
"I don't like the idea of Blair getting involved with people like that," Naomi said worriedly.

"Hello?"
"I miss you," Robbie sighed into his phone.
"I miss you too, baby," Andres grinned.
"Andres?" Robbie sat up. "Did I call you by mistake?"
"No, I answered Blair's phone when I saw it was you."
"Wait," Robbie said. "You're in Green Grove?"
"Yeah, I came up for the week since we're both off," Andres said. "I would have told you, bro, but he said you had to work, so it was best not to mention it." A thought crossed his mind. "Oh, man, I probably shouldn't have answered his phone."

An Admission of Weakness

"He told you not to tell me you were going up there?" Robbie frowned.
"He was afraid you'd feel bad you couldn't come too."
"And he has the whole week off?" Robbie said.
"Yeah," Andres said. "We're just gonna sleep in and lay around the pool at the country club while we drink strawberry margaritas. That's my drink now, remember?" he chuckled.
Robbie had introduced the big, burly man to the sweet beverage, and he became an instant fan.
"Well, at least you'll get a good tan," Robbie teased.
"I'll probably get fat, too, eating his mama's delicious home cooking," Andres chuckled.
"His dad's teaching me how to play golf. Oh, and he got us tickets to see Thad Hall's concert here in the park."
Thad Hall was one of the country's most popular singers and just happened to grow up in Green Grove.
"Are you sure you're not dating Blair?"
"His dick's too big for me," Andres joked. "I prefer the type that doesn't have a dick at all."
"That makes one of us," Robbie chuckled.
"The women here are all over him because of his tattoos, and some of the guys are too. You know Blair; he's eating it up," Andres said.
"His parents were really upset when they found out about them, though."

An Admission of Weakness

"I'll bet," Robbie said. "Well, tell him I called. I've got to get back to studying."
"I'll tell him," Andres said. "Take care, bro. We'll go for pizza when I get back next week."
"Sounds good," Robbie grinned. "Bye."
There was a knock on his door, and he looked up.
"Ya wanna go do something?" Major said.
"Sure," Robbie slammed his textbook closed. "I'm not in the mood to study anyway."

Robbie saw that Blair had called while he and Major were shooting hoops, but it was late, so he didn't call him back. He worked double shifts the rest of that week, so he was too tired for anything other than crashing in his bed at midnight so he could get up again at six.
By the end of the week, he realized that Blair hadn't called him, but he supposed that was because he and Andres were having too much fun together. After all, the two best friends were on vacation.

An Admission of Weakness

CHAPTER NINETEEN

The Fourth of July arrived and brought with it Rhett to Urbana. The two brothers rejoiced in being together again.
"Holy cow, look at you!" Robbie's eyes widened.
"Pwetty good, huh," Rhett grinned.
Over the last six months, he had done the daily exercises the university therapists recommended. That, along with the new brace, had made a big difference. The youth had gained ten pounds. He was still too thin, but there was a noticeable difference in his body mass. The limp was still there, but it was less apparent now.
"You look fantastic," Robbie said. "I'll bet the girls are all over you at school."
"Nah," Rhett said. "I'm still a geek to them. But that's okay. The wight girl will come along when the time's wight."
"And she's going to be as amazing as you are," Robbie assured him.
"Where's Blair?"
"He's at home in Green Grove for the summer," Robbie said. "He hoped to visit while you were here, but it didn't work out."
"So whose car is this?"
"I borrowed it from Andres," Robbie explained. "Come on, let's go eat. I have lots to tell you."

An Admission of Weakness

That night, as the two brothers settled in for the night, Robbie told him about all that had transpired during the spring semester since Blair was asked to pose for the photo book.
"Holy jeez-o-pete," Rhett's eyes were wide when he finished his tale. "That sounds like a movie or something."
"You're right," Robbie agreed.
"Awe you sure you can twust him after all that?" Rhett asked hesitantly. "I mean, he's gweat and all, but he weally hurt you; I don't want to see him do that again."
"I don't either," Robbie said. "And I don't trust him completely yet. He has to earn that back. But I don't want you to hold this against him. It was between him and me. If things work out between us, great. If they don't, that's okay too."
"But you love him," Rhett said. "It has to work out if you love each other. You'll be sad if it doesn't."
"You can't rely on other people for your happiness. I'll be happy with or without him. But forget Blair. Tell me what's going on at home."

Rhett thoroughly enjoyed the week he spent with Robbie. Andres and Major and other friends of Robbie's kept him entertained. He

An Admission of Weakness

became like a little brother to them, and they watched over him protectively.

The time passed too quickly, as all vacations do, and the night before Rhett had to leave, Robbie told him about the monetary gift from Blair.

"Awe you kidding?" Rhett said with astonishment. "Why would he do that?"

"He said he wanted someone worthy to have the money. You're his favorite person in the world, so he gave it to you."

"But you're his boyfwiend. You saved him; he should give it to you."

"No, it's yours," Robbie said. "What do you want to do with it?"

"What do you think?"

"Save it for college," Robbie said instantly.

"I don't think I'm going to go to college," Rhett said. "Maybe I'll get a car."

"Why aren't you going to college?"

"I'm not smawt enough," Rhett shrugged.

"Of course you are," Robbie said.

"I'm not dumb," Rhett agreed. "But I'm not college smawt."

"So what will you do?"

"I want to open up my own westauwant," Rhett said.

"In Toadback?"

"No way," Rhett shuddered. "I thought I'd go wherever you end up."

"Really?" Robbie grinned. "I'd like that."

An Admission of Weakness

"And you can help me wun the money side of the business."
"You bet I will, little brother."

Robbie returned to his room from the train station. He was feeling a little down after saying goodbye to his brother. It was going to be at least six months before he saw him again. He walked dejectedly down the hall and jumped when a voice suddenly spoke to him.
"Hey, handsome," Blair grinned. He was leaning lazily against the wall beside Robbie's door.
"Oh my god," Robbie ran and jumped into Blair's strong arms, wrapping his legs around him as well. "I can't believe you're here."
"I've missed you so much," Blair murmured emotionally into his neck.
He squeezed him, and Robbie squeezed back even tighter.
"I'm sorry it took me so long to get back here," Blair said. "I wanted to, but –"
"It doesn't matter as long as you're here now," Robbie said. "How long can you stay?"
"A couple of days if that's okay," Blair said.
"I have to work," Robbie said. "Why didn't you let me know you were coming?"
"I wanted it to be a surprise," Blair said ruefully. "I guess that wasn't such a good idea."

An Admission of Weakness

"I don't care," Robbie finally put his feet on the ground and pulled Blair into his room. "Come on."

The two men kissed feverishly for a while and then hastily removed their clothes. Fingers and lips roamed over their bodies in a desperate effort to get reacquainted.

"I love all these tattoos," Robbie panted as he knelt and kissed his way down Blair's torso.

"All the women back home did too," Blair grinned. "I'm glad Tiff insisted I get them for my modeling career. She picked them out, but I picked out the gold color for the ones on my side."

"You seriously had to mention that bitch?" Robbie abruptly stopped what he was doing.

"Oh god, I'm sorry," Blair groaned regretfully. "I wasn't thinking."

Robbie stood up and pulled Blair to the bed, where they lay side by side and stared at the ceiling.

"I guess I killed the mood, huh," Blair said.

"Definitely," Robbie said. "Let's just talk. How was your visit with Andres?"

"Look, the reason I didn't tell you he was coming up to Green Grove –"

"I know," Robbie said. "It's okay, although at first I thought you didn't want me to meet the rest of your family."

"That's not it," Blair said. "Camilla and Katie are fine with everything."

An Admission of Weakness

"What about your brother?"
"He can be pretty homophobic."
"Do you still get along with him now that he knows you're gay?"
"It's kinda complicated," Blair said evasively.
"The same with Dad."
"And your mom and grandmother?"
"I think they're okay with it," Blair said uneasily.
"You think?"
"We don't talk about it," Blair said.
Well, that was certainly true since the only people in his family who knew he was gay were Camilla and Katie.
"But they know about me, don't they?"
"Of course," Blair lied. "I just think it would be awkward to have you there. They need a little more time to get used to things."
"My dad will never get used to it; he's too backward. But I'm hoping Ma will eventually accept me for who I am."
"Do you think you could get someone to take your shifts while I'm here?" Blair changed the subject.
"Maybe Major would," Robbie said. "He's dying to meet you."
"I'd rather just hang with you," Blair said. "Why don't we wait until the semester starts in September to meet him?"
Robbie called Major, who was glad to take Robbie's shift for the next day. He was

An Admission of Weakness

disappointed that he wasn't going to meet his idol, but he understood that time was limited.

"Why does this guy idolize me so much?" Blair said.

"Because he's a gay football player like you," Robbie said.

"He's gay?" Blair frowned.

"I told you that," Robbie grinned.

"No, you didn't. Haven't the two of you been spending a lot of time together?"

"We work at the same restaurant," Robbie shrugged. "And I guess we do spend quite a bit of time together outside of work, now that you mention it."

"Why?"

"He's my friend," Robbie said. "He's actually pretty great, and he's so funny. He's seen the videos, and he thinks you're really hot."

Blair leaned up on one elbow and held up the other hand.

"Wait. How did he see the videos? No one knows my porn name."

"I don't know, but they're on a bunch of websites," Robbie said.

"Oh fuck!" Blair cried. "What if my family sees them?"

"The only way they'd find them is if they know your professional name: Dick Strong," Robbie said. "And I'm Bruce Dickinson."

"Holy shit! He's seen the videos you did too?"

An Admission of Weakness

"No, but the point is, no one will ever know," Robbie said. He grinned. "We just won't be able to run for political office."

"That's not funny," Blair scowled.

"Well, what do you want me to say? You're the one who got us involved in that mess. You had to know there would be consequences."

"I don't need to be reminded of what I did," Blair said irritably while he reached for his clothes.

"I'm sorry. I didn't think you'd have a problem with people seeing them," Robbie said. "Why are you getting dressed?"

"I don't know," Blair said agitatedly. "I just feel like I need to get out of here. It's like everyone knows what I did. I'm the laughing stock of the entire school."

"No, you're not," Robbie said soothingly. "If anything, people are envious of your body and your dick." He grinned and added, "You'd probably be a big star by now if you had stuck with it."

"What the hell kind of thing is that to say?" Blair scowled. "You wanted me to keep being a porn star?"

"Of course not," Robbie chuckled. "I'd have to change your nickname from D.J. to D.S. for Dick Strong. You probably prefer to go by your professional name."

"You're an asshole, Bruce," Blair finally grinned with him.

An Admission of Weakness

"I think Bruce Dickinson sounds kind of dignified," Robbie teased. "Like an author from the 1800s or something. I'd wear a monocle and smoke a pipe while I fuck people."

"Doesn't it upset you to know people are out there watching you having sex? You were gangbanged for over four hours straight that first day alone, for Christ's sake. You were even forced to swallow my piss. I'm really sorry about that."

"I just wish I'd been paid for it," Robbie grinned. "A hundred bucks for every thrust or every swallow. Too bad the cops caught them before I got a check."

"You're an idiot," Blair removed his clothes and lay back down to cuddle him.

"Actually, that's not true," Robbie chuckled. "I'm on the President's List."

"I love you so much," Blair said. "You always make everything okay. How do you do that?"

"It's my superpower," Robbie said cockily. He kissed Blair. "Like yours is fucking."

"That's not my superpower," Blair said wryly. "I've been told by more than one person that I'm not very good at it."

"Well, I'm telling you that you are my superhero when it comes to sex," Robbie said. Blair leaned over him and kissed him passionately. For the next two hours, they enjoyed each other's bodies in many different ways. Afterwards, they talked and cuddled until

An Admission of Weakness

they fell into a peaceful sleep with Blair's hard dick still in Robbie's ass.

The two spent the better part of the next day making beautiful and passionate love to one another. The rest of the time was spent eating pizza and burgers and talking. All the awkwardness from the night before was gone, and things felt back to normal. When it was time for Blair to leave, the two stood by his car.
"I don't want you to go," Robbie said.
"Me neither," Blair said. "When's your next two days off?"
"The middle of August," Robbie said. "I'll text you the dates."
"I'll try to come back then," Blair promised.
The two stared into each other's eyes without speaking. Finally, Robbie embraced him.
"I love you."
"I love you too," Blair said.
"Hey, brother!" some friends of Blair's from the education department called out as they made their way across the parking lot. "Yo, what's up, man?"
Blair pushed Robbie away and stuck his hands in his pockets.
"Hey, guys," he said gruffly.
The group of mostly Black men and women stopped to visit for a while. They eyed Robbie curiously while they discussed the upcoming

An Admission of Weakness

fall semester, but Blair didn't offer to introduce him.

"Did you sign up for Professor Satterwhite's seminars?" someone asked.

"I didn't think we could do that until September," Blair frowned.

"Dude, you're gonna get stuck with Sundays if you wait until then."

"You'd better go sign up now," someone suggested. "Gene forgot, too, so we're on our way to the department now. Come with."

"Thanks," Blair said. He extended his right hand toward Robbie. "Good to see ya, man. I'll catch ya later."

"Uh, yeah," Robbie frowned and reluctantly shook his hand. "I'll 'catch ya later'."

Blair and his friends walked away without a backward glance. Robbie watched them for a minute and then sighed before walking back to his dorm.

"Blair didn't stay long," Major commented before cramming a slice of pizza into his mouth.

"He only had two days," Robbie said. "He's working lots of hours at his parents' country club for the summer."

"Yeah, he's got it real tough," Andres said dryly. "He sucks up all the attention from the women at the pool, and then sleeps in on his

An Admission of Weakness

days off while his mama cooks his meals and does his laundry."

"Aw, let him enjoy being home as long as he can," Major said. "I wish I had a home to go to for the summer."

"Me too," Robbie said.

"I have one," Andres said. "But it ain't nothing compared to Blair's."

He described the three story English Tudor home while Robbie and Major listened wistfully.

"Granite countertops, crystal chandeliers, a library, a formal living room that's only used for guests. It's like something you'd see on TV."

"Did my name come up while you were there?" Robbie asked curiously.

"No," Andres said. "His dad kept bringing up his ex-girlfriend, though."

An Admission of Weakness

"Danielle," Robbie nodded. "Blair said she's a bitch."
"Why do nice guys always end up with bitchy girlfriends?" Major asked.
"Are you calling Robbie his bitchy girlfriend?" Andres grinned.
"Yeah," Robbie said indignantly. "That's not cool, man."
"I didn't mean –"
"Just because I slap him around..." Robbie said.
"And tell him what to do..." Andres added.
"Doesn't mean I'm a bitch," Robbie scowled.
"I'm sorry," Major said contritely. "I wasn't calling you a bitch, I swear. I think you're really nice."
The other two men stared woodenly at him until Robbie couldn't hide his grin any longer.
"You're both bitches," Major threw a mushroom at Andres and pulled Robbie into a headlock. "You're not nice at all."
The three of them laughed.
"You're so much fun to tease," Robbie pulled away from him and straightened his hair.
"That's because you're a genuinely nice guy."
"You're not, Bruce Dickinson," Andres chuckled. "I saw your videos. Whew, bro, you are a total whore."
"I work to my strengths," Robbie joked.

An Admission of Weakness

"How does one man swallow that much cum?" Andres asked. "And how the fuck did you swallow his piss?"

"You did that?" Major asked, wide-eyed. "I wanna see them."

"No, you don't," Robbie said.

"Just Google Bruce Dickinson," Andres said. "They're truly disturbing." He chuckled. "You think this guy is all nice and shit, but you see who he really is in those videos."

In less than a minute, Major was watching Robbie having sex on his phone.

"Holy fuck," he whistled. "Man, you are so hot."

He and Andres watched the video for a few minutes.

"Are you guys seriously getting off on watching me getting gangbanged?" Robbie asked.

"I will later," Major grinned.

"I can honestly say I'm not turned on in the slightest," Andres said. "But if I was to go that way, you'd be the guy I'd go for."

"That's why I fell for Blair," Robbie grinned. "He's the gay version of you."

"I suspected as much," Andres said.

"Can we please stop talking about sex?" Major frowned and turned his phone off. "I haven't been laid since last September."

"Well, I'll give you directions to Green Grove, and you can give Blair a visit," Andres

chuckled. "He'll fuck anyone. Robbie won't mind sharing him with you."
"I've already shared him enough, thanks," Robbie said dryly.

The three friends walked to Andres' car, laughing and talking all the way. At one point, Robbie jumped on Andres' back, but Andres wrestled him away.
"Get off me, you homo," he teased.
"Come on," Major said. "I'll give you a piggyback ride."
Robbie climbed on Major's back and stuck his tongue out at Andres. Major ran around in circles while Robbie struggled to hang on. When Major started walking normally, Andres got behind them and tickled the two of them. Soon, the three of them were helpless with laughter.
"Maybe you should ditch that tight-ass Blair for Major," Andres panted. "I'll bet Blair doesn't give piggyback rides like that."
"He gives me a different kind of ride," Robbie laughed. "I think I'll keep him. But Major, you're next in line if he fucks up again."

"He's so wonderful," Blair dropped down on Camilla's bed and stared wistfully at the new wall mural she was working on. "He knows exactly how I'm feeling, and he doesn't let me get away with anything."

An Admission of Weakness

"You shouldn't need to get away with anything," she said dryly.
"You know what I mean," Blair grinned. "He knows me so well, and he loves me anyway."
"He loves you because you're loveable," his sister said.
"I wasn't," Blair shuddered at the memory. "I was so awful to him; I can't believe he forgave me."
"Don't ever hurt him again," Camilla said. "He has the heart of an artist, and we're sensitive."
"I won't," Blair said. "Can I tell you something?"
"Of course," she frowned with annoyance at her last brush stroke.
"I had sex with all those other guys in those videos," he began.
"I don't really want to hear details about your sex life," she said.
"I just mean that I was always with women even though I knew I was attracted to men. And sex with those other guys was good, just because they were nice, good-looking guys."
"I hope you're coming to a point," she said.
"My point is that being with Robbie is so much better. Everyone told me I'm no good at sex, but Robbie said it's my superpower. It's like I'm a different person with him."
"You are," she smiled. "He lets you be your authentic self, and he doesn't judge you for it. That's the purest kind of love; it's

An Admission of Weakness

unconditional. You'd better hang on to it because it doesn't come along for everyone."
"The right man will come along for you," he said. "Dad brings Katie a new guy every time she's home. Maybe he'll do the same for you."
"I don't think I'd trust Dad's taste in men."
"Who's your ideal man?" he asked curiously.
"Hmm, let's see," she set her brush down. "He's kind and sweet, honest and loving, and he does something noble for a living. Maybe he's a doctor or someone who helps people. And most importantly, he's someone who loves me for who I am."
"If I could find Robbie, you'll find your guy too," he said.
He gave her a kiss on the cheek and left the room.

CHAPTER TWENTY

"How's that tough job of yours?" Andres asked.
"It's killing me, man," Blair joked. "Looking at half naked men all the time."
"You don't look at the women?"
"Sure I do," Blair said.
"You've screwed enough of them," Andres said. "I don't see how you can do both men and women."
"I've been with women all my life, so I'm used to it. It's not that bad," Blair said. "But as far as real attraction goes, I'm a lot more sexually attracted to men."
"I'm only attracted sexually to women," Andres frowned. "I can't imagine being with a man."
"I used to think I was attracted to women, but that was only because I assumed I was straight. Dad and Tiff played with my mind, but now that I know who I am, thanks to Robbie, I can honestly say I prefer men. When I was with Tiff, she made me take Ollie's boner pills. They keep you so hard, you can fuck anything for at least three hours."
"So you felt nothing when you were with her?"
"I didn't say that," Blair grinned. "Sex always feels good, no matter who it's with."

An Admission of Weakness

Robbie and Blair talked on the phone every evening for the next week.

"It doesn't look like I'm going to make it after all," Blair said. "Camilla is having her first exhibit that weekend at the Gallery. I kinda have to be here for it."

"That's exciting. Of course you have to be there," Robbie said. "Maybe I could come up and surprise her."

"No!" Blair said more vehemently than he intended. He toned his voice down. "I don't think Dad's ready yet."

"Maybe he'd come around faster if he met me in person," Robbie said. He grinned. "I'm kind of hard to dislike."

"That's true," Blair smiled. "But give me more time to talk you up."

"Okay," Robbie gave in. "I'm disappointed I won't get to see you, though."

"At least it will give you more time to study," Blair said.

"Actually, Major asked me to go to Indianapolis with him. I think I will."

"Indianapolis?" Blair frowned. "That's like three hours away."

"I know, but there's some big gay concert going on," Robbie said. "He offered to pay for the room and everything."

"The room? You're going to stay overnight?"

"The event is in the evening," Robbie said. "It'd be too late to drive back."

An Admission of Weakness

"Can you trust him?"
"What?" Robbie chuckled. "Of course I can trust him. He's a great guy."
"What's so great about him?"
"Well, he's very nice, and he's so funny. I don't know. We just get along really well. You'll like him."
"Is he good-looking?" Blair asked.
"I guess so," Robbie said thoughtfully. "I've never really thought about it. He's really tall, like six six, and he's pretty muscular."
"How'd you two become friends?" Blair asked suspiciously.
"From work," Robbie said. "Remember? I told you all this."
"You know, let me check with Camilla and see if I really have to be here."
"Of course you do," Robbie said. "Her first show is a really big deal. I just wish I could be there too. Tell her I wish her good luck."
"But –"
"I'll see you less than two weeks after that when you come back for football practice," Robbie said. "It will be fine."

"Time's running out, Grandma," Justin hissed. "I'm supposed to leave for college in two weeks. Have you heard from Mr. Price?"
Ruby was rinsing the dinner dishes at the kitchen sink.

An Admission of Weakness

"Not yet," she glanced around to make sure Carter wasn't within earshot. She dried her hands on a dishtowel and guided Justin out to the verandah.

"Dad has only one more week to get his money back," Justin said. "He's going to kill me if he loses all that tuition."

"Would you be willing to go to Rolling Hills part time?" Ruby asked him.

Rolling Hills Community College was located near the Interstate east of town.

"For what?"

"To get an associate's degree in business. That will show your father that you're serious about this."

"He'd never go for that," Justin said. "The only thing that will make him happy is if I'm a doctor."

"I'm not concerned with his happiness," she said dryly. "I only care about yours."

"I want him to be happy too," Justin said. "But I'd make a terrible doctor. I can't even stand the sight of blood."

"Let me make a phone call," she said. "Give me twenty-four hours and then we'll talk to your father again."

The next evening, Ruby and Justin knocked on Naomi and Carter's bedroom door.

"What are you going to say?" Justin whispered nervously while they waited in the hall.

An Admission of Weakness

"Don't worry," she said.
Carter opened the door in his silk robe and frowned at the two of them.
"Justin needs to talk to you," Ruby said.
"Fine," Carter said. "Justin, you can come in. Ruby, your bedroom is down the hall."
"Carter," Naomi scolded him. "Come in, Mama."
She sat up in bed as their guests entered the room.
"What's going on?" she asked worriedly.
"Go ahead, Justin," Ruby said.
"Mama, Dad, I don't want to be a doctor," Justin said tremulously.
"Not this again," Carter rolled his eyes and sat down on the foot of the bed.
"Carter, let him talk," Naomi said. She turned to her son, "Go ahead, dear."
"I don't want to go to college," Justin said. "That is, I want to go to Rolling Hills and study business. I've taken business classes in high school, so I know what it takes to run one."
"Don't be ridiculous," Carter said. "You leave for school in two weeks. Everything's already arranged."
"I know, but you can still get your money back," Justin said.
"I don't want my money back," Carter said angrily. "I want you to stop listening to your insane grandmother and go to school like we agreed."

An Admission of Weakness

"I never agreed to it," Justin said heatedly. "You agreed to it and told me I agreed to it. I never wanted to be a doctor. That was your dream."

"Justin, if you don't want to be a doctor, what do you want to do instead?" Naomi asked.

"I-I want to open a gym downtown that caters to older people," Justin eyed his father warily.

"I bought the old appliance store," Ruby said.

"You did what?" Carter said.

"You did?" Justin blinked with astonishment.

"It's perfect for what Justin wants," Ruby said. "We talked to Randall Price about renting it, but he wasn't keen on the idea."

"He wasn't?" Justin frowned. "When did you talk to him?"

"I talked to Brad Jameson," Ruby said. "He called Randall and discussed the situation with him."

"What situation?" Naomi looked confused.

"Justin showed Randall his business plan," Ruby said. "We asked if he would be interested in renting it since Justin is just out of high school and has no money."

"What did he say?" Justin asked.

"He didn't think renting was what was best for you, so he offered to sell the building for half what it's worth."

"Randall Price, the millionaire?" Naomi frowned.

An Admission of Weakness

"Yes," Ruby said. "He said he's been thinking about Justin's plan the whole time he's been in New York, and he believes it's a sound idea."

"So he sold it to you?" Justin said.

"Yes," Ruby smiled. "And not only that, he's going to remodel the interior the way you want it."

"Holy cow! That's freaking amazing!"

"Now wait a minute," Carter said. "You can throw your money away if you want, Ruby, but you can't force my son into some crazy plan. He's going to school to be a doctor."

"It's a good plan, dammit!" Justin snapped. "The only one who's forcing me into anything is you, Dad. You won't listen to me."

"I'm listening," Naomi said gently.

"I want to own my own gym," Justin told his mother. "I can do it, I know I can. I don't want to be a doctor. I don't like medical stuff, and the sight of blood makes me sick.

"I like business. I know about accounts payable, accounts receivable, monetization, margins, capital, overhead, key performance indicators.

"Once the business is a success here, I could franchise it. I know that's a long way off, but that's what I would be working toward."

"I think it sounds marvelous," Naomi smiled. "If you believe in it, that's good enough for me because I believe in you."

An Admission of Weakness

Justin grinned with relief. At least his mother understood.
"Just stop it, all of you!" Carter shouted. "Justin is going to be a doctor and that's all there is to it."
"No, I'm not!" Justin raised his voice as well. "If you want a doctor in the family, you go be one."
"I already am," Carter yelled. "I didn't pursue some ridiculous dream and throw my future away, and I won't allow you to either."
"Justin, you're serious about this?" Naomi said. "You understand what you're doing?"
"Yes, Mama."
"Then let me talk to your father," she said.
"There's nothing to talk about," Carter scowled. "You'll never convince me that he shouldn't become a doctor because I know what's best for him."
"Go on to bed, Justin," Naomi smiled gently.
"Thanks, Mama," he gratefully gave her a kiss on the cheek before he and his grandmother left the room.

"Carter, why is it so important to you that Justin become a doctor?" Naomi said.
"What kind of a future can he have owning a gym?" Carter paced up and down. "Think of what he could be. He could heal people, he could discover the next big cure."

An Admission of Weakness

"No, he couldn't," she said. "That's not what he wants. Do you really want him spending his life in a career he doesn't like?"

"He doesn't know if he likes it or not," Carter said. "He's just a boy, and he needs my guidance."

"He does need your guidance," she agreed. "But you can't guide him if you don't listen to him."

"I listened," he said indignantly. "I heard every foolish word that came out of his mouth."

"You heard the words, but you didn't hear him. They weren't foolish words to him."

"This is your mother's fault! She put these ideas into his head."

"There is no fault," she said. "And he just said this is his idea."

"So you want his life to be about him running a gym?"

"I want him to be happy," Naomi said. "He thinks this will make him happy. You know how he's practically lived at the gym either at school or at the country club. It's what he loves.

"And he will be helping people," she added. "He'll be helping them get healthier and in better shape. Isn't that a good thing?"

"You don't understand."

"Then explain it to me," she said.

When he didn't respond, she continued.

An Admission of Weakness

"You have your legacy, Carter. A great one. You have four beautiful, successful children, the respect of everyone in this town, and think of all the children you've guided over the years. Lots of them have you to thank for pointing them in the right direction. That should be enough for you."

He sat down on the bed, shoulders slumped.

"I've spent my life dedicated to my children," he said.

"I know you have."

"I want them to have a better life than I did."

"Katie has her master's in nursing, Blair is studying business, and Camilla is a gifted artist with her first show at the Gallery. She's helping people at the hospital.

"They're all good people, and that's because of you. You did everything right."

"Obviously not," he said dejectedly.

"Get your money back," she advised. "Let him try this for, say, a year. If it doesn't work out, he can go to school for something else."

"But –"

"You can't make him be a doctor if he doesn't want to be one," she said. "Let him live his own life."

"I had such dreams for him," Carter sighed.

She knelt behind him and put her arms around him.

"Your dream was for him to be happy, and he will be. That's all you can ask for."

An Admission of Weakness

Blair stood on the second floor balcony at the Gallery and put his phone back in his pocket. The place was crowded with people sipping champagne and eyeing Camilla's artwork. She had already sold a number of paintings, much to her surprise.

Blair was annoyed that Robbie hadn't answered his calls all weekend. What was he doing that he was too busy to take his boyfriend's calls? Okay, he knew he was being ridiculous. He had no reason to be jealous because no one was more loyal and honest than Robbie. Also, the irony of him being jealous wasn't lost on him. He had been with dozens of people over the last six months while Robbie was forced to stand by and watch.

Besides, they had never discussed whether or not their relationship was going to be exclusive. He was the one who canceled their weekend together, and Robbie had a perfect right to spend time with his friend. Still, it caused a pang in his stomach when he pictured Robbie sleeping in the same bed as some stranger.

Finally, around ten o'clock, Blair's phone rang.

"It's about time," Blair stepped out onto the sidewalk in front of the Gallery. "I've been calling you."

"I know," Robbie said over the loud music, laughter, and revelry going on in the background. "I'm sorry. We've just been so

An Admission of Weakness

busy. I've met so many people here. They keep buying me drinks."
"Don't drink anything that someone hands you," Blair said. "You don't know what might be in it."
"I know," Robbie laughed. "Major's been watching out for me."
"I'll bet he has. Where are you?"
"We're at some club," Robbie said vaguely.
"Robbie, come dance with me," a voice called out.
"Who's that?" Blair frowned.
"Major and some of the guys."
There was a brief scuffle, and then someone with a deep voice spoke.
"Robbie's got to go, whoever this is," he said into the phone. There was loud laughter followed by an abrupt silence.

Robbie called Blair Sunday evening.
"How was Camilla's show?" he asked.
"It was fine," Blair said. "She sold six paintings."
"That's fantastic."
"How was Indianapolis?"
"It was a blast," Robbie grinned. "We ate breakfast at two o'clock this morning with a bunch of Major's friends before going back to the hotel. We didn't get out of bed until noon."
"Did you sleep with him?"

An Admission of Weakness

"Yes," Robbie said. "But I was so drunk, I passed out, and Major had to take my clothes off for me."
"You were naked?"
"I guess so," Robbie chuckled. "I woke up that way."
"So you slept naked with another dude?"
"Are you jealous?" Robbie said.
"Of course not," Blair said. "I just wondered if he was any good."
"Well, if he was, I don't remember it," Robbie laughed.
"You think this is funny?"
"A little," Robbie said.
"I just want you to be careful if you sleep with other people," Blair said.
"Careful? You mean you want me to wear a condom with other people?" Robbie frowned.
"Don't you think you should?"
"Yeah, definitely," Robbie said. "Are you wearing condoms with other people?"
"Yeah, sure."
"Okay," Robbie said slowly. "I guess I didn't realize you were having sex with other people. So you want this to be an open relationship."
"I'm just saying that you have to be careful," Blair said.
"I will," Robbie said. "Listen, I've got to go. Major wants to fuck later, and I have to go buy extra-large condoms. I'll talk to you later."
"Robbie, wait –" but it was too late.

An Admission of Weakness

Robbie had ended the call.

"How long is Dad not going to speak to me?" Justin asked.
"I don't know," Naomi sighed. "You know how stubborn he can be."
"I know," Justin said. "But I didn't do this to hurt him."
"Of course you didn't," she said. "He'll get used to the idea eventually. You have to understand, he had all these plans for your life."
"But they weren't my plans."
"He understands that now. He's just disappointed. Not in you, but in the expectations he made for you."
She resumed her needlepoint and hummed a cheerful tune.
"You seem awfully happy these days," he observed.
"Why wouldn't I be happy?"
"I don't know," he shrugged. "Where do you go every day for hours at a time?"
"My sewing lessons," she said. "June and Billy are working with me."
"Isn't he that new clothing designer downtown?"
"Yes, he is," June smiled. "He's very nice, and he's very talented too."
"A guy that sews sounds faggy to me," he frowned.

An Admission of Weakness

"That's not a nice word," she said reprovingly. "Please don't use it again."
"Isn't he kinda young?"
"He's in his twenties, I believe," she said vaguely.
"Is June with you when you sew?"
"Sometimes," Naomi nodded. "But usually it's just me and Billy."
"He was in a biker gang, I heard," Justin scowled. "Doesn't he go by Snake?"
"I call him Billy," she said. "The name Snake seems wrong for such a good-looking young man."

"I think Mom's having an affair," Justin said ominously.
"No, she's not," Blair chuckled. "Where'd you get a crazy idea like that?"
"Haven't you noticed her humming a lot lately?"
"So?"
"She seems happier than usual, and she spends half the day at her 'sewing lessons'. Why does she need sewing lessons? She already knows how to sew."
"Maybe there are things she doesn't know," Blair suggested.
"She misses dinner sometimes. Why would a sewing lesson be more important than dinner?"
"I don't know," Blair admitted.

An Admission of Weakness

"And what about the guy she's taking lessons from?" Justin said darkly. "He goes by Snake, and he's young and handsome."

"I think he's gay," Blair frowned.

"That doesn't matter. Gay people only choose to be gay because it feels good to them. You know what Dad taught us about them. He's only gay when it suits him, and that means he can be straight when he wants to. What if he and Mom are having sex?"

"Ew!" Blair wrinkled his nose. "That's disgusting!"

"I know, but I think that's what's going on," Justin said. "Now tell me more about all those women you slept with. And don't leave out any details."

"Well, one of my favorites was this woman named Tina. She was so tight and had these enormous tits," Blair grinned lasciviously and raised an eyebrow. "I fucked her in this sling, and sometimes I'd just stand still and let her swing on and off my dick."

"Was she a screamer?" Justin's eyes grew wide.

"Like you wouldn't believe," Blair nodded. "Especially when I sucked on her tits while I was fucking her. Anyway, she had the hottest…"

He went on to give intimate descriptions about his encounters with Tina and Tiffany and a dozen other women he had been with while

An Admission of Weakness

Justin listened eagerly.

An Admission of Weakness

CHAPTER TWENTY-ONE

'Gay men sleep with other men because it feels good to them', Blair mused. But didn't straight men sleep with women because that felt good to them?

He'd heard from his father his entire life that gay men have no morals, but surely it wasn't true. Robbie was the most moral person he knew. Still, hearing his brother say it this time brought back the lectures the two of them had been subjected to as children:

"You stay away from homosexuals," his father had told them. "They are evil, conniving people who will stop at nothing to convert you to their sinful way of life."

"But why do they do that?" Blair asked.

"You see, son," Carter said. "Some people are drawn to sin like others crave chocolate. If all you did was eat chocolate, you'd be very unhealthy. It's the same with sex. They crave it with people of their own gender because it's like chocolate to them; they like it because they know it's bad for them."

"Can't they do what's right?"

"They can, but they don't want to," Carter explained. "You could eat a vegetable instead of chocolate, couldn't you?"

"Yes," the boys answered.

An Admission of Weakness

"It's the same thing. A man who sleeps with other men could have sex with a woman, which is what he knows he should do. But he's weak and gives in to his sinful nature because it's pleasurable, like chocolate is to you and me."

So was he sleeping with Robbie because he was weak? Robbie was the chocolate and women were the vegetables that he should be craving? That seemed like a sound argument. 'They choose to be gay because it's sinful.' Again, Robbie was upstanding and ethical and honest; he wasn't a sinner. And the two of them didn't choose to be gay because it was a sin; it's just who they were. Wasn't it?

Although, he had to admit, he was choosing to be with Robbie because it felt good, better than with a girl, the same way chocolate tasted better than vegetables. So if he was choosing homosexuality, did that mean he was really straight? If Robbie wasn't in the picture, would he choose to be with a woman?

Of course, he had been with women many times because that was what society told him was appropriate. He didn't enjoy it nearly as much as with men.

He preferred being with guys, but apparently that was only because it was like chocolate to him. Or was it? Damn, this was getting confusing! He had had it all figured out until Justin reminded him of what their father had

An Admission of Weakness

taught them all of their lives. So was he truly gay, or was he just weak?

Carter and Naomi helped Blair move back into his dorm room. Fortunately, Robbie wasn't around for them to meet, so he hurriedly threw his things in the room and then left with his parents to grab some lunch before they headed back home.

A little later, after he had his room set up the way he liked it, he walked over to the eatery where Robbie worked. Part of him wanted to see his boyfriend and part of him wanted to get a look at this Black god that seemed to be moving in on his territory.

Why had he given Robbie the impression that he was still sleeping around? That was a stupid thing to do. He wasn't sleeping with other people, and he didn't want to. It was like he had given Robbie permission to fuck whoever he wanted.

So if Robbie and this Major dude were having sex, he had no one to blame but himself.

Robbie had joked that he and Major were going to fuck later, but was it a joke? Maybe he thought if Blair was fucking around, he would too.

Was having a boyfriend supposed to be this complicated? This was all new territory for him, and he had no clue what he was doing.

An Admission of Weakness

Robbie and anyone who looked like he could be Major weren't at the restaurant, so he headed back to the dorm.

Just before nine o'clock that evening, Blair heard some loud noises coming down the hall, so he stepped out to see what was going on. He was taken aback at the sight of a huge dark man lumbering down the hall with Robbie on his back.

"Faster," Robbie laughed and smacked Major on the ass.

"That's it, daddy," Major grinned. "Spank my ass. Make it hurt."

"If anyone's the daddy, it's you," Robbie said. He lost his grip and fell to the floor, laughing all the while.

"Are you drunk again?" Blair demanded.

"Blair?" Robbie gazed up at him with astonishment. "You're here!"

He jumped to his feet and threw himself into Blair's arms, kissing his face all over.

"Oh my god, I'm so happy to see you!" he cried. "I love you so much!"

He finally released him when he realized Blair wasn't kissing him back.

"I thought you weren't coming until tomorrow," he said. He noticed the displeased expression on his face. "Oh, this is Major. Major, this is Blair, your hero."

An Admission of Weakness

"Robbie," Major frowned with embarrassment. He extended his right hand for a dap handshake. "Hey, man. It's nice to finally meet you."

"You too," Blair said stiffly. "Did I come back too soon? It looks like I'm interrupting something."

"Nah, we were just gonna order a pizza and watch a movie," Major said.

"He's never seen *The Goonies*," Robbie grinned. "Can you believe it?"

"No, I can't," Blair frowned.

"Uh, you know what?" Major eyed Blair uneasily and turned to Robbie. "Blair's back now, baby, so you guys should spend the evening together. We'll watch the movie some other time."

"At least stay and eat pizza," Robbie said.

"Yes, please stay," Blair said. "I don't want to mess up your plans."

Robbie took Major by the hand and pulled him into his room while Blair followed.

"It's a real honor to meet you," Major sat his large frame down on Robbie's bed while Robbie ordered the pizzas. "Robbie talks about you all the time."

"He talks about you too," Blair said coolly. "He said you spend a lot of time together."

"Yeah, we do," Major grinned. "He and Andres are like my best friends."

An Admission of Weakness

"Yeah, Andres mentioned you too. He said you're pretty fast on the field, so I guess we'll see who's faster."

"I'm not as good as you," Major grinned sheepishly. "I'm kinda nervous about starting practice."

"I wouldn't worry about it if I was you," Blair said. "With your build, you'll do fine."

The two discussed football until the pizzas arrived, and then the three of them sat back on the bed to watch *The Goonies* on Robbie's laptop. Blair sat between the two while the movie played.

"That's Josh Brolin?" Major said. "He looks so different."

"He was cute back then," Robbie said.

"Just watch the movie," Blair frowned.

When the movie ended and the pizza was gone, Blair excused himself for a moment to go to his room.

"I don't think he likes me," Major whispered.

"Sure, he does," Robbie said. "It just takes him a while to warm up to new people."

The door opened, and Blair reappeared completely naked.

"What the –"

"Are we doing this or what?" Blair said.

"Doing what?" Robbie frowned.

Blair walked over and yanked Major's shorts and underwear down before straddling him and kissing him passionately. He stroked Major's

An Admission of Weakness

large manhood while he placed one of Major's hands on his erect manhood. Major returned the kiss for a few seconds until Blair rose up and guided his dick into his ass.

"Holy fuck," Major breathed and closed his eyes.

It had been so long since he'd had sex, he didn't want it to stop. Finally, however, he forced Blair away.

"What's wrong?" Blair panted. "I thought I was your idol."

"What's going on?" Major looked between Robbie and Blair.

"He's fucking you, so I thought I'd join in," Blair said.

"Who's fucking me? You mean Robbie?"

"I'm not fucking him," Robbie said.

"You said you were," Blair said.

"I only said that because you said you were sleeping around," Robbie said.

"I'm not sleeping around," Blair said.

"It sure looks like you are," Robbie frowned.

"I'm not even sure I'm gay," Blair blurted out.

Robbie stared blankly at him for a moment.

"You're naked with a hard on while riding Major's dick, and you're not sure you're gay?"

Blair stood up and covered his groin with the laptop.

"As much fun as this was, I think I'd better go," Major said uncomfortably.

An Admission of Weakness

He arose and pulled his shorts up before giving Robbie a quick hug.
"Call me later, babe," he said.
"I will."

"What the hell was that all about?" Robbie said.
"I thought you and him were fucking around, so I decided I'd make it a three-way," Blair set the laptop down.
"He's just a friend," Robbie said. "Do you want this to be an open relationship?"
"Do you?"
"No, I don't," Robbie said. "But apparently you do."
"That's not what I want," Blair said.
"And yet thirty seconds ago, you were sitting on my friend's dick while I watched."
"I thought that was what you wanted."
"You never asked me what I wanted. We've never discussed monogamy, but I'm a one man kind of guy. I thought you knew that."
"I'm that way too."
"So you didn't sleep with anyone this summer?"
"No," Blair said. "I mean, I went out with several women from the club, but we didn't sleep together."
"Did they want to?"
"Oh yeah," Blair grinned at the memory of all the flirting he had been part of over the

summer. "They were practically begging for it."
"Did you want to?"
"Maybe some of them," Blair shrugged.
"So you wanted to sleep with them, but you didn't. Why not?"
"They were just turned on because of my tattoos," Blair said. "It's not like I would have gotten serious with any of them."
"You wouldn't have gotten serious with them? Did you really just say that to your boyfriend?"
"I just meant I only want to sleep with you."
"Okay, so we both want to be monogamous, even though you wanted to sleep with the women from this summer," Robbie said. "Do I have that right?"
"Absolutely," Blair grinned with relief.
"Fine," Robbie said. "Now let's talk about the other elephant in the room."
"What?"
"The 'I'm not sure I'm gay' elephant," Robbie said dryly. "At the end of last semester, you said you weren't attracted to women anymore. You said you had resolved that after the whole Tiffany debacle."
"I think my mom's having an affair," Blair said.
Robbie stared at him uncomprehendingly. "And...?"
"The guy she's having an affair with is my age, and he's gay."

An Admission of Weakness

"And…?"

"My dad says that people choose to be gay because it feels good to them."

"It does feel good to us, but we don't choose to be gay. You and I are proof of that."

"Then how is Snake able to sleep with my mom?"

"Maybe he's pansexual," Robbie shrugged. "Or maybe he's choosing to be gay when it suits him. Maybe that's what I'm doing with you. After all, I'm choosing to have sex with you.

"You're choosing to be attracted to men?" Robbie frowned.

"I'm choosing to act on it," Blair corrected him.

"That's the same thing," Robbie said.

"Not for me," Blair said. "I was sleeping with women before I met you."

"But you said you weren't attracted to them," Robbie said. "Was that a lie?"

"I was attracted to them, but only because I thought I was supposed to be."

"So are you still attracted to women?"

"I don't know. Maybe."

"'I don't know, maybe?'" Robbie said. "So if a beautiful woman came in here right now and took her clothes off, you wouldn't want to have sex with her."

"I'd rather have sex with you," Blair said.

An Admission of Weakness

"That's not an answer," Robbie said. "If I wasn't in the picture, and a beautiful woman took her clothes off, would you want to sleep with her?"

"I don't know," Blair said. "But that's not a fair question because I've slept with women for years, and you only fucked them in those videos."

"What's your point?" Robbie grimaced.

"I can sleep with a woman if I want to," Blair said.

"Are you trying to say you're bisexual?" Robbie looked confused.

"I don't know," Blair said. "Maybe I only like sleeping with you because I know it's wrong."

"Sleeping with me is wrong?" Robbie said incredulously. "Did you seriously just say that?"

"My dad said it's like chocolate and vegetables."

"I have no idea what chocolate and vegetables have to do with you being gay."

"Gay sex is like chocolate to some guys; we crave it like some people crave chocolate. But straight sex is like a vegetable because it's what we know we should be doing."

"Okay, that's the single stupidest thing I've ever heard," Robbie said. "Why would your father say something like that?"

"It makes sense if you think about it," Blair shrugged.

An Admission of Weakness

"No, it doesn't!" Robbie said sharply. "Not even in the least. Straight men sleep with women because they're attracted to them. Gay men sleep with other gay men because we are attracted to one another. We're not attracted to women. I understand that closeted gays guy might try sleeping with a woman to prove something to themselves, but that doesn't change the fact that they're gay.

"Being gay or straight is who people are. I know there are different degrees to that statement, but as far as I'm concerned, I'm one hundred percent gay. If a naked woman walked in here right now, I would not be aroused in the least."

"You wouldn't sleep with her because you prefer chocolate over vegetables. That means you're weak. I like chocolate, but I could eat a vegetable if necessary," Blair said.

"Wow," Robbie dropped down on the mattress. "You just called me weak because I'm gay?"

"You tried a lot of vegetables in those videos, and you were really into it. That tells me that you're choosing to eat chocolate because you're weak," Blair said.

"I was into it because I needed them to offer me a contract to save your ass!" Robbie snapped.

"So you did like it," Blair said. "I knew it."

"Okay, I'm totally confused now, but still not as much as you are," Robbie said. "You don't

An Admission of Weakness

know if you're gay or straight or bi because of some ignorant statement your homophobic dad made about vegetables and chocolate."

"He's a doctor," Blair said. "He's very smart."

"No, he's very stupid!" Robbie snapped. "A man who has a doctorate degree should know better than to use his prejudices against people he doesn't even know instead of listening to science."

"He's not stupid," Blair said heatedly.

"Did you sleep with any of those women this summer?" Robbie asked again.

"No," Blair said.

"So you didn't fuck them?"

"They wanted me to, but I didn't."

"What did you do?"

"Nothing, I swear."

Robbie stood up and paced the room with his hands to his face. Finally, he faced Blair.

"I only see one thing to do," he said.

"Me too," Blair grinned and tried to take him in his arms.

"Let go," Robbie said.

"What?"

"I'm not going to sleep with you like this," Robbie said.

"What? Why not?"

"Did you even miss me?" Robbie asked.

"Of course I did."

"Then why haven't you said so? When I saw you in the hall, I couldn't wait to jump into

An Admission of Weakness

your arms and tell you I love you," Robbie said. "But you haven't said a word. Were you still thinking about your girlfriends from this summer?"

"I was upset about Major," Blair said. "Of course I love you."

"I don't know if I can believe that. I think we need to take a break from being a couple," Robbie said.

"You don't mean that," Blair said. "I don't want to break up."

"I said a break, not break up," Robbie said.

"Why?"

"You've slept with lots of men and women, and you still don't know what your sexuality is," Robbie said. "You even wanted to fuck women this summer while we're supposed to be a couple."

"But I didn't fuck them."

"You might as well have," Robbie said. "I don't see how we can be a couple if you're unsure of things. I don't want us to be together and then suddenly have you say sorry pal, I'm not into guys anymore."

"That won't happen," Blair assured him.

"How do you know?" Robbie said. "I don't want to go through that again. I'd rather end things now."

"But you said you didn't want to break up."

An Admission of Weakness

"I don't, but I also don't want to be the guy you settled for because you couldn't find the right woman."

"I haven't settled for you," Blair said. "I love you."

"And I love you," Robbie said. "I never thought I'd love someone this much."

"Me either," Blair said.

Tears filled Robbie's eyes, and Blair brushed them away tenderly.

"So now what?"

"I'm giving you until November first to go out and date," Robbie's throat tightened. "See all the women you want. And if it turns out you fall for one of them, then we'll end things and you can have a future without me."

"I don't want a future without you," Blair said.

"You have two months to find out if that's true or not," Robbie said.

"What about you?" Blair frowned. "Are you going to see anyone? I guess if I'm dating other people, you should too."

"You're the one who's confused. I already know where my heart lies," Robbie smiled sadly. "Besides, I'll be busy with classes and cheerleading and work. Now you'd better go put some clothes on."

"We're still a couple, right?" Blair headed for the door.

"I hope so," Robbie said. "You tell me in November."

An Admission of Weakness

That was it, Robbie realized unhappily. Blair wasn't his and never had been. The fact that Blair had taken him up on his offer of two months told him that Blair was too messed up to be in an adult relationship. In his heart, he was setting him free, even though it hurt like hell to do so.

Justin met with Randall Price when he returned from New York. Together, they determined what changes were necessary to the building that Ruby had bought. True to his word, Randall agreed to pay for everything, including resurfacing the parking lot and installing a new roof, new furnace, and new air conditioning. Justin enjoyed his classes at the community college. High school had prepared him well, and he sailed through his lessons with straight A's.

The only worry he had was his parents. It wasn't as if he approved of his mother's affair, but he felt he understood it to a degree. His father had become distant and uncommunicative ever since he started his research for his book. It was obvious his mother was lonely and bored, so he didn't blame her for finding something to fill her time. He just needed to talk some sense into her. It was just unfortunate that she had encountered this Snake person. He was apparently one of

An Admission of Weakness

those fellows who took advantage of lonely married women trapped in loveless marriages. As for his father, the man had yet to speak to him after weeks of cold silences between them. It wasn't unexpected; his father's stubbornness was legendary.

Dinners were uncomfortable for him these days. His father wouldn't acknowledge him and refused to talk to anyone, and Camilla ate her food hastily so she could return to her painting. Ever since the success of her gallery show, her artistic spirit had been rekindled, and she couldn't find enough time to spend with her oils and canvases.

He felt awkward around his mother now that he knew her dark secret. The only conversation at the dinner table now was often between him and Grandma Ruby.

One evening he stopped by his sister's room.
"Camilla, can I talk to you?"
"Uh-huh," she said distractedly.
"Do you know what's going on with Mama?" he asked.
"Is something going on with Mama?" she frowned at the work in front of her.
"She's having an affair," Justin said.
"Uh-huh."
"Camilla!" Justin said. "Did you hear me?"
"Yes, Mama's having an affair," she said. She stopped and blinked when she realized what

An Admission of Weakness

she had said. "What? Mama's having an affair? Are you kidding?"

"Haven't you noticed her singing in the kitchen? How happy she seems lately? She's spending all her time with that dress designer, even missing dinner sometimes."

"Those are just sewing lessons," Camilla said scornfully.

"No, they're not," Justin said. "You know how Dad's all wrapped up in that book of his; he ignores Mom, and this guy convinced her to have an affair with him."

"How do you know?"

"It's obvious," he said. "Blair said the same thing."

"Oh my god," she set her brush down. "I can't believe she'd do something like that."

"She's lonely," Justin said. "It's Dad's fault as much as it is hers."

"Who is the guy?"

"His name is Billy Abernathy, and he goes by Snake. He's that new dress designer downtown."

"Oh him," Camilla relaxed. "He's gay."

"No, that's just what he wants people to think," Justin said. "He's probably having multiple affairs with women in town."

"That bastard!" she cried. "What are we going to do about it?"

"I don't know," he said. "I hoped you'd have an idea."

An Admission of Weakness

"We should confront Mama and tell her to stop it."

"We can't do that," Justin said. "She'd be humiliated if she thought we knew."

"That's true," she said. "Maybe we should talk to Katie. She's the oldest."

"I think the less people who know, the better."

"Let me give it some thought," she said thoughtfully.

An Admission of Weakness

CHAPTER TWENTY-TWO

"So he doesn't know if he's gay or not?" Major frowned. "How is that possible? I've known I was gay since I was five years old."

"Me too," Robbie said. "But everyone's different. I read about a guy who spent his life married to the same woman and didn't realize he was gay until he was in his sixties."

The two were lazing about in Major's room in the athletic department.

"Wow, talk about phoning it in at the last minute," Major grinned. "Think about all the dick he could have had all that time."

"I know," Robbie agreed and attempted a smile.

"I'm sorry," Major said. "I shouldn't have made light of it."

"That's okay," Robbie patted his leg. "I needed something to make me smile. I've spent the last two days crying."

"I can't decide if it's incredibly wise or stupid of you to give him two months to date other people."

"I have to know for sure that he's truly mine," Robbie said. "I can't be the guy he settled for because he was too confused to know what he wanted. Does that make sense?"

"I get it, baby," Major nodded. "Maybe exploring other avenues will make him realize that you're the one he wants."

An Admission of Weakness

"I'm pretty sure he's going to try to be straight for his father's sake. You watch, he'll end up engaged by November first."

"But he sat on my dick," Major said. "He can't pretend to be straight when he's going around fucking guys."

"Can I stay here for a while?" Robbie asked. "I don't want to run into him."

"Sure, but it's kinda cramped for two people, especially when one of them is as big as me."

"I don't mind," Robbie said.

"Why don't you stay here, and I'll stay in your room?" Major suggested.

"You'd seriously do that for me?" Robbie said.

"Sure. That's what friends are for."

"I love you," Robbie said emotionally.

"I love you too," Major gathered him into his massive arms.

For the next few minutes, Robbie allowed himself to be comforted by his dear friend. He was unaware of the tears in Major's eyes.

Robbie moved his things into Major's room the next day. He'd been there enough times that most of the guys knew him. The majority of them were friendly enough, although there were a few who were notoriously homophobic. It didn't matter to Robbie because it was a relief to be away from Blair.

An Admission of Weakness

It was only a matter of time before Blair found a woman to fall in love with if only to please his father. He didn't want to be around to see it. Maybe he was stupid to give Blair this time of freedom, but he didn't see what other option he had. How could he be with Blair knowing that the man wasn't truly in love with him?

"Hey, man," Blair said to Major in the dorm hallway.
"Brother," Major nodded.
"You here to see Robbie?"
"Robbie's living in my place," Major said. "I'm crashing here for a while."
"He's not living here?" Blair said, surprised. "Wow, he really doesn't want to see me, does he?"
"Of course he does," Major said. "That's what this whole thing is about. He wants to be with you, but only if he knows you're not having regrets about someone else."
"Speaking of regrets, I'm sorry about what happened in his room that night," Blair said.
"That's the first lap dance I ever got," Major chuckled. "And from my hero, no less."
"I'm nobody's hero, believe me," Blair said dryly.
"You are to the people who come to the football games."
"Being good at football doesn't make me heroic."

An Admission of Weakness

"I thought you were pretty awesome in your videos," Major said.

"Oh god, don't remind me," Blair groaned. "I can't believe you saw those."

"You've got it all, man," Major said. "You're handsome, hung, and a star football player. I'll bet every one of those people you fucked were thrilled to be with you."

"They were being paid, just like I was," Blair said. "I wish Robbie hadn't told you about that."

"Everyone makes mistakes. Besides, I'd have done the same thing if it paid good enough. Though I'm not good-looking enough to be a porn star."

"Sure you are; you got the body and the face for it. Did you see the one where I fucked the professor and her student, and then the janitor blew me? That showed my dick the best. And the one with Tina in the sling. That was great."

"What about the ones you did with Robbie?" Major said. "Those were by far the hottest videos I've ever seen."

"I'm glad you liked them," Blair said.

"The one where you were fucking Robbie and the neighbor couple came over showed off your body the best," Major grinned. "Or when you and the woman with the big tits tied him down."

"That was awesome," Blair chuckled.

An Admission of Weakness

"I can't believe all the stuff he did," Major said. "Are you both into watersports?"
"It was cool as far as I was concerned, but I don't think Robbie liked it."
"And to think, I got to touch your dick once. I haven't washed my hand since then."
"I hope that's not true," Blair chuckled.
"I couldn't be with a woman though," Major said. "How did Robbie do it?"
"We had some pharmaceutical help, but he was really into it."
"It grosses me out."
"It's not so bad," Blair shrugged. "Say, you wanna get a bite to eat?"
"I'm not sure," Major said uneasily. "Robbie might not like us spending time together."
"He wanted the three of us to be friends, remember," Blair said. "He won't care."
"I guess that's true," Major shrugged. "Okay, let's get a bite."
"Cool, brother. You can tell me what your favorite parts of my videos were," Blair grinned.

Robbie looked out Major's dorm room window and sighed. Suddenly school felt very lonely. Sure, he had his friends, his classmates, and his fellow cheerleaders, but without Blair, it seemed desolate and empty. It was the same as when Blair was off on his Tiffany/porn/modeling jag.

An Admission of Weakness

Major and Andres were still around, but they were involved in football again, so he didn't see them much unless it was at practice.
It didn't matter anyway. He was here for an education, not to socialize. At least he still had Rhett to talk to a couple of times a week, and his little brother always brightened his day.

"I'm gonna kick his ass the next time I see him," Rhett said angrily when Robbie explained what had happened.
"I'm the one who told him to date other people for two months," Robbie said.
"Yeah, but he didn't have to agwee to it," Rhett said. "You can't be with someone who's that messed up."
"I just hope he figures things out and comes back to me. But if he doesn't, he doesn't. Life will go on."
"His father is stupid, and he's stupid for listening to him," Rhett said.
"You're right. He is stupid. So why do I still love him so much?"
"Because there's no whyme or weason when it comes to love."
"You're pretty smart for a white trash Mississippi boy," Robbie teased.
"I thought you were smawt enough to not fall for the first pwetty face that came along."
"That was kinda dumb," Robbie sighed sadly.

An Admission of Weakness

"Don't worwy," Rhett said. "He may be stupid, but he's not that stupid; he won't thwow away the best thing that ever happened to him."

Some movement outside caught Robbie's eye. It was Blair walking down the sidewalk with a beautiful Black woman, and she had her arm linked in his. She was wearing heels and an elegant dress, while he was wearing one of the expensive suits Tiffany had bought him. They were obviously going on a date. As Robbie watched, she reached over and kissed his cheek, and Blair kissed her hand and put his arm around her.
Jeez, he hadn't wasted any time. He must have jumped on the first woman he saw and was going to ride her until another one came along.

"Where are Mama and Dad?" Blair asked Katie as they strolled along the sidewalk in the athletic department.
"Mama didn't come," Katie said. "She had some things to do."
Damn, she really was having an affair, Blair frowned. He couldn't remember a time that his mother wasn't at her children's games, recitals, and so on. It would take something really big to keep her away from his first game of the season. Ew, that put a picture in his mind that he couldn't shake.

An Admission of Weakness

"Have you noticed anything different about Mama?"
"What do you mean?" she frowned.
"Nothing," he said. "At least you and Dad are here. I can't believe you came home from California and didn't tell anyone."
"To be honest, I came to see Dillon," she grinned. "But I'm glad to see all of you too."
"Is Dad talking to Justin yet?"
"What do you think?" she said dryly. "But forget the family. I want to meet this boyfriend of yours. Camilla said he's adorable."
"We, uh, kind of broke up," he said uncomfortably.
"Oh no," she said. "What happened?"
"He wanted a break," he said evasively. "I've been seeing this girl."
"Oh no. Not another Danielle, I hope," she groaned.
"She's very nice and really pretty."
"But I thought you were gay," she frowned. "At least that's what you said. Are you pansexual?"
"I don't know," he sighed. "I'm trying to work through some things."
"Don't you love this guy?"
"Of course I do."
"If you're in love with him, what is there to work out?" she asked.
"He thinks I'm confused," Blair said.

An Admission of Weakness

"You must be if you're letting the man you love get away just so you can date a girl," she said. "Come on, let's go meet Dad."

"I can't believe I'm doing this," Naomi said. "It feels wicked."
"It's not wicked," Snake grinned. "Now hold still and let me do this."
"Oh, that's it," Naomi said. "That feels great."
"Good, because we've got a lot of work to do," Snake said. "The show's tomorrow, and we still have two dresses to finish."
"But I'm too old to wear a wedding dress," she said.
"Nonsense," June said. "You look gorgeous."
The three of them paused to gaze in the triple mirror at Naomi's reflection. She was wearing the lovely strapless gown she had first sewn for Snake. They had added the eight foot veil/headdress that flowed down her back to drag the floor with the gown's hemline. The dress was the perfect contrast to her unblemished brown skin.
"I'm missing Blair's first game for this," Naomi said ruefully. "I feel guilty."
"You shouldn't," June said. "You're doing something for yourself, and there's nothing wrong with that. Have you ever missed any of his games?"
"No, of course not."

An Admission of Weakness

"Then you're entitled," Snake said. "Besides, we can't do the show without you. I promise I'll make it up to you."

The Bridal Show was held the next evening at the Gallery. Naomi, June, and their teams had put everything else aside to sew the ten floor-length gowns as well as the ten shorter wedding dresses.

When Timothy, the director of the Gallery, told him this was the only date available for the next eight months, Snake had made the tough decision to go for it. For the next several weeks, the shop was a frenzy of activity with all hands working together.

The local florists, bakeries, party planners, and caterers had joined them as well, so the Gallery was sumptuously adorned with samples of flower arrangements, decorations, cakes, and desserts.

The dresses were the stars of the show, however. Their twenty models were all local women of various sizes and shapes. They each paraded in turn down the central open staircase and along the runway. Naomi was the final subject. Snake told her he was saving the best for last.

A string quintet from Taylor Academy of Fine Arts in Chicago performed music for the fashion show while other students circulated

An Admission of Weakness

among the crowd with champagne flutes and hors d'oeuvres.

It was an elegant affair, and most people were dressed up. The local newspaper sent a reporter and photographer to cover the lavish event. There were even television reporters and cameramen from Chicago, Bloomington, and Rockford. A professional videographer was on hand to video the show for the website.

"I wish Carter and the children were here," Naomi said nervously while June finished adjusting her veil so that it flowed evenly behind her.

"I know," June smiled sympathetically. "But they'll see the pictures in the paper."

"I hope not," Naomi said.

"Don't you think it's time to tell them about your career?"

"Carter would just make me stop," Naomi said with a hint of bitterness.

"Look at the woman in the mirror. Does she look like the kind of woman who lets a man tell her what to do?" June grinned mischievously. "Just look at you: strong, capable, independent, and stunningly beautiful. Carter and the children would be so proud of you."

"They'd think I'm being foolish," Naomi said dryly. "At least Mama's here. I'm thankful for that."

An Admission of Weakness

"She's sitting at the bottom of the stairs," June said. "I can't wait to see the look on her face when she sees you."

When it was Naomi's turn, she began trembling.
"Don't be nervous," Snake kissed her cheek. "You look absolutely beautiful. That's why I saved you for the finale."
They waited until the dress was introduced by Peter Johnson, the gregarious emcee.
"Okay, here we go," June said. "Now smile and enjoy yourself."
When Snake cued her, Naomi stepped to the top of the stairs. All eyes turned to her, and she gulped. The last time she had had this much attention was at her wedding.
In time to Wagner's Bridal Chorus, Naomi regally descended the stairs one at a time.
As one, the audience stood. Their eyes were transfixed, and their mouths were agape at the vision that she was. None was more taken aback by her beauty than her mother. Ruby stood with her hand to her breast and tears in her eyes.
Like a queen being presented to her subjects, Naomi made her way among the crowd with a serene smile on her pretty face. She heard oohs and aahs as she ambled along with her back straight and her head held high.

An Admission of Weakness

"She looks like a princess," Naomi heard someone whisper.
"Just beautiful," someone else said.
"Stunning," her friend Edna Johnson murmured to her husband.
"Like royalty," the mayor said to her husband.
Naomi reached the end of the runway and posed for pictures. Finally, she turned and returned the way she had come. When she reached her mother, she stretched out a gloved hand, and Ruby squeezed it while she dried her eyes.
"My beautiful girl," she smiled.
Naomi had tears of her own when she was finished. This was a momentous occasion in her life. She'd had others of course: her marriage and the birth of her children. But this was something just for her. Tonight she wasn't somebody's mother or wife. She was her own person, and this was something she had done for herself, the first thing in many years.

An Admission of Weakness

"Oh, my sweet baby," Ruby hurried over to her.
"It was okay, Mama?" Naomi said tremulously.
"You were the star of the show," Ruby said. "I wouldn't have missed this for anything in the world. You are so beautiful."
Snake made some final remarks, and then Naomi and the other models returned to the runway and were inundated with congratulations from dozens of well-wishers. Ruby stood by and watched with great pride and affection. It did her heart good to see her daughter get the praise and adoration she

An Admission of Weakness

deserved. Goodness knows, she didn't get any from her worthless husband.

An Admission of Weakness

CHAPTER TWENTY-THREE

The University of Illinois football team won their game that night. Robbie saw Blair at a distance with two young women and an older gentleman who must be his father. One of the women resembled the pictures of his sister Katie, but he didn't know the other. She was a pretty Black girl whom he had seen around campus. Blair kissed her, picked her up, and swung her around the way he used to do with him.
He swallowed with difficulty and made his way closer so he could overhear their conversation.
"Katie, Dad, this is Melissa, my girlfriend," Blair was saying.
"Nice to meet you, Melissa," Carter smiled and shook her hand. "Blair hasn't mentioned you. How long have you been seeing one another?"
"We dated last spring, but we didn't get serious until school started this semester," Melissa said.
What the hell, Robbie frowned? They dated last year? Their relationship was serious? Well, it appeared Blair had decided which sex he preferred, and in only a week's time. It wasn't a surprise to Robbie, but it still hurt him to his core.
"Didn't he play a fantastic game?" Melissa gushed and clung to Blair's arm.

An Admission of Weakness

Blair's family agreed, and while they were talking, Andres and Major ran over to join them. Major playfully tackled Blair, and the two wrestled and laughed until Carter broke them up.

"Come on," he said. "I'm taking everyone to dinner. Major, you and Andres come too."

"Let us go change," Blair gave Melissa a kiss. Robbie turned away as he and Major and Andres passed by on their way to the locker room, laughing and jostling one another good-naturedly. He watched Katie and Dr. Butterfield talk and laugh with Melissa like they'd known her all their lives.

"She's an education major," Andres said. "They started dating last semester. He told his dad they're serious."

"So all that bullshit about him not being attracted to women was a lie," Robbie said bitterly.

"You know Blair."

"I don't know Blair at all," Robbie said. "I guess it's a good thing I turned him loose. Sooner or later he'd have had an affair anyway."

"Probably," Andres said. "But if he's so into women, why did he have to take those pills to get hard when he was with Tiffany and all those other women in the videos? He said Tiffany used to get impatient with him."

An Admission of Weakness

"Please, I don't want to think about him being with women," Robbie flinched.
"You were with –"
"Don't say it!" Robbie held up a hand to stop him. "That never happened."
"Okay, if you say so," Andres grinned.
"It figures he'd go for someone named Melissa," Robbie said. "First Danielle, then Tiffany, now Melissa. Who's next? Brittainy? Amber?"
"I know, right?" Andres chuckled.
"Maybe he'll get Melissa pregnant and have to marry her. He'll end up with ten kids from ten different women before Melissa gets sick of him and kicks him out. He'll live in a one room apartment, a lonely old man who spends the rest of his life trying to pick up women half his age. All just to prove to his dad that he's straight. It would serve him right."
"He loves you, man," Andres said.
"No, he doesn't," Robbie snorted. "He was practically giddy when I gave him two months to date women, like he couldn't wait to fuck every one of them on campus. And then, in a week, he's practically engaged to Melissa."
"When I visited him this summer, all he could talk about was you."
"Then why didn't he come visit me?" Robbie said. "He asked you to come see him, but not me. He probably fucked around with those women while he was at home."

An Admission of Weakness

"They made over him like he was a Greek god. You know he can't resist that."
"Then when he got back to school, the first thing he did was put the moves on Major."
"He explained that."
"You weren't there," Robbie said. "He wanted Major, and he didn't care if I was there or not. By the way, when did they get to be such good friends?"
"During practice, I guess," Andres shrugged. "They live across the hall from each other now, don't forget."
"Maybe that wasn't such a good idea," Robbie said. "I've barely seen Major since then."
"You aren't jealous of Major, are you?"
"Of course not. Major would never get involved with him knowing what's going on with us."
"Look, don't worry about Melissa or Major. I know my man Blair; he's ninety-nine percent gay, and he loves you. All of this is because he's gullible and vain, and he's still trying to get daddy Carter's approval. It's what he's always done, and he doesn't know how to break the habit."
"Tell me about his dad," Robbie said.
"He's strong, obstinate, very opinionated, probably everything Blair told you he was. He loves his kids, but it's like he doesn't understand that they have lives of their own.

An Admission of Weakness

He's a nice guy, don't get me wrong, but I wouldn't want him as a dad."
"Great," Robbie sighed. "The man I love is a porn star, dating a girl named Melissa, and has daddy issues. Boy, I can really pick 'em, can't I?"

Carter and Katie dropped Melissa at her building and Andres at the athletic department. Lastly, they let Blair and Major out at their dorm. After saying good night, he and Katie headed back to their hotel.
"Why didn't Melissa stay over?" Major asked when they reached their rooms.
"I wasn't in the mood tonight, not with my dad and Katie here," Blair said.
"I don't understand why you're going out with her when you're supposed to be in love with Robbie."
"I'm trying to figure out whether I'm gay or straight or bi," Blair said.
"That doesn't mean you have to go out with Melissa. Don't you know this is hurting Robbie?"
"I'm doing this because of Robbie," Blair said. "He's the one who told me to date women."
"But you didn't have to take him up on that. I just don't see how you can fuck her while you're in love with Robbie."
"It's complicated. You want something to drink?"

An Admission of Weakness

"Sure," Major said.

The two settled on Blair's bed with a couple of beers while they talked about the game.

"What's it like to score the winning touchdown?" Major asked.

"Pretty fucking fantastic," Blair grinned. "But you should be proud; you played a great game. Want another beer?"

The two laughed and talked and wrestled playfully while they consumed beer after beer.

"Man, I gotta get some sleep," Major said finally at two o'clock in the morning. "I'm beat."

"Okay," Blair stood up and staggered a bit. "Good night, bro."

"Good night," Major stood up and stretched. Without thinking, Blair reached up and kissed him.

"You like the way I kiss?" he asked drunkenly.

"Sure," Major grinned. "You're a great kisser."

"Tiff and all those other girls said I was a lousy kisser," Blair said sourly.

"Maybe because you want to be kissing Robbie instead of them," Major said. "I'd kiss Robbie if he'd let me."

"Yeah, but Robbie's not here," Blair said sadly. "He doesn't want me anymore."

"He doesn't want me either."

"All I got is Melissa, and I don't want her," Blair eyed Major's lips dazedly. "If Robbie

An Admission of Weakness

doesn't want us, maybe we should kiss each other."
"Okay," Major shrugged.
The two men kissed feverishly for several minutes, but Major finally pushed him away. "Hey, man, we can't do this."
"I know," Blair nodded. He grew tearful. "I miss Robbie. I love him, you know."
"I love him too," Major said. "If he wasn't in love with you, I'd ask him to marry me."
"You wanna marry Robbie? So do I," Blair said with slurred speech. "You think he loves me?"
"Yeah, he loves you, but he's too good for you."
"Why do you say that?"
"Because you could be with him right now, but instead you're fuckin' a girl you say you don't want," Major said. "That's fucked up, bro."
"Wait, did you say you wanna marry Robbie?" Blair said. "Are you in love with him too?"
"It doesn't matter. He only likes me as a friend," Major reeled a bit. "You're the one he loves even though you treat him like shit. You say you love him, but you don't. If you did, you wouldn't be out there fucking everyone else.
"I don't think you know what love is. You love it when everyone kisses your ass because you're handsome and you play football. You act all tough like you're hot stuff. You pretend to be confused so you can fuck around, and he still loves you. That fuckin' sucks, man."

An Admission of Weakness

"I'm not pretending," Blair frowned. "Maybe I'm only gay because Robbie has me all messed up."

"Robbie isn't messing you up; your dad is," Major said. "Robbie's trying to make you wake up to the fact that you're a big, screaming, sissy queen. You know it's true, so why are you putting him through this bullshit?" He struggled to keep his eyes open. "I'll tell you why. It's all ego with you. You like it when dudes and pretty girls want you, and when they do, you don't care about anything else. You need to grow the fuck up, bro."

He stumbled across the hall and fumbled out of his clothes. Just as he turned out the light, Blair appeared in the doorway.

"Hey," he said huskily.

"Hey," Major replied.

"I love Robbie," Blair started crying.

"Me too," Major said sadly.

"I don't wanna be alone."

Major pulled back the blanket, and Blair climbed in beside him. He wept into Major's chest while the bigger man held him close. He had tears in his own eyes.

Dammit, it was so unfair that Robbie saw him only as a friend. He would make a much better partner than Blair; he would treat him like a king and make sure he knew how much he loved him every single day.

An Admission of Weakness

Blair finally dried his eyes and looked into Major's eyes. It took only a moment for them to strip off their underwear, and they made love until dawn. The bed proved too small, so they moved onto the floor.
"Man, I wanna fuck you," Major asked him.
"I'm usually a top," Blair said.
"Not tonight you're not," Major said. "It's not every day a guy gets to fuck his hero."
"I'm still your hero?" Blair said.
Major answered by taking Blair's thick, pendulous manhood into his mouth and deep-throating it all the way to the base.
"Holy fuck!" Blair cried.
Blair was eager to take Major's dick. It had been far too long since he'd been with a man. Major fucked him for half an hour, and then they sixty-nined for a while. Major was in heaven as he lay on his stomach while Blair rimmed and then fucked him. God, that felt amazing. Eventually, he fucked Blair again until his orgasm consumed him. he lay on his back while Blair fucked his mouth hard and fast until he climaxed mightily in Major's eager mouth.
After collapsing on top of him, he and Major fell asleep in each other's arms.

Robbie hesitated as he neared his former room. He glanced cautiously at Blair's door to make sure it was closed before tiptoeing closer. He eased his door open silently and stopped in shock at the scene before him. Major was lying naked on the floor, and Blair was in his arms with his legs intertwined with Major's.

As he watched, Blair gave Major an affectionate kiss. Major grinned and kissed him passionately in return. He rolled on top of Blair and pulled his legs up so that he could fuck him.

Robbie coughed, and Major noticed him at last. He instantly pulled out of Blair's ass.

"Oh shit!" he cried.

"Don't stop," Blair frowned. "Keep going, man."

Major snatched up the cum-stiffened towel from earlier and placed it over his groin.

"Don't stop on my account," Robbie said in a steely voice. "This is obviously what you guys wanted, so keep going. So now I understand why I never see you anymore, Major. What's it like to fuck a superhero? Did you enjoy it?"

"I-I –" Major sputtered.

"You know, don't answer that," Robbie said coldly. "Blair, did you tell him you like to have your nipples sucked and your armpits licked? Does Melissa know you're still sleeping with guys? Is Major the only one, or are there others?"

"Robbie –" Blair began.

An Admission of Weakness

"Don't speak to me!" Robbie glared at him. "We are so done, asshole. I hope the two of you fuck yourselves into oblivion!"
With that, he stormed from the room.

"We were drunk," Blair said.
"We still knew what we were doing," Major said.
"I was missing him so bad," Blair said. He covered his face with his hands. "God, he'll never forgive me for this. I might as well marry Melissa and get it over with. At least Dad will be happy."
"Oh shut up about Melissa and your stupid dad!" Major shouted angrily. "We have to figure out how to explain this to Robbie so he'll forgive us."
"He's never going to forgive us," Blair moaned.
"He has to," Major said. "Fuck, how could I do something so stupid?"
"I know how," Blair said. "We both love Robbie, we can't have Robbie, so we fucked each other."
"But you can have Robbie," Major said. "You could have been with him this whole time if you weren't such a fucked up piece of shit. Then none of this would have happened."
"I'm only doing what Robbie said to do," Blair said.

An Admission of Weakness

"So you're blaming Robbie? All he was trying to do was keep from having you break his heart again. You should try taking responsibility for once."

"Hey, no one forced you to shove your dick up my ass," Blair snapped.

"You only think about yourself. You never think about him," Major retorted. "And now we've both hurt him. Not just hurt him, but devastated him. Did you see the look on his face? He was brokenhearted."

"Maybe it's for the best," Blair said. "All I do is hurt him; he'll be better off without me."

"Quit feeling sorry for yourself, shithead!" Major said impatiently.

"I'm not. I just wish I'd never made that stupid comment about not being sure I'm gay."

"So now all of a sudden you're gay?" Major said. "Why couldn't you have admitted that a week ago?"

"I don't know if I'm gay or not," Blair said. "I thought I had it figured out after the whole thing with Tiff, but then I somehow got all confused again. If I was really gay, wouldn't I know it?"

"You should," Major said.

"All I know is that I always screw everything up between me and Robbie."

"That's your own fault. If he leaves you for good, you have nobody to blame but yourself."

"That's not fair," Blair frowned.

An Admission of Weakness

"Then whose fault is it? You think it's Robbie's fault. My fault? Andres' fault? Your dad's fault?"
"No," Blair said sullenly.
"That's right, because it's your fault! Why the fuck are you listening to your old man anyway? He's a homophobic prick for Christ's sake. And you're taking what he says about gay people like it's the Gospel According to Carter. He's always going to think the worst of gay people no matter what. If you want to be straight so bad to please your dad, go fuck Melissa and leave the rest of us alone."
"I don't want Melissa. I want Robbie."
"Then what the hell are you doing with Melissa?" Major said with exasperation.
"I don't know," Blair said helplessly.
"You'd better figure it out, or you're going to lose him for good," Major said.

"Well, that's that," Robbie dried his eyes. "I can't forgive this one no matter how much I love him."
"You'll forgive him because that's who you awe," Rhett said. "But you can't take him back anymore. He's a scwew up, and he'll always be a scwew up."
"I know," Robbie sighed. "I've learned my lesson."
"I hope so, because I can't stand seeing you hurt," Rhett said.

An Admission of Weakness

Robbie packed up his things in a clothes basket and returned to his own dorm room. Major looked up when he opened the door.
"Get out," Robbie barked at him.
"Robbie, I'm so –"
"Nope, don't want to hear it," Robbie shook his head firmly. "Get out. Now."
"Fine, I'll go," Major said.
He began to gather his things while Robbie moved closer to the window. Major unexpectedly closed the door and leaned his considerable weight against it.
"You don't want to hear it, but I need to say it."
"Fine. Talk all you want, but I'm not going to listen," Robbie donned his noise-canceling headphones.
Major wrestled them away from him and held them behind his back. Robbie scowled and folded his arms.
"You know, maybe I'll do the talking," Robbie said angrily. "I can't believe, I just cannot fathom how you could do something like this to me. Do you have any idea or even care how much this hurt? My best friend and my boyfriend fucking behind my back? A true friend would never do something like that. I trusted you and loved you, and this is how you repaid me."
"That right there," Major said sharply. "That's the problem that led to last night."

An Admission of Weakness

"No, what led to last night was you wanted to be with my boyfriend, so you manipulated the situation so you could be across the hall from him day and night."

"You asked me to change rooms, remember?" Major said. "That wasn't my idea."

"I asked to stay with you; you're the one who wanted to change rooms!"

"Oh right," Major said.

"It doesn't matter. You wanted Blair, and now you have him. I hope you'll be happy together. Just watch out for when he gets tired of your dick and wants a pussy instead."

"I don't have Blair," Major said. "I don't have anyone."

"Why? Did he already dump you for Melissa? Wow, that was fast, even for him."

"He didn't dump me because I was never his. You're the one he loves. You're the one we both love."

"I don't need friends with your kind of love," Robbie said bitterly.

"It's my kind of love that led to this whole mess," Major said. "If you'll just shut up and listen, I'll tell you."

"You should have just stabbed me through the heart with a knife," Robbie said theatrically. "That would have hurt less."

His eyes filled with tears.

"You made me lose my best friend *and* my boyfriend," he said. "Goddammit!"

An Admission of Weakness

He started throwing items from his clothes basket until he couldn't see anything through his tears. Major sat down beside him and gathered him into his arms.

"Get off me, you big stupid bastard!" Robbie fought against him.

"I'm not letting you go, so just sit there and take it," Major said.

Robbie stopped fighting against him. Instead, he clung to him and cried.

"How could you do this to me?"

"I'm so sorry," Major said. "Just let me explain something to you, and maybe you'll understand."

"I'll never understand how someone could hurt another person like this. I would never do this to you."

Robbie finally forced Major away from him. Major stepped back in front of the door, just in case Robbie tried to make a run for it.

"What I did last night was the worst thing I've ever done in my life, and I will regret it for as long as I live."

"Good," Robbie said coldly.

"You said you love me –"

"Loved, not love," Robbie corrected him.

"Fine. Loved. And I appreciated that. I loved you too."

"No, you didn't."

"Yes, I did, but the way I loved you wasn't the same way you loved me," Major said.

An Admission of Weakness

Robbie looked at him curiously.
"I'm in love with you, Robbie," Major stared down at the floor. "You only see me as a friend, the guy you talk to about Blair, the one who gives you piggyback rides, the one you help with his homework. We go out to eat together, we watch movies, and the whole time it's killing me inside that I can't tell you how I really feel.
"I'm not in love with Blair. I'm in love with you. I want to be your boyfriend and make love to you. I want you to love me the way you love Blair.
"And that's why last night happened. I went out to dinner with Blair and his family. They treated me so nice, like I was a decent human being. That doesn't happen very often to me.
"Blair and I were just coming off the win, and we were high from that. We drank a bunch of beer in his room, and then I said good night. I went to my room – your room – and turned out the light, and then he came over, crying and saying he missed you. I let him get in bed with me, and that's when stuff happened. We were drunk and stupid, and I know that's no excuse, but I'm sorry. I never meant to hurt you."
"Were you drunk this morning when you were fucking him?"
"No," Major said honestly.
"So what else did you do? Did you let him fuck you? Did you rim him?"

An Admission of Weakness

"We –"
"Stop! I don't want to hear about it," Robbie cringed with pain.
"Look, I'm not perfect. I got issues and so does Blair. You know that. We screwed up big time, but that doesn't mean we don't both love you."
"I don't believe you," Robbie said flatly.
"I know," Major said. "I got no excuse, and I don't expect you to forgive me. I wish more than anything that we could still be friends, even if you don't love me the way I want."
Robbie merely stared down at the floor and crossed his arms. When he didn't say anything, Major finished gathering up his things and left the room.

An Admission of Weakness

CHAPTER TWENTY-FOUR

"Will you take these shoulder pads back to Major for me?" Robbie asked.
"Why don't you take them?" Andres said.
It had been two weeks since Robbie found Major and Blair in each other's arms. Since then, Robbie had seen no sign of either of them, much to his relief. They seemed to be making a conscious effort to avoid him. He figured that Blair was more than likely living with either Major or Melissa now.
"Before I'd do that, I'd throw them in the garbage first," Robbie snorted.
"No, you wouldn't," Andres grinned.
"You think this is funny?" Robbie scowled.
"No, I think it's sad," Andres sobered.
"Then talk to your friends," Robbie said. "They knew what they were doing."
"I'm talking about what you're doing," Andres said.
"Me?" Robbie said indignantly. "I haven't done anything to anyone. Haven't you been paying attention to what those assholes did to me?"
"They didn't do it to you," Andres said. "They did it because of you."
"If you're going to sit there and defend them, you can leave," Robbie pointed at his dorm room door.
"I'm not excusing them, especially Blair. But both of them are brokenhearted over you. They

An Admission of Weakness

both love you for some reason. Maybe it's the blue eyes. I don't know."

"Right," Robbie said sarcastically. "My friend and boyfriend are so in love with me that they fell in bed together and fucked their brains out."

"That's right," Andres said calmly.

"You believe that idiotic story of Major's? You really are a sucker."

"You love them both, and you know it," Andres said. "You'd do anything for either of them."

"Not anymore."

"Blondie, I hate to tell you this, but you are a nice guy. You forgive people, and you give them second chances. In the case of Blair, third and fourth and fifth chances."

"I can't forgive this."

"Yes, you can."

"If I do, then I'm nothing more than a doormat, and they'll just keep wiping their feet on me over and over again."

"Then be a doormat for a while. Major would never hurt you on purpose," Andres said. "He's one of the nicest people on the planet. And so are you. As for Blair, he has a lot of growing up to do, but even as imperfect as he is, you love him with all your heart."

"The heart that he keeps breaking."

"Do what you want with Blair. But go see Major. He's really suffering, man."

An Admission of Weakness

"So am I."
"He won't leave his room. He won't go to class or to practice. He's gonna lose his football scholarship if he doesn't show up to the next practice. Is that what you want?"
"Of course not," Robbie said.
"See, you still love him," Andres grinned. "So go talk to him and settle this thing."

Robbie walked down the hall of Major's dorm. He thought about opening Major's door and tossing the shoulder pads inside. Perhaps that's what he would do. No sense risking seeing him and Blair fucking again.
Three tall, lanky men approached him from the opposite direction.
"Hey, faggot," one of them sneered. "You here to see your boyfriend?"
They laughed together.
"Why is that funny?" Robbie frowned. "I'm here to return these to Major."
One of them snatched the shoulder pads away and held them aloft.
"Why don't you guys grow up?" Robbie rolled his eyes.
The man in the middle shoved him, and Robbie pushed back. He used the same technique that he had used on Blair and toppled the guy to the floor.
"You look a lot shorter laying down," Robbie smirked.

An Admission of Weakness

Before he could react, the other two were on him. He tried to defend himself, but they were ruthless with their fists and feet. Finally, he was forced to curl into a fetal position to protect himself while they kicked him repeatedly, shouting homophobic epithets all the while. The barrage abruptly stopped, and Robbie looked up to see Major pick each man up and literally throw them down the hall. They got up and challenged him but backed down when he revealed his true size.

"I was raised in the ghetto," Major said in his toughest voice. "I know how to fight little ol' white boys like you. I'll snap the three of you like twigs.

"I'm also gonna report the three of you for hate crimes," he went on. "You can kiss your scholarships goodbye."

"We were just messin' around," one man said. Major lunged at them, and they took off running as fast as they could while he grinned. Finally, he knelt beside Robbie.

"You weren't raised in the ghetto," Robbie grimaced.

"'Course not," Major chuckled. "But racists pigs like that would think so just because I'm Black."

"Ow!" Robbie winced and held his ribcage.

"Come on," Major said. "I'm taking you to the Infirmary."

An Admission of Weakness

Other people walked up and down the hall and eyed the two of them curiously.
"I'm fine," Robbie said. "Just get me out of this hallway."

"You're gonna have a black eye," Major said. He raised Robbie's shirt. "And you're bruising all over. I think you should see a doctor."
"I don't care what you think," Robbie suddenly remembered that he was angry with Major.
"I just saved your life," Major reminded him.
"I didn't ask you to," Robbie said sullenly.
"In that case, you want me to call those guys back and let them finish what they started?"
"Just shut up," Robbie said. "Why aren't you going to football practice?"
"Why do you care?"
"I don't. But Andres said you're going to lose your scholarship if you miss one more practice."
"I don't care," Major shrugged. "I'm ready to get the fuck outa here and go back home."
"You don't have a home to go back to," Robbie said.
"I'm gonna stay with a friend until I can find a job," Major said indifferently. "The Wal-Mart is hiring."
"You want to be a football coach," Robbie said. "You have to finish your degree."
"I'll take night classes," Major said.

An Admission of Weakness

"No," Robbie said firmly. "You're going to stay here and finish your degree. I'll stay out of your way. You never have to see me again."

"You think that's what I want? Man, you don't know me at all."

"What do you want?"

"I want to go back to how it was before. I want us to be friends again. I can't stand having you hate me."

"I don't hate you," Robbie said hesitantly.

"Why not? You have every right to after what I did."

"You didn't do it alone," Robbie said. "He was there with you. He's the one who instigated it."

"That's not true. I'm the one who invited him into my bed. I figured if I couldn't have you, being with him was the next best thing."

"Is that how he felt too?" Robbie frowned.

"He was crying over you because he loves you. He's only confused because of his stupid dad."

"I know why he's doing it," Robbie said dryly. "But he's a grown man who needs to tell his father to fuck off."

"I told him that, and so did Andres," Major said. "We said you're the best thing that could happen to him, and he was a fool to let you go."

"You told him that?"

"What choice did I have?" Major shrugged.

"You had a choice," Robbie stood up and gingerly hugged the big man. "Ow, I hurt all over."

An Admission of Weakness

Major put his arms around him and held him.
"I love you, you big, stupid bastard," Robbie said.
"Does that mean we can be friends again?"
"Yes, although I should beat you up for what you did," Robbie said.
"Fine," Major stood back and spread his legs. "Kick me in the balls. I deserve it."
"I'm not going to kick you in the balls," Robbie grinned.
"Go ahead. Kick me as hard as you want. I won't resist, I promise."
"This is what I want," Robbie held him close. "I've missed you."

"So how's Blair?" Robbie asked. "I haven't seen him for two weeks."
"He's staying with Melissa," Major said. "He's avoiding you."
"That's good," Robbie said. "I don't want to see him either."
"He wants to see you. He's just afraid to."
"He should be," Robbie said.
"He knows how all the shit he's pulled has hurt you, and he thinks you're better off with someone else," Major explained.
"He's right. I'm not taking him back this time," Robbie said. "Since all that matters to him is pleasing his dad, he should marry Melissa and have a family."
"That's not all that matters to him," Major said.

An Admission of Weakness

"You're right. I forgot to mention his dick and his ego," Robbie said dryly.
"I meant you, stupid," Major said.

Naomi picked up the newspaper from the front steps and leafed through it eagerly. Sure enough, there was the full color insert with the pictures from the bridal show. She tucked it under her arm and set the paper on her husband's desk.
"Is it here?" her mother looked up from her crossword puzzle.
"It's here," Naomi nodded excitedly.
The two of them sat down on Ruby's bed and scanned through the glossy pages.
"How beautiful," Naomi said.
She told her mother all the details about working on each dress and even helping design some aspects of them.
They got to the centerfold and turned it sideways. There, in high-resolution color, was a photograph of Naomi. She was standing in a half turn with a bright smile and shining eyes.
"You look absolutely radiant," Ruby breathed. "You were the star of the show."
"I felt like a queen," Naomi admitted.
"When are you going to show it to Carter?"
"I'm not," Naomi said. "He'd only disapprove."
"Why on earth did you marry him in the first place?"

An Admission of Weakness

"I loved him, Mama. I still do."
"To each their own, I guess," Ruby wrinkled her nose.
"Mama," her daughter frowned reprovingly. "Are you at least going to show this to your children?"
"No, and neither are you," Naomi said. "This is just for me."
"I know," her mother squeezed her hand. "But the family is going to find out eventually."
"Until then, it's something that's just mine."

"I had several people tell me today they saw your picture in the newspaper," Carter said that evening at the dinner table. "What were they talking about?"
"I have no idea," Naomi said. "Justin, eat your salad."
"They said to tell you congratulations," Carter added. "What have you done that deserves congratulations?"
"She's put up with you for thirty years," Ruby said. "She deserves the Nobel Peace Prize for that."
"Good one, Grandma," Justin chuckled.
He sobered at the look on his father's face.
"That's enough from you," Carter scowled.
"Wow, you talked to me," Justin said. "I can't believe it."
"Leave my table if you can't speak to me with more respect," Carter said.

An Admission of Weakness

"I think you should leave the table if you can't speak to me with more respect," Justin said boldly.
"I've lost my appetite anyway," Carter frowned. "I have work to do."
He wiped his mouth with the linen napkin and left the room.

Blair lay on the narrow bed with Melissa snuggled up beside him. Sex between them had failed miserably. Even focusing on Robbie hadn't done it for him this time. He went through the motions of going down on her, sucking her nipples, and fucking her in several different positions, but no matter how hard he tried, he couldn't bring either of them to an orgasm.
He explained it away by telling Melissa that he was too stressed, what with football and classes and ending his friendship with Robbie. Thankfully, she said she understood. That didn't stop her from trying to entice him every night, however.
"Isn't Robbie Lee that gay cheerleader?" she frowned after he rolled off of her and onto his back. "I'm surprised you'd be friends with someone like that."
"Why?" he panted.
"You're so macho," she said. "Men like you usually don't like gay guys."

An Admission of Weakness

"I don't like gay guys," Blair said. "But Robbie's okay."

"I was taught that being gay is a sin," she said. "I don't like the idea of two men together."

"Me neither," Blair said. "My dad says it's a choice."

"Of course it is," she said. "What I don't understand is why anyone would choose to be gay? Don't they know how hard their lives are going to be?"

"I guess it's because they're too weak to do what's right."

"I suppose," she agreed as she took his manhood into her mouth.

Blair's father was quite taken with Melissa. Of course, why wouldn't he be? She was sweet and pretty, and she came from a good family. Ever since Carter met her, he had called Blair every other day to see how the relationship was going. Blair surmised that he had given up on the idea of Danielle as a daughter-in-law, and he probably phoned more often because he wasn't currently speaking to his younger son. Blair had been staying with Melissa ever since he slept with Major. He couldn't bear to run in to Robbie, not because he was afraid to face him, but because he knew a confrontation would do neither him nor Robbie any good. Now he was entangled in this relationship with Melissa that he didn't want. She was obviously

An Admission of Weakness

falling for him, and he feared that he was going to end up proposing to her just to make her and his father happy.

What was wrong with him that he kept letting his father run his life? Was his father correct about the whole gay thing? He was a brilliant man, and he wouldn't tell his sons something that wasn't true.

In all of his life, he had never stood up to his dad, even when he disagreed with him, which was most of the time. He'd become so accustomed to kowtowing to the man that it was second nature to him now. Come to think of it, it was likely his poor self-esteem that was the root of his issues. His father expected him to marry a woman, and that was probably why he kept sabotaging a relationship with the most wonderful guy in the world.

If he couldn't allow himself to be with Robbie, maybe he was better off with a woman. He could certainly do worse than Melissa.

The cheerleaders threw a dance in October for themselves and the football team as a way for new members to become acquainted. It was held in a modest ballroom on campus. The women wore evening gowns or party dresses, whereas the men dressed in suits or at least jackets and ties.

Robbie introduced Major to a friend of his, a pleasant young man from South Africa named

An Admission of Weakness

Simon. Simon was only too eager to go out with Major and immediately agreed to be his date. It was entertaining to watch Major become all tongue-tied around Simon, while Simon's dark face lit up with pleasure whenever Major was present.

Meanwhile, he invited an acquaintance from one of his business classes to the dance, an older student named Elliot.

"Do you want the four of us to go together?" Robbie asked Major.

"Um, I would, but Blair asked me and Simon to go with them," Major frowned uncomfortably.

"Oh," Robbie nodded. "I didn't know you and Blair were still speaking."

"We never stopped," Major shrugged. "It's all good."

"Okay, I guess I'll see if Andres wants to go with us."

"Actually, Andres and his girlfriend are going with us too," Major said.

"Oh. Then I guess it will be just Elliot and me."

"I can't believe Simon agreed to go with me," Major grinned.

"Are you kidding?" Robbie chuckled. "When I told him I was going to introduce the two of you, he practically did a cartwheel right there on the spot."

"I'd have been glad to go with you, you know," Major said.

An Admission of Weakness

"It's time you met some new people," Robbie said. "I'm yesterday's news."
"You'll always be today's news to me," Major pulled him into a bone-crushing embrace.

The dance was in full swing when Robbie and Elliot arrived. They donned their name tags and strolled over to the refreshment table. Robbie glanced around and waved and smiled at Coach Wilkensen and his wife. He knew most everyone here with a few exceptions.
Robbie was wearing the only nice clothes he owned: a frayed silk tie, a hand-me-down brown jacket, an age-yellowed white shirt, a dated pair of pleated khaki slacks, and his one pair of good shoes. He didn't look anywhere nearly as sharp as this crowd, but he was at least presentable.
Elliot was nattily dressed in a new suit and stylish shoes, and his auburn hair was fashionably cut and arranged just so. He was an English major with a Business Minor, tall and slender, nice but pretentious.
"Is this the best you have to wear?" he frowned when Robbie stopped at his door.
"It's this or my cheerleading outfit," Robbie joked. "I figured I should dress up."
"Maybe no one will notice," Elliot shrugged.
Robbie saw Major and Simon sitting at a table across the room. Major was wearing a black suit, white shirt, and a dark gray tie. Jeez, he

was kinda hot all dressed up, Robbie thought. Simon looked totally adorable as always. He was wearing beige slacks with a navy satin vest and tie. Tonight, he wore a bright smile.

"There's Major," Robbie pointed. "Let's go talk to them."

They made their way across the room. Andres and his date were sitting with the pair.

"Hey, guys," Robbie grinned. "You all look amazing."

"So do you, bro," Major stood up and hugged him.

"This is Elliot," Robbie said. "Elliot, this is Major and Simon. This is Andres and…"

"Tiffany," Andres said with a straight face. Robbie's eyes widened, and Andres laughed. "I'm just joking, man. This is Ebony."

"Hi," Elliot smiled.

"I love your name," Robbie shook her hand. She was tall and svelte with a dazzling smile. Her formfitting gown was gold and navy and sparkly. "Oh my god, you are gorgeous. I'd almost consider switching teams for you."

"Thanks," she chuckled. "That's high praise coming from a gay man."

Blair and Melissa walked up and sat down at the table with plates laden with food. He purposely avoided looking at Robbie. Everyone sat down except for Robbie and Elliot.

An Admission of Weakness

Robbie's heart broke a little more when he saw Blair. He looked so handsome in a tailored suit that Tiffany had bought him.

"Hi, Blair," he tried to sound cordial. "You're looking well."

"Oh my god, you're Blair Butterfield!" Elliot exclaimed. "You made two touchdowns in the first game of the season."

"Uh, yeah, that's me," Blair frowned uncomfortably.

"I scored two touchdowns too," Andres said wryly.

"I'm Elliot," Elliot ignored Andres and reached across the table to shake Blair's hand. "I'm a huge fan of yours. On the field and off."

Oh god, another fan of his porn videos, Blair sighed. Andres and Major nodded knowingly at each other.

"In fact, the whole reason I agreed to come with Robbie tonight is because of your movies."

"Hi, I'm Melissa," Melissa said, annoyed that no one was going to introduce her. "I'm Blair's fiancée."

"His what?" Robbie said.

That did it, he thought. His heart was officially broken beyond repair.

"His fi-an-cée," Melissa repeated the word slowly. "It means we're engaged."

An Admission of Weakness

"Why am I not surprised?" Robbie glared at Blair. "So I guess you're not confused anymore, are you?"
"Robbie, don't," Blair frowned.
"Uh, Robbie, why don't we get some punch?" Major said.
"No thanks," Robbie moved around the table to talk to Melissa. "I want to hear all about how you and Blair became engaged."
"Oh, you're Robbie?" Melissa frowned. "I didn't know you were friends with Major too. I'm surprised he didn't tell you about the wedding. He and Andres are going to be the best men."
"Are they?" Robbie gritted his teeth. "And yet neither of them thought to tell me. Well, I'll just have to scold them later, won't I?"
"I was going to tell you…" Major began.
"But you didn't," Robbie finished. "I wonder why?"
"So what was it like being in those videos?" Elliot pulled up a chair inches from Blair.
"You didn't tell me you were in movies, silly," Melissa smacked Blair's arm lightly.
"I'll bet there are lots of things he hasn't told you," Robbie said dryly. "If you ever want to see the ones he and I were in together, I'll be glad to show you."
"No!" Blair said sharply.
"Why not?" Robbie said innocently.
"I think she'd enjoy it," Andres said.

An Admission of Weakness

"No, she wouldn't!" Blair snapped.
"Just Google Dick Strong," Elliot told Melissa.
"Who's Dick Strong?" she frowned.
"They're teasing you," Blair said. "Just forget it."
"So how did you two crazy kids get engaged?" Robbie asked. "I'm just dying to hear the whole story. Don't leave anything out."
"Robbie..." Blair began.
"Be quiet, Melissa's talking," Robbie looked daggers at him. "Honey, your makeup is flawless; I can barely tell that you're really a man."
"She's not a man, and you know it," Blair frowned while Andres and Ebony choked back a laugh.
"Shhh, everyone," Robbie said curtly. "I want to hear this story."
"It was so cute," Melissa said. "His parents were visiting for the last home game, and Carter – who's just a doll by the way – took us all out to dinner afterwards. He made a toast to Blair and me and then handed him Grandmother Butterfield's wedding ring. See?" She held out her left hand to show a lovely one carat marquise shaped diamond solitaire. "He said to Blair, don't you have a question to ask Melissa, and Blair pretended to be all embarrassed and confused, and then he got down on one knee at the table – after his father told him what to do – and he asked me to marry

An Admission of Weakness

him. Of course I said yes. He had the same look in his eye then as he does right now."
"Yeah, it was a magical moment," Andres said dryly.
"You are the luckiest woman on the planet!" Elliot breathed. "I'd marry him in a heartbeat if he'd ask me."
"Oh, Blair isn't gay," she said.
"No, he's definitely not," Robbie agreed.
"Robbie, do you want to dance?" Major asked.
"No thanks," Robbie said. "No, of course Blair's not gay. He's a man's man, all full of testosterone and road rage like any decent American man. Does he call you his little woman and smash beer cans on his forehead?"
"Oh, I see," Melissa frowned. "You're jealous, aren't you? Are you in love with him too?"
"Are you kidding?" Robbie chuckled. "I can barely stand the sight of him. Trust me, the only thing I think of Blair is what a son of a –"
"Robbie!" Major said loudly. "Come on."
He grasped his wrist and hauled him away from the table.
"Don't make a scene," Major said.
"You and Andres were there when he proposed, and you agreed to be his best men," Robbie wrenched his arm away furiously. "But you forgot to tell me, is that it?"
"We didn't see what good could come of it," Major said.

An Admission of Weakness

"Tell me, Major, how many times have you slept with Blair since that first time?"
"Robbie, it wasn't like that," Major said awkwardly. "We were just horny."
"Oh my fucking god," Robbie turned to go. "I'm so out of here."
"You can't leave your date," Major stopped him.
"He'll never notice I'm gone," Robbie said bitterly. "Neither will Blair because he's got another worshiper to welcome to the flock."
"You still can't go off and leave Elliot here," Major said firmly. "Come on, let's dance."
"Go dance with Simon," Robbie waved him away. "I'll be fine. I promise I won't leave, and I won't make a scene."
Major and Simon stepped out onto the dance floor, and Robbie sat down reluctantly next to Elliot, who was engrossed in a flirtatious conversation with Blair. He sipped on his margarita and glared at Andres before turning to stare out at the dance floor.
"I don't mean to be all judgy or anything," Melissa pulled her chair closer. "But don't you realize it's a sin to have sex with another man?"
"It is?" Robbie looked astonished and crossed his eyes at Blair. "Since when?"
"Since Bible times," she said. "You should really think about dating a woman."
"Oh, like Blair did," Robbie said sarcastically.

An Admission of Weakness

"Blair's always dated women," she said. "He doesn't approve of gay people either."
"Now that surprises me," he said. "I thought he was all about his gay friends."
"He doesn't have gay friends because he doesn't like gay people," Melissa said. "No offense."
"How could that possibly offend me?" he said.
"You would like being with a woman," she said and then giggled. "Blair's an incredible lover."
"I hear he's especially good at anal," he said dryly.
"Robbie," Andres said warningly.
"So you'll think about dating a woman?" Melissa said.
"You know, you've convinced me," he said. He stood up with his shoulders back and his head held high. His voice grew louder and louder. "From now on, it's only women for me. No more men. I'm tired of them anyway. All they do is lie and cheat." He looked pointedly at Blair and Andres as people around them turned to frown. "They're all weak and spineless and stupid.
"Really stupid," he yelled. "I mean, some of the stories I could tell you about the stupid men I've slept with. There was this one in particular —"
"We don't need to hear your disgusting stories," Blair scowled. "Just sit down and stop talking."

An Admission of Weakness

"Sit down, Robbie," Andres frowned.

"Why do you want me to stop talking, Blair?" Robbie said. "Are you afraid I might tell Melissa some of your secrets?"

"Just sit down and shut up," Blair rolled his eyes.

"Did you just roll your eyes at me?" Robbie demanded angrily.

"Come on, Melissa," Blair stood up. "Let's dance."

"I'm dancing with Melissa," Robbie took her hand and dragged her to the dance floor.

An Admission of Weakness

CHAPTER TWENTY-FIVE

"This isn't exactly what I meant when I said you should be with a woman," Melissa said. "Although I'm gratified to see you take such an initiative. You see, I'm not available; I'm engaged to Blair. I love him."
"I'm sure you do," Robbie said. "I thought I did too."
"See, you're confused again," she said. "He's not gay."
"I guess that *is* where I'm confused," he nodded thoughtfully. "Because I thought all those times we slept togeth–"
"I'm cutting in," Blair pulled him away gruffly.
"I thought you'd never ask," Robbie tried to take him in his arms.
"Robbie, I asked you to drop this," Blair glared at him. "Please, just stop this."
"Come on and dance," Robbie insisted.
This time, Blair shoved him, and Robbie careened into another couple.
"Hey, look out, man," the man scowled.
Robbie ignored him and rushed at Blair. The two sparred until Blair finally dealt him a right cross that sent him reeling.
"Stay the fuck away from me!" he shouted.
"You sonofabitch!" Andres whirled him around.

An Admission of Weakness

"You fucking bastard," Robbie seethed and wiped the blood from his lip. "Pretending you aren't gay when everyone here knows –"
With a roar, Blair tackled him and knocked him to the floor, where he straddled him and began hitting him. Major and Andres swiftly intervened and hauled him off, but not before he got a few heavy punches in. Simon rushed to Robbie's aid and helped him sit up. His clothes were torn and his lip swollen. His eye was already starting to bruise, and his nose was bleeding.
"What the fuck's the matter with you?" Coach Wilkensen jabbed a finger in Blair's chest. "I ought to kick you out of school right now!"
"And I ought to beat the shit outa you," Andres added.
"This was a fucking hate crime, asshole," Major said angrily.
"Kick his ass out of school, Coach," Robbie got to his feet. "See if his precious beard will still want to marry him then."
Blair tried to rush him again, but Andres held him back.
"She's not my beard," Blair addressed the crowd. "Melissa is the woman I love, and we're getting married."
There was a smattering of uncertain applause as a burly security officer arrived and escorted Robbie roughly from the dance floor.

An Admission of Weakness

"Get out of here," the man pushed him toward the door. "And stay out."
"Fine," Robbie said. "I'm done with everyone here anyway."
He adjusted his torn clothing and limped from the building while Andres, Major, Simon, and Blair watched.
"Butterfield, I want you in my office first thing Monday morning," Coach Wilkensen said grimly. "And you'd better by god be scared."

"I'm getting sick of seeing you in my office, Butterfield," Coach Wilkensen scowled. "What is with you guys and Robbie Lee?"
"I don't know what you mean," Blair said sullenly.
"The three basketball players that Major reported. They beat him pretty severely, and they've lost their scholarships and their education."
"That was Robbie?" Blair looked surprised.
"What was it about this time?" the coach sighed.
"He tried to dance with me in front of my fiancée," Blair said.
"So? He's the one who saved your ass with those pornographers, isn't he?"
"He thinks he's in love with me," Blair said.
"I know that," Coach Wilkensen said impatiently. "You two were a couple, I thought."

An Admission of Weakness

"Not anymore. He threatened to tell Melissa about the videos," Blair said. "How am I going to put the past behind me if he's out there telling people?"

"Holy shit, this is worse than one of my wife's soap operas," the coach rolled his eyes.

"Yes, sir."

"Wait. He was in the videos too," the coach frowned. "Are you saying he's blackmailing you?"

"Not exactly," Blair said uneasily.

"Then I don't see what the problem is."

"I just want him to stay away so I can marry Melissa."

"Have you thought about being honest with your fiancée? The truth goes a long way in fixing things, you know."

"She'd dump me if she knew."

"She should dump you if you're going to lie to her. Why would she want to marry a gay man, and why do you want to marry a woman?"

"I'm not a liar, and I'm not gay," Blair said.

"You sure the fuck are," Coach Wilkensen snorted.

"It was just a phase," Blair said. "But if she finds out about it, I'll lose her."

"Then my question would be does she really love you? Robbie clearly does. And my second question is, why are you pretending it was just a phase? Six months ago you told me

An Admission of Weakness

specifically you were gay. I've seen the videos, remember."

"It's hard to explain."

"Give it a try anyway," the coach said dryly.

"Being gay is a sin," Blair said. "My dad says it's a choice."

"With all due respect to your father, it's not a choice," the coach said. "And it's not a sin."

"How do you know that?"

"Because I know gay people, and I've educated myself. You think you're the first gay student to come through here? Homosexuality is part of nature. Do you think giraffes and penguins and horses 'choose' to be gay? Of course they don't, and people don't either."

"But I chose to be with Robbie and Major," Blair said.

"You're sleeping with Major while you're engaged to this Melissa? Holy jeez," the coach groaned. "Are you sleeping with Melissa too?"

"Yes."

"Good god, you are one messed up motherfucker."

"I'm trying to be honest with myself," Blair said.

"So you think that because you made a conscious choice to sleep with Robbie and Major, that means you're really straight?"

"I guess so."

"That's the stupidest fucking thing I've ever heard," the coach said.

An Admission of Weakness

"No, it's not," Blair said. "See, just because a straight man chooses to fuck another man doesn't mean he's gay."
"How do you figure that?"
"It's like vegetables and chocolate," Blair explained. "Women are vegetables and men are chocolate. I want chocolate, but I should stick with vegetables because they're good for me and chocolate isn't."
"So you're saying you want to sleep with Major and Robbie but you have to sleep with women?"
"Yes."
"Do you have any idea how stupid you are?" Coach Wilkensen said. "Seriously. I've never heard anything so idiotic in my life."
"I'm straight," Blair attempted to explain. "But I wanted to sleep with guys because I like doing something I know is wrong for me."
"If we're going with that reasoning, does the fact that you chose to sleep with a woman mean you're gay?" the coach asked wryly.
"Of course not. That doesn't make any sense."
"So you chose to sleep with men, and you chose to sleep with women," the coach said. "It sounds like you're choosing to be both gay and straight."
"But I'm supposed to sleep with women."
"Says who?"
"My dad."

An Admission of Weakness

"If you were straight and slept with men, that would be a choice. If you're gay and slept with women, that's a choice. That's not a hard concept to understand."
Blair stared at him blankly.
"How are you not getting this? It's basic human biology."
Again the coach received a blank stare.
"Why did you sleep with Major and Robbie?"
"I wanted to," Blair said.
"Because you're attracted to them physically?"
"Yes, sir."
"Is that why you're sleeping with Melissa?"
"It's not quite the same thing."
"Are you saying you're not attracted to Melissa physically? You sleep with her because it's a way to get off?"
"I guess so," Blair said.
"So you enjoy sex with a man more than a woman?"
"Sure," Blair shrugged.
"Then you're gay," the coach said bluntly.
"Break it off with Melissa and make up with Robbie Lee."
"My dad would never accept that."
"Oh, I see what this is all about," the coach nodded. "You want to make your dad happy."
"Yes."
"Does he live his life to please you?" the coach asked. "Does he have to have your approval before he buys a car or paints the house?"

An Admission of Weakness

"Of course not."

"You're a grown man, Blair. You don't need his approval either because it's your life, not his. Someday you're going to look back with a lot of regrets if you live for him instead of yourself. How can you not understand that?"

"I've never questioned him."

"Once you become a man, it's your job to question everything, including your parents," the coach said. "And one more thing, Butterfield. You need to stop putting your dick in everyone who tells you how great you are. Stop being so goddammed arrogant. That's a great quality on the gridiron, but not in real life. It's past time you were realizing that."

Coach Wilkensen's fatherly tone disappeared, and he became deadly serious.

"I warned you that one more infraction of any kind, and you would be out of here."

"I understand, sir," Blair swallowed with difficulty. "I'll be off campus by tonight."

"Shut the fuck up until I'm done talking," the coach said impatiently.

"Yes, sir."

"This incident is going to appear on your permanent record, but I'm going to hold it back until you graduate. Otherwise, I'd have no choice but to end your college career at the University of Illinois right now."

"Thank you, sir," Blair said, relieved.

An Admission of Weakness

"Thank me by getting your personal life straightened out so I don't have to hear about it ever again. Now get the hell out of my office!"

Robbie got permission to attend his classes remotely over the next few weeks, so he left his room only to eat and attend cheerleading practice. His door remained locked at all times. Andres and Major knocked on it a few times a day at first, but he never spoke to them. They eventually stopped coming by, although he heard them laughing and talking in Blair's room. He supposed Major and Blair were still sleeping together. He should never have introduced Simon to Major; the poor guy was undoubtedly going to get his heart broken. Simon, Major, and Andres called and texted his phone, but he never answered, and he deleted their texts without reading them.

He had been called before the Administrative Board and given a stern rebuke after his disgraceful public brawl. After that, he had no desire to see anyone unless he absolutely had to.

He saw Andres and Major and Blair at the football games, of course, but he stayed far away from them. The three of them received lots of attention from their fans, so they didn't seek him out, thankfully.

An Admission of Weakness

"We need to deal with the source of the problem," Andres said.
"What's that?" Major frowned.
"Blair," Andres said. "It's because of him that Robbie won't speak to us."
"Some of that's on me," Major said ruefully. "I slept with Blair two more times after Robbie caught us."
"Why the hell would you tell Robbie that, you dumbfuck? God, you're as stupid as Blair."
"No, he's not," Simon took Major's hand and squeezed it soothingly.
"If all of you had kept your dicks in your pants," Andres said disgustedly, "we wouldn't be in this mess."
"I think the best thing is to just stay out of it and let nature take its course," Simon said. "If Blair and Robbie are meant to be together, they will be."
"I'm talking about us and Robbie, not Blair and Robbie," Andres said. "Blair can do whatever the fuck he wants. I don't care anymore."
"A friend of mine is having a Halloween party at her house," Simon said thoughtfully. "Maybe we could get Robbie to go. Then we could ambush him."
"We want to be his friends again," Andres said wryly. "Not take him prisoner."
"You can't make him be friends if he doesn't want to," Simon said. "He feels like you guys betrayed him."

An Admission of Weakness

"We were protecting him," Andres said.
"Which in hindsight was pretty dumb."
"I'm still going to invite him to the party,"
Simon said. "He needs to get out of that room."

The public fight with Robbie had a profound
effect on Blair, as had the coach's words.
Something clicked in his brain, and he
suddenly realized it was time to stop acting like
a teenager and take responsibility for himself. It
was time to stop hurting the people in his life
with his lies and confusion.
Ever since coming to college, he had made a
mess of everything. He lied to his family about
his major, slept with a dozen female students to
prove his heterosexuality to himself, decided he
was gay and then decided he wasn't, gotten
himself entangled in a pornography ring and
had sex with dozens of men and women, gotten
his innocent boyfriend involved with a pair of
seedy pornographers, nearly got kicked out of
college, slept with more women, gotten
engaged to a woman, slept with his boyfriend's
best friend three times, beaten up his boyfriend,
nearly been kicked out of school again, and
broken his boyfriend's heart over and over.
It was beyond ridiculous, and it was time for it
all to stop. He wasn't confused anymore, and
he was going to be honest from here on out. He
was gay, and that's all there was to it.

An Admission of Weakness

He didn't want to marry Melissa, and he needed to be upfront with her. He also needed to be honest with his family about his sexuality and his field of study. His father would be furious, but it didn't matter what his father thought anymore. He grinned with relief at that thought. It was like a weight had lifted from his shoulders. Somehow Coach Wilkensen's words had gotten through to him when no one else could.

This was his life, and he needed to make the most of it. He could start by apologizing to the people he had hurt.

"Melissa, there's something I have to tell you," Blair said. "It's not going to be easy to hear."

"Why don't you tell me later?" she smiled coyly.

She slid under the blanket and took him in her mouth. It was nothing like Major's blow job, but it still had the desired effect. He closed his eyes and enjoyed the sensation until she moved up to kiss him passionately. After a few minutes, he rolled them over and nursed on her breasts for a while. They sixty-nined one another until finally, he raised her legs and inserted his dick into her.

"Fuck, that feels good," he grunted as he pistoned in and out of her.

"Oh, Blair, you're fantastic," she murmured. "I love you."

An Admission of Weakness

He leaned down to kiss her so she'd stop talking while he fucked her. For the next twenty minutes, he lay on top of her, got behind her, and let her sit on him until he finally climaxed inside her.

"That was amazing," she grinned as she lay on top of him with his penis still inside her.

"Melissa, I need to talk to you about something."

"What is it?" she frowned.

"I haven't been completely honest with you," he said.

"You've lied to me? Why would you do that?"

"I have lied to you," he admitted, "but it's only because I was lying to myself. You know that our sex life hasn't been that great."

"You've been under a lot of stress," she said. "I understand."

"That's not it," he said. "The truth is, I don't like having sex with women. I'd rather be with men."

"You're telling me this while your dick is still inside me?"

"Yes?" he said uncomfortably. He lifted her up so he could slip from her vagina.

"Are you asking me or telling me? Because you don't sound very sure of yourself."

"I am sure that I'm gay."

"Why would you choose to be gay? Is it because of something I've done?"

An Admission of Weakness

"This has nothing to do with you," he said. "And no one chooses to be gay. It's simply who we are. I'm gay, not by choice, but by design. I didn't fully understand that until recently.

"I've pretended to be straight to make my dad happy, but it's not who I am, and I can't lie about it anymore. It wouldn't be fair to you for us to get married."

"You don't want to marry me?"

"I can't marry you because I'm gay. And you don't want to marry someone who can't give you the love you deserve."

"Is this because of Robbie? Has he somehow corrupted you?"

"He didn't corrupt me. All he ever did is love me, and I love him. As beautiful as you are, he's more beautiful to me."

"Then why did you beat him up?"

"Because I was still lying to myself. But I'm not lying anymore."

"We literally just fucked," she said. "Your cum is still in me."

"I know, but –"

"He'll never be with you again after what you did," she said. "You might as well marry me. God and I will help you be straight."

"I don't think even God can make me straight."

She reached down and stroked his penis until it became firm again. She lowered herself onto it once again.

An Admission of Weakness

"See," she said. "God is already making you straight."

He fucked her for the next ten minutes, but finally he lifted her off of him.

"I can't keep doing this."

"You love fucking me, and you know it."

"I like it, but I don't love it," he said.

"Then why did you insist we do it? Why did you fuck me so hard and kiss me so passionately? You can't tell me you're gay when you make love to me like it's the first time every time."

"First of all, you insisted on it," he said. "And I'm passionate because I'm usually thinking about guys."

"Ew," she said. "You think about men while we're doing it?"

"Sometimes," he said.

"Well, it's not ideal," she shrugged, "but if that's what it takes…"

"I don't want to do that anymore," Blair said. "I want to be with a man."

"Fine," she sighed and slipped off the engagement ring. She handed it to him.

"You're making a big mistake. You're going to burn in hell."

"I'll take that chance," he said dryly.

"Call me when you change your mind," she said. "I'm going to pray for God to change you, and He will. So I'll be waiting."

An Admission of Weakness

"Okay, but in case it's God's will that I'm gay, don't wait too long. There's a wonderful man out there who can give you the love and passion you deserve."
"You'll see I'm right," she kissed him and snuggled closer.

"I'm gay," Blair said.
"Don't tell me, you've met some new guy who's convinced you you're in love with him?" Andres said dryly.
"No. I just wanted to tell you that I know now that I'm gay."
"I kinda figured that out the first time we slept together," Major said dryly.
"You stupid dickhead," Andres said. "It took you twenty-one years to figure out what it took us ten minutes to know."
"I always knew it," Blair said.
"You could have fooled us," Andres snorted.
"I mean I knew it, but I let my dad and my brother get in my head, and Melissa didn't help any."
"*This above all: to thine own self be true. And it must follow, as the night the day, Thou canst not then be false to any man,*" Major quoted.
Blair and Andres looked at him like he was crazy.
"What?" Major said defensively. "That's Shakespeare."

An Admission of Weakness

"I know," Andres said. "I'm just surprised you knew."

"I'm not as dumb as you think," Major frowned.

"Okay, smart guy, what does it mean?" Blair said.

"It means that if you're honest with yourself, you can be honest with others," Major said. "You lied to everyone else because you were lying to yourself."

"That's why things are so screwed up, fuckwad," Andres said. "If you'd been honest to begin with, you and Robbie would be together now, and no one wouldn't be speaking to anyone else."

"Huh?" Blair looked puzzled.

"He means that you're a stupid, narcissistic, motherfucking asshole," Major said.

"I know," Blair said. "But I'm starting over by being honest with everyone. I broke it off with Melissa, and now I'm telling you."

"Well, don't expect any miracles with Robbie," Major said. "He's one hundred percent done with you."

"You really burned your bridges there, bro," Andres agreed. "You not only built them and then burned them, but you built them again, burned them again, and just to make sure, you bombed them too."

"I know it's too late with Robbie," Blair said unhappily. "But I still need to talk to him."

An Admission of Weakness

"He doesn't care what any of us have to say," Andres said.

"Thank god I don't have to be best man," Major said. "When the minister asks if anyone has any objections, I'd have to raise my hand and tell him all the shit you've pulled."

"You know, Robbie is going to that costume party on Halloween night," Andres said. "Maybe we should go too."

"What good will that do?" Blair said. "He'll just avoid us."

"Not if he doesn't know it's us," Andres grinned.

"I'm a six and a half foot tall, two hundred eighty pound Black man," Major said. "There's no costume in the world that will disguise me."

"Yeah, me neither," Andres looked down at himself.

"He might not recognize me if I'm covered enough," Blair said. "It's worth a try anyway."

An Admission of Weakness

CHAPTER TWENTY-SIX

Rhett knocked on Robbie's door.
"No one's home, so go the fuck away," Robbie barked.
"Not even for your little bwother?"
The door burst open a moment later, and Robbie grabbed his brother and lifted him off the ground.
"What are you...how...when...?"
"Put me down and I'll tell you," Rhett laughed.
When the two were settled with the door securely locked again, Rhett explained.
"After we talked last, I couldn't stand the thought of you being here all alone, so I saved up my money and got on a twain. I even got an Uber dwiver to bwing me here."
"What about your job?"
"Ma told them it was a family emergency, and they gave me the time off."
"Ma did that?" Robbie said, astonished.
"I know, wight?"
"What about the girls?"
"Vaneeta's seventeen now," Rhett said. "She's watching them."
"I forget how grown up you are," Robbie said.
"I'm nineteen," Rhett reminded him.
"I'm sorry I wasn't there for your graduation," Robbie apologized.
"There, uh, was no gwaduation," Rhett said uncomfortably.

An Admission of Weakness

"Why not?"
"Wobbie, I have to tell you something."
"What?"
"I, uh, didn't gwaduate," Rhett said uneasily.
"You didn't graduate?" Robbie frowned.
"I flunked out. I'm sorwy to let you down."
"How could you flunk out? You're smart."
"Not weally. The only way I made it as far as I did was because you helped me."
"Why didn't you tell me? I'd have helped you from here."
"You had enough to worwy about," Rhett said. "I didn't want to be a burden."
"You are never a burden to me."
"It doesn't matter. I'll be fine."
"You're going to graduate," Robbie said firmly. "How long can you stay?"
"As long as I need to, I guess."
"Good. Then we'll study and get your GED."
"If you say so," Rhett grinned. "Now tell me evwything that's happened so far."
The brothers talked for hours, ordered a pizza and some ice cream, and then talked for a few more hours.
"I'm supposed to go to a party on Halloween," Robbie said.
"That sounds fun."
"Why don't you come with me?" Robbie said. "We'll dress up in costumes and everything. You can say you went to your first college party."

An Admission of Weakness

"Cool," Rhett grinned. "You be a piwate, and I'll be a cowboy."

Robbie and Rhett borrowed cowboy boots, a black cowboy hat, flannel shirt, and a western belt with a huge silver buckle from Robbie's friends. Some of his gay friends even had spurs, chaps, and a lasso for him to use.
"Is this a gay pawty?" Rhett asked.
"There will be a lot of gay people there," Robbie said.
"Then I want to look gay."
"You already look like one of the Village People," Robbie laughed.
They found a purple feather boa, and Rhett wrapped it around his neck and threw the end over his shoulder. He donned his black eye mask.
"There," he grinned. "Now I'm the gay Lone Wanger."
Coming up with a pirate outfit seemed too complicated, so Robbie decided to wear his cheerleading outfit with a simple black mask over his eyes.

Blair may have been honest with Melissa, but she wasn't taking no for an answer. He nursed from a nipple while she rode his hard manhood. She cried out in ecstasy as he pounded his dick deeply into her.
"Aw fuck," he groaned into her breast.

An Admission of Weakness

They changed position several times until she was leaning over the side of the bed with Blair fucking her from behind. In his mind he was picturing Robbie's beautiful hairy ass and chest, so it didn't take long for him to climax.
"I think I'll go as an angel," she said while she was still impaled on his dick.
He had moved back to his own room after breaking things off with her, and she had followed. The two of them were still having frequent sex, mostly at her insistence. He figured it was at least a way for him to get off.
"I didn't know you were going to the party," Blair frowned.
"Well, of course I am, silly," she said. "Who else would you take?"
"I figured since we broke up –"
"That's just temporary," she chuckled. "I'll be wearing that ring again very soon."
She kissed him, making his manhood swell once again. In no time, they were making love again.

The party venue was far grander than Robbie expected. It was a three story brick mansion with tall columns and a brick driveway curving before the front door.
"Who lives here?" he asked with awe.
"My friend's dad is Dr. Oliphant," Simon said, referring to the renowned trauma surgeon.
"Why isn't Major here tonight?"

An Admission of Weakness

"He and Andres and Blair went to the football team's party," Simon shrugged. "I wanted to go with you and Rhett." He chuckled at Rhett's purple boa. "I always thought the Lone Ranger needed a splash of color."

"Try to keep Melissa occupied," Blair whispered to his friends. "If Robbie sees her with me, he'll know who I am."
"We'll all keep our distance until you talk to him," Andres said.
"Make it fast," Major added. "This costume is fucking uncomfortable."
"Yeah, but you're the best looking Shrek ever," Andres teased him.
He and Blair laughed while Major grinned sheepishly.
"I look ridiculous," he said. "Why do you guys get to look so great and I look like a monster?"
"You're not a monster; you're an ogre," Blair grinned. "Get your fictional characters straight."
He was wearing an elaborate African costume with a full wooden face mask. His tattoos were covered or disguised so they wouldn't give him away.
Andres was wearing a black suit with a cape and top hat. A *Phantom of the Opera* mask covered two-thirds of his face, making him unrecognizable.

An Admission of Weakness

"Why did you bring Melissa?" Major frowned. "You said you broke up with her."
"I can't get rid of her," Blair said.
"Try having Major fuck you in front of her," Andres said dryly.
"I don't think even that would faze her," Blair said. "God, I want Robbie back."
"That's not going to happen, bro," Andres said. "You need to be realistic and move on."
"Maybe Simon knows someone for you to date," Major suggested.
"I'm through dating for a while," Blair shook his head. "I'm clearly not very good at it."

An Admission of Weakness

"Not when you let flattery go to your head," Andres said. "The second anyone says something nice to you, you follow your dick right into their asses or pussies."

"Ew, no more vaginas," Blair wrinkled his nose. "I've seen more than enough of those for ten lifetimes."

"And yet you're still fucking Melissa," Andres said. "God, you're a mess."

"Why do you like pussies?" Major asked Andres curiously. "I've only seen a few, but I think they're disgusting."

"Dicks are definitely better looking than vaginas," Blair added.

"Dicks are cool," Andres shrugged. "I'm very fond of mine. I just don't want one in my ass or mouth."

"That's exactly what we do want," Major chuckled.

"Preach it, Brother Major," Blair raised his hands in the air like he was at a revival tent meeting. "Glory, hallelujah, lord send me some dick."

"Holy fuck, you really are gay," Andres grinned. "Gay at last, gay at last, thank God Almighty you're gay at last."

Robbie and Rhett warily followed Simon into the mansion.

"Jeez-o-pete," Rhett whistled. "I've never seen anything like this before."

An Admission of Weakness

"Me neither," his brother said. He pulled Simon aside. "You're sure they're not here?"

"Would I bring you to this party if they were?" Simon frowned. "Now come on, girls; Mama needs a drink."

Simon selected a bottle of Corona for himself and handed another to Robbie, while Rhett settled for a soft drink. Rhett gazed around delightedly at all the people in their funny costumes in this opulent environment. Most people were wearing masks, so he didn't expect to recognize anyone. He was astonished when several people from the cheerleading squad called him over. He waved excitedly at them.

"Can I go?" he asked his brother.

"You don't need my permission," Robbie chuckled. "Go have fun. Just no alcohol."

"K, bye," Rhett was off like a flash, or at least a flash with a limp.

Robbie sighed. He was still in disfavor with the entire athletic department for ruining the dance, as he could see by his peers' glares from across the room.

"There's my friends," Simon tugged on his arm and led him into the billiard room.

Simon and his companions laughed, drank, and acted silly while they played pool or danced to the peppy music being played over speakers somewhere. Robbie danced for a while with Simon and then went in search of his brother. He found him finally out by the heated pool

An Admission of Weakness

with a couple of male cheerleaders and four members of the football team. Rhett seemed to be the center of attention and was regaling them all with some humorous story. These football players were too macho to wear costumes, and the cheerleaders were clad the same as he was with similar masks, so they were easy to recognize.

That was odd. Simon said the football team was having their own party tonight, so what were these guys doing here?

Oh well, at least Rhett was having fun. These people had become quite fond of him during his earlier visits, and he relaxed knowing they would treat him right.

He headed back into the house and helped himself to a soda and a few dozen hors d'oeuvres. Several classmates stopped him for a brief chat, hoping to fool him with their hidden identities.

A big, lumbering green Shrek bumped into him as he passed. Robbie paused to chuckle at the sight of the big man in such a silly costume. Shrek was followed by a pretty Black angel dressed all in white with white wings. She paused when she noticed him.

"Robbie," she frowned. "I want to talk to you."

"Melissa," Robbie greeted her. "How are you?"

"I'm fine."

"Still engaged to Blair?"

"Of course," she said. "Why wouldn't I be?"

An Admission of Weakness

"No reason I can think of," Robbie said dryly. "He told me you're in love with him, but I need you to tell me you're not anymore."

"Don't worry," he said. "There's no danger of me trying to steal him away from you. He's all yours, and good riddance to him."

"I hope this means you've turned things over to God," she said. "Have you found yourself a nice woman yet?"

"I have, as a matter of fact," Robbie said.

"I knew it," she beamed. "My prayers worked."

"Yes, God is in control, and all's well with my dick and her vagina," Robbie said sarcastically.

"And doesn't it feel better to be right with the Lord?"

"I feel like a weight of two hundred and ten pounds has been miraculously lifted from my shoulders," Robbie said.

"That's because God took Blair away from you. I prayed that He would, and He did," she said proudly. "When Blair and I started dating, I knew God had sent him to me. And now everyone's happy," she beamed. "Blair and I are in love, and you won't burn in a lake of fire for all eternity."

"I guess I really dodged a bullet, huh," he said. "It's a good thing God listened to you. Otherwise I'd have been stuck with the worthless bastard forever."

"So, uh, is your girlfriend here?" she asked uncomfortably.

An Admission of Weakness

Robbie glanced around until he saw a freckle-faced youth dressed as Dorothy from *The Wizard of Oz*. He seized him by the arm and pulled him close.
"This is Dorothy, my girlfriend," he smiled wickedly. "Say hi to Melissa, Dorothy."
"Hi, Melissa," the young man said awkwardly.
"Hello," Melissa frowned.
"Okay, I'll see ya later, sweetie," Robbie kissed his cheek and shoved him back to his friends.
"Oh, Robbie, you poor thing," Melissa said. "I don't think that's an actual woman."
"She isn't?" Robbie frowned over at the young man. "She said her name was Dorothy. Isn't that a woman's name?"
"Yes, but I'm pretty sure that was a man in a dress."
"Well, damn," he said, chagrined. "Now what am I going to do?"
"Don't worry," she patted his arm. "Now that you're on the proper path, God will provide the right woman for you."
"You think so?"
"Of course," she said. "Well, good luck. I need to go find Blair. We got separated when we got here, and I've been looking for him ever since."
"Wait," he reached out a hand to stop her. "Blair's here?"
So that was why Simon invited him to this party, he thought shrewdly.

An Admission of Weakness

"Oh, I think I see him," she smiled and waved as she walked away. "See ya later."
He watched her for a moment, barely noticing the Black phantom of the opera standing nearby.

Robbie walked around the vast house until he found Simon.
"I'm going," he called over the loud music.
"What? Why?"
"Blair's here," Robbie said.
"No, he's not," Simon said.
"Melissa told me he's here," Robbie said dryly. "Like you didn't know."
Shrek, he thought suddenly. Was that Blair?
"Is he dressed like Shrek?" he asked.
"Blair's not here," Simon said. "Stop being so paranoid."
"Never mind," Robbie said. "I'll tell Rhett we're going."
"He's having fun," Simon frowned. "Don't spoil his first big party."
"Fine. If he wants to stay, will you look after him and see that he gets back to the dorm?"
"You can't leave just because Blair is here," Simon said. "You've said repeatedly that you don't care about him anymore. He's engaged to Melissa, so he's not going to bother you. Stay and have fun."
"Just promise you'll look out for Rhett."

An Admission of Weakness

Robbie wandered through the crowded house and found Rhett playing beer pong with a group of twenty-somethings on the dining room table.

"What do you think you're doing?" he demanded.

"Don't worwy," Rhett grinned. "I'm not dwinking. They put Coke in mine."

His face was flushed, and it was clear from the light in his eyes and wide smile on his face that he was having the time of his life.

"But I don't see why I can't dwink if I want to," he added.

"Because you're not twenty-one," Robbie said. "Anyway, I think we should go. Blair's here."

"I don't want to leave," Rhett frowned. "I'm having fun."

"Fine," Robbie relented.

"Come play with us," Rhett said. He turned to the others. "Hey, evwyone, Wobbie's gonna play."

A cheer went up, and Robbie joined the game. He forgot everything else for a while and permitted himself to have fun until he looked up and saw Shrek and Simon walk by.

"Hey!" he called to him. "Shrek."

The pair tried to hurry away, but Robbie was too quick for them.

"Who are you?" Robbie demanded. Even as he asked the question, he realized who it was.

"Never mind," he scowled and turned away.

An Admission of Weakness

"Robbie, it's me," Major said.

"So you didn't know they were here?" Robbie frowned at Simon. "Where's Andres?"

"I'm here," the phantom of the opera said from behind him. "We just want to talk to you."

"Now you want to talk? What about when you agreed to be Blair's best men and didn't tell me he was marrying Melissa? You didn't care to talk then."

"What good would it have done?" Andres said. "It wouldn't have changed anything; it would only have hurt you."

"We were trying to keep you from getting hurt," Major said.

"I don't need to be protected," Robbie said. "What else haven't you told me?"

"Well, you're not going to like it, but Melissa's pregnant with triplets. We don't know whether Blair or Major is the father," Andres said. "They're all having sex together, so the chances are fifty-fifty."

"Oh my god!" Robbie's eyes widened. "Major, you said you could never sleep with a woman."

"There's more," Simon added. "Melissa doesn't know it yet, but Blair and Major got married."

"She told me she and Blair are still enga..." Robbie's voice trailed off, and he rolled his eyes. "You're all assholes. I've got to go. Rhett, Simon's going to take you home

An Admission of Weakness

whenever you're ready to go. I'll see you back at the dorm."

Robbie sat down on the bottom step of the grand staircase while he waited for his ancient phone to open the Uber app. He noted how beautiful the enormous crystal chandelier high above him was. He glanced over at an incredibly lifelike African warrior in full regalia with a spear and wooden face mask. What was its significance, he wondered as he studied it? Who had worn it, and where was it from?
For some reason, it seemed familiar to him. Wasn't there another just like it in the billiard room? And yet another in the dining room, living room, and by the pool? What the hell? At that moment, the barefoot figure suddenly came alive and crouched like a panther with its spear pointed threateningly at Robbie. Startled, Robbie dropped his phone, and the warrior grunted and picked it up. He studied it uncomprehendingly and then jabbed his spear in Robbie's direction. Robbie was too taken aback by this apparition to do anything but put his hands up and back away up the stairs.

An Admission of Weakness

CHAPTER TWENTY-SEVEN

The warrior jabbed at him again and made guttural sounds. He crept closer, forcing Robbie up the stairs. The two made their way to the second floor while Robbie glanced desperately out of the corners of his eyes for a means of escape.

What the hell was happening? Was he drunk, or was he hallucinating? Fuck, someone probably put something in the beer, and he had been foolish enough to drink it without question. That must be it, he decided, because there was no way he was in his right mind. A statue didn't just move around the mansion as if by magic, and it most certainly didn't come to life and threaten people.

Yes, this was most definitely a hallucination. A hallucination can't hurt you, he reasoned. He just needed to stay calm until it passed.

He continued to walk backward up the stairs with the spear pointed at his throat. The creature – man, warrior, statue, whatever it was – continued making deep, throaty sounds as it forced him upstairs.

When they reached the landing, his attacker guided him to the first door they came to. He backed Robbie up against it and gestured for him to open it.

They entered a large bedroom with paneled walls, thick wool carpets, a fireplace, and a

An Admission of Weakness

huge four poster bed. The warrior kicked the door shut and padded around Robbie like a cat circling its prey. He jabbed the spear at him and growled in some unknown language.

"I don't know what's going on here," Robbie kept turning to face him. "I don't know what you want. I just want to get my brother and go home."

The soldier suddenly stopped and stood up straight.

"Rhett's here?" he leaned his spear against the wall, his voice muffled by the mask.

"What?" Robbie frowned.

Blair took off the mask.

"Rhett's here?" he repeated.

"Blair?" Robbie blinked. His anger grew swiftly. "What the fuck are you doing? You scared me to death!"

"I'm sorry," Blair said. "I needed to get you alone so I could talk to you."

"What makes you think I want to hear anything you have to say?"

"Because you still love me."

Robbie glanced around and picked up a heavy bronze Buddha.

"You'd better use that spear to defend yourself because I'm going to kill you!"

"Now hold on," Blair said. "I know you're mad at me, and you have every right because I'm a screw up, but I love you and I want to explain."

An Admission of Weakness

"There's no need," Robbie said. "You made everything clear when you told me you were engaged and then beat the shit out of me."
"I'm not engaged anymore."
"Yeah, right," Robbie snorted. "Melissa just told me that you're still engaged. And she's staying with you in your dorm room. I heard the two of you going at it this morning. You still make that grunting sound when you cum, or was that her?"
"Alright, we're still having sex. But that's because she won't leave. She refuses to accept that it's over, but I did break up with her, I swear."
"So the only reason you're having sex with your ex-fiancée is because she won't leave? Yeah, that makes perfect sense."
"She still thinks God is going to make me straight," Blair said.
"You're already straight, remember? How many times have we been through this?"
"Please just give me a chance to talk and I'll tell you about it," Blair said. "I'm not straight."
"So now you're gay again, even though you're still having sex with your fiancée," Robbie nodded. He added sarcastically, "Naturally, I absolutely believe you."
"I was never straight," Blair said. "I've just pretended to be to make my dad happy."
Robbie's eyes widened.
"You told me you came out to your dad."

An Admission of Weakness

"Not exactly."
"So you lied again," Robbie said.
"Katie and Camilla are the only ones in the family who know," Blair admitted. "I've wanted to tell Mama and Dad, but I just –"
"Why would you be honest with them when you can't even be honest with yourself?" Robbie said dryly. "Your dad must be thrilled with Melissa. She's Black, pretty, not too bright. I heard she's pregnant with triplets. That should make Papa Butterfield ecstatic."
"She can't be pregnant," Blair said scornfully. "She's taking birth control pills."
"Okay, that just finished this conversation for me," Robbie moved toward the door.
Blair quickly blocked his way.
"We're not done."
"We were done a long time ago because you're a self-involved, narcissistic, egotistical, lying moron who has to have daddy's approval before you do anything. And let's face it, I'm the last thing Carter Butterfield would ever approve of. You're better off sticking with Melissa."
"So I have some issues," Blair said. "So I'm a slow learner. Everybody has something, don't they?"
"Blair, I'm so done with this," Robbie said wearily. "I know you're sorry for being a dumbass, and I accept your apology. But I'm

not taking you back. You've screwed me way too many times."

"What do you mean take me back?" Blair said. "You gave me two months to figure things out, and that's what I've done. The two months isn't up until midnight tonight, so I'm still within the window. That means we're still together."

"You're too messed up. You're straight, you're gay, you're pansexual, you're gay, you're straight again. I'm not playing this game with you," Robbie sighed. "I should have known better than to get involved with someone who was still in the closet."

"But you did, and you fell in love with me," Blair said. "And I'm in love with you too. I've never loved anyone else.

"You're right; I've always done what Dad wanted, never questioned it even when I didn't agree with it. But I finally realize it's my life, not his. He doesn't live his life for me, and I'm not going to live mine for him. I want to live it for us."

"If everything you do is for your dad, is anything you've ever said or done been real?" Robbie asked.

"I'm being real right now."

"You're wearing an antique African warrior costume, and you're telling me this is real?" Blair stripped off the costume and stood there in only his tight boxers.

An Admission of Weakness

"Is this real enough for you?" He turned in a circle with his arms out. "This is the real me."
"Is this supposed to convince me of something?" Robbie said skeptically. He was finding it nearly impossible to keep from staring at Blair's muscular body, perfect round ass, and bulging crotch. He noticed that some of his tattoos had been covered over with makeup that was now smeared.
"Listen. I've never fully enjoyed sex with women, and I never understood why, but I do now. It's not meant for me because I'm not straight, simple as that. Pussy is okay, but I love dick. I love your dick, your hairy chest. I love your hairy ass and armpits, I love your muscles. I love the way you smell, all musky after cheerleading practice or after we've fucked.

"I love your sweetness, your kindness, your strength. I love how smart you are, the way you look after Rhett and your sisters. How you never let anything stop you.

"You're the only person in the whole world that makes me feel right, like you see me for who I'm supposed to be. I've been with a lot of men and women, and that's how I know you're the only one that's right for me."
He gazed searchingly into Robbie's eyes, hoping against hope to see understanding there. Robbie stared back at him and was surprised at the sincerity he saw in his face.

An Admission of Weakness

"Those are wonderful words, and I've waited a long time to hear you say them," he said at last. "But don't you see the irony of you telling me you're gay when you just fucked your fiancée this morning?"

"She's not my fiancée."

"It doesn't matter. Tomorrow you're going to change your mind again and be off with some other woman. Or maybe you'll marry Melissa or sleep with Major again and decide he's the only one that's right for you. I'm not going to stick around to see whether it's Melissa or Major or god knows who else you end up with. I just know it won't be me."

"Please," Blair said desperately. "I know you have no reason to believe me. But I know in my heart that this is who I am for real. The experiences of the last couple of years have hit me over the head time and again, trying to get me to listen, and I finally have. I've stopped being a child."

"You know what might prove that you've actually grown up?" Robbie said.

"What? Whatever it is, I'll do it," Blair said eagerly.

"Come out to your dad and tell him about me," Robbie said. "You do that, and I'll consider taking you back."

"Technically, we're still together," Blair reminded him.

An Admission of Weakness

"Then I'm breaking up with you now," Robbie said. "You tell your family about me, and then we'll see."
"Thanksgiving is in three weeks," Blair said.
"I'll tell them then. I think I have to do it in person."
"You promise?"
"I promise. My dad will probably kick me out of the house, but it will be worth it."
"He won't do that," Robbie said. "He loves you."
"He's still not speaking to Justin, and it's been over two months," Blair said dryly.
He took Robbie in his arms and tried to kiss him, but Robbie pulled back.
"You think the last ten minutes are going to fix everything?" he frowned.
"They at least made a difference, didn't they?"
"Yes, I suppose so," Robbie said grudgingly.
He put his arms around Blair and kissed him.
"Oh my god, why did I ever walk away from you?" Blair said.
"Because you're a –"
"A fucking idiot, I know," Blair grinned. "An idiot that loves you more than I've ever loved anyone."
They kissed again, more passionately this time, and didn't hear the door open.
"Uh, Wobbie?" Rhett coughed.
"Aaaaahh!" Melissa screamed.

An Admission of Weakness

Robbie and Blair jumped and turned toward the doorway. Within seconds, the room was filled with curious spectators.

"What are you doing?" Melissa cried angrily. "You said you didn't love him."

"Who are you talking to?" Robbie asked. "Me or Blair?"

"Both of you."

"Well, I lied when I told you that," Robbie hid a smile. "I can't answer for Blair."

"Blair?" Melissa placed her hands on her hips.

"I tried to tell you," Blair shrugged. "I'm gay, and I'm in love with Robbie. Looks like this is God's will for me after all."

"That's Satan talking," she said coldly. "God hates homosexuality."

"Then why did he make gay sex so much fun?" Robbie asked.

"It's way more fun than straight sex," Blair added.

"You're both disgusting," she scowled. "I thought I could help you both, but you're hopeless. Blair, I don't want to see you ever again. And Robbie, you're a pathetic liar!"

"No, he's not!" Rhett said hotly. "He's the best bwother in the whole world!"

"Oh what do you know, you ignorant hayseed?" she snapped. "Why don't you learn to talk right?"

"Hey!" Blair said sharply. "You can't talk to him like that."

An Admission of Weakness

"Melissa," Robbie said, eyes blazing, "maybe you think I won't punch you because I'm a man, but I'm also gay, so I will hit you, and then I'll scratch your fucking eyes out! Now apologize to my brother!"
Melissa screamed in anger and frustration and stormed through the crowd and out the door.

"Go back to the party," Andres addressed the spectators and shooed them toward the door. Once everyone was gone except for Rhett, Andres, Major, and Simon, Andres closed the door.
"Does this mean you two have finally made peace?" he asked.
"I think so," Blair grinned.
"Wobbie, you can't take him back after all he did to you," Rhett frowned. "He'll just hurt you again."
"I won't, I promise," Blair said.
"Wobbie, you surely don't twust him."
"It's okay," Robbie said. "I haven't taken him back. We're just going to talk about it for a while, and then we'll see."
"Technically, we never broke up," Blair said.
"You should have," Rhett scowled. "Why is he wehwing just his underwear? And why were you kissing him?"
"Come on, guys," Simon said. "Let's let Robbie and Blair talk. Rhett, some of the guys said you're an expert at beer pong. Me and

An Admission of Weakness

Major are going to take on you and Andres. We'll beat the pants off of you."
"That's a good idea," Major chuckled. "Strip beer pong. Losers have to do two bare-assed laps around the house."
"Fine," Andres grinned. "I hope you and Simon don't mind being naked in front of a crowd."
"You're on," Major said. "You'll be showing your dicks before we will."
"We're not scared," Rhett said boldly.
The four of them left the room with Andres' arm fondly around Rhett's shoulders.

Blair locked the door and stripped off his underwear. His manhood was already hard.
"What are you doing?" Robbie gulped at the sight of his perfect penis. God, he had missed that!
"We haven't been together since July," Blair backed him toward the bed.
"Whose fault is that?"
"Yours," Blair grinned.
"How do you figure that?"
By now, Robbie was pinned between the bed and Blair.
"You turned me loose for two months," Blair said. "You should have known I was going to do something stupid."
"So it's my fault you got engaged to Melissa?"
"That's okay," Blair said. "I forgive you."

"Gee, thanks," Robbie said dryly. "You seriously think I'm going to sleep with you on some stranger's very expensive sheets?"
"Aren't you?"
"Yes, I am, but only to show you what you're going to miss if you ever screw up again," Robbie said.

He eagerly doffed his clothes and climbed onto the tall bed. Blair crawled over him, slowly kissing and licking his body from his feet to his groin. He paused there and took Robbie's

An Admission of Weakness

manhood down his throat several times while Robbie moaned with bliss. Next, he moved up to nurse from his nipples, to suck and lick his hairy armpits, nuzzle his neck, and finally kiss his lips ravenously. Robbie in turn did the same things to him, and for the next hour, they rolled about the bed until Blair forced Robbie's legs apart with his knees. Slowly but forcefully, he inserted himself into Robbie's ass.

"Oh god," Robbie groaned at the oversized intrusion.

"No one has an ass like yours," Blair panted.

"Or a vagina?" Robbie said.

"Shut up," Blair grinned. "That word is a boner killer now."

"It wasn't this morning," Robbie said.

"Do you really want to talk vaginas?" Blair panted.

"Good point," Robbie grunted.

Blair fucked Robbie slowly and gently at first, but his thrusts became harder and faster as his lust grew. This was who he was meant to be fucking, he realized. Not a woman, and not another man. Just Robbie.

Robbie pulled him down and kissed him ravenously. They moved from the bed to the floor to a chair, from the bathtub to up against a window. Blair was under him, behind him, on top of him, and over him until they both shouted out their pained pleasure when they climaxed.

An Admission of Weakness

"That was fantastic," Blair gasped and wiped the sweat from his forehead.
Robbie started to pull away, but Blair held him firmly in place with his dick still up his ass.
"That was just round one," he grinned.
A knock came at the door.
"Blair, we're taking Rhett home," Andres said through the door. "I hope you're using this time wisely.
"We definitely are," Robbie called back.
"By the way, Major and Simon are taking some naked laps around the house. Rhett's recording it."
He laughed and walked away.

"This doesn't mean everything's okay, you know," Robbie snuggled into Blair's chest.
"I know," Blair said. "Can we at least see each other?"
"On one condition," Robbie grinned. "Tell your teammates that I'm your boyfriend. Then I'll go out with you."
"Done!"

"Guys, I have an announcement to make," Blair stood on a bench in the men's locker room with Robbie by his side.
"What? You guys made another porn?" someone joked.
"Was Melissa in it?" Slick said. "She's hot."

An Admission of Weakness

"You should have told us," a third man laughed. "We'd have all fucked her with you."
"She needs a man with a big dick like mine. Melissa told me she never felt that little baby cock of his."
"Shut the fuck up," Blair retorted good-naturedly. "I have something important to tell you."
"Go ahead, bro," Andres said.
"Hurry up, Butterfield," Coach Wilkensen said impatiently. "Practice started five minutes ago."
"I'm not engaged to Melissa anymore," Blair said.
"She finally wised up?" Slick said, and everyone laughed.
"I broke up with her because I'm in love with someone else," Blair said.
"We don't care," someone called out.
"Michelle Obama's already married, man."
"I'm gay, and I'm in love with Robbie Lee," Blair said.
Robbie grinned and took his hand.
"We know," a couple of guys shouted.
"I never understood why you got engaged to Melissa while you're with him," someone said.
"I was trying to be something I'm not, and I want to tell all of you that I'm not confused anymore. I'm one hundred percent gay."

An Admission of Weakness

"Anyone got a problem with that?" Major stood up and folded his arms as if daring anyone to speak up.
"I think it's great," Andres said.
"Me too," a few guys added.
"I think he should stick with Melissa," Slick frowned. "He could do better than Blondie."
"Robbie's okay," someone said. "Leave him alone."
"I still don't care," another person said, and everyone laughed.
"Okay, are we done sharing, ladies?" the coach said sarcastically. "Then get your girly butts out to the field."

"Dad, I need you to come get me," Justin said into the phone.
He listened for a moment.
"I'm at the police station," he said dourly. "I've been arrested."

An Admission of Weakness

CHAPTER TWENTY-EIGHT

Forty-five minutes earlier, Justin opened the door of the W.H. Abernathy House of Fashion at the east end of Green Grove's downtown. He glanced around uncertainly. The large room featured a half dozen mannequins wearing finished evening gowns, party dresses, and wedding gowns on display in the front windows. There were four sewing machines, four dress forms, three drafting tables, two fabric steamers, and a reception desk with two computer monitors.

The room was deserted except for one man standing at a drafting table. He had long, wavy, light-brown hair, a beard and mustache, numerous tattoos, and was attractive in a rugged, thuggish sort of way. He was staring down at the paper before him, but he looked up when the door opened.

"Hi," he smiled. "Can I help you?"

"I'm looking for Snake," Justin said.

"I'm Snake. Is there something I can do for you?"

"Yeah," Justin said coldly. "You can stay away from my mom."

He slammed his fist into the side of Snake's face and sent the man reeling. Snake was caught off guard, but he was no stranger to fighting, so he came back up quickly with his fists in the air.

An Admission of Weakness

"What the fuck's the matter with you?" he scowled.

"What the fuck's the matter with you?" Justin jabbed at him again, but Snake moved out of range.

"Let's just talk for a minute, man," Snake said. "I don't want to fight you."

"Then stay away from my mom," Justin said.

"I don't even know who your mom is."

"Naomi Butterfield," Justin said.

"Oh. You must be Justin," Snake dropped his fists. "Naomi's told me all about you and the gym you're setting up. She's very proud of you."

"You keep her name out yo mouth," Justin spat. "I know what you're doing with her, and it fucking makes me sick."

"Look, I'm not making her do anything she doesn't want to do," Snake said. "She's enjoying herself, and there's nothing wrong with that."

"You son of a bitch!" Justin said furiously. He started throwing punches hard and fast. Snake defended himself and even returned a few punches of his own.

In the middle of this brawl, Officer Riley Shaw entered the building and saw what was happening. Riley was a descendent of the town's founding family, June Shaw's son, and a policeman with the Green Grove force. In

An Admission of Weakness

spite of being diminutive in size, he was strong and well versed in karate and judo.
He was also Snake's husband and was stopping by to take him home.
Acting quickly, he wrestled Justin to the floor and held him down with a knee while he handcuffed him. He and Snake picked him up and held him by the arms.
"What the hell's going on?" Riley demanded.
"I don't know," Snake panted. "He just came in and started fighting me."
"Justin, what's this all about?"
"Ask him," Justin said sullenly. "He knows what he's doing, and he doesn't care that it's destroying our family."
"How is Naomi being here with me destroying your family?" Snake looked puzzled. "Surely she's a grown woman; she can do what she wants."
"See what I mean?" Justin glowered. "God, she's practically old enough to be your mother."
"I know," Snake said. "That's one reason I love her. She reminds me of my own mom."
"Fuck, man, you are really twisted!" Justin wrenched his arm from Snake's grasp.
"Come on," Riley said. "I'm taking you to the station."

An Admission of Weakness

Carter arrived at the police station and demanded to know why his son had been arrested.
"He hasn't been arrested," Chief Warner said soothingly. "He's just been detained."
He was a stocky, middle-aged man with short, thinning hair and was well liked and respected in town. The citizens knew him to be honest, compassionate, and fair.
"Then what the hell's going on?" Carter said irritably. "Why's he here?"
"He started a fight with Billy Abernathy," the chief said. "Fortunately, Billy has chosen not to press charges. I gave Justin a stern talking-to, but I think his father needs to talk to him. He seems to think Snake is interfering with your family in some way."
"I don't even know a Billy Abernathy," Carter said with annoyance. "If he was doing something to harm my family, I'd know about it."
"As you say," the chief shrugged. "This is between you and Justin. I'll get him for you."

The car ride home was stony silent, but when Carter closed his study door, he had plenty to say.
"Justin, what the hell is wrong with you? Is this what you're doing now? Fighting strangers? You should be in college earning a degree, but

An Admission of Weakness

instead I'm picking you up from the police station.

"Do you have any idea how serious this is? You're a Black man, for god's sake. One misstep now can affect the rest of your life. If we were in any other town, you might have ended up dead at the hands of the police. You don't even have to commit a crime to be murdered in cold blood by the very people who are sworn to protect and serve.

"Well, I can tell you from experience, the police are not there for people like us. Their entire culture is built on racism; the original concept of the police was to protect slave owners from the people they owned. They were also hired to hunt down runaway slaves.

"Black people are not citizens to the police. We are suspects, animals, potential criminals that need to be hunted down like we were still slaves."

"I know all that, Dad," Justin said sarcastically.

"Do you? You've never experienced it, but I have."

"Is that the only reason you're speaking to me? To tell me how awful the world's been to you?"

"To all Black people, and don't ever sass me again," Carter said sternly. "The point is, if you were studying pre-med like I told you to, none of this would have happened. How do you think I felt getting a call telling me my son had been arrested? If this Abernathy fellow had

An Admission of Weakness

chosen to press charges, you could have gone to prison. Do you understand that?

"There's no compassion in the judicial system for a young Black man in this country, no matter how innocent you are. Once you've been arrested, you're a marked man.

"Don't think they won't be watching you, hoping to catch you in some compromising position so they can arrest you, or worse. Do you know how many innocent Black men and women have been murdered just for being Black?"

"I know about racism. I don't need a fucking lecture from you."

"Language!" Carter snapped. "I will not tolerate that word in this house."

"I'm a grown man; you can't tell me what to do anymore."

"I can while you're living in this house."

"Then maybe I'll move out," Justin said belligerently.

"How? You have no money. You're in over your head as it is with this ridiculous gym of yours."

"Stop calling it ridiculous!" Justin snapped. "Why can't you be supportive of my dream? Why do you have to mock it?"

"Because you are capable of so much more than this, Justin," his father said. "Why can't you understand that you're wasting your

An Admission of Weakness

potential? I can't just stand by and watch you destroy your future."

"Then don't watch," Justin stood up. "From now on, just forget you have a son named Justin. I'll get my own place and then you'll never have to see me again."

He walked to the door and looked back.

"Sorry to be such a disappointment to you," he said. "But you're a disappointment to me too, so I guess we're even."

"Don't mention being arrested to your mother," Carter called after him. "There's no sense upsetting her."

But Justin was gone.

"What did you say to Justin?" Ruby confronted Carter the next morning with her hands on her hips.

"What I say to my son has nothing to do with you," he leisurely sipped his coffee.

"He's moving out!" Ruby said angrily. "And it's your fault."

"He's a grown man," Carter shrugged. "If he wants to move out, that's his prerogative."

"He's starting a new business and going to school. How the hell do you think he's going to support himself?"

"That's not my problem," Carter said. "He doesn't have to move out; he's choosing to. If he's foolish enough to leave when he can't

support himself, then he'll have to live with the consequences."
"How can you treat your own son like this?" she demanded. "He's trying to follow his dream, and you're actively trying to crush it."
"I'll still pay for his schooling if he comes to his senses and studies to be a doctor," Carter said. "I think that's pretty generous considering how he's treated me."
"Oh my god!" she exclaimed disgustedly. "You truly believe that because he isn't letting you run his life, that makes him selfish? It isn't up to you to tell him what he wants. He knows what he wants, and that's what he's trying to do in spite of you. He'd rather do it with your support, but obviously you're too pig-headed to give him that. You're a disgrace as a father!"
"How dare you talk to me like that!" he set his cup down and stood up indignantly. "It's your fault that he's making the biggest mistake of his life. So if he wants to leave, why don't you go with him?"
"You know, that's a good idea," she said coldly. "If he goes, then I'll go too."
"Good," he said.
"Let's see what Naomi has to say about this," she said.
"She thinks what I tell her to think," Carter said dismissively.
"You're a Neanderthal!"

An Admission of Weakness

The renovations to the new gym were finished, and the decor was stunning. All of Justin's ideas had come to fruition, and he was overjoyed with the results.

The floors were covered with a warm, wood laminate and rubber mats. Neon dumbbell and fitness machine signs, white LED Christmas lights, pictures of fit, older men and women, and motivational sayings adorned the walls. The lighting was soft and indirect.

He had commissioned Camilla to turn the entire wall opposite the front windows into a colorful mural depicting key moments in Black history, and the result was astonishingly beautiful.

The second workout room was mirrored all around for those that liked to watch themselves while they exercised. The lighting was brighter here and less forgiving.

Throughout both rooms were dozens of treadmills, barbell sets, dumbbell sets, training benches, stationary bikes, rowing machines, and much more. There was a nutrition center in one corner that offered healthy drinks and snacks.

The locker rooms were done in black and white tile with urinals, toilets, and open showers with rainfall shower heads.

Randall Price had gone above and beyond with the renovation, Justin thought gratefully. He had spared no expense, insisting on the best of everything.

An Admission of Weakness

"You save money in the long run by buying the best," he told Justin. "And you'll be more satisfied with the results."
That included remodeling the apartment above the gym. Randall had gutted it and fitted it with a luxurious contemporary kitchen, expensive fixtures, new windows and doors, and so on. Justin was extremely satisfied with the results. It was almost more than he could comprehend that his dream was actually coming true.
Now if only things could be straightened out with his parents. His father unsupportive and cold, his mother having an affair with a white man half her age; could things get any worse?

"What did you fight about?" Naomi demanded.
"I don't fight with my children," Carter said.
"Then why does he insist on moving out?"
"It was his decision," Carter shrugged. "I offered to pay for medical school, but he still refused."
"He's not going to medical school," Naomi said. "We've already been through that."
"Then it's time for him to go," Carter said. "I'm not going to let a freeloader live here for nothing. Although I've been doing it for thirty years for your mother."
"Do *not* call Justin or Mama freeloaders!" Naomi snapped. "Justin is working hard every day at school and in getting his new business

An Admission of Weakness

ready. And Mama worked all her life for me, so it's the least we can do now for her."

"She didn't raise me," Carter reminded her. "I don't see why I have to use my money to support her."

"Your money?"

"Yes, my money," he repeated.

"So everything I've done to raise your children, care for this house, do your laundry, and cook your meals was worth nothing to you?"

"That's not what I said," he said impatiently.

"Yes, it is," Naomi scowled. "Maybe I should go with Justin and Mama. At least I'd have someone to talk to!"

She turned on her heel and walked away.

"Justin, you are not moving out of this house," Naomi said. "I don't care what your father said."

"There's an apartment above the gym," Justin shrugged. "I'm moving there."

"And I'm going with him," Ruby said firmly.

"No," Naomi said. "I don't want either of you to leave."

"We know," Justin said. "But he's made it impossible to stay here."

"We'll stay if you'll have Carter committed," Ruby said. "I hear the psychiatric unit at Cook County Hospital is just lovely."

"That's tempting," Naomi couldn't resist a smile. "But no."

An Admission of Weakness

"I told Justin I'd cover his expenses until the business gets going," Ruby said. "My pension is more than enough for us to live quite comfortably."

"I know this isn't what you want, Mama, but it's something I have to do," Justin said. "I'd be leaving home eventually anyway. And once I'm not around, maybe Dad will spend more time with you."

"That won't happen until his book is finished," Naomi said dryly. "But I don't care about that."

With that statement, Justin realized his mother didn't love his dad anymore. She must have fallen in love with Snake. Damn, he never thought he'd end up coming from a broken home.

But how could he blame her? If she and Snake were in love, didn't they deserve to be happy? Mama clearly wasn't content with his dad, so maybe the best thing for everyone was if they divorced so she could get on with her life. She was still reasonably young and attractive, and although Snake was white and a bit rough, he was good-looking. Jeez, his future stepfather wasn't much older than him. How weird was that going to be?

"Mama, I'm just around the corner from Snake's shop," he said. "You can come visit whenever you're there for your...your sewing lesson."

An Admission of Weakness

"What kind of furniture is in this apartment?" Naomi sighed resignedly. "I won't have you two sleeping on the floor."
"There's nothing there right now," Justin said. "But you should see it, Mama. It's really nice."
"Randall did a magnificent job remodeling it," Ruby said.

The next day, Naomi and Ruby met Justin after his classes. There was a large furniture outlet across the highway from the community college, so the three picked out enough furniture to fill the two-bedroom apartment.
"And how will you be paying for this today?" the friendly clerk asked.
Naomi handed him a credit card.
"I won't be paying for it," she smiled. "My husband will."

An Admission of Weakness

CHAPTER TWENTY-NINE

Naomi and Ruby spent the next few days supervising delivery of the truckloads of new furniture and then arranging everything just so. They bought dishes, towels, bedroom linens, and groceries, sparing no expense. Naomi seemed to get quite a lot of satisfaction spending her husband's money.

In the meantime, Justin oversaw delivery and setup of lots of new exercise equipment in between attending classes and studying.

"This is for your first apartment," Naomi handed a wrapped present to her son.

"Mama, you've already done too much," Justin protested.

He opened the package to find a framed picture of the family. It had been taken just before Blair left for college and was the most recent one in which they were all together.

"Thanks, Mama," he grinned. "I love it."

She gathered him into her arms and squeezed, unwilling to let him go.

"I'm so proud of you," she whispered tearfully. "I love you very much."

"I love you too," he said. After a moment, he squeaked out breathlessly, "Mama, I can't breathe."

She released him.

"If there's anything you need, you let me know," she dried her eyes.

An Admission of Weakness

"And if you need me, let me know," he said, "even if it's just to talk."
"I will," she said.
"Whatever you have to do to be happy, I'll support you," he added. "It may take me some time to accept it, but I'll be there for you, I promise."

Most evenings it was just Naomi and Carter in the big house for dinner. Camilla was usually out with friends or on a date. As was his habit, Carter would disappear into his study afterwards to work on his book. Sometimes, Naomi would use the alone time to return to the studio to work on a project.

One evening, Camilla dropped by the gym with a flier in her hand.
"Have you seen this?" she demanded.
Justin examined the first few pages and handed it back to her.
"I don't care about wedding dresses," he snorted. "Especially if they're designed by Snake."
"You'd better care," she opened to the centerfold and showed it to him. "Look at this."
"Holy shit!" he swore at the picture of their mother in a beautiful wedding dress. "Where'd you get this?"
"Some of the patients at the hospital showed it to me," she said.

An Admission of Weakness

"What does it mean?"
"She was in a bridal show and didn't tell us," Camilla said.
"I think it means she's going to divorce Dad and marry Snake," he said grimly.
"Why do you say that?"
"I talked to him," Justin confessed. "I told him to stay away from her."
"What did he say?"
"He said he was into older women and that it was what she wanted," Justin shrugged. "He also said he's in love with her."
"Oh god," she said. "She's really going to leave Dad for this guy, isn't she?"
"It looks like it," he gestured to the glossy page.
"Did he at least seem nice?" she asked.
"Well, he didn't press charges against me when I got arrested for fighting him."
"You were arrested?" she asked with astonishment.
He explained what had transpired when he confronted Snake.
"Obviously, he can't press charges against the son of the woman he's going to marry," she reasoned. "He must really love her."
"I just hope he treats her right," Justin said. "It's going to be weird having a stepfather that's younger than our oldest sister."
"I don't even want to think about it," she wrinkled her nose.

An Admission of Weakness

For three weeks, Robbie tutored Rhett in preparation for his GED.
"I'm too stupid," Rhett sat back on the bed in frustration. "It's too hawd."
"You are not stupid," Robbie said firmly. "You used to get B's and C's when I helped you before."
"Maybe you were a better tutor back then," Blair suggested.
"You are such a funny man," Robbie grinned.
"Maybe it's funny to you, but it's not to me!" Rhett snapped at Blair. "You don't know what it's like to be dumb and ugly and not be able to talk wight."
"Hey, you are none of those things," Robbie said sharply. "You're just feeling stressed from all this studying. I'm working you too hard."
"I'm sorry, Rhett," Blair apologized. "I wasn't making fun. Getting a GED isn't easy. I've been listening, and I don't know some of the stuff you have to learn."
He sat up from lying on his side on the floor of Robbie's dorm room.
"Why doesn't Robbie tutor both of us? We could learn it together."
"That's stupid," Rhett snorted. "You alweady gwaduated."
"No, that's a good idea," Robbie said. "It's always easier to learn with someone else."

An Admission of Weakness

And from that time on, the three of them worked on Rhett's lessons together unless there was a game or practice to interfere. On those evenings, the football team or the cheerleaders were only too happy to take Rhett under their wing. He spent time on the field or in the locker room with them, and they made him an honorary member of the squad and the team, which boosted his ego significantly. Major and Andres were especially doting on the young man.

"The test is tomorrow," Robbie said one evening.

"Let's take the night off and celebrate," Blair suggested. "Whatever you want to do, it's my treat."

"I think I'll study," Rhett said coolly.

"Oh," Blair said. "Sure. That's probably the smart thing to do."

"Don't you have other fwiends?" Rhett frowned. "You've been hanging awound here evwy night."

"Uh, of course I do," Blair said. "You know, I should spend time with Andres and Major. You guys probably want time alone. I should have thought of that. I'll see you later."

He picked up his shoes and other items and left the room.

"He's never going to forgive me, is he?" Blair said unhappily.

An Admission of Weakness

"Sure he will," Robbie assured him.
"I can't blame him after everything I've done," Blair sighed. "And then I horned in on every moment you've spent together. I wasn't thinking; I was just so happy to be back together."
"We're not back together," Robbie said.
"We're just friends with benefits for now."
"I don't like the sound of that," Blair frowned. "It makes it sound like I'm nothing special to you."
"You once called us friends with benefits," Robbie reminded him. "Let's see how it goes at Thanksgiving with your family."
"I promised I would tell them," Blair said. "Don't you believe me?"
"I'd like to," Robbie shrugged.
"Fine, so I don't have the greatest track record," Blair said. "I'm not the same guy I was before."
"The greatest track record?" Robbie grinned. "You didn't even make the race. You're still stuck in traffic trying to get to the race. That's how bad your track record is."

Robbie waited for Rhett to come out of the exam room. When he did, he studied his face anxiously.
"How did you do?" he asked.
"I don't know," Rhett shrugged. "I'll find out tomohwow."

An Admission of Weakness

Rhett packed his things to return to Toadback.
"Blair offered to take us out for dinner tonight," Robbie said.
"No thanks," Rhett said. "But you should go. I can hang out with Andwes or Simon and Major."
"You know, it's okay to like Blair," Robbie said.
"I don't want to like him!" Rhett said harshly. "He made you sad too many times."
"But that's between him and me," Robbie said. "He's never done anything to you."
"Whatever he did to you, he did to me," Rhett said.
"You are such a good brother," Robbie hugged him. "That's why I love you so much."
"I love you too," Rhett said.
"All I'm asking is that you give him a chance, like I'm doing. He knows if he screws up again, it's really over. There are no more chances."
"I hope you mean that."

The GED scores were posted the next afternoon, and Rhett was beyond thrilled to see that he passed.
"I can't believe it!" he shouted gleefully. "I did it!"
"You sure did," Robbie laughed. "I'm so proud of you."

An Admission of Weakness

"I'm pwoud of us," Rhett said. "I'm a high school gwaduate, and you awe almost a college gwaduate."

Rhett headed back to Texas on the train that afternoon. He wanted to stay with Robbie for Thanksgiving in case Blair didn't come through on his promise, but he felt he should be with his mother and sisters for the holiday.

Robbie and Blair slept together that night for the first time since their reunion at the Halloween party. It seemed inappropriate before with Rhett there.
"I leave tomorrow for home," Blair laid his head on Robbie's hairy chest. "I'm going to miss you."
"Me too," Robbie sighed. "Do you know what you're going to say?"
"I thought I'd just say I suck dick and fuck guys up the ass," Blair shrugged. "And then once Dad's out of the hospital after his heart attack –"
"I'm serious."
"As serious as a heart attack?" Blair chuckled.
"Just answer the question."
"I thought I'd say it at the dinner table on Friday. All the aunts, uncles, and cousins will be there on Thursday, and I don't want to ruin that for Mama and Gran. They love the holidays when everyone's together."

An Admission of Weakness

"Will you call me after you talk to them?" Robbie said.
"You don't think I'll do it, do you?" Blair sat up and frowned down at him.
"No, I just want to know what their reaction is."
"If you don't hear from me, that means their reaction was bad and I'm on my way back to school," Blair said wryly.
"I think it will be okay," Robbie said.
"Like it was with your family?"
"My dad's a crazy, ignorant, redneck Trumper," Robbie said. "Your family is educated, and educated people tend to have less problems with gay people."

"Justin and Gran moved out?" Blair looked shocked. "Are you freaking kidding me?"
"And that's not all," Camilla said. "You won't believe what's going on with Mama."
She explained about the wedding dress, Justin's confrontation with Snake, and the impending divorce and remarriage of their mother.
"She told you she's divorcing Dad?"
"She doesn't know we know," Camilla said. "But Snake told Justin he's in love with her and then had her make her own wedding dress."
"It makes sense," Blair nodded.
"Tell me what's going on with Robbie?"

An Admission of Weakness

"It's all good," he grinned. "We're not officially back together; he calls us friends with benefits."

"That doesn't sound good at all," she frowned. "It sounds like he's stringing you along."

"No, he's not," Blair said. "He's just being careful. After all, I have screwed up an awful lot. I don't blame him for not trusting me. That's why this week has to go well."

"Why?"

"I promised him I'd come out to the family while I'm home. He said if I did that it would show him I'm serious about being gay."

"I didn't think being gay was something to be serious about. Isn't it just who you are?"

"I just mean I'm serious about him," Blair explained.

"And are you?"

"I love him more than I can tell you," he said.

"I'm glad," she said. "I liked him. I think he'll be good for you. As for telling Dad, I don't know. He's already in a bad mood from Justin moving out, and Gran hasn't made it any easier."

"Why didn't anyone tell me what was going on up here?" he asked.

"We didn't want to upset you," she said. "Oh god, Dad's going to be so angry about Melissa. And then when you tell him you're gay…all I can say is, you'd better wear your running shoes because he's going to kill you."

An Admission of Weakness

Thanksgiving Day was hectic for Naomi and her mother. There was so much food to prepare for the fifty or so family members who would be in attendance. Camilla and Blair made sure the house was spotless, the bathrooms were stocked with toilet paper, coasters set out on every available surface, and all the beds made. Justin spent the morning in the gym. He didn't want to spend any more time than necessary around his father.

Carter avoided the kitchen and his mother-in-law. He went to the garage and hand washed the black Mercedes E-Class sedan that he was so proud of.

Katie stayed in L.A. for the holiday. Instead, Dillon flew to California for a few days. The city wasn't particularly to his liking since he was a small town boy, but he enjoyed spending the time with Katie.

Dozens of Butterfields arrived, and the day passed without incident. Justin didn't speak to his father, Carter refused to speak to Ruby, but otherwise it was a pleasant time with family.

Friday evening arrived, and Blair and Camilla helped heat up leftovers from the Thanksgiving feast. Ruby and Justin joined the family at Naomi's insistence.

Conversation was stilted and superficial. They were all feeling the tension in the air. Camilla,

An Admission of Weakness

Justin, and Blair were picturing their mother with a white man twenty-five years her junior. Camilla and Blair were nervous about Blair's impending revelation. Justin and Ruby were still angry with Carter, and vice-versa. Naomi remained upset with her husband over her mother and son moving out, not to mention his remark about 'his' money.

Blair talked about school, Justin invited him to see the gym, and Ruby told them humorous stories about some of her tutoring students.

"How's Melissa?" Carter asked. "I was sorry she couldn't come home with you."

"She's fine as far as I know," Blair said uncomfortably.

"You should certainly know how your girlfriend is doing," Carter frowned.

"That's the thing," Blair hesitated. "You see, we, uh, broke up."

"What?!" Carter scowled. "What did you do to her?"

"Why do you assume I did something to her?" Blair said.

"I know you, Blair," his dad said. "You did something to screw things up. You always manage to find a way to –"

"I didn't screw anything up!" Blair interrupted him heatedly. "Just once, couldn't you be on my side?"

"That's a laugh," Justin snorted.

"Tell us what happened, dear," Naomi said.

An Admission of Weakness

"I told her I was in love with someone else," Blair said. "She didn't want to accept that, but she finally dumped me when she saw us kissing."

"You cheated on your fiancée with another girl?" Justin grinned and high-fived him. "Playa!"

"Don't call him 'playa'. Cheating is nothing to be proud of," Camilla scolded him.

She glanced briefly at her mother.

"That's right," Naomi agreed. She turned back to Blair. "Go on."

"Who were you kissing?" Carter demanded. "And why would you ask Melissa to marry you when you knew you were already in love with another woman?"

"I never wanted to marry Melissa," Blair said. "That was all your idea."

He reached in his jeans pocket and pulled out his grandmother's ring. He handed it to his dad. "Here, let Justin have this. I don't need it."

"I don't need it," Justin said. "I'm not getting married."

"You're saying that I wanted you to marry Melissa?" Carter snatched the ring from Blair.

"You practically made me do it," Blair said.

"I wanted you to marry Danielle," Carter said. "I still do. She's the perfect girl for you."

"There is no perfect girl for me," Blair said.

"Why not?" Naomi asked gently.

469

An Admission of Weakness

"That's why I don't want to get married," Justin grinned. "I'm just going to sleep around. Why settle for one girl when there are millions of them out there?"
"You'd make a great gigolo," Camilla rolled her eyes.
"Thanks," Justin said.
"It wasn't a compliment."
"Why is there no perfect woman for you, Blair?" Naomi asked again.
"Who were you kissing?" Carter repeated.
"It was just someone," Blair said tentatively.
"The point is, I didn't love Melissa."
"Who do you love?" Ruby asked.
"Um, no one, really, I guess," Blair said uneasily. "I just didn't want to marry Melissa."
"Tell them why not," Camilla prodded.
"I still want to know who you were kissing," Justin said. "I'll bet she has big –"
"Justin," Naomi shook her head at him.
"It was just a random gir– person at a party," Blair said.
"Tell them who it was," Camilla said.
"It doesn't matter who it was," Blair said. "Melissa wasn't the right woman for me, and that's all there is to it."
"I'll call Danielle," Carter said. "That's the girl for you."
"No, Dad," Blair said irritably. "I don't want Danielle. She's a bitch."

An Admission of Weakness

"She comes from a wealthy family," Carter said dismissively.

"Look, I need you all to listen to me," Blair said. He took a deep breath and blurted out the words, "I'm not into women. I like guys."

Carter and Justin stared at him with slack jaws.

"What did you say?" Justin frowned.

"I like guys," Blair repeated. "That's why I couldn't marry Melissa. I don't like women."

"So you're gay," Naomi said. It wasn't a question.

"I'm gay," Blair said. "But it doesn't change anything. I'm still the same person I've always been."

"You're not gay," Carter shook his head dismissively.

"I am gay. I was confused at first; I didn't understand the feelings I was having. But I do now, and I'm definitely gay."

"Of course you're not," Carter said firmly. "You're still confused."

"He's not confused anymore, Dad," Camilla said. "He knows how he feels."

"Nonsense," Carter said. "It's just that Melissa wasn't the one. I thought she was, but it appears I was wrong. I'll call Danielle, or we'll find another woman for you."

"Blair, are you okay?" Naomi asked. "I'm sure this must be a traumatic time for you. I wish I'd known you were having those feelings."

An Admission of Weakness

"It wouldn't have made any difference," he said. "It was something I had to figure out for myself."

"And you feel confident that this is who you are?" Ruby asked.

"I've never been so sure of anything in my life," Blair said firmly. "I know who I am now."

"I think that's wonderful," Ruby smiled. "Now you can be your authentic self."

"Thanks, Gran," Blair said gratefully. "Mama?"

"It's fine, sweetheart," Naomi smiled. She stood and gave him a hug from behind. "I always kind of knew, but I'm glad you finally told us."

"I'm not," Justin scowled. "I can't believe my own brother is a fag."

"Do not use that word!" Camilla said.

"Why not? That's what he is," Justin threw down his napkin and stood up. "What the hell is wrong with this family? Blair's a sexual deviant, Dad's a fucking prick, and Mama is –"

"Justin," Ruby said. "That's enough."

"It is enough," he agreed. "I can't sit here with a goddamn faggot."

He spat in his brother's direction.

"I have no brother anymore," he said coldly. "You might as well be dead for all I care!"

With that, he kicked his chair over and strode from the room. A moment later, they heard the back door slam hard enough to rattle their dishes.

"He'll come around, dear," Naomi said. "It's just new to him. Don't give it another thought."

"I'll talk to him," Ruby patted his hand. "It will be okay."

"It will not be okay," Carter stood and pushed his chair back. "If Blair insists on pursuing this aberrant lifestyle, he will not be welcome in this house."

"Dad, you don't mean that!" Camilla cried.

"I do mean it."

"I'm not 'pursuing' anything," Blair said. "This is just who I am. Gay people don't choose to be gay any more than straight people choose to be straight."

"We don't have to choose to be straight," Carter said icily. "It's how we're born, how we're supposed to be."

"And this is how I was born," Blair said. "It's how I'm supposed to be."

"I won't listen to this garbage any longer," Carter said. "I don't want you here in the morning when I get up. Go back to that school and your perverted friends. I'm sure that's how you got caught up in this despicable lifestyle."

"Fine," Blair said. "If you don't want me here, I'll leave, and I won't be back."

"Now let's just all calm down," Naomi said. Blair ignored her and walked to the door and looked back.

An Admission of Weakness

"I should have known this is how you were going to react. Fuck you, Dad."

An Admission of Weakness

CHAPTER THIRTY

Naomi hurried after Blair as he ran up the stairs to his bedroom.
"Don't listen to your father and your brother," she said while she watched him pack his things. "Please don't leave."
"I can't stay here," he said. "Justin hates me, Dad hates me."
"They don't hate you," she said. "They just don't understand."
"Do you have a problem with me being gay?"
"Of course not," she said. "I love you for who you are, and I always have. And so does your grandmother and Katie and Camilla."
"Wait," he frowned. "How did you know they knew about me?"
"Katie may have let it slip, but it was an accident," Naomi said. "She told me about Robbie, and she said he's very nice."
"Well, if dad hates me, he's really going to hate Robbie. So if I have to choose between the two, I'll choose Robbie. I love him with all my heart."
"I'm glad. And he feels the same way?"
"Yes, he does," Blair said. "We have some things to work out, but any problems we've had are my fault. That's why I'm trying to be honest with everyone, especially him. I was a total dick to him, and yet he stood by me. He's the best thing that ever happened to me."

An Admission of Weakness

"If you love him, then I love him too," she said. "But a white Mississippi boy named Robert E. Lee? Seriously?"

She grinned impishly, and he smiled back and gave her a hug.

"I love you, Mama," he said.

"So will you stay and let us try to work this out?"

"Okay," he said. "I'll stay for you and Gran. But if Dad pulls any bullshit…"

"It's four against two," she said. "We have the truth on our side, so we can't lose."

"Are you on your way back to school?" Robbie asked.

"Mama talked me out of it," Blair flopped back on his bed.

"It was that bad?"

Blair described the scene at dinner.

"What did they say when you told them about me?"

"Um, the way you'd expect," Blair said evasively.

"I'm sorry," Robbie said. "But at least it's done. They know who you are now, and they know we're in love."

"It didn't get any better," Blair said when he returned to Urbana. "Dad and Justin refused to listen, and Justin said he wished I was dead instead of gay."

An Admission of Weakness

"At least he didn't try to shoot you," Robbie said wryly.
"He might have if he'd had a gun," Blair said. "What are you going to do about Christmas?"
"I promised Mama I'd come home. She said that gives her a whole month to work on them."

The month passed quickly for Blair and Robbie. There were football games, studying, and final exams to get through before the Christmas break.
Robbie, as usual, planned to work and spend time with Andres and a few other friends.
Major and Simon were going to Simon's house for the holiday.
"Am I still just a friend with benefits?" Blair asked one night.
"I think we can promote you now," Robbie said. "How does 'guy I'm dating' sound?"
"Not great."
"Guy I'm dating who I'm also sleeping with?" Robbie suggested.
"No."
"Boyfriend with a question mark?"
"How about just boyfriend?" Blair said.
"Boyfriend, huh?" Robbie said thoughtfully. "That does have a nice ring to it."
Blair began tickling him.
"Say it," he said sternly. "Say I'm your boyfriend."

An Admission of Weakness

"I'm your boyfriend," Robbie giggled and gasped out the words while he tried to push Blair away.

"You're my boyfriend," Blair said. "Say it."

"You're my boyfriend, you're my boyfriend," Robbie said.

"There," Blair released him. "Was that so hard?"

"It wasn't, but it is now," Robbie pulled back the sheet over them to reveal his erect manhood.

Blair took it in his mouth for a few minutes until Robbie begged him to stop before he came. Blair grinned wickedly and then lowered his ass onto it.

"Holy fuck, you're tight," Robbie groaned.

"I'm not used to bottoming," Blair grunted while he adjusted to Robbie's length.

"You did your fair share of it in the videos," Robbie reminded him. "You did your fair share of everything."

"You were right there with me for three days," Blair said. "You did things even I couldn't do, you animal."

"What can I say?" Robbie grinned. "I'm a multi-talented guy."

"I'll say," Blair said. "You impressed the hell out of me. You'd have been the bigger star if we'd stuck with it."

"You want me to call Ollie? I'll bet he's still got our contracts."

An Admission of Weakness

"I don't think so," Blair leaned down and kissed him. "But there is one thing you did that I want to try sometime."

Blair remained at school a few extra days to celebrate Christmas with Robbie.
"This past month has been the happiest of my life," he said. "I finally know who I am, what I want, and who I want. And most of that is thanks to you."
"I'm glad if I helped," Robbie said. "But the journey was always yours alone. You're the one who did it."
"Here," Blair extracted a package from under his bed. "Merry Christmas."
Robbie grinned and hurried across the hall to his own room. He returned a moment later with a gift in his hands.
"Merry Christmas to you too."
"You first," Blair said.
Robbie ripped the paper off and opened the small box. Inside was a silver watch with a silver band and a rectangular, navy blue face.
"It's beautiful," Robbie breathed.
"Look at the back."
Robbie turned it over and squinted:
To Robbie Lee, the only man I'll ever love
"See," Blair said. "I put it in writing."
"This is the nicest gift I've ever gotten," Robbie said. "Thank you."

An Admission of Weakness

They kissed, and then Robbie told him to open his present.

"It's perfect," Blair chuckled. "I love it."

He held up the red, apple-shaped mug that said 'world's greatest teacher' on the side. It featured a comical green worm for a handle.

"I wish we could be together for Christmas," he gave Robbie a kiss. "I hate the thought of you being alone."

"I'm used to it," Robbie shrugged. "Mama says Dad's doing a lot better about me being gay. Gran's been educating him and Justin, so it sounds promising."

"I think it would help if they met me," Robbie said. "Once they see that we're in love and happy together, they might look at things differently."

"You're probably right," Blair acknowledged. "But you have to work, and there will always be other chances to meet them."

Blair arrived home in the middle of the afternoon on Christmas Eve. He was in a funk at leaving Robbie for the remainder of Christmas break. Also, he wasn't expecting much from his father or Justin in spite of his mother's words. And he couldn't help but wonder when she was going to announce that she was leaving his dad and marrying Snake. Jeez, he was going to have a stepfather named Snake!

An Admission of Weakness

He stepped in through the back door and tossed his dirty laundry bag onto the laundry room floor. He shivered and threw his coat and gloves on the washing machine.

"I'm home," he said and took a deep breath. The house smelled heavenly of gingerbread, Douglas fir trees, his mother's rib roast, and Christmas spices.

His mother and grandmother looked up and smiled, but before they could greet him, someone else ran up and leaped into his arms.

"Ooohh!" she squealed with delight. "I'm so happy to see you!"

He held her at arm's length, and his eyes widened.

"Danielle? What are you doing here?"

"You see, I told you he'd be thrilled to see me," Danielle said to Naomi and Ruby. "I knew you missed me as much as I've missed you."

"What are you doing here?" he repeated as she embraced him again and he pushed her away.

"I'm here so we can start making wedding plans, silly," she clung to his arm.

"Who's getting married?" he frowned.

"We are, of course."

"Where did you get an idea like that?"

"Shame on you, acting like you didn't propose," she scolded him. "Your dad told me how you begged him to call me because you were tired of seeing other people, and now it's time for us to get serious about our future."

An Admission of Weakness

"Mama?" Blair turned to her.
"Don't ask me," Naomi shrugged. "Ask your father."
The front doorbell rang.
"Blair, dear, will you get that?" Ruby asked.
"I'll come with you," Danielle took his hand and pulled him through the house, leaving Ruby and Naomi to glance knowingly at each other.
The house was decorated festively for the holiday. One seven-foot live Douglas fir stood in the living room picture window covered in hundreds of ornaments and white lights. Another tree stood at one end of the dining room in the bay window with multi-colored lights, and a third tree stood on the second floor landing, visible from the foyer and front door. The stairway banister was adorned with evergreen boughs, red bows, and white Christmas lights. There were poinsettias scattered throughout the house along with a multitude of other Christmas decorations.
Blair opened the front door.
"Hi," he said. "Can I help you?"
"Hello. My name is Ashura Otieno," the dark-skinned stranger shivered. He spoke in a dignified Kenyan accent. Smiling warmly, he extended his hand. "Dr. Ashura Otieno."
"Hi," Blair shook his hand. "Come in out of the cold."
Katie hurried down the stairs at that moment.

An Admission of Weakness

"Blair!" she said.

The two hugged, and Blair had to forcibly remove his hand from Danielle's so he could embrace his sister. Camilla joined them from the living room and hugged her siblings. She looked curiously at Ashura.

"And who is this?" she asked.

"I am Dr. Ashura Otieno," Ashura smiled. When they all continued to look at him questioningly, he continued. "I spoke at your high school last month. Dr. Butterfield invited me to Christmas Eve dinner."

"How nice," Camilla said.

"That is a lovely boubou," Ashura complimented her.

"Thanks," she smiled. "Well, take your coat off and come stand in front of the fireplace. You look frozen."

She took his coat and duffel bag and led him and the others into the living room. She walked on to the kitchen.

"Mama, Dr. Otieno is here."

"Who?" Naomi frowned.

"Dr. Otieno," Camilla repeated. "He's here for Christmas Eve dinner, he said. He's carrying a duffel bag."

Ruby and Naomi turned to one another and shook their heads.

"Dad invited him," Camilla said.

"Go tell your father he's here," Ruby said.

After Camilla walked away, she added, "Of all

An Admission of Weakness

the nerve, inviting two extra people for dinner without telling us."

"I hope that's all," Naomi said grimly. "This rib roast will only go so far."

Danielle picked up Blair's bag from the kitchen floor and pulled him up to his bedroom. She began unpacking his things for him.

"So my father invited you?" he looked puzzled. "Why?"

"He told me how brokenhearted you've been ever since graduation," she folded his underwear and socks and put them away. "He said you've become sexually confused because of some terrible people you're involved with."

"I was confused," Blair admitted. "But I'm not anymore. And they're not terrible people."

"When he told me you proposed," she continued dreamily as if he hadn't spoken, "I said yes immediately and agreed to come for Christmas."

She reached over and kissed him.

"Danielle, I didn't propose," he said.

"Yes, you did," she smiled. "Why else would I be wearing your grandmother's ring?"

"He gave you the ring?" Blair examined the glittering jewel on her finger. "God, he must be truly insane."

"I would have preferred to get it from you, but he couldn't wait for me to have it."

An Admission of Weakness

"Danielle, I'm gay, and my father's crazy. I'm sorry he got you here under false pretenses, but I'm not going to marry you."

"You are not gay," she laughed and hung a shirt in the closet. "I had to rearrange your things so mine would fit."

He looked in the closet and his dresser drawers. Dozens of her panties, bras, dresses, blouses, and skirts were neatly arranged alongside his own.

"What the fuck?" he scowled. "You've moved in."

"Just for now," she said. "Once we're married, Mother and Dad will set us up in one of their houses close to your new job."

"What new job?"

"Whatever Mother has you doing with the firm," she shrugged. "Eventually, you'll be the CEO of Morgan Enterprises."

"Danielle, I don't know the first thing about business. I'm an education major."

"No, you're not," she frowned. "You're a business major."

"I only told Mama and Dad that," he said. "I'm studying education. I want to be a teacher."

"Why? Teachers don't make any money. They barely make a living wage."

"It's not about the money," he said.

"Everything's about money," she snorted. "Don't worry. Mother will get you the training you need to run the company."

An Admission of Weakness

"I'm not going to work for your mother," he said. "We are not getting married because I'm gay. I suck dick and fuck guys up the ass."
"Please," she said dismissively. "You and I had sex more times than I can count, not to mention all the other stuff we did. You can't tell me you're gay because I know better."

When Blair and Danielle came downstairs, Carter was involved in a conversation with Ashura in the living room.
"Dad, I need to speak to you," Blair tried to speak civilly.
"After the holidays," Carter said. "You can thank me then."
"I don't want to thank you," Blair said.
"Blair, can't you see I'm speaking with our guest here? We'll talk after the holidays."
Katie and Camilla were setting the dining room table while their mother and grandmother continued dinner preparations in the kitchen. Justin had arrived and was helping them. He was barely speaking to any of the family at this point.
The front doorbell rang just before dinner, and Blair and Danielle answered it hand in hand.
"Grandpa," she smiled. "You made it."
"When someone offers me a free meal, I'm there," her grandfather joked. "Blair, it's good to see you again, young man."

An Admission of Weakness

Charles Morgan was a distinguished looking, seventy year old gentleman with graying hair and twinkling eyes. He was a retired captain in the Army and had been wounded in Vietnam, causing him to have a slight limp for which he used a cane. His days were spent gardening, painting, or playing the piano when he wasn't volunteering at the school.

"Hello, sir," Blair grinned. He remembered the older man's dry sense of humor. "You're looking well. That's a sharp outfit."

Charles was wearing black slacks, a black silk shirt with a plum colored vest over it, a plum bowtie, brown and black shoes, and a brown and black knee length overcoat. Atop his head was a black fedora with a dashing plum feather in the band.

"You've got to dress how you feel," Charles grinned. "And I'm feeling jaunty."

"That's just the word for how you look," Blair chuckled. "Come on in."

Charles hugged his granddaughter and Blair. "Where is that gorgeous grandmother of yours?"

"She's in the kitchen," Blair grinned.

"You're looking fit," Charles felt Blair's bicep. "My goodness, football certainly agrees with you. I've been following the games. Maybe you should think about a professional career."

"He's going to work for Mother," Danielle said.

An Admission of Weakness

"Hmm," Charles winked at Blair. "Lucky boy."
"Um, Camilla's done a lot more of her mural since you were here last," Blair changed the subject.
"I definitely want to see that," Charles winked knowingly at him. "Now lead me to the food and the beautiful women, and leave me alone the rest of the night."
"Grandpa," Danielle scolded him.

"Charles, what the hell are you doing here?" Ruby scowled when he stepped into the kitchen.
"Mama!" Naomi frowned. "Don't talk to guests like that. You knew he was coming."
"I was hoping the senile old fool would forget," Ruby said dryly.
"It's nice to see you too, Ruby," Charles grinned. "I'm surprised you're still sober this time of day."
"Too bad for me," she said huffily and carried a bowl of sweet potatoes to the dining room.
"Charles, it's lovely to see you," Naomi smiled and kissed his cheek.
"You're more beautiful than ever, Naomi," he said. "I can still picture you at the bridal show in that wedding dress. You stole the show."
"Let's keep that under our hats," Naomi glanced around. "Mama's the only one in the family who knows about it."
"It's our secret," he winked.

An Admission of Weakness

"Charles, why don't you make yourself useful instead of standing there using up valuable oxygen?" Ruby scowled. "Help me bring some wine up from the cellar."
"Do I look like your hired hand?" he frowned. "I came here to eat, not to wait tables."
He followed her to the wine cellar and held the basket while she selected four bottles of red wine.
"You're looking lovely as ever," he grinned.
"And you look quite dashing tonight," she smiled. "You just keep getting more handsome, you beautiful man."
She caressed his cheek, and he kissed her hand. He set the basket down, and the two kissed passionately.

An Admission of Weakness

CHAPTER THIRTY-ONE

"Have you all been introduced to Dr. Otieno?" Carter asked after everyone found a seat at the dining room table.

"Please call me Ashura," their guest smiled.

"Ashura spoke at the high school about being an immigrant," Carter said. "When he told me he's all alone, I insisted he come spend the holiday with us."

"We're so pleased you could come, Ashura," Naomi said graciously. "Where are you from?"

"Nairobi," he said in his precise, accented voice. "I was orphaned there. A couple from Kitisuru paid for me to go to university, and I came to the United States to study medicine."

"That's impressive," Carter said. "And wasn't it polite of you to accept their generosity in paying for you to become a doctor. It just shows what some dedication and vision will do for one's future."

"Subtle," Justin rolled his eyes.

"Katie, you and Ashura have a lot in common," Carter said. "I thought you'd enjoy talking to him since he's a doctor, while you chose to only become a nurse."

"Are you working here in the States?" Katie ignored him.

"Yes, I have a clinic on Chicago's Southside," Ashura smiled. "I became a citizen of this country last year and wanted to give something back to the people here who have been so kind to me."

"That's wonderful," Katie smiled. "I think helping people is so important. It beats what I do."

"Camilla, I want to see your mural," Charles said. "Blair tells me you've added to it."

"Of course," Camilla said. "Are you still painting?"

"I dabble," he said. "I'm not as talented as you though."

"I'd enjoy seeing your murals too," Ashura said.

"If you'd like," Camilla smiled.

"You're very talented, Grandpa," Danielle said. "And you play the piano so beautifully."

"So do you," he winked at her. "I miss hearing you."

"What are you studying at Dartmouth, Danielle?" Ruby asked.

"African American Studies," Danielle replied.

"I'll bet that's interesting," Katie said. "We should all know our history."

"Why?" Justin asked. "It won't change anything."

"Those who don't know their history are doomed to repeat it," Charles said.

"Tell that to white people," Justin said sarcastically. "They're the colonizers, the land stealers, the mass-murderers. We aren't."

An Admission of Weakness

"We should all know our history," Carter said firmly. "If we want to better ourselves, we must learn from the past."

"I *am* bettering myself," Justin said.

"Danielle, have you made some good friends at Dartmouth?" Naomi quickly changed the subject.

"Yes, quite a few," Danielle said. She went on to talk at length about some of them.

"I'm surprised you didn't study music," Ruby said. "You're so gifted."

"I tried to get her to," Charles said.

"Mother wouldn't hear of it," Danielle said. "She said music can only take you so far."

"It's nice you recognize your mother has your best interests at heart," Carter said.

"Oh my god," Ruby murmured.

"Perhaps you and your grandfather will perform for us after dinner," Naomi shot a frown at her husband.

"Your father's trumpet solos were legendary in high school," Carter said. "He had the talent to go all the way to the top."

"So it's okay for him to follow his dream, but not me?" Justin said.

"My point is, he knew better than to follow a foolish dream. Instead, he was responsible and married well, and now he's part owner of a multi-million dollar company."

"There's more to success than wealth," Charles said. "Money doesn't bring happiness."

An Admission of Weakness

"Then you must be the happiest man on the planet," Ruby said.

"What would a sourpuss like you know about happiness?" he retorted.

"Mama," Naomi said.

"Grandpa," Danielle said. She changed the subject. "Blair will make a great addition to Mother's company. He was always so smart in school."

"He's acing his business classes," Carter said. "He'll make a brilliant business man someday. You know, I was just remembering how close you two have been since middle school. I'll bet you're glad to rekindle the old flame."

"Glad isn't the word," Blair said dryly.

"Ecstatic is more like it," Danielle grinned. "I can't believe how much I've missed him. And all of you, of course. I can't wait to be part of your family, Dr. Butterfield."

"Please call me Carter," he smiled.

"Blair and you getting married? That's a laugh," Justin snorted and glared at his brother. "Blair's not the marrying kind. At least not to a woman."

"Justin, I've been hearing good things about your new business," Charles said.

"It's magnificent," Ruby said.

"It really is," Naomi smiled proudly. "I'm thinking about getting a membership myself."

An Admission of Weakness

"Stop by anytime, Mr. Morgan," Justin said. "I'll give you a tour personally. I'd say Dad could give you one, but he's never been there."
"Mama, these sweet potatoes are so good," Katie said.
"Do you like to cook?" Ashura asked.
"Mama's tried to teach me," Katie grinned. "But I'm hopeless."
"No, you're not," Naomi said. "You're just not as interested in it as I am."
"I hope she's not as interested in 'sewing' as you are," Justin muttered.
"What's that?" Katie said.
"I said you don't like sewing like Mama does either," Justin said. "I hear she has a real talent for it. That's what Snake says."
"Shut up, Justin," Camilla said grimly.
"When did you talk to Snake?" Naomi frowned. "I didn't know you knew him."
"He said he loves you because you remind him of his mother," Justin watched her for her reaction.
"Isn't that sweet?" she smiled. "He's a lovely young man."
"That doesn't creep you out?" Justin said incredulously.
"Why would it?" his mother looked confused. "It's a very nice compliment."
"I'd like to hear more about Ashura's clinic," Camilla said hurriedly.
"Are you also a nurse?" Ashura asked.

An Admission of Weakness

"I'm a nursing assistant at the hospital."
"A very noble profession," he smiled.
"Katie is the head of nursing at one of those big Los Angeles hospitals," Carter said.
"That must be a rewarding job," Ashura said.
"It's a lot paperwork," Katie shrugged. "I miss working with patients."
"Nonsense," Carter said. "You're far too educated to be doing menial work."
"There's nothing wrong with menial work," she said evenly.
"I didn't say there was anything wrong with menial work. Camilla's very suited to it," Carter said. "But you should have a job commiserate with your education. You have an executive education, and that's the job you've taken.
"Fortunately, your brother's education in business will make it possible for him to take on an executive position in Danielle's family business."
"Dad –" Blair began.
"I'm glad Blair's going to marry Danielle," Justin interrupted him. "She's still the prettiest girl in Green Grove. If she can't fix him, no one can."
"Justin," Naomi shook her head at him.
"Would anyone like more wine?" Ruby held up a bottle. "I for one need mine in a Big Gulp."

An Admission of Weakness

After dinner, Camilla showed Ashura and Charles the mural-covered walls of her bedroom. Blair and Danielle accompanied them, holding hands the entire time. Ashura and Charles were quite complimentary of Camilla's work and became involved in an in-depth discussion about art in general.

Danielle pulled Blair to his room and wrapped her arms around him while she kissed him.

"It's been too long," she said. "I swear we won't ever be separated again."

"Danielle, I'm seeing someone," he said.

"I know," she said. "Melissa something or other. Obviously, you have to dump her before we get married."

"I already dumped her," he said.

"Wonderful," she grinned. "Then there's nothing to stop us."

"I'm seeing someone else," he said.

"It doesn't matter," she said. "Whoever she is, she can't be as pretty as me."

"It's a he, and he is prettier than you," he said dryly.

"Not this again," she sighed. "Once we're married, you'll forget all that nonsense. I'm here to take away your confusion." She smiled impishly. "You certainly weren't confused back when we were together. You were an animal."

"I was just a kid then, but I've grown up," he said.

An Admission of Weakness

"Do you remember when we did it at the Victoria?" she chuckled. "It's a miracle we didn't get caught. Or in Coach Dobson's office?"

"I remember," he chuckled. "How about in the bathroom at Molly's or in the backseat of your grandfather's Chevy?"

"Oh my god," she laughed. "I almost forgot that."

"You used to go crazy when I'd suck your tits while I fucked you," he grinned. "You even liked it when I fucked you in the ass."

"I still like that," she said coyly. She grew serious for a moment. "The time I remember the most fondly was the first time we did it right here in this room. We were fourteen. You were so nervous, but you knew I was too, so you acted strong for me. You were so passionate and made me feel like I was the prettiest girl in the whole world. Those were such wonderful times."

"Danielle –"

Before he could say any more, she dropped to her knees, unzipped his jeans, and took him in her mouth. It didn't take long for him to get hard.

"Oh fuck," he moaned and closed his eyes as she expertly tended to him.

"This will take away your confusion," she said before returning to the job at hand.

After another minute, she spoke again.

An Admission of Weakness

"I'm thinking a June wedding at Mother and Daddy's mansion on the lake."
"That sounds perfect," he gasped.
She removed her slacks and panties and backed up to him.
"Danielle, I'm not going to fuck you," he frowned.
"Yes, you are," she said.
She used the voice that always allowed her to successfully manipulate him into doing whatever she wanted him to do. Blair used to call it 'the voice', and he had been helpless against it.
"Okay," he moved into position, but before he could do more than slide into her body, someone knocked on their door.
"Danielle, we want to hear you and your grandfather play for us," Ruby said.
"Damn," he scowled.
"Don't worry," she grinned. "We'll finish this later."

Charles played some jazzy tunes on the grand piano in the living room, and then the family gathered around to sing Christmas carols. Afterwards, Danielle performed Beethoven's 'Pathetique Sonata' and Mozart's 'Rondo in D Major'.
"Magnificent," Charles said. "You should be performing in public."
"That's what Ian says," she said modestly.

An Admission of Weakness

"Who's Ian?"
"He's just one of the friends I was telling you about."
"I'd like to hear 'O Holy Night'," Ruby said. Charles sat down at the piano once again, and Danielle stood beside it and cleared her throat. Once her grandfather played an introduction, she began the song in her flawless soprano. The others listened in awe as the duo performed the beautiful song, which climaxed on a high C-Sharp.
"That was lovely," Ruby said. "My dear, you belong on the stage with that voice."
"You absolutely do," Naomi agreed.
"Blair, it's a good thing you're not letting this girl get away again," Carter said. "She's one in a million."

They all returned to the dining room for coffee and dessert. Blair helped his mother carry things from the kitchen and took her aside.
"Did you know Dad gave Danielle grandmother Butterfield's wedding ring?"
"Yes, I knew," her mother said. "I tried to talk him out of it, but he wouldn't listen."
"She thinks I'm going to marry her," Blair said.
"You don't have to if you don't want to."
"I'm gay, Mama," he said frustratedly. "I'm not going to marry Danielle. I'm in love with Robbie. God, I finally get things figured out,

and he throws me right back into it again! Damn him."

"I know it's frustrating."

"He's doing what he always does," Blair said. "He's forcing me into a situation like he did with Melissa. Between Dad and Danielle, I'm going to get all confused again. I can already feel it. How the hell am I supposed to get out of this?"

"I'll talk to him again, but I doubt it will do any good."

Justin ate his chocolate cake and sweet potato pie quickly and then said a curt goodbye.

"I'll be staying here tonight," Ruby said. "Naomi and I have a lot of work to do in the morning."

"That's fine," Justin said. He looked pointedly at Blair. "I'm going to Winnie's to find a woman. That's what a real man does. But I guess you wouldn't know anything about that, would you, Blair?"

Winnie's was a popular, upscale tavern/eatery on the west side of town.

"You don't have a clue what a real man is, little brother," Blair said. "Going out and sleeping with random women isn't it."

"At least I sleep with women," Justin said.

"Real men aren't threatened by other people's sexuality," Blair said. "Maybe you should look at yourself if you have a problem with me."

An Admission of Weakness

"Maybe I should kick your ass," Justin said grimly.
"Fine," Blair stood up. "Let's see you try."
"There will be no fighting, you two," Ruby said sternly.
"It wouldn't be much of one anyway," Justin snorted.
Blair headed for the kitchen and the back door.
"You coming? Or are you all talk?" he demanded.

The two brothers circled one another warily in the snowy back yard.
"Justin, Blair, stop this!" Naomi called from the back door. "Come in this house at once."
"Let them fight it out," Carter pulled her back inside. "Maybe it will teach Blair a lesson."
"And what lesson is that?" she snapped. "That fighting makes you more of a man?"
"Exactly."
"That's the stupidest thing I've ever heard," she glared at him and walked away.
Outside, Justin threw a punch and missed, and Blair slugged him in the stomach. There was more hitting and then the two grappled for supremacy on the ground. Blair pulled away and kept his fists up. Justin hit him with a right cross, and Blair retaliated with one of his own. After several minutes of this, Justin ended up on the ground with Blair sitting on his back and holding his arm behind him.

An Admission of Weakness

"Have you had enough?" Blair panted.
"Get off me, faggot!" Justin spat into the snow.
"Not until you say you won't call me that name anymore," Blair said.
"Faggot!" Justin said defiantly.
Blair wrenched his arm higher, causing Justin to cry out in pain.
"Say you won't call me that name anymore," Blair repeated.
"Faggot," Justin said with a little less conviction.
"You want me to break this arm?" Blair said. "Because I will, and how's that going to look to your customers? You'd have to tell them you got beat up by your gay brother. You'll be the laughing stock of Green Grove."
He waited, but Justin remained silent.
"Say it," Blair said through gritted teeth, "or I swear to god I'm going to break your arm."
He wrenched the arm even higher.
"Ow!" Justin yelled. "You're gonna break my arm!"
"That's the whole idea, stupid," Blair said. "You think beating someone in a fight or sleeping with random women makes you more manly than a gay guy, but you're dead wrong. A gay guy just beat the shit out of you, so what does that make you? I guess you're less of a man than I am, huh?
"Look, I've slept with lots of women, and I tried to like it. I gave it more than a fair chance,

An Admission of Weakness

but it's not for me. This is the way I was born. I didn't choose it, and there's nothing I can do to change it. God knows I tried. Man, did I try. But this is who I am, and you'll just have to deal with it. And if you can't, then that's your problem, not mine. I don't need you; I can live my life very happily without you. But I'd like to have a brother. So say you won't call me a faggot again."

"No," Justin said.

"Then I guess you can go looking for a woman with a broken arm," Blair sighed.

Just as he started to increase the pressure on Justin's arm, Justin spoke up.

"Okay, okay," he said hastily.

"Okay what?"

"I won't call you that anymore," Justin said.

"You promise?"

"I promise already!" Justin snapped.

"Good," Blair said. "Now was that so hard?" He shoved Justin's face deeper into the snow and then released him. Justin stood up and rubbed his sore arm. He glowered at Blair.

"It doesn't matter what I call you," he said. "You're still a faggot."

Blair ran at him, but Justin turned and ran for his car. Blair chased him for a moment and then watched him jump hurriedly into his car and squeal his tires on the driveway.

An Admission of Weakness

It was bedtime on Christmas Eve. The Butterfield custom was to stay up until midnight to welcome Christmas day with a cup of eggnog. The atmosphere was a bit subdued this year, and after finishing their eggnog, they bid each other good night.

Naomi and Ruby showed Ashura the guestroom, and then Ruby asked Charles to help her with some linens kept in the cedar closet on the third floor.

"Why do we have to keep up this charade?" he asked as he took her in his arms and kissed her neck and face. "I want the whole world to know I love you."

"I do too," she said. "But this is still new to both of us. I want it to be just you and me for a while. I don't want anyone else's opinions on what we're doing. And now it seems things have rekindled with Blair and Danielle. Let things settle with the family, and then we'll tell them."

"You do love me, don't you?" he frowned.
"Of course I do," she said. "And we'll tell the whole world when the time is right. Just not yet."

Charles said goodnight to the Butterfield family and drove home to his immaculately kept bungalow in his mint condition '76 Chevrolet Caprice sedan.

An Admission of Weakness

Naomi told Ashura to make himself at home and then said good night. She and Carter closed the door to their room, and Ruby settled into her old bedroom as well.

Katie and Camilla headed to their bedrooms, and Blair reluctantly allowed Danielle to stay with him in his room. He was never able to say no to her when they were in school, and apparently, he still couldn't.

"Wouldn't you rather stay with your grandfather?" he said. "You rarely get to see him these days."

"I came home for you," she said. "I'm obviously going to sleep with my fiancé."

"Danielle, I told you I'm gay," he said uneasily.

"You are so funny," she chuckled. "We proved you're straight earlier; no gay man is going to get an erection with a woman like that."

"You take my bed," he said. "I'll sleep on the couch in the den."

"Don't be silly," she began undressing. "Come to bed. It will be like old times."

"It can't be like old times," he said. "I'm not the same man I was."

She removed his shirt and then unfastened his jeans while she used 'the voice'.

"You know this is what you want, so stop fighting it. Tonight you'll realize once and for all that I'm the only one for you."

She helped him undress and then quickly disrobed until they were both naked.

An Admission of Weakness

"You see," she grinned. "You're already getting aroused." She fondled his genitals, placed his hand on her breast, and kissed him passionately.

Against his will, Blair found himself getting hard. She took his hand when he was fully erect and led him to the bed.

"Now lay down," she said. She remembered his sexual preferences, so she licked his armpits, sucked his nipples, and fingered his ass while she blew him and sucked on his balls. He had done this dozens of times with her, so it was second nature to suck her nipples while she straddled his groin and carefully inserted his manhood into her. She sighed contentedly as she sat down on him. "You see, this is who you are. You are not gay."

"Danielle, I'm not wearing a condom."

"Shhh," she leaned down to kiss him. "Just fuck me. Let's make a baby tonight."

Ashura descended the stairs in his robe and pajamas and tentatively walked to the kitchen. He just had to have another bite of that incredible sweet potato pie.

He cut himself a piece, poured a glass of milk, and sat down on a barstool at the center island. The only light came from the large vent hood over the industrial range, leaving most of the room in shadows.

An Admission of Weakness

"Oh!" Camilla jumped when she noticed him. "I wasn't expecting anyone to be down here." She was wearing a flannel nightgown and slippers.
"I'm sorry," he stood up. "I will go."
"Don't be silly," she smiled. "It looks like you had the same idea I did."
He sat back down and resumed eating his pie while she cut herself a slice.
"I couldn't resist," he said. "I'm not used to such wonderful cooking."
"Do you cook?" she settled down beside him.
"Some," he said. "But not like this."
"It must get lonely for you, all alone in the city," she said.
"Sometimes," he nodded.
"Tell me about your patients," she said. "Your work sounds fascinating."
The two talked for an hour about Ashura's patients and their mutual desire to help people. The kitchen lights came on, and they looked up to see Katie enter the room wearing a frumpy chenille bathrobe and fuzzy slippers.
"What are you two doing?" she asked curiously as she helped herself to a bottle of cold water from the refrigerator.
"Talking about Ashura's work," Camilla said. "Come join us."
The three of them discussed their views on healthcare for a while.

An Admission of Weakness

"I'm sorry your brothers are fighting," Ashura said. "Am I correct in thinking that Blair is gay?"

"He is."

"Then what is Danielle doing here?"

"Dad is determined that Blair is going to marry Danielle," Katie said. "And once he has his sights set on something, he won't give up until he accomplishes it."

"Danielle seems determined to marry Blair as well," Camilla said. "He's got an uphill battle on his hands."

"So that is why Danielle and Blair are sleeping together now? I don't understand. If he's gay, then how can he sleep with a woman?"

"Blair was confused about his sexuality for a long time, mostly because he felt he had to have Dad's approval. He's just now coming to terms with it, and Dad is doing his best to prevent that."

"He's in love with a man named Robbie from school," Camilla added. "I met him, and he's wonderful."

"I'm sorry," Ashura shook his head. "I still don't understand."

"Join the club," Katie sighed. "I think Blair's still confused, so I don't know what the hell's going to happen."

"Katie, do you know why your father asked me here?"

An Admission of Weakness

"So you wouldn't be alone, he said," Katie said.

"That was partly it," he said. "I promised I wouldn't tell you, but I cannot repay your kindness to me with lies. You see, your father –"

"What's going on here?" Carter stepped into the room in his robe and reached into the refrigerator for a soda.

"We're just talking," Katie said.

"That's nice," Carter said. "Camilla, don't you think you should go to bed and let Katie and Ashura talk alone?"

"No," Camilla said.

"Then let me rephrase that," her father said sternly. "Go to bed."

"Fine," she stood up and put her dishes in the dishwasher. "I'm tired anyway."

"I should go to bed too," Ashura said.

"No, you two talk," Carter urged him. "Get to know one another."

He took his soda and escorted Camilla from the room.

"Of course," Katie said. "You're here for me, aren't you?"

"I'm afraid so," he nodded. "I hope you are not angry."

"I'm angry with Dad, but not you," she said. "I should have known he was up to something. Ashura, you are a lovely man, but I already have a fiancé."

An Admission of Weakness

"Then why would your father ask me here?"

"He doesn't like Dillon," she said. "We've been affianced secretly for a few years."

"Why keep it secret? Are you ashamed of him?"

"Not at all," she said. "Dad is a difficult man to stand up to, but Dillon is coming to dinner tomorrow, and we're finally going to tell everyone that we're getting married."

"And if your father doesn't accept it?"

"I've learned that whatever issue he has with Dillon is his problem. I can live without Dad if that's how he wants it, but I won't live without Dillon. I'll still have Mama and Gran and the rest."

"Good for you," he said. "It is a courageous thing you are doing. There is a saying: lying is an admission of weakness. Telling the truth is being strong and true."

"I'm done with being weak. Dillon and I deserve better than this. Tomorrow, a new chapter starts for the two of us."

An Admission of Weakness

CHAPTER THIRTY-TWO

Naomi and Ruby made biscuits and gravy, bacon, eggs, and fruit the next morning and then called everyone down to eat. Charles returned to join them, but Justin was a no show. Snow had fallen during the night, dropping three inches of the pristine, powdery substance over the town.
"How did everyone sleep?" Carter asked.
"Like a log," Camilla said.
"We didn't get much sleep, did we, baby?" Danielle grinned mischievously and squeezed Blair while she clung to him.
"That's good to hear," Carter said approvingly. "Katie, what about you and Ashura?"
"We didn't get much sleep either," Katie nudged Ashura. "Did we?"
"That's right," Ashura grinned. "She gave me quite the workout."
"I'm glad to hear that," Carter smiled. "Well, let's eat so we can get to the gifts."

"Blair, what are you doing?" Camilla took him aside. "Did you sleep with Danielle?"
"Yes, but I didn't cum. I'm just pretending to go along with things until New Year's."
"You're leading her on? That's not fair."
"I've told her repeatedly that I'm gay," he said. "She won't listen. We'll stay for Dad's New

An Admission of Weakness

Year's Party and then I'll go back to school and Robbie."

"Dad's still going to expect you to marry her," she pointed out.

"I won't be back home until Spring Break. Maybe by then, I'll think of some way out of it."

"But –"

"Look, Dad and Danielle never listen to a word I say," Blair said frustratedly. "The only thing I can do for now is keep them happy until I can get away from here."

"Are you sure they aren't playing with your mind?" she asked worriedly. "It's bad enough when Dad manipulates you, but now it's two against one."

"I just have to hold out for a week," he said.

After breakfast, the family gathered around the tree in the living room. Blair and Danielle sat squeezed together in a chair with their arms around each other. Charles sat on the sofa next to Ruby.

"You two make out up in your room," Ruby scolded Blair.

"Sorry, Gran," Blair stopped kissing Danielle.

"We can't open presents without Justin," Naomi said. "Someone text him and tell him we're waiting for him."

An Admission of Weakness

"I'll text him," Ruby picked up her phone just as someone knocked on the front door in the foyer.

"Who would be coming by on Christmas morning?" Carter said.

He opened the front door and frowned at the stranger standing there in the heavily falling snow.

"Can I help you?"

"Hi, I'm Robbie," Robbie said.

"Whatever you're selling, we're not interested, and I think it's in poor taste to go door to door on Christmas Day."

He started to close the door, but Robbie stopped him.

"I'm Robbie Lee," he said. "Is Blair here?"

"You know Blair?" Carter said. He sighed. "Fine. Come in. He's in the living room."

Robbie brushed the snow from his hair and coat and followed Carter through the wide living room doorway and smiled at the group of people staring back at him. His smile faded when he saw Blair sitting cozily with a woman curled up on his lap with their arms around one another. They were kissing and giggling.

"Blair, there's someone here to see you," Carter said. "He said his name is Robbie."

Blair turned to stare at Robbie with a look of horror. He unceremoniously shoved Danielle off of him, and she landed on the floor.

An Admission of Weakness

"R-Ro-Robbie?" he stammered. "What are you doing here?"
"This is Robbie?" Naomi said.
"Robbie!" Camilla cried. She jumped up and ran to give him a hug.
"Hi, Camilla," he embraced her distractedly. "It's good to see you again."
"What are you doing here?" Blair frowned.
"I-I thought I'd surprise you," Robbie gulped. "I, uh, wanted to meet your family."
"Robbie, I'm Naomi, Blair's mother," she graciously shook his hand.
"It's so nice to finally meet you," Robbie smiled. "I've heard so much about you. You're even prettier than he said."
"Thank you, dear," she said. "Let me introduce you to everyone. This is my mother Ruby, and that's Charles Morgan, a friend of the family. You know Camilla, and this is Katie, my oldest."
Robbie smiled and shook each of their hands.
"It's nice to meet you," Katie smiled.
"Justin isn't here yet," Naomi continued, "but he's due any minute. This is Dr. Ashura Otieno, a friend of my husband's. And this is my husband Carter."
"Nice to meet you, sir," Robbie shook his hand.
"Yes," Carter frowned suspiciously at him. "Robbie Lee. What's your full name?"
"It's, um, Robert Eustace Lee," Robbie said hesitantly.

An Admission of Weakness

"And so it begins," Ruby muttered while she and Charles eyed one another uncomfortably.

"Robert E. Lee?" Carter's eyes widened, and he dropped Robbie's hand. "Your name is Robert E. Lee? Where are you from?"
"Toadback, Mississippi."
"A southern white boy named Robert E. Lee," Charles whistled in disbelief. "Is this a joke?"
"Where's a glass of wine when you need one?" Ruby murmured.
"What are you doing here?" Blair asked impatiently. "You said you had to work."
"I, uh, took some time off."
"You haven't met our other guest yet," Carter said. "This is Danielle, Blair's fiancée."
Danielle stepped forward and shook his hand.
"You mean ex-fiancée," Robbie corrected him.
"Oh no," Danielle said. She extended her left hand to show off the magnificent marquis diamond on her ring finger. "I'm his fiancée."
Robbie merely stared at her blankly.
"It's so nice to meet you," she gushed. "Are you a friend of Blair's?"
"Yes, he's a friend from school," Blair answered. "I didn't know he was coming."
"You've got to be kidding me," Robbie said. "You're engaged again?"
"Yes, we just announced it yesterday," Danielle said. "Isn't that fabulous news?"

An Admission of Weakness

"You know, I'm interrupting your Christmas," Robbie swallowed with difficulty. "I'm sorry. I-I'll go."

"Nonsense," Naomi said. "Come and join us. You drove all that way."

"This snow is supposed to turn into a blizzard any time now," Charles said. "You'd better stay."

"If I leave now, I should be able to beat the snow back to Urbana," Robbie backed toward the door. "Again, I'm so sorry for bothering you all on Christmas morning."

He turned and fled out the front door with Blair hurrying after him.

"Robbie, wait!"

"I can't believe I fell for it again," Robbie paused in the heavily falling snow to pace in a circle and rub his forehead with his gloved hand. "Oh my god, I must be the stupidest person on the face of the earth."

"She's not my fiancée," Blair said.

"She's wearing the fucking ring you gave Melissa," Robbie snapped. "You know, don't even try to explain because I refuse to listen to any more lies."

"Dad gave her the ring before I got here," Blair said. "He told her I proposed. I didn't even know she was going to be here until I got home yesterday."

"Did you sleep with her?"

"Yes, but nothing happened."

An Admission of Weakness

"You slept in the same bed with her, and nothing happened?" Robbie said skeptically. "Next you're going to tell me I just imagined she was sitting on your lap while you were making out. Goodbye, Blair."

He opened the car door.

"Robbie, I'm telling you the truth," Blair said.

"You wouldn't know the truth if it hit you over the head!" Robbie yelled angrily. He snatched up handfuls of snow and hurled them at Blair. "God, Rhett was right all along when he said not to trust you. He told me over and over not to take you back, but I wouldn't listen.

"You didn't even tell them about me," he gestured to the house. "They have no fucking idea who I am. You lied again. They don't even know you're gay, do they?"

"They know I'm gay. I told them at Thanksgiving, just like I said," Blair said. "And Mama knows about you. Obviously, I didn't tell Dad about you, but that's because he wouldn't listen. He never listens to me."

Robbie looked up at the big flakes falling around them and tried to keep the tears from falling.

"Why did I have to fall in love with you?" he asked the sky. "Why not someone I could trust?"

"You can trust me," Blair said. "Come back in, and we'll tell them who you are together."

An Admission of Weakness

"Who am I? I'm nobody," Robbie said. "Just a poor, white trash boy from Toadback. I'm not your boyfriend, I'm just a 'friend' from college."

"Robbie, I love you!" Blair exclaimed. "This is all a big mess created by my dad. I'm just playing along until I go back to school."

"And that obviously included sleeping with Danielle," Robbie said sarcastically. "You had no choice."

"I could have slept on the sofa," Blair admitted.

"But you didn't. Were you naked?"

"You weren't there," Blair said. "Danielle always gets her way, and she insisted I sleep with her. I can't say no to her."

"So you were both naked in the same bed, and she wanted sex."

"But she didn't get any. I mean, she did, but I didn't cum. I just played along to keep her happy."

"So you had sex with her, just hours after you and I made love yesterday morning."

"It wasn't real. I was just pretending."

"Of course you were. She's a beautiful woman, so you 'pretended' to fuck her."

"I did pretend!" Blair said indignantly. "I spent most of the night fighting her off."

"And the rest of it was spent plowing her into the mattress. I know your history, remember?" Robbie said dryly.

An Admission of Weakness

A late model pickup pulled into the driveway, and a man got out.

"Hey, Blair," Dillon said. "Thought I'd come a little early to beat the snow. It's really getting bad out there."

"Katie's in the house," Blair nodded. "Go on in."

"I've got to go," Robbie got in the car and started the engine.

Blair ran to stand behind the automobile with his arms crossed defiantly.

"Get out of the way!" Robbie rolled the window down and shouted at him.

"No! You're staying here, and we're going to get this whole thing straightened out. We'll tell Dad who you are."

"No, we won't," Robbie said. "Now get out of the way."

"You heard Dillon," Blair said. "The roads are getting bad. It's not safe for you to drive back to school. You're not used to the snow. You'll end up dead."

"I'd rather be dead than with a lying piece of shit like you," Robbie said.

He put the transmission in reverse and inched the car closer to his ex-boyfriend. Blair refused to budge.

"I'll run you over," Robbie threatened.

"No, you won't," Blair said.

Robbie kept a foot on the brake and revved the engine.

An Admission of Weakness

"I'm warning you," he said.
"You are so cute when you try to be tough," Blair chuckled.
Robbie sighed and put the car in park. Blair walked up and opened his door.
"An inch of snow has fallen while we've been out here," he said. "There's no way you're driving home in this."
He removed Robbie's battered suitcase from the backseat and walked to the house.
"Come on," he said. "I'm freezing."

Another car pulled into the driveway as Blair and Robbie entered the house. It was an old, rusted Toyota Corolla with Maryland plates. A young, attractive Black man with long hair got out and looked around before knocking on the front door.
"It's like Grand Central Station around here," Ruby frowned as she walked through the foyer. "Don't people stay home on Christmas anymore?"
She opened the door.
"Yes?" she said.
"Hi, I'm Ian Bailey," the stranger said. "I'm looking for Danielle."
"Ian? From Dartmouth?"
"That's me," he grinned.
"Yes, she mentioned you," Ruby said. "Come in and join the circus."

An Admission of Weakness

"Ian, what are you doing here?" Danielle quickly removed her arms from around Blair. She had latched on to him as soon as he walked back in the house with Robbie. "How did you find me?"

"You never answered my calls, so I called your dad, and he told me where you were. I couldn't let you face this alone, so I took off work and drove here."

"All the way from New Hampshire?" Charles said, surprised.

"Yes, sir," Ian nodded. He turned back to Danielle. "Did you make it in time?"

"In time for what?" Blair asked.

"Before her aunt passed –"

"Before the snow started," Danielle answered hastily.

"Hi, I'm Danielle's fiancé," Blair frowned and shook Ian's hand.

"You're her what?" Robbie scowled.

"I mean her ex-fiancé," Blair corrected himself. "We dated all through school."

"Oh right," Ian said. "I'm glad the Marines let you come home."

"Uh, yeah," Blair said uncertainly. "You and Danielle go to school together?"

"That's how we met," Ian nodded. "We're in most of the same music classes."

"I didn't know you were taking any music classes, Danielle," Charles said. "I'm glad to hear it."

An Admission of Weakness

"You're Dannie's grandfather?" Ian shook his hand. "You're even more distinguished than she said, sir."

"Well, aren't you perceptive," Charles grinned.

"You're classmates?" Blair asked suspiciously.

"Yes, he's a classmate," Danielle said truthfully.

"Why do you care?" Robbie asked Blair.

"I don't," Blair shrugged. "I was just asking."

"Uh-huh," Robbie muttered. "Are you ready to talk to your dad?"

"In a minute," Blair brushed him aside.

"Talk to me about what?" Carter frowned.

"Nothing, Dad," Blair said impatiently.

"Actually, Dannie and I are much more than classmates," Ian began.

"Are you dating or something?" Blair scowled.

"Blair?" Robbie said.

"Blair?" Carter said.

"Danielle?" Blair ignored them and scowled at his fianceé and Ian. "Are the two of you dating?"

"I need a drink," Robbie said.

"It's not even noon yet," Carter said. "I don't know how they do it in Mississippi, but we don't indulge in alcohol until evening around here."

"It's five o'clock somewhere," Ruby muttered. "Robbie, come with me; I hate to drink alone."

"That's never stopped you before," Charles called after her.

An Admission of Weakness

"Go crawl under your rock," Ruby retorted.

Ruby and Robbie sat down at the kitchen table, and she poured them each a small glass of white wine.
"So you're Robbie," she looked him up and down. "It's nice to finally meet you. Forgive me, but could you be any whiter?"
"Probably not," he said ruefully. "What's whiter than a poor, blonde-haired, white-trash boy from the rural south whose dad is a maga Trumper that wears confederate flag shirts everywhere he goes?"
"How about a poor, white, trailer-trash southern boy from Toadback named Robert E. Lee?" she said wryly.
"And there you have it," he held his glass up. "I'm officially the whitest guy in America."
"You didn't know about Danielle, did you?"
"I knew he dated her in high school, not that they're getting married," he said.
"To be fair, that came as a surprise to Blair as well."
"So he really is engaged to her? Because he said he's not."
"No, he is."
"Then how could that be a surprise to him?" he asked. "Because it would be totally like him to have been dating her this whole time while he was seeing me."

An Admission of Weakness

"Once you've gotten to know Carter, you'll understand a few things about Blair," she said.
"It doesn't matter anymore," he said. "As soon as the weather clears, I'm out of here."
"Why?"
"Did you see Blair interrogate Ian out there? He's jealous of him. He's never been jealous of me. He had sex with Danielle last night just hours after leaving me, and they were all over each other when I first got here. If I hadn't showed up when I did, they probably would have run off and eloped."
"Do all gay men have sex with women?" she asked curiously. "It seems like that would defeat the whole point of being gay."
"Gay men don't sleep with women," Robbie said. "If they do, they're either bisexual or trying to prove something to themselves."
"Which is Blair?"
"He's just an egotistical troglodyte," Blair said.
"Your accent gets much stronger when you're upset," she observed.
"That's it," he downed his wine. "I can't do this anymore. This isn't even the first time he's been engaged to a woman while we were dating. Do you know he's slept with more women than I can count since I've known him?"
"I did not know that," she frowned.
"Well, it's true, and there are videos to prove it. Look, is there a motel here in town?"

An Admission of Weakness

"There are two," she nodded. "But they're always booked for the holidays."

"I can't stay here and watch him and Danielle celebrate their engagement," he said. "I never should have come here."

"But you're here," she said. "You might as well make the best of it. He may surprise you and stand up to Danielle and his father."

The back door burst open, and Justin stepped inside and shook the snow from himself. He shivered and threw his coat haphazardly on the washing machine before kicking off his snow boots.

"Damn, it's cold out there," he rubbed his hands together. "I just heard they're closing the highways and the Interstate, Grandma. Who's the white guy?"

He poured himself a cup of coffee.

"This is Robert E. Lee," Ruby said wryly.

"Is that supposed to be funny?" he said. "Like he's not white enough."

Ruby couldn't resist laughing, and Robbie joined her.

"What's so funny?"

"I was just telling him he's the whitest person I know," she said.

"So who is he?"

"I go to school with Blair," Robbie said. "I just stopped by to wish him and Danielle all the happiness in the world."

An Admission of Weakness

"He's gonna need more than well wishes to be happy in that marriage," Justin snorted. "You a faggot like him?"

"Justin!" Ruby scolded him sharply.

"I see that toxic masculinity runs in the family," Robbie said. "Although your case seems even more severe than your asshole brother's."

Naomi and Camilla entered the kitchen just then, preventing Justin from uttering an angry retort.

"We've got a meal to prepare," Naomi said. "Everyone out so I can figure out how I'm going to feed this crowd."

"Did you already open gifts?" Justin asked.

"Don't worry, your toy fire truck is still under the tree," Ruby said dryly.

She led her grandson and Robbie from the room. Justin disappeared upstairs, and Ruby squeezed Robbie's arm in solidarity.

"Be patient with Blair," she said. "This is his father's doing, not his."

"So why does he act like he's head over heels for his soon to be bride?" Robbie said.

"He's a good actor?" she suggested.

"Well, at least finding out like this gives me time to buy them a wedding present," Robbie said.

"How about a wedding cake laced with arsenic?" she said with a grin.

"Perfect," he agreed.

An Admission of Weakness

"Can we help?" Ashura and Charles asked Naomi.
"Ashura, you can help Camilla make the pasta salad," Naomi said. "Double the recipe, Camilla, dear."
"Yes, Mama."
"Tell me what to do, Chef," Ashura rolled up his sleeves and grinned at Camilla.
"What about me?" Charles asked.
"Help Mama with the cornbread," Naomi said.
"What does he know about cornbread?" Ruby said.
"I know mine tastes a whole lot better than yours," he said.
Naomi watched while the two older people picked and groused at one another. Who did her mother think she was fooling?

"Dillon, don't you need to get back to that little farm of yours?" Carter frowned. "I can't imagine what was so important to make you leave your family on Christmas Day. Or is your family not that close?"
"We're very close," Dillon said calmly. "And that little farm is actually a thriving horse ranch. Perhaps you should stop by sometime, and I'll give you a tour."
"I've seen horses before," Carter said. "Katie, why don't you go help Ashura in the kitchen?"
"Who's Ashura?" Dillon frowned.

An Admission of Weakness

"Dr. Ashura Otieno," Carter said. "He and Katie hit it off quite nicely."

"He's a doctor friend of Dad's from Chicago," Katie explained.

"He and Katie spent the night together," Carter said. "They said it was wild."

"Dad! Why would you say something like that?"

"It's true," Carter said. "You both told me you had a wild night together."

"What was so wild about it?" Dillon scowled.

"Use your imagination," Carter said. "And while you're doing that, wake up to the fact that you're wasting your time sniffing around here. Katie is not interested. So go on home and don't bother coming around here again.

"Katie, do as I say; go on out to the kitchen and talk to Ashura. Build on what happened last night."

"Yes, Katie, go build on the good time you had last night," Dillon said grimly. "Obviously, I was wrong to come here today."

"Dillon, nothing happened," Katie said, but Dillon walked away. She turned to her father. "Thanks a lot."

"I didn't expect a thanks so soon," he said. "But I'll take it anyway."

CHAPTER THIRTY-THREE

Blair, Danielle, and Ian were sitting on the upholstered window seat of the dining room bay window when Robbie left the kitchen.
"Blair, it's time we talked to your father," he said.
"How long have you two known each other?" Blair ignored Robbie and focused on Ian.
Robbie leaned against the dining room doorway and watched the trio.
"Three years," Ian said. "I'm sorry to change the subject, but I was wondering what's happening with your aunt, Dannie?"
"Oh, uh, she made a complete recovery," Danielle said. "It's a miracle, really."
"I'm glad," Ian grasped her hand and squeezed. "You must be very relieved."
"What are you majoring in, Ian?" Blair asked.
"French horn," Ian said. "I want to lead an orchestra someday. I recently played a solo with the New York City Orchestra."
"You must be very good," Blair said with displeasure.
"I'm working on it," Ian said modestly.
"Where are you from?"
"Bethesda, Maryland. I got a partial scholarship, and I work in the cafeteria to help pay for school. What about you? Being in the Marines must be a tough job. But you have the build for it."

An Admission of Weakness

Blair flexed his biceps and nodded.
"You must not work out much," he observed.
"Blair, what are you doing?" Robbie scowled.
"Do you work out?" Blair ignored him.
"Not much," Ian said. "Between classes, practice, working, and spending time with Dannie, I don't have time for anything else."
"What did you mean earlier when you said you're more than classmates?" Blair frowned.
"I'm his accompanist," Danielle said hastily. "He's very talented."
"What he wants to know, Ian, is if you and Danielle are sleeping together," Robbie interjected dryly.
"We've been a couple for almost –" Ian began.
"Sleeping together?" Danielle interrupted him. "Don't be silly. Ian and I are just close friends."
"We are?" Ian frowned. "I'm just a close friend to you?"
"Oh, Ian, you're so funny," Danielle chuckled nervously. "Why don't we talk about something else?"
"Danielle?" Blair frowned.
"Blair, let's talk to your dad," Robbie said, becoming angrier by the minute.
"Robbie, will you just wait a minute!" Blair exclaimed with annoyance.
That did it, Robbie decided. Blair was clearly more concerned with Ian and Danielle's relationship than his with Robbie. He turned on

An Admission of Weakness

his heel and walked into the living room, where Carter was looking through a newspaper.

"Dr. Butterfield, can I talk to you for a minute?"

"Why?" Carter said with annoyance.

"I have something to say that you need to hear," Robbie said patiently.

"I doubt that very much."

"I'm in love with your son," Robbie said.

"How dare you make such a ridiculous statement," Carter scowled. "I'm not going to sit here and listen to this."

He stood up to leave the room, but Robbie blocked his way.

"Please, just let me talk."

"You're wasting your time saying such foolish things," Carter said. "The very idea that Blair would fall for someone like you is laughable, even if he was homosexual. Blair's in love with Danielle."

"Maybe. But I came here so I could tell you that I love him."

"It's obvious you're only here to convert him to your evil way of life," Carter said. "He's going to marry Danielle."

"He said you arranged that."

"I had nothing to do with it. And now that they're getting married, I think it's in very poor taste for you to come here on Christmas Day to try to spoil his happiness."

An Admission of Weakness

"He said he told you he was gay at Thanksgiving," Robbie said. "Is that true?"

"This is the first I'm hearing of it," Carter said sourly. "Are you finished?"

"He never told you about me, did he?" Robbie said.

"If I thought he was gay and in love with someone like you, he wouldn't be welcome in this house."

"Well, maybe he doesn't love me like I thought he did, but I have loved him for three years. And whether he says he's straight or not, he and I have been in a physical relationship.

"No matter what you think, a man can love another man romantically. Being gay is not a sin, and it's not a choice. Believe me, my life in Mississippi would have been a hell of a lot easier if I'd been able to be straight, but that wasn't who I was. People don't choose their sexuality any more than they choose the color of their skin or hair.

"I pretended to be straight so I could stay alive. A gay boy in Toadback wouldn't have lasted long, trust me. That's why I hid who I was until I could get the hell out of there.

"My own father used a shotgun to force me out of our house the night I left. He shot a hole the size of a toaster in the wall right next to where I was standing. That's how much he hated me. You actually remind me a lot of him."

An Admission of Weakness

Carter glared witheringly at him, but Robbie forged ahead.

"I didn't want to be an outsider all my life, but I didn't have a choice. You do have a choice," he went on. "You can choose to accept your son for who he is, or you can pick up a gun and threaten his life. I can tell you this, if you don't accept him for who he is, you're going to lose him forever. He may play straight so you'll love him, but he's going to be miserable his whole life. As a father, I'd think you'd want him to be happy. Surely you don't want your children to live unhappy lives.

"Blair wants your love more than anything in the world, and he's willing to destroy his own life to get it. Why don't you give it freely so he doesn't have to do that? Because if he spends his life unhappily with Danielle or some other woman, that will be your fault, and I don't think you want to live with that."

Carter merely stared at him impassively.

"That's all I have to say," Robbie said. "I love Blair, and I think he loves me. We'd like to have your blessing. And he needs your acceptance."

"That's enough!" Carter exclaimed angrily. "How dare you come into my house and spew your vile lies! I want you out of here now." He took Robbie by the elbow and propelled him roughly toward the front door.

An Admission of Weakness

"Carter, what are you doing?" Naomi frowned. She had just walked into the living room to ask him to get the leaves for the dining room table from the attic.

"This young man is leaving this house right now," Carter said grimly. "I won't have him under this roof a second longer."

"Where is he supposed to go?" his wife demanded. "There's a blizzard out there."

"I don't care where he goes, but he's not staying here."

"Carter, Robbie is a guest in our home," she said. "He's welcome here."

"He most certainly is not! He's a homosexual who's spent the last three years trying to corrupt our son," Carter said. "Are you going to just stand by and allow him to do that?"

"Robbie, would you excuse my husband and me?"

Robbie returned to the dining room.

"Carter Butterfield, what is the matter with you?" Naomi snapped. "Have you forgotten every good manner you were ever taught?"

"That boy was sent by the devil to ruin Blair and Danielle's happiness," Carter said. "You can see in his eyes that he's pure evil."

"All I see is a sweet young man who came to visit his friend," Naomi said.

"He is not staying under my roof," Carter scowled.

An Admission of Weakness

"Fine," she said. "If you're going to send him out into the blizzard, I'm going with him." With those words, she turned on her heel and strode away.

"Danielle, could I ask you a question?" Robbie returned to the dining room, where Blair was still grilling Ian.

"Uh, sure," Danielle arose reluctantly.

She and Robbie walked to the foyer.

"This is none of my business, but when did Blair propose to you?" he asked.

"He asked his father to give me the ring while he was home for Thanksgiving," she said. "Why?"

"No reason," Robbie said. "And since he got home yesterday, he said he still wants to marry you?"

"Yes, of course. He said he was tired of being with other people. Why else would I have the ring?"

"I know this is a personal question, but did the two of you sleep together last night?"

"I suppose he had to brag about it like a typical man," she smiled. "It was wonderful. He was so passionate."

"So you had sex?"

"Of course," she said. "All night long." She leaned in and whispered conspiratorially.

"We're trying to get pregnant."

An Admission of Weakness

"Really?" Robbie blinked with surprise. "Has he said anything to you or the family about being gay?"

"Blair's not gay," she chuckled. "Where'd you ever get an idea like that?"

"So the two of you are in love?"

"Very much so," she said. "Oh, I see where this is going. You were hoping I was available. I'm sorry, but obviously I'm not. Camilla's single, though. I could put in a good word for you, if you like."

"Yes, if you would, that would be great," Robbie said dryly. "You're a peach."

"I know," she said. "And if I'm honest, sweetie, you would never have had a chance with someone like me in the first place."

"Thanks for being honest," he resisted the urge to strangle the bitch.

Robbie climbed to the top of the stairs and sat down. He watched the Christmas tree lights twinkle on the upstairs tree and listened to the wind whistle around the corners of the house while he thought about things.

So Blair had lied again and again and again. The man had no shame, no morals, and he would sleep with anyone and everyone. Maybe it was a good thing he came here after all; at least this way, he was able to confirm with Blair's own family that he was a liar.

An Admission of Weakness

Dillon took the stairs two at a time and nearly ran over Robbie before he noticed him.
"Sorry," he apologized. "I didn't see you there."
"I shouldn't have been in your way," Robbie said.
"Why are you sitting here?"
"I needed to get away from everyone for a while," Robbie said.
"Me too," Dillon said. "I'm Dillon."
"I'm Robbie," he shook his hand. "Nice to meet you."
"Are you friends of…who are you exactly?"
"I came here to surprise Blair, but I'm the one who got the surprise."
"I got a shock when I got here too," Dillon said.
"Was yours as bad as mine?" Robbie asked.
"Probably," Dillon said. "Katie and I were supposed to announce our engagement tonight, but I found out she spent the night with some doctor who's staying here."
"Dr. Otieno," Robbie nodded. "I met him briefly. He seemed very nice."
"Great," Dillon sat down dejectedly. "I've spent the last fifteen years waiting to marry Katie, and the night before we announce it, she meets a doctor and sleeps with him."
"Damn," Robbie frowned. "I'm sorry."
"What was your surprise?" Dillon asked curiously.

An Admission of Weakness

"I thought Blair and I were in love, but I come here and find out he's engaged to Danielle, and they had hot, sweaty sex all night long last night, trying to make a baby."

"That doesn't sound very gay to me. No offense, bro."

"He's not," Robbie said. "Or I guess he's pansexual. Hell, I don't know what the fuck he is. He's lied about everything from the day we met, and yet I stupidly fell in love with the bastard."

"So what are you going to do?" Dillon asked.

"I want to leave, but apparently I'm stuck here because of the blizzard."

"I have a four-wheel-drive truck outside," Dillon said. "We could try to make it to my parents' ranch. I don't feel like sticking around here either."

"You'd let me stay with you? I'm a complete stranger to you."

"I recognize a kindred spirit," Dillon grinned. "Come on. Let's go."

Dillon eased his big truck onto the street and put it in four wheel drive. The snow was coming down heavily now, and the wind was whipping it into fantastically shaped drifts. Visibility was near zero. Cars were being covered, and many of the streets were impassable.

An Admission of Weakness

It took nearly an hour, but they managed to get to Market Street before they were forced to turn around.
"Damn it," Dillon cursed.
"You know, maybe you ought to go back and confront Dr. Otieno," Robbie suggested. "After all, fifteen years is a lot of time to waste. I mean, if you really love her."
"You know, you're right," Dillon frowned. "What the hell am I doing? Running away like a scared rabbit? And you should confront Danielle."
"I already did," Robbie said regretfully. "Unfortunately, she and Dr. Butterfield confirmed everything I was afraid of."
"I'm sorry," Dillon said. "But if it helps, I think Blair would be better off with you than that bitch. We call her the barracuda."
"Thanks," Robbie made an effort to smile.

Blair and Danielle were setting the dining room table when Dillon and Robbie returned to the Butterfield house.
"Well, there's the happy couple now," Robbie said sarcastically. "Did you make Ian leave so you wouldn't be so threatened, Blair?"
"I don't know what you're talking about," Blair frowned.
"Of course you don't," Robbie said. "Did you even notice I was gone?"
"You were?"

An Admission of Weakness

"Oh my god," Robbie rolled his eyes and walked on to the kitchen.
"There you are," Naomi smiled at him.
"I'm so sorry for showing up like this and intruding on your Christmas."
"So are we," Justin said.
Ruby smacked him on the back of the head.
"Ow!" he scowled and moved away from her.
"Nonsense," Naomi said. "Now I didn't know your food preferences, so I hope you like what we've prepared."
"He's obviously not too picky about what he puts in his mouth," Justin said.
This time Charles slapped him on the side of the head.
"Stop it!" Justin cried indignantly.
"Anything you make will be fine," Robbie said. "It all smells fantastic."
"A Mississippi boy like you is probably used to good old southern cooking," Ruby said.
"I love southern cooking," Robbie said. "Homemade buttermilk biscuits, collard greens, okra, chitlins, black-eyed peas, fried chicken, sweet potato pie. Northern people don't know what good food is."
"So now he's a food expert," Justin snorted.
"Justin, will you go and call the family to the table?" Naomi said impatiently.
"Fine," he rolled his eyes and left the room.

An Admission of Weakness

"How do you feel about cornbread?" Ruby held up a hot cornbread in a cast iron skillet from the oven.
"No meal's complete without it," he grinned.
"Mine's better than hers," Charles said.
"Is there such a thing as bad cornbread?" Robbie said.
"I knew I liked you," Ruby twinkled at him.

The dining room table sat ten, so the family, Ashura, Charles, and Danielle took their places while Robbie, Dillon, and Ian sat at a separate table.
"You could sit with me, you know," Robbie said to Blair.
"I can't not sit with the family," Blair frowned.
"You're right," Robbie said. "You and your fiancée should definitely sit with the family."
"Robbie," Blair sighed. "She's not my fiancée."
"It's fine. I don't mind," Robbie waved him away. "Just pretend I'm not even here. You've been doing a good job of that since I arrived, so keep it up."
"I didn't know you were coming," Blair said irritably. "What do you want me to do? Make a scene in front of everyone?"
"And risk upsetting Danielle? You sure wouldn't want your future bride to be unhappy. By the way, she told me all about last night, so you don't have to pretend anymore."
"What did she say?"

An Admission of Weakness

"That she hopes you made a baby," Robbie said. "The point is, as soon as I can leave here, I'm going back to school, and you are never, ever to speak to me again."
"Robbie, I was just pretending," Blair said. "I didn't cum, and she knows it. Who are you going to believe? Your boyfriend or a girl you just met."
"That's an interesting question," Robbie said. "And the answer is, I choose her. You couldn't tell the truth if your life depended on it."

"Blair and Danielle aren't really engaged, are they?" Ian whispered to Dillon.
"No," Dillon said. "That's just what Blair's dad wants. Blair's gay from what I understand."
"Well, that's a relief," Ian said.

Naomi finished carrying the bowls and platters of food to the table before she sat down.
"Blair, shouldn't you sit with your friend? He came all the way from Urbana just to see you," she frowned.
"Blair gets the jitters if he's too far away from Danielle," Robbie said dryly.
"Robbie," Blair said grimly. "Be quiet."
"Did you seriously just tell me to be quiet?" Robbie said incredulously. He stood up. "You know, I'm not hungry after all."
He left the room in the direction of the foyer.

An Admission of Weakness

"Blair?" Ruby gestured toward the foyer with her eyes.
"What?" Blair said. "I'm hungry."
"Dannie, don't you want to sit with me?" Ian frowned.
"I would, but the family expects me to sit with them," she said.
"I drove a thousand miles to be here," he reminded her.
"I can't be rude," she said.
"She's fine where she is," Blair said firmly.
Ian sat down crossly at the card table with his arms folded.
"Dillon, come sit beside me," Katie said.
"Where will your new boyfriend sit if I do that?" Dillon asked sarcastically.
"Okay, fine," she stood up and pulled him into the kitchen.
"You're being ridiculous. I didn't have sex with Ashura," she said indignantly. "We told Dad that as a joke. We sat up most of the night playing rummy, eating sweet potato pie, and talking about you and his life in Nairobi."
"But your dad said –"
"And why do you suppose he said that to you?" she said dryly. "Could it possibly be to upset you so you'd stop 'sniffing around' me?"
"So you swear nothing happened?"
"I swear that nothing happened," she said.
"He's a very nice guy, but you should know by

now that there's no other man for me but you. I love you, you idiot."
The swinging kitchen door opened.
"Dillon?" Ashura poked his head into the room.
"What?" Dillon scowled at him.
"I sense that you may have a problem with me, and I just want to set your mind at ease. Obviously, Katie is a very special woman, but all she could talk about last night was how much she loves you. She and I have no interest in each other, and besides, I don't sleep with a woman on the same day I met her.
"Your relationship with her is not threatened by me. However, you should know that Katie plays a mean game of rummy, although I think she cheats."
He extended his hand to Dillon, who shook it sheepishly.
"Are we good?"
"We're good, Dr. Otieno," Dillon said.
"Then why don't we all sit down together? And Dillon, I insist you sit next to Katie," Ashura said.
The three reentered the dining room.
"Can we all please sit down and eat before everything gets cold?" Carter said with annoyance.
Justin finished filling his plate and stood up.
"Dillon can have my seat," he said. "I'm eating in the den to watch the game."
"You most certainly will not," Naomi said.

An Admission of Weakness

"I'm a grown man," Justin said. "You can't tell me what to do."
"Don't talk to Mama like that!" Blair said sharply.
"I'll do what I want," Justin said. "Mind your own fucking business."
"Justin, that's enough!" Ruby said angrily. "If that's how you're going to behave, you can just go home!"
"You can sit with a faggot and a liar and a cheater if you want, but I won't," Justin said.
"Do you mind if I join you?" Ian asked.
"Come on, bro," Justin shrugged.

CHAPTER THIRTY-FOUR

Everyone silently found their seats again while Ian and Justin disappeared into the den.

"What about Robbie?" Camilla frowned. "Are we really going to let a guest go without dinner?"

"He said he isn't hungry," Carter said. "Let him do without."

"Blair?" Katie turned to her brother. "Are you seriously not going to go after him?"

"He's not hungry," Blair shrugged.

"Blair, go get him and bring him back," Naomi said.

"Our food is too spicy for a white boy," Danielle chuckled. "Maybe he can have a sandwich later."

"Danielle, what kind of a racist remark is that?" Charles said heatedly. "You should know better!"

Camilla picked up a plate and filled it with food.

"What are you doing?" Carter said.

"I'm going to eat with Robbie since Blair's too cowardly to do the right thing," she picked up her own plate.

"Sit down," Carter said sternly. "Your place is at the table with your family."

"My place is with Robbie so he doesn't have to be alone," Camilla glared pointedly at Blair.

An Admission of Weakness

She left the room in search of Robbie and found him at the top of the stairs.

"Here," she handed him the plate and sat down beside him.

"I'm not hungry," he said.

"Of course you are," she said. "And Mama's cooking is too good to miss."

"I'm sorry about ruining your Christmas," he said ruefully. "I pictured this going so much differently."

"I know you did," she said. "And I'm sorry Blair's being such a jerk."

"I'm not really surprised, I guess," he said. "He's not the problem. I'm the one who keeps coming back to him."

"You love him," she said. "You know him for all that he is, and you love him anyway. I hope I find someone who loves me that much."

"I think I must be a masochist," he said. "Somewhere deep down I must get off on this kind of rejection."

"I don't think that's it," she said. "And I think you know he really loves you. He's just weak. He lets people push him into things he doesn't want. And believe me when I tell you he doesn't want Danielle."

"He had sex with her last night, he was holding her in her lap and kissing her when I got here, and he's barely spoken to me since I got here."

"That's because Ian showed up," she said. "Blair doesn't want Danielle, but he also

An Admission of Weakness

doesn't want Ian to have her. In his mind, she belongs to him."
"And he can have her," Robbie said bitterly. "He obviously doesn't want me."
"He wants you very much. But he knows you'll always be around, so he's not focusing on you at the moment. He's a little boy defending what he considers his property."
"Then I shouldn't be around," Robbie said.
"I think if you and Ian got to know each other better, Blair and Danielle would turn their focus on the two of you," she grinned impishly.
"Ian's straight."
"I wouldn't be so sure of that," she said.

"Charles, get off your fat ass and let's sit with Robbie and Camilla," Ruby said.
"Were you ever part of the Gestapo?" Charles asked. "You'd have made a fantastic officer."
"Why thank you. That's the nicest thing you've ever said to me," she said.
The two found Camilla and Robbie and sat down on the steps below them.
"This is nice," Ruby said. "I've never eaten on the stairs before."
"Please don't let me keep you from your family," Robbie said.
"Don't worry about it," Ruby said. "I'd rather sit with you than Carter."

An Admission of Weakness

"So this is how we're eating Christmas dinner?" Carter scowled. "With the family split up in different rooms?"

"Apparently," Naomi sighed unhappily and gazed around at the empty chairs.

"This is nonsense," Carter stood up. He yelled, "Justin, get in here and eat with your family. Camilla, return to the table. Dillon can sit with Robert E. Lee."

"I'll be glad to," Dillon stood as well.

"If you go, I'm going too," Katie stood up.

"Look, we can all fit around the table if we squeeze in a little," Naomi said. "Come on, everyone, let's all sit together."

She called Charles and Ruby back to their seats, and Camilla moved her chair aside so Robbie could sit next to her.

"I'm sorry for inconveniencing everyone," Robbie eyed Blair and Danielle uncomfortably. "I should never have come here."

"You're right," Carter said. "You should have thought twice before going to someone's house uninvited on Christmas Day."

"Carter!" Naomi said sharply before turning to their guest. She smiled kindly. "Robbie, you're very welcome. We're delighted you're here. Why don't you tell us about your classes?"

"I'm a business major," Robbie said. "It's challenging, but I enjoy it."

"What made you come to Illinois for college?" Charles asked.

An Admission of Weakness

"A scholarship," Robbie said.
"You must be very smart," Camilla said.
"I've got a 4.0," Robbie shrugged.
"Your parents must be very proud of you," Naomi said.
"They must be," Robbie agreed noncommittally.
"Any brothers or sisters?" Ruby asked.
Robbie told them briefly about his family.
"I feel like I know all of you," he said. "I've heard so much about you. Andres thinks very highly of you."
"You know Andres?" Carter said.
"He's a good friend."
"He doesn't know what you are, I take it," Carter said.
"Carter, shut up," Ruby snapped.
"I'm a who, not a what," Robbie said. "And he knows very well who I am. It doesn't bother him because he's secure with his sexuality, unlike some people."
"Are you insinuating something?" Carter scowled.
"I'm just saying that men who aren't questioning their sexuality don't have a problem with gay people. You know, men like Charles and Dillon. Oh, and of course, you and your sons too. You're obviously comfortable with your masculinity."
He glared at Blair while Ruby and Charles grinned at one another.

An Admission of Weakness

"My sons and I understand what it means to be a man," Carter said coldly.

"Yes, Blair certainly knows how to take it like a man," Robbie said sarcastically. "I've seen that for myself dozens of times."

"Robbie, just stop it," Blair frowned. "This isn't the time."

"Blair, isn't there something you wanted to say to your father?" Robbie said.

"No," Blair glanced at Danielle and then stared down at his plate.

"I didn't think so," Robbie said. "Why don't we talk about Blair and Danielle getting married? I think that's very exciting, and I couldn't be happier for the two of them."

"Thank you," Danielle smiled. She took Blair's hand and kissed him.

"I hope you'll invite me to the wedding," Robbie went on. "Hopefully the two of you made a baby last night like you wanted, Danielle. In fact, I'm surprised he hasn't fathered lots of children. He's an animal in bed. The guy can't get enough sex. You wouldn't believe how many women he's bedded in the years I've known him. I hear them going at it every night. He even does it with more than one at a time."

"Robbie, stop it!" Blair scowled.

"Blair, is that true?" Naomi frowned.

"Of course not, Mama," Blair said.

An Admission of Weakness

Robbie continued talking as if no one had spoken.

"But of course, Danielle, your family has money, so naturally Dr. Butterfield wants him to marry you. After all, someone majoring in education and drama isn't going to make a lot of money."

"Shut up, Robbie," Blair scowled.

"No," Naomi said. "Blair's majoring in business administration like you."

"Oh, is he?" Robbie said innocently. "I guess I thought all those education classes he's taking meant he was an education major. My mistake."

"I love this kid," Charles chuckled, and Dillon joined him.

"Blair, what is he talking about?" Carter demanded gruffly.

"I have no idea," Blair looked daggers at Robbie.

"Blair is majoring in business because he's going to be the CEO of Mother's company one day," Danielle told Robbie.

"Is he?" Robbie said. "Well, I must be mistaken then. He would never lie to you. I mean, what kind of a marriage would it be where the couple keeps secrets from one another?"

"Blair, what is your major?" Carter demanded.

"It's business," Blair said firmly.

An Admission of Weakness

"And there you said you weren't going to live your life for your dad anymore," Robbie said. "I knew you didn't mean it."
"Robbie, please drop this," Blair pleaded, trying to keep his voice even.
"What are you going to do when graduation rolls around, Blair? How are you going to hide the truth from your family then?"
"Will you just stop it?" Blair shouted angrily. "Why are you doing this to me?"
"I'm not doing anything," Robbie said. "I'm just congratulating you on marrying a rich wife, which is clearly what's important to you. That and making your dad happy.
"Now that I know our relationship was a complete sham, I'm happy that you've found someone like Danielle to spend your life with. How many kids are you thinking of having? Knowing how much you like sex, I figure you'll have at least ten children, five boys and five girls. I can see it now, you coming home from a hard day at the office to your loving wife and doting children. And every night, you and Danielle can have hot, passionate sex. It will all be just what you deserve."
"Robbie, you should have never come here," Blair said. "All of this would have worked itself out if you'd let me handle it the way I planned."
"And what way was that? Do everything that Father Butterfield said: marry Danielle, go to

work for her Mother, get rich and be a big success. Have a boytoy or two on the side to satisfy those nasty homosexual urges you can't control. And then, when you're eighty, finally decide that daddy's approval wasn't all it was cracked up to be."

"Blair is not gay!" Carter yelled. "I won't have it! He's as straight as I am."

"If that's true, then you must have fucked a lot of men in your day," Robbie said.

Carter knocked his chair over in a fit of rage and rushed at Robbie. Camilla attempted to hold him back, but before anyone could stop him, he cold-cocked Robbie with one blow.

"Carter!" Naomi screamed. "What have you done?!"

"Robbie!" Blair rushed to his side.

Robbie lay flat on his back on the floor.

"Why the fuck did you do that?" Blair shouted furiously at his father.

He shoved him, and the two grappled against one another while Dillon, Ashura, and Charles tried to separate them. It became a melee with Blair and Carter striking out blindly at everyone in their personal space. Charles was knocked to the floor, and Dillon was literally thrown across the table.

"Charles!" Ruby hurried to help him up.

Chairs were knocked over, the tablecloth was askew with dishes and food falling to the floor, and people were screaming and shouting.

An Admission of Weakness

Camilla dragged a senseless Robbie out of the fray. Katie ran to Dillon and helped him to his feet. Naomi shouted at her husband and attempted to pull him away from Blair, but he pushed her aside, and she fell against the table, crying out in pain.

"Naomi!" Ruby cried with alarm.

Angrily, she picked up the bowl of pasta salad and threw it in Carter's face before helping her daughter to a chair.

"Are you alright?" she examined her daughter's side. It was already starting to bruise.

"I'm fine, Mama," Naomi said. "See if Robbie's okay."

Camilla and Ashura were tending to the unconscious young man.

"Is he okay?" Blair demanded as he knelt beside Robbie. "Dr. Otieno, is he okay?"

"He's going to be fine," Ashura said soothingly. "Camilla, prop his feet up on a chair."

The fight seemed to have gone out of Carter, and he panted and leaned against the table while he wiped the pasta and sauce out of his eyes. Ruby turned to him, angrier than she had ever been in her life. She slapped him across the face with all her strength, sending sauce and fragments of wet pasta across the room.

"If you ever harm my daughter again, I will kill you," she seethed. "I will take a gun, and I will shoot you in the head. And if you think I'm joking, just try me."

"Mama, I'm alright," Naomi said. She stood up and faced her husband. "I'm done, Carter. I've taken all I can, so I'm done."

Ruby made sure Charles was okay and then she and Naomi left the room and climbed the stairs to Ruby's bedroom.

Blair got to his feet, panting for breath.

Danielle rushed to his side and rubbed his arm soothingly.

"You poor darling," she said. "It was so brave of you to rush to his defense, especially after the horrid things he said. You may think he's your friend, but he's not. He's only here to stir up trouble.

"Come on, let's go up to your room, and I'll make you comfortable."

"I need to make sure he's okay," Blair brushed her aside.

"The doctor said he's fine," Danielle said in 'the voice'. "Now come with me so I can make sure you're okay."

"Okay," he gave in, as she knew he would.

She supported him while he limped up the stairs.

Katie and Dillon headed up to Katie's bedroom, and Carter walked to his study and closed the door.

Dr. Otieno helped Robbie sit up.

An Admission of Weakness

"What happened?" Robbie rubbed the side of his sore head.

"Well, let's see, Dad hit you," Camilla said grimly. "Blair threw Dillon across the room, Mr. Morgan got shoved to the floor, Mama got pushed against the table, and Grandma threatened to kill Dad. It's not exactly your typical Christmas."

"I pushed things too far," Robbie said. "I owe you all an apology."

"You were quite entertaining," Ashura said wryly.

He checked Robbie's eyes and turned his head carefully this way and that.

"You're okay," he said. "Let's put some ice on your face. It's going to swell, I'm afraid."

"Where's Blair?" Robbie glanced around.

"Danielle took him upstairs," Camilla said.

"Of course she did," Robbie shook his head disgustedly.

"But the good news is that Blair came to your defense. That's what started all the fighting."

"Fighting?"

"I'll explain it to you while we get some ice for your face," she said.

Justin ignored the shouting coming from the dining room.

"So who are you again?" he asked while he dug into the delicious dinner.

An Admission of Weakness

"I'm Ian. I came from New Hampshire because Danielle's aunt was dying, but apparently she made a full recovery."
"How do you know Danielle?"
"We've been dating for the past three years," Ian said. "I thought this would be a good time to propose to her, but she seems more interested in her ex-boyfriend. Evidently what she and I have isn't what I thought it was. Everyone's saying they're engaged."
"Nah," Justin said. "He's a fag."
"You're sure?"
"I'm sure," Justin said. "He's just playing with Danielle. He has no intention of marrying her. He likes this Robbie guy."
He shivered with revulsion.
"That's good," Ian said. "Because I couldn't compete with someone as good-looking as him."
"You're not much of a man if you're too afraid to fight for the woman you love."
"Blair could beat me to a pulp in two minutes," Ian said. "Besides, if she loves him, I want her to be happy." He changed the subject. "Who exactly is Robbie?"
"Some fag friend of Blair's," Justin shrugged.
"You like that word, don't you?"
"It's not my word," Justin said. "It's what they are. Faggots."
"They're gay. There's no reason to insult them by calling them names."

An Admission of Weakness

"I don't like fags," Justin said.
"Why not?"
"They're unnatural. It's a sin to be that way when you don't have to be."
"Everything you just said is completely wrong," Ian said. "Homosexuality is not unnatural; it's actually part of nature. There are thousands of gay species all across the planet. Elephants, penguins, horses, and so on.
"And no person or animal chooses to be gay. It's simply who we are."
"We? Don't tell me you're queer too?"
"No offense, but that's the kind of question someone asks when they have no argument to offer."
"Are you calling me stupid?" Justin scowled.
"No, just ignorant," Ian said.
"That's the same thing."
"No, it's not," Ian said. "Stupidity can't be fixed, but ignorance can. You're reacting to homosexuality with ignorance because you don't know the facts. Once you know the facts, you can react more rationally.
"Do some research," Ian advised him. "Don't listen to homophobes who only want you to hate the same people they do. You're too smart for that."
"You just said I'm ignorant."
"For now. But you can choose to be educated if you want to. And just for the record, I like guys as well as girls."

An Admission of Weakness

"Are you fucking kidding me?" Justin scowled. "I'm serious. You may want to scoot to the other end of the sofa. You might catch it if you sit too close."

An Admission of Weakness

CHAPTER THIRTY-FIVE

"Ashura is very nice, don't you think?" Camilla said in a hushed voice while Ashura stepped across the kitchen to answer his phone. "He looks like Sidney Poitier."
"Yes, he does," Robbie agreed. "He seems to like you."
"Dad brought him here for Katie."
"Katie has Dillon, doesn't she?" Robbie said.
"Yes, but Ashura would never want to be with someone like me."
"Why not?"
"Because he's a doctor, and I'm just a CNA," she said.
"So?" Robbie frowned.
"He should be with someone like Katie, someone with an education. That's why Dad brought him here," she said.
"Do you all do everything your father says?"
"We were raised to believe his will is our command. That's why Blair is going to marry Danielle, why he hasn't told Mama and Dad he wants to be a teacher, why Katie got a degree and a job she didn't want, why she and Dillon have kept their relationship hidden for fifteen years, why Justin and Dad haven't spoken for six months, why Mama's having an affair with a man half her age, and why I'll never be good enough for the most wonderful man I've ever met."

An Admission of Weakness

"Your mother's having an affair?" Robbie said with astonishment.
"Oh dear. I shouldn't have told you that," she said ruefully.
"But you're all adults," Robbie said. "Stop letting your father control you."
"Resisting is harder than you think. Why do you think Blair was finally able to be himself at college? Why do you think he went through all that stuff the last few years in an effort to find himself?"
"Why?"
"Because he was away from here and because of you," she said. "The second he left you and came home to this house, he turned back into jellyfish Blair. And then add in Ian trying to take what belongs to him, and it's the perfect storm."
"So the only way I can have a relationship with Blair is to get him away from here?"
"No," she said. "He was angry at the things you said, but he ran to your defense when Dad hit you. You almost reached him; you just have to keep up the pressure until he breaks."
"You just said he's going to marry Danielle, so what's the point?" Robbie said.
"You don't think the man you love is worth it?"
"I don't know anymore," Robbie sighed.
"Robbie, you're the only person who can save him from himself."

An Admission of Weakness

"Ian, can I talk to you?" Camilla said.
Justin had left the den to get whatever dessert he could scrape off the tablecloth.
"Sure."
"Do you understand what's happening with Blair and Danielle?"
"I think so. He's pretending to be engaged to her to please his father."
"He's not pretending," she said. "He's going to marry her even though he's in love with Robbie."
"But why would he do that?"
"Because he can't stand up to Dad when Dad forces him into situations like this. And then add in Danielle pressuring him, he's going to lose the battle.
"What you need to understand is that she's under as much pressure from her mother as Blair is from Dad. That's why she's here for Blair and why she hasn't told anyone she's majoring in music."
"How do you know all this?" he said, surprised.
"I listen when people talk," she grinned. "The point is, Blair and Danielle don't love each other, but they're playing the roles they're expected to play because it's second nature to them."
"So I've lost her to him, haven't I?" he frowned.
"Yes. But if you want her back, you need to put on a little play of your own."

An Admission of Weakness

The house was silent. Naomi had locked herself in her room, Ruby and Charles were in her bedroom, Blair and Danielle were lying on Blair's bed, Camilla and Ashura were having a private conversation in the living room, Katie and Dillon were in her room, Carter was in his study, and Justin was in the den watching football. Robbie and Ian were sitting on the bottom step of the stairway talking quietly.

Blair stared up at the ceiling while Danielle kissed her way down his body. What was happening to him? He had come home resolute and strong, secure in his sexuality, and now here he was slipping right back to where he was while he was in high school. Only it was worse now because he was engaged to a woman he didn't even like, and he was treating his boyfriend like shit.
"Danielle, I don't want to do this," he said feebly.
"It's just sex," she said.
"I'm not talking about that," he said. "I don't want to get married."
"Blair, you can't let what Robbie said upset you. He's just jealous. You know you want to be with me."
"I don't —"
"Blair, we're doing this," she said sternly. "I'm going to make you so happy that you'll forget

everything else. All this confusion of yours will disappear."

"Are you sure?"

"Of course I'm sure," she said. "Now just relax and let me love you."

She continued making love to his body while he put an arm over his face.

God, why was he such a spineless idiot? Here he was in bed with a woman again when what he wanted more than anything was to be with Robbie. Why couldn't he say no to Danielle or his father? He should be checking on Robbie to make sure he was okay, so why wasn't he?

He had grown so much in the last year, like he was finally coming into his own. One day under his father's roof with Danielle, and all his progress was destroyed.

Of course, it wasn't his father's or Danielle's fault; it was his own. They were just being themselves, but he had a choice as to how to react to them. Maybe he needed a psychiatrist to help him get over his self-destructive desire for his father's approval.

Even as that thought occurred to him, he knew what it was that he truly needed: Robbie. Robbie was the man he loved, the one who made him want to be a better version of himself.

Somehow, he needed to get back to the Blair who was strong, independent, and confidently gay.

An Admission of Weakness

He started to push Danielle away and get up, but instead, he groaned as Danielle's body sank down onto his hard manhood. He grasped her hips and lifted her up so that he could piston in and out of her. She bent down to kiss him ravenously.

"Fuck," he gasped with pleasure as he pictured himself kissing Robbie while his dick filled Robbie's tight, furry ass.

"Cum in me," Danielle whispered into his ear. He rolled them over so he could pound her harder.

"Oh fuck yeah," he grunted.

"Oh yes," she cried out. "Fuck me, Blair!"

Just then, the mellow tones of a French horn wafted through the house.

"What's that?" she cocked her head to the side.

"Oh fuck, I'm gonna cum!" he shouted out as he thrust ever deeper.

"Stop!" she pushed him aside just as he shot load after load onto her abdomen and the sheets. "It's Ian. He's playing Tchaikovsky's 'Sleeping Beauty Waltz'."

She hastily wiped the semen off of her body and donned her clothes.

"What the fuck?" he frowned. "You said you wanted me to cum in you. I thought you wanted to get pregnant."

"Just get dressed," she impatiently threw him his underwear before hurrying from the room.

An Admission of Weakness

Ashura, Camilla, and Robbie sat on the sofa enthralled while Ian played the romantic tune. He was sitting on a straight-backed chair next to the piano bench with the French horn in his left hand and his right hand inside the bell. The sweet, warm tones rippled throughout the house.

As he played, he saw first Danielle and then Blair enter the room looking disheveled. They were followed by Katie and Dillon and then Ruby and Charles. Naomi joined them a moment later, and Carter came as far as the wide doorway to listen. Justin remained in the den by himself.

For once, Danielle didn't climb on Blair's lap. Instead, she sat on the floor across the room from him. What no one knew except Danielle and Ian was that the 'Sleeping Beauty Waltz' was the first song they had collaborated on when they started school three years ago. It was a favorite of theirs and had become 'their song'.

Damn Ian, she thought. Didn't he know what he was doing? He was going to spoil everything with Blair, and then what would her mother say?

"You marry that Butterfield boy no matter what," her mother had said to her after

An Admission of Weakness

receiving Carter's phone call. "I don't care if you have to get pregnant to do it, just do it."
"I'll try, Mother," she said. "But what if he doesn't want –?"
"No excuses," her mother said. "He's from a good family, and he'll make a good head of the company someday."
"Ian is a wonderful –" Danielle began.
"He's a musician," her mother snapped. "I won't have you married to a lazy, unmotivated boy-band reject. He'll never make anything of himself, but Blair has potential. He's crude and raw right now, but I can fix that. A few years under my wing and I'll have him fit to run the company. So marry him, or don't come home again!"

Why did this have to be so hard? Why couldn't she love Blair, and why couldn't he be straight? She saw for herself that he was in love with Robbie. Why did she have to fall in love with a sweet, kind musician who would probably never be rich and successful? And why did her mother have to be such a fucking bitch?!

Ian's song ended, and the appreciative audience applauded.
"That was lovely, Ian," Naomi said.
"Do you know 'Gabriel's Oboe'?" Charles limped over to the piano. "That's one of my favorites."

An Admission of Weakness

"I love that song," Ian smiled.
They played the emotive song together, and then Ruby asked for some Christmas carols.
"It *is* Christmas, even if it doesn't feel like it," she said.
Charles, Danielle, and Ian performed singly, in pairs, and as a trio for the next hour. Robbie was in awe of the tremendous talent in front of him. He had no musical gift himself, and he was envious of those who were blessed in such a way. He had to admit that Danielle's rich, flawless soprano voice gave him goosebumps. Danielle watched him and Blair eye one another surreptitiously. There was a deep connection there, and Robbie was a nice fellow, but she couldn't allow him to interfere with what she knew she had to do.
"Why don't I fix us something to eat?" Naomi said at last. "Maybe some turkey sandwiches?"
"Camilla and I will help you," Ashura said.
"And we'll clean up the dining room," Katie took Dillon's hand.
Carter scowled and returned to his study.
"Robbie, you and Ian have a lot in common," Camilla said. "You should get to know one another."
Ian set his French horn down and joined Robbie on the sofa, ignoring Danielle and Blair.
"I've been admiring the color of your hair," Ian said. "I've thought about dying mine blonde."

An Admission of Weakness

Ian's long, braided dreadlocks were tied back in a low ponytail that cascaded down his back.
"I think Black guys with blonde hair are hot," Robbie said. "Especially with piercings like yours."
"He'd look ridiculous," Danielle frowned. "I've told him his hair is perfect just as it is."
"Why do you care how he wears his hair?" Blair frowned.
"I don't," she shrugged.
"You should get your ears pierced," Ian ignored her. "A hoop in one and a diamond in the other."
"I think I will," Robbie said.
"I suggested that last year, but you said no," Blair said.
"So I've changed my mind," Robbie shrugged.
"You have the most beautiful blue eyes," Ian said to Robbie. "Oh wait. You have an eyelash."
He removed the errant hair from Robbie's cheek and held it on his finger tip.
"Make a wish."
Robbie thought a moment and then blew the lash from Ian's hand. The two laughed together and then became involved in an earnest conversation. Danielle took Blair's hand and led him away.
Someone put on a Johnny Mathis Christmas CD. His smooth, comforting voice filled the

An Admission of Weakness

house, and the tension in the air noticeably lessened.

Robbie and Ian continued their conversation while they walked to the dining room when Naomi called everyone to eat. They took their sandwiches to the window seat and sat down together.

To their surprise, they found they really did have a lot in common. Robbie enjoyed learning about the music world, and Ian was a charming teacher. For the first time since his arrival, Robbie forgot about Blair, and he laughed at Ian's funny stories.

"What are they so happy about?" Blair muttered.

"Why do you care?" Katie said. "You're engaged, remember?"

"That's right," Danielle said loudly. "We are definitely getting married."

Robbie and Ian looked up for a moment and then resumed their conversation.

"Maybe we'll elope," Blair said.

He looked over at Robbie, but Robbie merely continued talking to Ian.

"That's the first sane thing I've heard in this house today," Carter said. "I think it should be as soon as possible."

"I do too," Blair said.

"I am a licensed minister," Ashura said. "I could marry you right now if you like."

An Admission of Weakness

"There you go, Blair," Robbie said. "You want to get married so bad, I say go for it."

"We can't get married without Danielle's family here," Blair said.

"Aw, they won't mind," Robbie said. "You can have another ceremony for them."

"We don't have the marriage license," Blair said.

"Yes, we do," Danielle said. "Mother got it for us. But she'll be upset if I get married without her here."

"I'll explain it to her," Carter said. "We'll do it in front of the living room fireplace after we eat."

"No!" Blair said sharply. "We're going to wait, and that's the end of it."

"Coward," Robbie mouthed the word to Blair before turning back to Ian.

"We're apparently getting to them," Ian whispered and made a point of laughing loudly.

"Looks like it," Robbie laughed and slapped his knee as if Ian had just said something hysterically funny.

He reached over and wiped a spot from the corner of Ian's mouth. Ian responded by scooting closer to him and whispering something in his ear. Robbie nodded and glanced briefly at Blair's scowling face before saying something into Ian's ear.

An Admission of Weakness

After their pieced-together meal, most of them gravitated to the living room. Ian sat on the sofa with his arm around Robbie while Blair settled in a chair with Danielle on his lap. He scowled at Robbie and then began ardently kissing her.

"Danielle, why don't you take that upstairs?" Charles frowned. "I'd rather not watch my granddaughter make out."

"That's okay," Blair glared at Robbie. "We can wait until tonight."

"Why wait?" Robbie shrugged. "We'll throw down a blanket, and you two can go at it right now."

"Come on, Robbie," Ian said. "Let's go upstairs. They're grossing me out."

He took Robbie's hand, and the two of them left the room.

"Why are those two so chummy all of a sudden?" Blair asked sourly. "They don't have anything in common."

"I know there's one thing they both like," Camilla grinned mischievously. "You said you liked it too, but I guess you were wrong."

"Ian's straight," Blair said scornfully.

"He's actually pan," Danielle said uneasily. "He had just broken up with a guy when we started dating."

"So you are dating him?" Blair frowned. "You're engaged to me."

An Admission of Weakness

"It was just a casual thing. I would never fall for the artistic type," she scoffed. "You know me better than that."

A little later, Naomi said good night.
"Mama, why don't you stay in my room and let Charles have your bed?"
"I don't want to put you out," Charles said. "I'll be fine on a sofa somewhere."
"How about out in the garage," Ruby said.
"Mama," Naomi said. "You take Mama's bed, and she'll sleep with me."
"What about Carter?"
"Carter can sleep wherever he wants," Naomi said, "as long as it isn't with me.
"Ashura, you take the guest room. Danielle, I suppose you're with Blair, unless Blair and Robbie –"
"Obviously I'm going to sleep with my fiancé," Danielle glared at Robbie and took Blair's arm.
"Robbie and I will be fine here in front of the fireplace," Ian grasped Robbie's hand.
"Are you sure, dear?" she frowned. "Robbie?"
"That's up to Blair," Robbie said.
"Robbie, I –" Blair began.
"Blair's sleeping with me!" Danielle said sharply. "Aren't you?"
"If that's what you want," Blair gave in.
"Fine," Robbie said defiantly. "Then Ian and I will sleep together and get to know one another better. Is that okay with you, Blair?"

An Admission of Weakness

"Why would he care where you sleep?" Danielle said.

"Danielle, why would you sleep with your ex-boyfriend when your current boyfriend is standing right in front of you?" Ian said.

"She's my fiancée," Blair balled his hands into fists.

"I can see that," Ian said grimly. "Well, have fun tonight. Although I have a feeling you've already been having fun. Am I right, Dannie?"

"Come on, Blair," Danielle pulled him forcibly from the room.

"Dillon –" Naomi hesitated.

"I'll find a spot for Dillon, Mama," Katie said.

"Justin hasn't come out of the den," Naomi said. "So I suppose he can sleep there. Carter has his study, so I think we're all taken care of."

Ian and Robbie settled side by side on the floor in front of the dying fire. It was the only light in the dark room.

"I enjoyed talking to you today," Robbie said.

"Me too," Ian grinned. "I know we were trying to make them jealous, but I'd have spent the evening with you anyway."

"I can't believe they're up there again having sex," Robbie frowned.

"If they are, they are," Ian shrugged. "I figure if they're meant to be, then there's someone better for us."

An Admission of Weakness

"That's a good way to look at it," Robbie said. "But it doesn't make it hurt any less. I love him."

"And I love her," Ian said. "But we can't make them love us or be the people we want them to be. Maybe it's too late for them to break free from their parents. They might have to settle for one another for the rest of their lives."

"That's a sad thought," Robbie said.

"It is," Ian stood up and removed his clothes. "I hope you don't mind, but I sleep naked."

"I don't mind."

"Why don't you get comfortable?" Ian said. "We have our blankets if anyone comes down here."

Robbie hesitated and then stripped off his clothes as well. He lay down, and Ian inched closer.

"There," he said. "That's better."

The two talked until they drifted off to sleep. An hour later, Robbie awoke to find Ian's arm across his chest and his leg bent over his own. He shrugged and closed his eyes again.

"Robbie?" Ian whispered. "Can I make love to you?"

"Uh, okay," Robbie said tentatively.

What the hell, he decided. Blair was doing god knows what with Danielle, so he supposed he was free to do as he pleased.

Ian rolled on top of Robbie and kissed him zealously. Eventually, he moved down and

An Admission of Weakness

nursed from a nipple for a while. Robbie grimaced with pleasure and took one of Ian's nipples into his mouth. They moved onto armpits and then sixty-nined one another for several minutes.
"You have a beautiful cock," Ian grinned before raising Robbie's legs in the air to rim him. "Hmm, nothing I like better than a hairy ass or a shaved pussy."
Ew, Robbie wrinkled his nose as he pictured the female anatomy.
"Can we please not talk about pussy?" he shivered with distaste.

Ashura knocked on Camilla's door.
"I'm sorry to waken you," he whispered when she opened it.
"I wasn't asleep," she said.
"I wondered if you would like another midnight snack," he said.
"That sounds great," she grinned.

"I'm just going to make sure Charles is settled in okay," Ruby said.
"You might see if he had enough to eat," Naomi said. "Maybe he's in the mood for a little brown sugar."
"Naomi!" Ruby looked shocked. "Why would you say such a foolish thing? I can't stand the man."
"I know," Naomi said. "I'm sorry, Mama."

An Admission of Weakness

"I'm just being a good host," Ruby said.
"That's very commendable," Naomi grinned. "Especially since you 'can't stand the man'."
"Go to sleep," Ruby said as she headed out the door. "I'll be back when I get back."

"Stop thinking about Robbie," Danielle said as Blair fucked her.
The two of them had been going at it since they came upstairs.
"How did you know I was thinking about him?" Blair said with astonishment.
"I want you to think about me," she said. "I'm the one you're fucking. Forget all this gay nonsense."
"I've tried, but it's who I am."
"Just keep going," she said. "I want to get pregnant tonight."
He stopped moving.
"Why are you so anxious to get pregnant?"
"I want to have a baby with you. Once I'm pregnant and we're married, then we won't have to worry about you being gay."
"Whether we're married or not isn't going to change the way I feel," Blair said. "I'll always be gay."
"You weren't gay before."
"Yes, I was," Blair said. "But I repressed those feelings, and I can't do that anymore."
"How can you be gay when your dick is in me?" she said.

An Admission of Weakness

"I can fuck women, but I want to be with men. I want to be with Robbie."

"Well, you can't be with him, so you're going to have to get used to being with me."

His dick softened and slipped from her body.

"I can't do this anymore," he sat up on the side of the bed. "I love Robbie. He's the one I should be with. What I'm doing with you is a lie, and we both know it."

"Look at it this way. Your dad is going to be furious when you tell him he's been paying for an education degree with a drama minor," she said. "Add on the fact that you're gay, and he'll disown you."

"I know, but –"

"Everyone is counting on you to be straight," she snapped. "Me, my parents, your father, the rest of your family. You have no choice but to be straight. We have to go through with this marriage."

"But I can't marry you when I'm in love with Robbie."

"The same Robbie who's downstairs right now having sex with Ian?"

"We don't know they're having sex," Blair said uneasily.

"Of course they are," she said. "Ian's sexual appetite is voracious. He wants it two or three times a night. I guarantee he and Robbie are fucking at this exact moment."

"Doesn't that bother you in the least?"

An Admission of Weakness

"No," her voice wavered. "He's nothing to me."
"He must mean something," he said dryly. "He drove a thousand miles to be here for you."
"It doesn't matter," she said impatiently.
"You're the one I have to marry."
She put on his bathrobe.
"Come on. We're getting married this minute."

An Admission of Weakness

CHAPTER THIRTY-SIX

Blair and Danielle found Ashura and Camilla in the kitchen.
"We want to get married right now," she said. "Camilla can be our witness."
"What about Robbie?" Camilla frowned.
"What about Ian?"
"What about them?" Danielle said. "They have nothing to do with this."
"Hang on a sec," Blair said.
He tiptoed through the dining room and peered into the living room. He gulped when he saw two naked, perspiring bodies moving in the dim firelight. Sure enough, Ian was fucking Robbie as Danielle predicted.
"Oh fuck, you've got the tightest ass," Ian gasped as he slid in and out of Robbie's body.
"Don't stop," Robbie panted and pulled him down to kiss him passionately, determined to forget about Blair and Danielle upstairs.
"Don't cum yet," Ian said. "I want you to fuck me next."
He increased his efforts, and as Blair watched, he threw his head back and grunted loudly.
"Aw shit!" Ian cried. "I'm gonna fuckin' cum inside you."
Sadly, Blair returned to the kitchen.
"Fine," he said resignedly. "Let's do this."

An Admission of Weakness

The storm broke during the night, and road crews were already out clearing the streets and roads. The sun shone blindingly on the glistening snow, and in typically extreme Midwest weather, the temperature was already well on its way to forty-three degrees.

When Naomi headed down the stairs to the kitchen, she observed Ian and Robbie in each other's arms, kissing and grinding their nude bodies together. Oh dear, she thought, things just keep getting more and more complicated. She peered into the study and found Carter sleeping fitfully on the leather sofa with a throw over him. Justin was asleep on the couch in the den.

Blair and Danielle walked boldly into the living room, where Robbie and Ian were making love to one another. Robbie's hairy legs were in the air, and Ian was fucking him. His ass was covered with a blanket.
"Did you really need to make all that noise?" Ian paused. "You're making it hard to concentrate here."
"I can't believe you're fucking him," Blair said coldly.
"Are you talking to me or Robbie?" Ian said.
"You should have been here for rounds one and two," Robbie said.

An Admission of Weakness

"We had plenty of sex ourselves," Danielle said loftily. "All night long."

"Well, good for you," Robbie's throat tightened, but his face showed indifference. "You'd better get used to that, Blair. That's what you're going to have to face for the rest of your life."

"Oh, he knows," Danielle smiled sweetly. "That's why he insisted we get married last night."

Ian had resumed thrusting in and out of Robbie, but he pulled out and turned to her.

"You didn't get married," he scoffed. "He's gay."

"Trust me, we've had sex a dozen times since Christmas Eve, so I know for a fact he isn't," Danielle said. "And we decided not to wait, so we woke Dr. Otieno in the middle of the night, and he married us."

Ian and Robbie's jaws dropped.

"No, you didn't," Robbie gulped.

"You actually got married?" Ian scowled. "Why would you do that?"

"Did I hear that you two got married?" Carter walked into the room just then. He heaved a sigh of relief. "Well, thank God. At least something's working out for my children."

Robbie's phone rang while the family gathered around the table and he and Ian dressed. Carter was all smiles as he stood and held up his glass of orange juice.

"I'd like to make a toast. For those of you who don't know, Blair and Danielle got married last night."

"What?!" Naomi, Katie, and Ruby all exclaimed at once.

"I can't believe you actually went through with it," Justin rolled his eyes at his brother. "Damn, you are one desperate motherfucker."

"Yes, it's finally done," Carter said. "Now Blair will have a secure future, and things can get back to normal around here."

"Nothing around here is normal," Robbie said sourly from the doorway. He ended the call on his phone and tucked it into his pocket. "This family is even more screwed up than mine, and most of it is Carter's fault."

"There's no point in being a sore loser," Carter said sternly. "Blair was never going to be your boyfriend."

"I'm not talking about Blair," Robbie said heatedly. "Although he just ruined his life, and yet you stand there congratulating him."

"His life isn't ruined," Carter said.

"Sure it is," Robbie said. "Because Blair is gay, only he's too much of a coward to tell you. He loved me, and I loved him, but he was willing to throw all that away just to please you."

Blair merely stared down at the table.

An Admission of Weakness

"Danielle doesn't love him; she loves Ian. She only married Blair to stay in her mother's good graces.
Danielle took Blair's hand and avoided everyone's eye.
"And the rest of your family is doing the same thing."
"I don't know what you're talking about," Carter said huffily.
"Yes, you do, you sanctimonious ass, but you don't care as long as you're getting your way," Robbie said. "Blair married someone he doesn't love because he's a child who had to make sure Ian didn't take his toy away and so he could prove to you he's straight. He can't even admit to you that he's an education major with a drama minor. Look at him sitting there beside his wife. He can't even look at me.
"Katie and Dillon have been seeing each other for fifteen years, but they've kept it a secret all that time so they wouldn't upset you."
"That's ridi–" Carter began, but Robbie plowed ahead.
"You haven't spoken to Justin for six months simply for going against your wishes and following his dream, which was to open his own gym.
"And it's because of you that he's a misogynistic, homophobic, racist prick."
"Shut your fucking –" Justin began, but Robbie swept on.

An Admission of Weakness

"Camilla has fallen for Ashura, but she thinks he's too good for her because she knows you wouldn't approve. So she's going to let a chance for love pass her by and never tell him how she feels.

"And your wife of thirty years is so unhappy with you that she's having an affair with a man half her age."

"What?" Naomi looked scandalized.

"And Danielle, you're so desperate to please your mother that you haven't told her you're actually majoring in music and not African-American Studies. You're willing to marry a gay man for her and sacrifice a future with Ian. Don't you care that he loves you? He drove a thousand miles to comfort you, and he was even going to propose to you. But you just went and shit all over him!

"And Ruby, I love you, but why on earth are you keeping your relationship with Charles a secret? We all know what's going on. What do you care what Carter thinks?"

"There," he took a deep breath. "Either I made things better for you, or I made them much, much worse."

Every face stared back at him silently with slack jaws.

"Now if you'll excuse me," he said flatly. "I just found out my dad died, and I have to go bury him."

An Admission of Weakness

He picked up his battered suitcase, and it immediately fell apart. He gathered most of his things into his arms and strode through the front door with as much dignity as he could muster.

Robbie was still brushing the snow off his borrowed car when Dillon and Ashura arrived to help him.
"I'm so sorry, man," Dillon said.
"Me too," Ashura nodded. "Is there anything we can do?"
"Just straighten things out in there," Robbie said. "And tell Blair to stay the fuck away from me."
He got in the car and drove away.

Inside the house, everyone was shouting at once.
"That's enough!" Carter slammed his fist on the table. "Now we are going to sit down and calmly discuss all of this."
They all sat down and eyed each other uneasily.
"First of all, I am not having an affair," Naomi said emphatically.
"Yes, you are," Justin said. "I got arrested because of you and Snake."
"You got arrested?"
"I got into a fight with him to make him stop seeing you."
"You did what?!" she cried.

An Admission of Weakness

"I told him I knew you two were sleeping together, and I wanted him to stop it," Justin said. "He said he was in love with you and you were two consenting adults."

"He said nothing of the sort!" she snapped. "Because we are not having an affair. Goodness gracious, he's twenty-five years old."

"That's what he said," Justin said stubbornly.

"You told me he said I reminded him of his mother," Naomi said. "That's all he meant when he said he loved me. I love him too – like a son, not a lover."

"Then what are you doing with him?" Camilla frowned.

"I'm working as a seamstress and consultant for his bridal line," Naomi said. "He and June Shaw came to me and asked for my help."

"Ohhh…so that's what the picture in the paper was for," Katie said.

"You saw that picture?"

"What picture?" Carter demanded.

"This one," Justin reached into the breakfront and pulled out the glossy flyer with Naomi's photograph as the centerfold.

"Mama, you look gorgeous," Camilla smiled. "And I'm so relieved you're not having an affair."

"I told you all I was taking sewing lessons because I knew how your father would feel about me working outside the home. So I lied."

"You lied to me?" Carter said angrily.

An Admission of Weakness

"Yes, I did," Naomi said defiantly. "You want to make something of it?"

"I-I'll speak to you later about this," he backed down. "Now what's this nonsense about Katie and Dillon?"

"It's not nonsense," Katie said heatedly. "And it's already done, Dad, so you can't do anything about it."

"What's done?" Carter scowled. "You'd better not be married too."

"I've quit my job in Los Angeles and taken a job as a floor nurse here at the hospital. I'm moving out to the ranch with Dillon. We're getting married in June."

"How marvelous!" Ruby cried. "I'm so happy to hear that."

"After the expensive education I paid for?" Carter said angrily. "And this is how you repay me?"

"I didn't know there were conditions to you paying for school," Katie said.

"You knew exactly what was expected of you," Carter said. "If you're going to throw your future away so you can shack up with him, what are you still doing here? Get out of my house."

"Dr. Butterfield, if you'd just listen –" Dillon began.

"Get out!" Carter yelled.

"Fine," Katie and Dillon headed for the stairs to go pack. "If you come to your senses, you

An Admission of Weakness

know where I'll be. Otherwise, have a nice life, Dad."

The two left the room.

"Camilla, you knew what I expected of you –"

"Don't even start, Dr. Butterfield," Ashura held up a hand to stop him. "Camilla, I like you very much, and I hope Robbie was correct when he said you liked me too. Can we go up to your room and talk?"

"Uh, sure," Camilla blinked with surprise.

He took her hand and guided her up the staircase while Carter sat quietly seething. He spoke at last.

"At least Blair hasn't disappointed –" he said.

"Hold on just a minute, sir," Ian interrupted him and turned to Danielle. "You are some piece of work. You knew how I felt about you. I told you I loved you before you left to come here, and yet you lied to me so you could come here and marry another man."

"Ian, if you'd just let me explain," she said.

"There's no need," he said. "I understand all about your mother and Dr. Butterfield. You did what you felt you had to do, and I'm not going to stand here and judge you. But I will tell you that I don't date married women, so when you get back to Dartmouth, get all your shit out of my apartment.

"I hope this works out for you because this is clearly what you wanted all along. I can't

An Admission of Weakness

imagine you being happy with a gay guy who doesn't love you, but you made your choice." He picked up his duffel bag and left the house. Danielle burst into tears and ran upstairs with Blair following close behind. After a moment of silence, Naomi spoke.

"Mama, I've known about you and Charles all along," she said. "Why didn't you tell me?"

"I don't know. It's been so long since I've been in love, I wanted to enjoy it all by myself for a while," Ruby said. "But I was going to tell you."

"We'll talk about it later," Naomi said. "I have to go up and pack."

"Where are you going?" Ruby asked.

"I'll either stay with you and Justin or Katie and Dillon until I figure out what I'm going to do."

"You are not leaving this house," Carter said firmly. "I won't have it."

"You're not going to give up your job, are you?" Ruby ignored him.

"Of course not," Naomi said. "I love that job. At least I'm appreciated there."

She and Ruby and Charles walked up the stairs. Justin stood up and stretched.

"Good going, Dad," he said before leaving the room. "You were right, and we were all wrong."

An Admission of Weakness

CHAPTER THIRTY-SEVEN

Robbie returned Andres's car to him and then caught the train to Mississippi. Rhett met him at the station and drove them to Toadback.
"How's everyone doing?" Robbie asked.
"We're okay," Rhett said. "How awe you and Blair?"
"Blair married his high school girlfriend, so there is no more Blair to worry about. But I don't want to talk about him. Let's just get through this funeral."

Robbie handled the interment details for his mother, who seemed in a state of shock. His sisters were concerned for her, but they weren't especially sad that their father was dead.
"So what happened?" Robbie asked.
"He was dwunk at work and slipped in some pig blood," Rhett shrugged. "Just a normal day for him, except this time there was a table full of meat saws and knives where it wasn't supposed to be, and –"
"That's enough. I get the picture," Robbie cringed.

"Ma, I can skip a semester and stay here to help out," Robbie said.
"You ain't a'gonna do that," Flora said. "Yor Aint Rosetta is gonna let me and the girls move in with her."

An Admission of Weakness

"Well, that's good news," Robbie said.
Of all his relatives, his mother's sister Rosetta was the most educated. She was widowed and worked as a legal secretary in a nearby town. She owned a nice brick home and a car with all the hubcaps, a rarity in their area.
"There's just one problem," Flora said. "She ain't got no room for Rhett."
"What's he going to do? He can't stay here by himself," Robbie glanced around at the crumbling house. "I see the hole's still there."
"Your pa was proud of that," she said. "Said it would serve as a warnin' to people like you to stay away."
"Gee, that's nice to hear," Robbie said sarcastically.
"I never met a stupider man in my life," Flora sighed. "Why the hell did I ever git mixed up with him in the first place?"
"You thought he was stupid?"
"'Course I did," she snorted. "What kind o' nut shoots a damn hole in the side of the house?"
He couldn't resist laughing, and she laughed with him.
"You can't come back here," she said. "These locals'd kill you, and I couldn't bear that."
"You couldn't?"
"'Course not," she said. "I ain't a'gonna bury no child o'mine afore their time."
She caressed his cheek affectionately.
"It ain't your fault, ya know," she said.

An Admission of Weakness

"What's not?"

"You bein' gay," she said.

"I know," he said.

"In fact, they ain't no need for blame a'tall. It's just how some people are."

"You're right," he said. "I'm surprised you knew that."

"I been a'doin' my research since you come out," she said. "I know all about it, 'cept I don't quite understand what goes in where when you're goin' at it."

"It's probably better if you don't," he said. "Thanks, Ma. I never thought you'd understand."

"I know I ain't much, Robbie," she said emotionally, "but I love my children, and I'm always gonna look out for 'em.

"And that brings me to Rhett. I was a'hopin' he could come stay with you til he's ready to be out on his own."

"Uh, sure," Robbie blinked. "He's always welcome to stay with me."

"He tole me a little about yer feller," she frowned. "I don't think he's good enough for you. You deserve the best, and don't you never forget it."

"I won't," he said emotionally and gave her a hug. "I love you, Ma."

"I love you," she said. "And if anyone tries to put you down for bein' gay, you bring 'em here, and I'll whoop their asses."

An Admission of Weakness

Two weeks later, after Flora and the girls were settled into Aunt Rosetta's house, Rhett and Robbie set out for Urbana in their father's old Ford truck.

As soon as they arrived at school, Robbie requested a new room as far from Blair as possible. He explained to his advisor about his father's death and his brother's need for somewhere to stay, and the man was kind enough to arrange a job for Rhett as a therapy tech with the same team who had provided him with his new brace. As an employee, he was granted special permission to stay with his brother in his dorm room.

Robbie was offered a job at the library, which was a much needed change from fast food. He knew Blair never visited the building, so he ran no risk of running into him.

Rhett befriended a sweet young therapy tech with auburn hair named Vanessa, and the two of them began to spend time together. As for Robbie, he swore off men that semester. He wanted to focus on his studies and his brother. He forewent going to any sports related parties and get-togethers, although he was still required to attend the home games. Fortunately, he never ran into Blair.

He rarely saw Andres or Major these days. Major and Simon had their own circle of couple friends, and Andres spent his time with

An Admission of Weakness

his girlfriend Ebony. It was just as well; they only reminded him of Blair.
He still loved him, and he missed what they had had together. But at least it was finally over. Blair was married, and there was no coming back from that.

Ruby brought supper over and set it in front of Carter at the kitchen table. It was a week before Blair was to return to school.
"No Camilla this weekend?" she said.
"She's with Ashura," Carter said briefly.
"I see. Where are Blair and Danielle?"
"They're meeting with Cheryl Morgan."
"Why?"
"Is that any of your business, nosey?" he said grumpily.
"Eat your salad first," she said. "It's laced with broken glass."
"Fine," he sighed. "They're going over the renovation plans for the house she's giving them in Kenilworth."
"My goodness," she said. "I wish Naomi had met a guy with a sugar-mama like Cheryl Morgan when she was in college."
"Will you please just go home?"
"This was my home until you screwed everything up," she said. "In fact, a lot of people used to call this house home. But then Carter had to have his way and drove everyone out."

An Admission of Weakness

"This was not my fault."
"Of course not," she agreed. "It's Naomi's and Blair's and Justin's and Katie's. They were all in the wrong while you were just trying to help."
"You're being sarcastic, but you're not wrong," he said.
"You manipulated your children to get them to do your bidding. Justin managed to escape some of it thanks to me, but the others weren't so lucky."
"Yes, you were a big help with Justin," he said sarcastically. "Thank you very much."
"Don't mention it. So when does Blair go back to school?"
"He isn't going back."
"Why not?"
"What's the point of him getting a degree that will do him no good at Morgan Enterprises?" Carter said testily.
"He'll need that degree whenever this marriage goes belly-up, which is only a matter of time."
"He and Danielle will do just fine," he said.
"Well, your marriage is certainly a good example for them," she said dryly.
"Speaking of that, is Naomi okay?"
"She's great," Ruby said. "This is the happiest I've seen her in years."
"If all you're going to do is insult me, stop coming over here."

An Admission of Weakness

"Okay," she said agreeably. "If you get lonely for someone to talk to, you can always call one of your children. Oh wait, none of them are speaking to you."
"Go away."

"Blair, you have to finish your degree," Ruby took him aside.
"I don't see why," he said. "Danielle's mother is already setting up a team to train me in everything I need to know to run Morgan Enterprises."
"What will happen if you and Danielle get a divorce down the road?" Ruby asked.
"Gran, that's not going to happen," he said.
"Oh, you love her that much, do you?"
"Sure," he shrugged.
"Then why did you break up with her after high school?"
"I didn't technically break up with her. I said we should see other people. And you can see where that got me."
"No, what got you to where you are now is listening to your father instead of your heart."
"And Dad was right," he said. "I'm going to be living in a big mansion with a six figure income."
"With a woman you don't even like," she said.
"She's okay," Blair shrugged. "Besides, I'll be working sixty hours a week, so we won't see each other that much."

An Admission of Weakness

"That will help, I'm sure," she said dryly.

"Dude, don't be so fucking stupid," Justin said to his brother. The two were standing in Blair and Danielle's bedroom.
"Wow, those are the nicest words you've said to me in months," Blair said.
"Grandma says you're not going back to school. Why wouldn't you finish your degree while you have the chance?"
"You don't even have a degree," Blair said.
"We're talking about you, not me," Justin said. "Why don't you admit the real reason you don't want to go back to the U of I?"
"Because I have a job waiting for me making more money than you'll ever see?" Blair said.
"That's not it," Justin said. "You don't want to run into the faggot."
"I don't care if I see him again," Blair said. "I'm married now."
"You're still queer," Justin said.
"Do you want to go to the back yard again like we did on Christmas Eve?"
"You fought me that night to prove that being gay doesn't make you less of a man."
"And I proved it."
"But you're proving the opposite now," Justin said. "You're a gay pussy."
"I'm not gay, and I'm not a pussy!" Blair snapped.

An Admission of Weakness

"If you were gay then, you're gay now," Justin said. "You can't choose your sexuality, you know. You are what you are."

"Not according to you and Dad."

"I know better now," Justin said. "I may not like it, but you're gay and you're not going to change. So why you married Danielle when there was a guy right in this house who said he loved you is beyond me.

"I take that back. I do know why. It's because you're a pussy, just like I said."

Blair balled his hands into fists.

"You were afraid to go against Dad, afraid to show the faggot you loved him, afraid not to marry Danielle, and now you're afraid to face him again."

"What's the point of facing him?" Blair sat down dejectedly on the bed.

"You could at least have some closure," Justin said. "You're going to see nothing but pussy for the next fifty years, so man up and talk to him. Maybe you can still work something out."

"Like what?"

"Fuck him on the side," Justin shrugged. "Hell, fuck a different guy every day. Because I know you aren't going to be able to fuck Danielle. Maybe I'll fuck her for you while you're fucking your boyfriend."

"You're not going to fuck my wife!" Blair said indignantly.

An Admission of Weakness

"Well, somebody should, and it's not going to be you," Justin said.
"I'm still fucking her," Blair said. "She wants a baby, so we're fucking every night."
"Dude, why would you have a baby with someone you don't love? Are you fucking nuts?"
"She wants a baby," Blair said. "It's my duty to give her one."

Blair managed to convince Cheryl Morgan to let him finish his degree at the U of I while Danielle completed her education at Dartmouth.
"Danielle married you because I need someone to take over this company someday," Cheryl said grimly. "You'd better not let me down."
"No, ma'am," he gulped.

Blair returned to the university and knocked on the door across from his dorm room. He was surprised when a young Asian man answered it.
"Yes?"
"Is, uh, Robbie here?"
"There's no Robbie here," the man frowned.
"He lives here," Blair said. "Robbie Lee. Blonde, tall, good-looking, talks with a southern accent."
"Not a clue what you're talking about, dude," the man closed the door in his face.

An Admission of Weakness

Blair asked Major and Simon and Andres about Robbie, but none of them had seen him. He decided at last to let it go. No point in bringing up the past now that he was married.
Oh god, he was married! The thought gave him a jolt in the pit of his stomach every time he remembered it.

"I'm glad things worked out for you," Robbie smiled into the phone after he finished the spring semester's final exams.
"Thanks to you," Katie said. "After you left the house that day, we brought everything out into the open. Dad wasn't happy, of course. I've spoken to him a few times, but he won't acknowledge Dillon or the wedding. And that's why I'm calling. We want you to come."
"It's nice of you to invite me," he said. "But I can't. I have to work, there's my brother, and –"
"And Blair and Danielle will be here," she finished for him.
"I'd rather not see them again."
"That's perfectly understandable," she said. "But it might be a chance to clear the air."
"I think I'd rather leave things the way they are," Robbie said. "There's no point in reliving everything."
"Are you dating anyone?"
"Nope. I've sworn off men," he said.

An Admission of Weakness

"Oh no, don't tell me you're going straight too," she chuckled.

"No," he laughed. "I just think I'm one of those guys who's always a bridesmaid, never a bride."

"Blair called me the other night," Katie said. "He misses you. He was crying."

"He had every opportunity to fix things while I was there."

"You know he can't be pushed," Katie said. "And you pushed kind of hard."

"I know," he sighed. "I was a big hit with your whole family, wasn't I?"

"Actually, you were," she said. "Did you know that Justin is the one who convinced Blair to go back and finish his degree? He's finally come around to the whole gay thing because of you."

"I'm surprised."

"So don't give up on Blair," she said. "Miracles can happen."

Carter stopped by the W.H. Abernathy House of Fashion a few days before the wedding.

"Hello, Carter," June smiled. "It's been a long time."

"Yes, it has," he said tentatively. "Is Naomi here?"

Naomi walked in from the back room just then.

"Carter, what are you doing here?" she frowned.

"Naomi, it's nice to see you," he said.

An Admission of Weakness

"What are you doing here?" she repeated.

"I was wondering if you knew where my silver cufflinks are."

"Are you actually going to the wedding?" she looked surprised.

"I am the bride's father. I have a right to be there."

"But you don't have the right to ruin your daughter's special day," Naomi said.

"Do you know where the damn cufflinks are?"

"Wear your gold ones," she said. "They're in the jewelry case in the safe."

"Is that the dress you wore?" he gestured to a nearby mannequin.

"It's being fitted for Katie," she nodded. "And then perhaps Camilla will want to wear it too someday."

"How much is that costing me?" he eyed the dress appraisingly.

"It's not costing *you* a dime," she said, annoyed. "Billy gave it to me as a gift for the work *I* did."

"I didn't mean…I meant…"

"I know what you meant," she said. "The same thing you meant when you talked about 'your' money."

"It's our money, and you know it."

"The only thing I know is that I worked for thirty years as your personal servant, and you have yet to say thank you."

An Admission of Weakness

"I always appreciated everything you did," he said.

"No, you took it for granted. I was your wife, and it was my duty to look after the children and the house and the finances.

"Well, I'm a woman, Carter, first and foremost, and I'm a wife and mother second. Do you understand that at all yet?"

"Marriages have defined roles," he began.

"Oh my god," she shook her head. "You know what, I don't care what cufflinks you wear or if you even go to the wedding."

With that, she turned on her heel and left the room.

The wedding was held at the ranch on a cloudless June day. Naomi and Marci and Ruby worked for weeks on the decorations and the food. Katie and Dillon specifically kept the guest list down to a few hundred family and friends.

It was a rustic but elegant affair held on the front lawn of the main house, and the food was delicious comfort food per Dillon's request. He and his father wore black tuxedos with purple accents. Camilla, as the maid of honor, was dressed in a lovely purple strapless gown from the Abernathy collection. Naomi, Marci, and Ruby were dressed in purple as well. Charles looked quite dapper in a royal blue shirt and tie, brown and black plaid slacks, brown

An Admission of Weakness

suspenders, and brown saddle shoes. Topping if off was a snazzy brown fedora with a royal blue feather.

"You look lovely, Danielle," Carter greeted her with a kiss on the cheek.

"I hate this dress," Danielle picked at the bodice crossly. "Mother picked it out. I mean, of course she picked it out. She picks out everything. She runs my life. I have no say in anything."

"I'm sorry," Carter said uncomfortably.

Blair took him aside.

"Stay away from her. She's been in a mood since she got home from school. Nothing's good enough, she hates everything, she hates her mother, she hates me, and the list goes on. I stay in my own bedroom and try to avoid her as much as possible."

"You're sleeping in separate bedrooms?" Carter frowned. "Perhaps I should talk to her and explain the roles of husband and wife. Newlyweds sometimes have trouble communi–"

"No thanks," Blair said dryly. "I think you've done enough."

"Dr. Butterfield, there are some of my family I want you to meet," Dillon approached him warily. "And if you could be polite, I would appreciate it; I want them to like Katie's family."

An Admission of Weakness

"Of course I'll be polite," Carter scowled. "When have I ever been impolite?"
"Try every time I've seen you for the past fifteen years," Dillon said. "To be honest, I didn't even think you'd show today."
"I wouldn't miss my daughter's wedding."
"Well, it's my wedding too, so don't do anything to mess it up. I want it perfect for Katie."
"Carter, if you do anything to make Katie cry today, so help me god, I will rip your hemorrhoids out through your mouth," Ruby said.
"I'm not a monster, you know," Carter said indignantly.
"See that you aren't today," Naomi said sternly.
"Oh, I see you went with the silver cufflinks."

Camilla's phone rang just as they were ready to get started. She stepped away and returned a moment later.
"Ashura's going to be late," she said.
"Something came up."

Ashura ended the call with Camilla and gulped. How was he ever going to explain this? The Butterfields would never understand, and he might lose Camilla over it. Still, he had to do the right thing and tell them the truth.

An Admission of Weakness

CHAPTER THIRTY-EIGHT

Blair danced with his mother at the reception to one of Nat King Cole's ballads.
"Danielle looks nice tonight," Naomi said.
"She may look it, but she isn't acting it," Blair said grimly.
"I sense things aren't terrific with the newlyweds," Naomi said worriedly.
"I try to avoid her since she got home from school. She's angry at everything. Nothing I do is right."
"Are things okay in the bedroom department?" she asked hesitantly. "I only ask because of, you know, Robbie."
"I told her before we got married that I was gay," Blair said.
"Not this again," Naomi frowned and stopped dancing. "You were straight, then you were gay, then at Christmas you were suddenly straight again. Now you say you're gay. Son, you need to make up your mind."
"I'm gay, Mama," he said. "I've always been gay, but I didn't understand it for a long time. I had everything figured out at Thanksgiving and then I came home for Christmas, and Dad had Danielle and me engaged with Grandmother's ring and everything, and Robbie and Ian showed up, and I screwed everything up again. I don't know why I ever agreed to marry her."

An Admission of Weakness

"I thought she agreed to marry you," Naomi said.
"She's the one who insisted on it," Blair said. "I wanted to wait."
"If you knew you were gay, why on earth would you do this? Why would you push Robbie away? He loved you."
"I don't know," Blair threw his hands in the air. "I'm a screw-up, Mama. I'm an arrogant, stupid, narcissistic asshole who threw away the sweetest, most loving man in the world to make dad and Danielle happy. I'm possibly the most fucking idiotic human being who ever existed." He dropped his hands hopelessly.
"And now I'm married, and he's gone, and it's too late. He was right, Mama; I ruined my life." His eyes filled with tears, and Naomi held him in her arms while he cried.
Carter swallowed with difficulty and turned away with the glasses of punch he had been bringing his wife and son.

Ashura beckoned to Camilla from the edge of the dance floor, where she was dancing with Justin.
"You made it," she beamed. "Come on, let's dance."
"Millie, I have to talk to you," Ashura said. "There's something I have to tell you, and you're not going to like it."

An Admission of Weakness

"Okay," her smile faded. "You know you can be honest with me about anything."

"Come with me," he pulled her to the side and showed her a couple of papers. He gesticulated wildly with his hands.

"Oh my god," she said, her eyes wide. "This can't be happening."

"What will your father say?"

"He's going to be furious," she said. "We'd better take him out to the stable to break the news."

Camilla rounded up her parents, grandmother, Charles Morgan, Katie and Dillon, and Blair and Danielle and herded them out to the big stable building. She closed the door behind them and took a deep breath.

"Ashura has something to tell you, and I want you all to stay calm."

"What is it?" Carter said impatiently.

"I made a mistake," Ashura said hesitantly. "In fact, I made a couple of mistakes."

"And?" Ruby prodded. "Can we move this along? There's a piece of wedding cake out there with my name on it."

"Okay, you remember that I married Blair and Danielle at Christmas."

"Yes, of course," Naomi said.

"The thing is, I may not have been exactly licensed to perform a wedding in Illinois."

"What?" Carter exploded. "You said you were."

An Admission of Weakness

"I am in New York," Ashura said uneasily. "I didn't realize I wasn't licensed in all fifty states."

"Oh my god," Danielle said.

"You said a couple of mistakes," Naomi said patiently.

"Well, the license application was made in Cook County."

"Yeah, so?" Danielle frowned. "Mother pulled some strings with the clerk's office and got it for us."

"Yes, I know," Ashura said. "And that's the problem. The application was made in Cook County, but the wedding took place in Green Grove County."

"What's wrong with that?" Blair asked.

"You have to marry in the county where the application was made," Carter said grimly.

"Fine. We'll just say the wedding took place in Cook County. No one will know the difference."

"Also…" Ashura said.

"There's more?" Charles said. "Oh my god."

Ashura held up the papers in his hand.

"I, uh, forgot to register the marriage with the clerk's office. I was supposed to do that within ten days, but I got busy with the clinic, and time got away from me. As a result, the Illinois government has no record of the marriage."

"So they're not married?" Naomi's eyes lit up.

An Admission of Weakness

"That's the good news," Ashura said. "I can take the certificate to Cook County and see if they'll make an exception. With Danielle's family's pull, it's very possible."

"No!" Blair and Danielle cried at the same time.

"What do you mean no?" Carter said. "You've made a commitment to each other and to Morgan Enterprises."

"Fuck Morgan Enterprises," Danielle smiled for the first time in months. "Fuck Mother, and fuck the State of Illinois."

She turned to Blair.

"We're not married," she said. "We're free!"

"What will we tell your mother?" Blair said.

"Who cares? I'll let Daddy deal with her," Danielle said. She gave Blair a fervent embrace. "I love you, Blair, but I don't want to be your wife. I'm in love with Ian, and you're in love with Robbie."

Blair hugged her back and spun her around. "I'm not your husband!" he exclaimed joyfully. "I'm nobody's husband!"

"And I'm nobody's wife!" she laughed.

They danced in a circle for a minute or two.

"That's the first time you've laughed in weeks," Blair chuckled.

"Don't you see?" she said happily. "Mother can't control my life anymore. I never have to see her again if I don't want to. This is the happiest I've been in twenty years!"

An Admission of Weakness

She took Blair's hand and dragged him to the limousine her parents hired.
"Where are we going?" he asked.
"Home," she giggled. "To pack our shit and get the hell out of there!"

"Well, this is a disaster," Carter said angrily. "Ashura, I'm very disappointed in you."
"But look how relieved Blair and Danielle are," Ruby grinned at the pair running to the car.
"Blair?" Naomi called after him. He looked back at her. "You've been given a once in a lifetime chance to start over. Don't screw it up!"
"I won't, Mama, I swear!" he waved happily and climbed into the long car.

On the way to Kenilworth, Blair tried Robbie's phone, but Robbie had obviously blocked him. Rhett must have done the same thing because his call was rejected as well.
He sat back in the seat and smiled. Oh well, he would find Robbie and make things right. The important thing now was that he was no longer married.
He had never felt such a sense of relief in his life. His mother was right; he had been given a second chance, and he couldn't screw it up.

"Would you like to dance?" Carter asked Naomi when they returned to the party.

An Admission of Weakness

"I suppose," Naomi said reluctantly.
The two moved gracefully around the dance floor.
"You look lovely tonight," Carter said.
"Thanks," she said dryly.
"What?" he frowned.
"Nothing," she said. "It's just that that's the first time you've complimented me in fifteen years."
"That's not true."
"Yes, it is," she said. She changed the subject. "It's a relief about Blair and Danielle."
"A relief? Are you kidding? His whole future with Morgan Enterprises is gone. His mansion and Mercedes are gone. Danielle is gone."
"You care about those things, but he doesn't. He never loved Danielle, and he never wanted to be a businessman."
"Oh, he'll still be a businessman," Carter said firmly. "I'll see to that."
"You have a son who's already a businessman, and you have yet to set foot in his place of business."
"That's different," Carter said. "He had the potential to be a –"
"Stop it," she said. "Justin wanted to be a businessman, but that wasn't good enough for you. Blair wants to be a teacher, but that's not good enough either. Just let them live their lives. Couldn't you see how miserable Blair

An Admission of Weakness

and Danielle were in the marriage you pushed them into?"
"They just needed time to adjust," Carter said.
"Blair is gay, Carter. You're going to have to accept it and the fact that he's in love with a southern white boy named Robert E. Lee."
"I will never accept that," he said stiffly.
"Then stay in that big house all by yourself," she pushed him away. "Because unless you learn to accept the people you claim to love for who we are, you are going to lose us for good."
She walked away from him into the crowd.

"Robbie, I have some news for you," Katie said.
"You're pregnant already?"
"Not that I know of," she chuckled.
"How was the wedding?" he asked. "I wish I could have been there."
"As it turns out, you could have been," she said.
"What?" he sounded puzzled.
"Blair and Danielle are not married," she said excitedly. "They never were."
"You mean they lied? Oh my god, he will go to any length to pretend to be straight. This is because I was with Ian that night, isn't it? Blair was jealous, which he has no right to be after all the shit he's pulled."
"Robbie, listen," she said. "They didn't lie. It was a mistake. Ashura didn't…you know

An Admission of Weakness

what? It's too complicated to explain. The point is, Blair and Danielle thought they were married, but they never were. Blair is single."

"Well, don't worry," Robbie said sarcastically. "He'll find another woman to marry in no time. I'll keep my fingers crossed that third time's the charm."

"Robbie, he's not straight, and he's not confused. He knows who he is. He just got sucked into Dad's vortex of manipulation. You saw how powerful that is. But he's out of it now. He's free, and you're free. This is your chance to be together."

"No," Robbie said. "We've had more than enough chances to be together, and it's never worked out. The universe is trying to tell us something, and it's time we listened."

"Robbie, I'm only going to say this once, and I speak from experience. Don't throw away a chance like this. Dillon put up with fifteen years of my bullshit, and I'm lucky he's still here. You've put up with three years of Blair's bullshit, so why give up now? You've come this far, it's time to go all the way."

The summer flew by for Robbie. He worked and studied hard as usual. Rhett was flourishing in this collegiate environment. Besides Vanessa, he made a number of other good friends with whom he spent most of his free time.

An Admission of Weakness

That was good, Robbie thought. Rhett deserved the chance to blossom on his own.

Robbie kept to himself for the most part. He met most of his hall mates, but they were freshmen who were only interested in partying and drinking.

When the fall semester began, he threw himself into his classes, determined to ace each one. Without the distraction of friends or a boyfriend, he was better able to focus on his studies.

He heard nothing from Blair. Katie had said he was eager to get back together with him, but if that was true, where was he?

Knowing Blair, he had probably gotten himself engaged to some woman or fallen for another guy. The love he professed for Robbie was apparently nothing but a joke.

Dillon and Katie lived in wedded bliss all summer in their cabin. She thoroughly enjoyed her new job at the Green Grove Hospital as well as the horses and the rolling green hills surrounding the ranch.

Justin's business was beginning to take off. Once people over thirty realized it was a much more pleasant atmosphere without the know-it-all twenty-somethings around, they were eager to switch their memberships.

Justin insisted that Ruby be a full partner since she was in large part responsible for his

An Admission of Weakness

success. She took no money, but she helped him with the financial aspect of the business and worked a few hours every day at the gym. To her surprise, she found that she enjoyed it very much.

Now that the secret of her relationship with Charles was out, the two spent nearly all their time together.

Camilla and Ashura were inseparable as well. Their open, warm, and selfless personalities blended well, and she spent as much time in Chicago with him as possible. It was awkward for him to come to the Butterfield house because Carter was still displeased with him over Blair's marriage debacle.

"Dad, you need to let that go," Camilla said to him one evening.

"Blair's whole future was destroyed by the man's ineptness," Carter scowled.

"He's not inept," she said. "He made a mistake. Alright, a couple of mistakes. Why do you insist on holding this grudge? And speaking of grudges, are you ever going to speak to Justin again?"

"As soon as he realizes what a mistake he's made, I will be happy to talk to him."

"You haven't even been to the gym to see what he's done," she said. "It's astonishing what he's accomplished."

"With a lot of help," Carter snorted.

An Admission of Weakness

"And wasn't he lucky that Mr. Price and Gran were willing to help him," she said. "If only his father had been that supportive. Here, eat your supper."
She turned to leave the dining room, but she paused and looked back.
"Dad, I'll be moving out soon, and you're going to be in this house all alone. Is that really what you want?"
"I want my family to appreciate the fact that I only want what's best for them."
"We do appreciate it, and we love you," she said. "But you want our complete obedience for the rest of our lives, and we can't give that to you. Our lives belong to us."

In September, Naomi drove over to the Butterfield house.
"Carter, I came over here to speak to you," Naomi said. "Can you stop working on your book for five minutes and look at me?"
"I was wondering when you'd come to your senses," he removed his reading glasses and sat back in his desk chair.
"I'm getting my own place," she said. "I can't impose on Mama and Justin any longer."
"I see," he carefully hid his dismay. "Where will you go?"
"There's a small house next to Anthony Miller and his husband Jacob that is for rent. It's already furnished and is quite charming."

An Admission of Weakness

"You have a perfectly good house here," he said.

"*You* have a perfectly good house," she corrected him. "I don't have anything."

"That's nonsense."

"It was bought with your money," she said. "You paid the mortgage and for the upkeep. You bought the furniture. It all belongs to you."

"Here we go again," he sighed.

"I'm here to tell you that the children will be coming to my house for Thanksgiving," she ignored him.

"Nonsense," he frowned. "Thanksgiving must be held here."

"It must?"

"It won't be Thanksgiving without everyone gathered here as usual."

"Well, the family wants to come to my house, so that's what's going to happen. I will have Mama or Charles bring you over a plate." She got to her feet.

"You have your book and your self-righteousness to keep you company, so you won't miss the rest of us.

"And just so you know, I'm thinking about getting a divorce."

"Naomi, there's no need for that," he said. "I don't want a divorce."

"Neither do I. But you refuse to consider anyone else's opinions or dreams unless they agree with your own. You think of me as a

An Admission of Weakness

servant instead of a partner. So until those things change, I won't be back, and neither will the children.
"I hope it's worth it to you, always being right about everything even when the proof that you're not is staring you right in the face. That sense of satisfaction will be your only companion from now on."

"I've emailed him, I've sent him notes, I tried calling, but I can't get through to him," Blair said. "I've even sat outside his dorm room waiting for him to come home. I can never catch him."
"Which room are you talking about?" Andres said.
"What do you mean, which room?" Blair frowned.
"He and Rhett have moved a few times," Andres explained.
"Rhett's here?"
"He's living with Robbie now after their dad died."
"I didn't know that," Blair said. "So that means I've been asking strangers to forgive me and take me back."
"Looks like it," Andres chuckled.
"I went to his job, but they said he quit."
"Because he got a new job," Andres said.
"Where's he working?"
"I don't know," Andres lied.

An Admission of Weakness

"Why haven't you told me any of this?" Blair demanded.

"He told me not to," Andres shrugged. "He doesn't want anything to do with you."

"Dammit."

"Give it up, bro," Andres advised. "You screwed the pooch too many times. He's never going to take you back."

"He has to."

"No, he doesn't, and he doesn't want to," Andres said. "So move on."

"I've tried," Blair said. "I've spent the last five months getting my act together. I've been talking to the team psychologist twice a week, and I know who I am now. And it's more clear to me now than ever before that Robbie and I belong together."

"You've said that before," Andres said dryly.

"I know. But then I went home, and my dad got into my head again."

"Which he will do every time you go home," Andres said. "So you might as well just go back to Danielle and work for her mom, because your dad's just gonna nag you until you do. You'll give in to him; you always do."

"Not anymore. It's different now."

"Sure it is," Andres rolled his eyes.

"Look, I've spent every day of the last five months growing up," Blair insisted. "Dad can't push me around anymore. He can't push any of us around now, thanks to Robbie."

An Admission of Weakness

"What's Robbie got to do with it?"
"He destroyed our family," Blair said.
"And that's a good thing?"
"It freed us all from my dad," Blair said. "Me, Katie, Camilla, Justin, and even Mama. We've all left him."
"I just don't see that your dad was that bad. He was always nice to me."
"He's not a bad man, and I know he loves us, but it's the way he's always manipulated us to get us to do what he wants."
"What's going to stop him from doing it again?"
"We confronted him," Blair said. "Justin's doing his own thing, Katie and Dillon are married, Camilla's dating a really nice guy, and I'm no longer married to Danielle."
"The only reason you're not married to her is because the minister screwed up," Andres reminded him. "You never confronted your dad about anything. Trust me, you'll do whatever he tells you to do next. And if it isn't him, it will be another porn director or worse."
"At least tell me if Robbie's dating anyone."
"I don't know," Andres said. "I don't see much of him anymore."
"Please tell me where he lives."
"I can't," Andres said. "I already told you more than I should have."
"You don't care that we love each other?"

An Admission of Weakness

"You may think you love him, but I doubt you know what love is," Andres said. "And I'm pretty sure he feels nothing for you but contempt, not that I blame him."
"Will you at least give him a message for me?"
"Ask your sisters," Andres said. "You said they've been talking to him."
"They gave him my messages, but he ignored them. Please, Andres, I'm begging you."
"No," Andres said impatiently. "Brother, give it up already. Find yourself some nice woman that will make your dad happy, or go make some more porn, or whatever, but leave Robbie alone. He's been through enough."

Blair pleaded with Major and Simon to give him Robbie's address, tell him where he was working, or get a message to him, but they refused. He wandered through the business department, hoping to see Robbie there, but without success. He spoke to his classmates and friends, but they all said they hadn't seen him. One of them finally told him she thought Robbie was taking most of his classes online. He had been watching for Robbie at the football games and at practice, but he never seemed to be there. The cheerleading coach told him that Robbie was injured at the first game and had been benched for the rest of the season.

An Admission of Weakness

It was a lost cause, he feared. Robbie had written him off completely, and he had run out of ideas of how to find him.

An Admission of Weakness

CHAPTER THIRTY-NINE

Blair made a stop at the library between classes to pick up a book for Andres that was being held at the main desk. He got in line and studied his phone while he waited.
"Next," a familiar voice said.
He looked up and came face to face with Robbie. The two stared at each other with astonishment.
"Hi," Blair said at last.
"What do you need?" Robbie asked briskly.
"How are you?" Blair asked.
"Do you have a book being held for you?"
"Uh, for Andres," Blair said.
Robbie extracted a book from a nearby shelf.
"Here," he said curtly. "Next."
"Wait," Blair said. "Can I talk to you?"
"No," Robbie said. "Next."
"Please?"
"I can take over for a while, Robbie," another library employee said. "Go talk to your friend."

"What do you want?" Robbie folded his arms
"First of all, I've been trying to find you, but no one would tell me where you were," Blair said.
"I know. What do you want?"
"I'm not married anymore," Blair said. "I never was."
"I know that. So are you here to tell me you and Danielle have reconciled and are expecting

An Admission of Weakness

twins? Or are you engaged to some other woman?
"Wait, I know. You got involved with another pornographer and need my help to make more videos. You're suddenly gay again. Or have you already turned back to straight? Did you come to tell me you slept with my best friend again? Do you want me back for the twentieth time? Is that it? Or am I invited to your house so you can ignore me and have sex with your fiancée while I'm forced to watch?
"Or better yet, you've come up with some brand new way to break my heart, and you just can't wait to see the pain on my face so you can sit back and laugh."
"I'm sorry for all of it," Blair said. "That's all I wanted to say."
"Well, I forgive you," Robbie said sarcastically. "Now let's kiss and make up and live happily ever after."
"I'm not asking you to forgive me," Blair said. "And I'm not asking you to take me back."
"You're not?" Robbie's eyes narrowed suspiciously. "Oh, I see. You found someone new to torture. Well, good for you, and good luck to you and her or him or it or them."
"There's no one new," Blair said. "The only person for me is you, but I blew that, so I guess I'll be alone the rest of my life."

An Admission of Weakness

"Please," Robbie snorted. "You'll probably sleep with someone and be engaged before you get out of the library."

"Look, I want you back more than anything in the world," Blair said sincerely. "I won't deny that. But I know you won't take me back, so I'm not going to ask. I just came here to apologize for everything I did and for spoiling the good thing we had.

"This isn't some trick to get you back so I can hurt you again. There is no other man in my life, and there will never be another woman."

"At least until tomorrow?"

"I was with Danielle at Christmas because I was trying to go along with her and Dad until I could get out of there," Blair said. "And the only reason I married her – thought I married her – was because I knew I had pushed you too far when I saw you and Ian having sex in the living room."

"Well, marrying her would be the natural next step in that situation," Robbie said dryly.

"I haven't been with anyone since Katie's wedding."

"Have you run out of new conquests already?" Robbie said.

"I'm not even going to try to explain," Blair said hopelessly, "because you wouldn't believe me anyway."

"That's true."

An Admission of Weakness

"I thought maybe I could give us both some closure by seeing you," Blair said. "But I see now that this was a mistake."
He turned to go, but paused and looked back. "I'm sorry about your dad," he said. "Is your family okay? Rhett, the girls, your mom?"
"They're fine," Robbie said.
"Good. Tell Rhett I said...never mind. He wouldn't want to hear it.
"It doesn't matter anymore, but I will always love you," his throat constricted until he could barely speak. "Have a happy life. I know it's going to be great for you."
He walked away.

"This is the worst game in the history of this university!" Coach Wilkensen shouted at his team in the locker room at halftime.
"Butterfield, you can hit the showers because you're out for the rest of the game. I've never seen so many consecutive fumbles in my thirty years of coaching; I think you set a new record for the University. I hope you're happy.
"Now get the fuck out of my sight," he added disgustedly. "I can't even look at you."
Blair avoided looking at his teammates as he headed for the shower room. He was humiliated, but he didn't care anymore now that reconciliation with Robbie was no longer possible.

An Admission of Weakness

Ever since he and Danielle split up, he had felt a new optimism about the future. He would apologize, Robbie would forgive him, and they would live happily ever after. It hadn't occurred to him that Robbie wouldn't forgive him. Apparently, Andres was right when he said that Robbie felt nothing for him but contempt.

He showered and dressed in his street clothes and went to join his father. The family was taking turns coming to his games this semester. Sometimes it was Katie and Dillon or Camilla and Ashura, sometimes it was his mom and grandmother and Charles, and once even Justin came to watch him.

He got to the bleachers and was astonished to see both of his parents sitting together. He explained about being removed from the game, so the three of them walked to the parking lot.

"I can't believe you both came," he said. "Does this mean…I mean are things better?"

"I didn't know she was coming," Carter said.

"We drove separately," Naomi explained. "I couldn't miss another game, and I didn't see why your father being here should stop me from coming."

"Come on, let's go eat," Carter scowled. "We can take my car."

"Which one?" Naomi pointed to the black Mercedes E-Class and the white Cadillac CT5 sitting a few cars apart. "They're both yours."

An Admission of Weakness

"Oh my god," Carter sighed and unlocked the Mercedes.

"What happened tonight?" Carter said after they were seated at their favorite upscale restaurant. "You haven't fumbled the ball like that since you were a boy."
"Nothing happened," Blair said. "I was just having a bad game, that's all."
"Everything okay, dear?" Naomi asked worriedly. "You look tired."
"I haven't been sleeping," Blair admitted.
"Is it a woman?" Carter asked.
"Carter," Naomi shook her head.
"It's not a woman, Dad," Blair said. "And just for future reference, it will never be a woman again."
"Now you can't give up hope," Carter said. "I spoke to Charles Morgan Jr., and he said –"
"Dad, I'm not getting back together with Danielle. She loves Ian, and I'm gay. Remember?"
"But Charles Jr. said that Ian hasn't proposed," Carter said. "That means she's still on the market."
"On the market?" Naomi said angrily. "Did you just compare a woman to a prized hog?"
"Dad, Danielle isn't interested in me," Blair said.
"I heard her say she loves you at Katie's wedding," Carter said. "If we could just –"

631

An Admission of Weakness

"Dad!" Blair exclaimed. "I'm fucking gay for Christ's sake!"
"Fine," Carter said. "If not Danielle, I'm sure there are any number of young women who would be –"
"Carter, will you please just shut the fuck up!" Naomi shouted exasperatedly.
The other diners looked around in alarm.
"Blair is gay!" she went on, heedless of the disruption she was causing. "When will you get that through your stupid skull?"
"Folks," their waiter frowned.
"Don't worry," Naomi picked up her purse and got to her feet. "We're leaving."
She turned to the other customers.
"I'm so sorry," she smiled pleasantly. "Please enjoy your dinners. My husband will be paying for your meals tonight."
With that, she strode through the exit doors, followed by her son, while her apoplectic husband fished a credit card from his wallet and handed it to the smirking waiter.

"Do you want to talk about it?" Naomi asked.
"First, did you say fuck in the restaurant just now?" Blair asked.
"Yes, I did," she said.
"I thought I might have hallucinated."
"Your father brings out my darker side these days," she grinned and then became serious. "So what happened?"

An Admission of Weakness

"I saw Robbie," he said.
"Uh-oh," she frowned. "That doesn't sound promising."
"It's over, Mama," Blair said sadly. "I hurt him too badly and too many times."
"He turned you down when you asked him to take you back?"
"I couldn't even ask," he said. "You should have seen the look on his face when I tried to talk to him. He hates me."
"What did you say to him?"
"I apologized for everything and said I was sorry about his dad."
"What did he say?"
"Remember how he talked to Dad right before he left last Christmas? It was kind of like that."
"Oh dear," she said sympathetically. "I'm sorry."
He wiped a tear from his cheek.
"There's nothing left for me to do," he said. "It's definitely over."
She hugged him, and he buried his face in her shoulder.
"I don't know what to do," he wept. "I can't eat, I can't sleep. I'm literally up all night."
"I know," she said soothingly.
Carter walked over to join them.
"What's this about?" he mouthed to his wife.
"Robbie," she mouthed back.
"Oh god," he groaned. "Not again."

An Admission of Weakness

"Honey, why don't you come home for a few days?" she disregarded her husband. "You can stay with me, and I'll make all your favorite foods."

"Thanks," Blair dried his eyes. "But I can't miss any more class. I'm barely holding my own as it is."

"You're failing?" Carter frowned. "Do you know what that will mean to your scholarship?"

"I know, Dad. Why do you care? You don't want me to be a teacher anyway."

"I want you to succeed," Carter said.

"All that means to you is that I marry Danielle again and work for her mother," Blair said. "Well, I don't know how many more times I'm going to have to tell you this, but I'm not in love with Danielle, I don't want to work for her mother, I don't want to live in Kenilworth, and I'm gay."

"You're just upset," Carter unlocked the car. "We'll talk about it later."

"No, we won't, because no matter how many times we talk about it, you don't hear a word I say. So just forget it. And don't come back here anymore. I don't want you to come to my games from now on."

"Fine," Carter shrugged. "I won't. But don't expect any more money from me."

"I don't want your money," Blair said. "I'll get a job."

An Admission of Weakness

"Concentrate on your studies," Naomi said. "You have your whole life to work at a job. Right now, school is your job. Whatever money you need, I'll give you."

Blair went home for Thanksgiving and Christmas and stayed with his mother. It was good to be with his family. Justin had come around on his views of Blair's sexuality, although he still disapproved of Robbie. Surprisingly, Justin had a steady girlfriend, a very nice local woman named Isabella. Her mother was a police officer, and her father was the finance manager at the Cadillac dealership. Not surprisingly, Camilla and Ashura announced that they were engaged, and perhaps the biggest announcement of all was when Katie and Dillon told them all they were going to have twins.

"When are you going to get married, Gran?" Katie asked.

"Why would I marry her?" Charles frowned. "This is a friends with benefits kind of relationship. I got what I wanted out of it."

"And why would I want to be saddled with an old goat like him?" Ruby said. "My other boyfriends would be very upset if I went and got married on them."

"Mama," Naomi grinned and shook her head.

An Admission of Weakness

"The truth is, I asked her to marry me, and she said she wanted to see what other offers came in before she answered."
"Charles, be serious," Naomi said.
"Fine," Ruby said. "If you all must know, and I know you must, we are engaged but haven't set a date yet."
There were cheers and hugs and words of congratulations for the next few minutes.
"I hate to admit this, but she's the best thing that ever happened to me," Charles kissed her hand.
"And I suppose he's not so bad," Ruby shrugged and grinned like a schoolgirl.

The Butterfield house was dark when Ruby stopped by.
"Here's your Christmas dinner, Scrooge," she turned on some lights and set the covered tray in front of Carter.
"Thanks," he wearily pushed it away. "I'm not hungry."
"Why not?"
"Please go away," he struggled to stand up from the table. He was wearing only a pair of boxers, socks, and a dirty tee shirt.
"Are you okay?" she frowned worriedly.
He looked as if he had aged twenty years since Thanksgiving.

An Admission of Weakness

"I'm fine," he said. "Why wouldn't I be? My wife hates me, my children hate me, I have no one."

"I don't know why or how, but your family doesn't hate you. They actually love you."

"So where are they?"

"They're waiting for you to come to your senses and love them for who they are, not for who you want them to be."

"No man in the world loves their family more than I do," Carter said. "So I pushed too hard. Is that a crime?"

"The way you did it, it should be," she said.

"I just wanted them to be happy," he said tearfully. "I didn't want them to struggle like my parents and grandparents did.

"You of all people know they can't just do well. They have to be exceptional to succeed in this country simply because they're Black, and that's not fair."

Tears streamed down his face.

"My children deserve every happiness, and this cruel society doesn't want them to have it. That's why I pushed them. I want them to go out into the world and say, 'Fuck you. You tried to hold me down, but you failed. I won, you white sonsofbitches, and you can all go straight to hell!'"

"Carter, I understand how you feel," she said more kindly. "That's how I felt when I was raising Naomi. But I had to let her find her own

An Admission of Weakness

way. All I could do is support her and pray that she'd make it. She did make it, and so have your children. You did an amazing job as their father, but you weren't willing to let them find their own path. You tried to choose it for them, and that was a mistake. That's why they aren't here right now. It isn't because they don't love you, because they do. And so does Naomi."

He dropped to his knees and covered his face with his hands. She knelt beside him and held him while he wept.

"Naomi, please come home. I love you so much," he sobbed. "I'm sorry I made a mess of things."

"Shhh," she whispered as she rocked him back and forth. "It's okay. You can still fix things; it's not too late."

When his tears were done, she fetched him a box of tissues.

"This should go into that book of yours," she said. "Your grandchildren should know the story of how their grandfather finally admitted to his mother-in-law that he's an idiot."

"It's done," he wiped his eyes.

"What's done?"

"The book is done," he said. "And the part about Carter being an idiot features prominently in the final chapter."

"Can you put in there that I called you an idiot?" she asked. "I'd like that to be a direct quote."

An Admission of Weakness

"Sure," he said and started crying again.
She put an arm around him and squeezed affectionately.

Robbie and Rhett stayed in Urbana for Thanksgiving, but they made the trip home to Mississippi for Christmas. It was a more joyful holiday than they were used to when their father was alive. Aunt Rosetta had a great sense of humor and kept everyone in stitches.
Robbie was amazed when he saw his mother and sister for the first time since the funeral. They were all wearing nice, new clothes, with stylish hairdos and makeup.
"Ma, you look amazing!" Rhett said delightedly.
Indeed, Flora looked ten years younger, and she frequently wore a smile. For the first time in her adult life, she actually felt happy and worthwhile as a woman.
On Christmas morning, Aunt Rosetta handed her a large envelope.
"Merry Christmas, Sis," she grinned.
"What's this?" Flora frowned. "I told you not to get me nothin'."
"Just open it," Aunt Rosetta said.
Flora scanned the documents uncomprehendingly.
"I don't git it. What am I a'lookin' at?"

An Admission of Weakness

"It's a wrongful death settlement for Otis," Aunt Rosetta explained. "From the meat packing plant."
"But I didn't —"
"No, but I did," Aunt Rosetta chuckled. "I gave all the information to the lawyers I work for, and they pursued it on your behalf."
"They're agivin' me money?"
"Look at the amount," Aunt Rosetta turned to the final page.
"Aaahhh!" Flora screamed. "Is this a joke?"
"It's no joke. The money is yours."
"How much is it, Ma?" the girls clamored.
"It says t-two m-million dollars," Flora stammered.
"That makes you a woman of independent means, Sis," Aunt Rosetta smiled. "And no one deserves it more."

Blair visited the library every chance he got. He sat at a table near the front desk just to be near Robbie. He knew it was over between them, but he couldn't seem to stay away.
Robbie would frown at him every so often and go about his work.
"You can't loiter here," a security officer said.
"I'm reading," Blair said.
"You don't have a book," the man pointed out.
Blair removed a book from a nearby shelf.
"Now I do," he said.

An Admission of Weakness

"You're reading a book from the Women's Studies section?" the guard said doubtfully.
"Are you implying I don't appreciate women for the strong and independent people they are?"
"Yes, I am," the man said. "Although reading that might do you some good. I know all about your reputation where women are concerned."
"What reputation?"
"I saw the video where you and your friends gangbang the woman with the broken-down car," the security man said dryly.

An Admission of Weakness

CHAPTER FORTY

Robbie was uncomfortable under Blair's constant scrutiny. He tried to do as much work among the shelves as possible. But no matter where he went in the building, Blair was always there.

"I thought you understood that it's over," he said impatiently one day.

"I do," Blair said. "I just want to be near you."

"That's considered stalking, you know."

"Yes, I know," Blair nodded. "But look at it this way: it isn't just anyone who can say he has a stalker."

"You think it's funny?"

"There's nothing funny about two people with broken hearts."

"Please," Robbie snorted. "You have to have a heart before it can be broken."

"I have one," Blair said. "And I finally started listening to it instead of my dad."

"For now, maybe."

"I've stopped talking to him," Blair said. "We all have except for Gran."

"Why?"

"Because he won't let any of us live our own lives. Mama's even left him; they may get divorced."

"Because of what I said last Christmas? That makes me feel bad."

An Admission of Weakness

"Don't," Blair said. "Everyone's happy now except for Dad. Camilla's engaged to Dr. Otieno, Justin's business is booming, Gran's engaged, Katie's pregnant…"

"Katie's pregnant?" Robbie grinned. "I'll bet they're thrilled."

He quickly toned down his enthusiasm.

"I mean, that's nice for her," he shrugged. "And for Camilla and Ruby too."

"Mama was in a fashion show," Blair pulled out his phone. "You wanna see?"

"No thanks."

Blair held out his phone anyway, and Robbie took it.

"Oh my god, she looks incredible," he said. "She is a beautiful woman. So classy and elegant. I can't believe she wants to divorce your dad. I feel responsible for telling everyone she was having an affair."

"She actually wasn't. She was just working for the fashion place but didn't tell anyone because she knew Dad would make her quit."

"I couldn't picture her cheating on your dad," Robbie said. "I'm glad I was wrong. So why did she leave him?"

"Because of how controlling he is. He controlled her as much as he did us kids, and I guess she finally had enough of it. She seems really happy. Everyone's happy except for me."

An Admission of Weakness

"You'll get over it," Robbie said dryly. "You'll sleep with some random and marry her so you can work at her parents' company."

"I was living in a mansion, you know," Blair said. "For a little while, I had a fancy car and a six figure income, and I was never more miserable in my life, unless you count right now."

"Sorry if I'm less than sympathetic."

"I'm not asking for sympathy," Blair said. "I'm only here because I want to be near you."

"What good is that doing you?"

"I feel better about myself when I'm with you. I'm a better person."

"Well, good for you," Robbie rolled his eyes.

"I can't eat anymore, and I can't sleep, I can't play football," Blair grew emotional.

"Nothing's any good without you.

"I ruined my life by listening to Dad. You were the best thing to ever happen to me, and I pushed you away."

"You certainly did," Robbie said.

"I'm sorry," Blair dried his eyes and stood up. "I'd better go."

"He's a mess," Andres said. "He won't eat, he doesn't sleep but maybe an hour or two a night, and he's close to getting kicked off the team. He barely goes to class anymore. Nothing matters to him. I've tried to fix him up with people, and he won't go."

An Admission of Weakness

"Why would you fix him up with someone?" Robbie said sharply.
"Why not?"
"I-I don't think he's ready to meet someone new."
"Why do you care?" Andres said. "You said in no uncertain terms that you're done with him."
"I am," Robbie said. "But why would you want to inflict him on some innocent man or woman?"
"I want him to get over you and not flunk out of school," Andres said. "The only way to do that is for him to meet someone else and move on."

Blair watched Robbie put books back on the shelves. He could barely hold his head up.
"You look like a zombie," Robbie frowned. "Why don't you go home and sleep?"
"I can't sleep."
"You surely have something better to do," Robbie said.
"Probably," Blair said tiredly.
"You should at least be studying. Andres said you're about to flunk out."
"So?"
"Are you kidding? You're willing to throw the last four years down the drain?"
"All the last four years have done is show me what an idiot I am," Blair shrugged.
"What classes are you failing?"

An Admission of Weakness

Blair told him about the two classes he was behind in.
"Go get your books," Robbie sighed resignedly. "You might as well study while you're just sitting here. I'll help you catch up."
"You'd do that?"
"If you don't graduate, you'll probably end up on skid-row drinking bourbon out of a brown paper bag, and I don't want that on my conscience."

Robbie oversaw Blair's work while he studied in the library. Frequently, he would sit down and go over review questions with him or help him figure out a problem.
"You really are smart," Blair said admiringly.
"You're smart," Robbie said. "You're just not focused."
"That's your fault," Blair said. "You're the only thing I can think about. I don't care about any of this stuff; I only care about you."
"You care about what your dad wants," Robbie said.
"I really don't," Blair said. "After talking to the psychologist –"
"You talked to a psychologist?"
"For six months," Blair nodded. "He showed me how to think for myself instead of letting Dad do it for me."
"But you'll go home at spring break, and you'll be right back where you started."

An Admission of Weakness

"No, I don't think so," Blair said. "Now that I understand how Dad has manipulated all of us, he doesn't have a hold over me anymore. Katie and Justin and Camilla and Mama; we're all living our lives for us."
"Are you trying to convince you or me?" Robbie said.
"Me, I guess," Blair said. "I know I can't convince you of anything until you see it for yourself."
"We're going to graduate in a couple of months," Robbie reminded him. "We'll never see one another again."
He flinched as an unexpected sensation pierced his stomach. Blair visibly cringed at those words.
"I guess you're right," he gulped. "You know, I think this is enough for tonight. I'm gonna go."
He swiftly gathered up his things and fled the library.

Blair aced his midterm exams and was in no more danger of flunking out thanks to Robbie's help.
"Thank you for all you did," Blair said. "I wouldn't have made it without you."
"I'd have done the same for anyone else," Robbie shrugged.
"Oh sure," Blair said. "Uh, are you going home for break?"

An Admission of Weakness

"I'll be working," Robbie said. "Rhett and Vanessa are going to spend a couple of days with her family in Carbondale."

"You're welcome to come home with me," Blair said without thinking. "I mean…that is, you have to work, and you don't want to spend any more time with me than you have to. I shouldn't have offered. I'm sorry."

"It's okay. Enjoy yourself at home," Robbie said.

The evening before Rhett and Vanessa were to leave for Carbondale, a well-dressed, middle-aged Black man walked into the nearly deserted locker room and looked around.

"Blair," he bellowed. "Where are you?"

Rhett stepped out from the supply room and frowned.

"Can I help you?" he asked.

"This place is like a maze," Carter staggered and bumped against the wall.

"Awe you looking for someone?"

"I'm looking for Bl-blair Bu-butterfield," Carter hiccoughed. "Where is he?"

"He's not here," Rhett frowned.

"Why not? This is where he's supposed to be."

"I think he went home for spwing bweak."

"I need to talk to him," Carter stumbled and hung on to Rhett to keep from falling. "He's my son."

"You're Dr. Butterfield?"

An Admission of Weakness

"Blair's my dad," Carter said. He added sadly, "He won't speak to me. He blames me for everything. Did I just call him my son? I meant he's my dad. Anyway, I have to talk to him. Tell me where he is."
"He's not here," Rhett repeated uneasily. "Have you been dwinking?"
"I don't drink," Carter slurred. "Oh, I might have a glass of sherry after supper sometimes, but it's not like I've started drinking since my family ran out on me. Are you implying I have a drinking problem?"
"No, but you seem dwunk."
"Maybe Blair's in his room."
"He went home to Gween Gwove."
"Why would he do that?"
"Spwing bweak?" Rhett said uncertainly.
"I'd better go home then," Carter turned to go but fell to his knees. "I need to talk to him."
"I think I should take you to see Wobbie," Rhett said uneasily. "You can't dwive."
"I can dwive just fine," Carter tried to stand but couldn't seem to figure out how. He looked down with surprise. "What I can't seem to do is walk. Give me a hand, Naomi."

Rhett and Carter stumbled to the parking lot, and Rhett set him in the passenger seat of the Mercedes. The front right quarter panel was crumpled and scraped with yellow paint from a safety pylon that Carter had struck earlier.

An Admission of Weakness

Rhett nervously drove the expensive car to the building in which he and Robbie shared a room. He managed to climb the stairs with Carter clinging to him, barely conscious by now. Robbie looked up with astonishment when the two entered the room. Rhett managed to get Carter to the bed, where they both collapsed.

"Dr. Butterfield?"

"He's dwunk," Rhett panted from his exertion. "I didn't know what else to do with him."

"What's he doing here?"

"He said he's looking for Blair."

"Blair's in Green Grove," Robbie said.

"I told him that, and he said he was going to dwive home."

"This makes no sense," Robbie looked perplexed. "He should know Blair's at home." Or maybe not, he mused. Blair said he was going to stay with his mother and wasn't speaking to his father, so perhaps Carter was unaware of his son's schedule.

He and Rhett stared down at their guest, who was currently lying on his back, snoring lightly and dead to the world.

"I guess we should make him comfortable," he sighed.

Together, they removed his tie and shoes and covered him with a blanket.

"I'll call Vanessa and cancel ouwuh twip," Rhett said.

An Admission of Weakness

"There's no need for that," Robbie said. "Go on and have fun. You've been looking forward to it since January."

"I can't leave you alone with him. What if he's mean to you again?"

"I'm not afraid of him," Robbie said dryly.

"Maybe we should tie him up," Rhett suggested.

"That would look good, wouldn't it?" Robbie chuckled. "His gay son's ex-lover tying him up in an anonymous location. Maybe we should take his clothes off first. That will confuse the hell out of him."

The brothers laughed hysterically while they invented different scenarios in which Carter might wake up and find himself. Finally, Rhett gathered up his things and said goodbye. He and Vanessa wanted to get an early start the next morning, so they planned to leave from her apartment.

Robbie felt through the pockets of Carter's suit jacket until he found his phone. He scrolled through the contacts to find Naomi's number and hit speed dial.

"Hello?" Naomi answered.

"Mrs. Butterfield, this is Robbie Lee."

"Robbie?" she frowned. "What are you doing on Carter's phone?"

"He's actually here in Urbana," Robbie said.

"What is he doing there? Blair is here."

"I don't think he realized that."

An Admission of Weakness

"Let me talk to him," she sighed.

"He's kind of passed out," Robbie said uncomfortably.

He explained that Carter had come to the athletic department in search of Blair, and Rhett brought him to Robbie when he realized the man was quite intoxicated.

"I can drive right down," Naomi said. "I'm sorry he's inconveniencing you."

"I don't think you need to do that," Robbie said. "Let him sleep it off, and then I'll send him home."

"Very well," she said. "Robbie, Blair told me how you helped him pass his midterms. I want you to know I'm grateful to you."

"No need to be," he said uncomfortably.

"Still, it was quite charitable of you after everything that happened between you."

"Is he feeling better now that he's at home with the family?"

"I'm afraid not," she said. "He's done nothing but lie in his room and stare at the ceiling. I can't get him to do anything. He doesn't sleep, and I've fixed all his favorite foods, but he won't eat."

"I heard about Katie and Dillon," he changed the subject. "Congratulations on becoming a grandmother."

"It's going to be twins," Naomi smiled. "We're very excited."

An Admission of Weakness

"I'll bet," Robbie said. He hesitated before continuing. "Mrs. Butterfield, I'm sorry for what I said about you that day at your house. I was just repeating what I'd heard."

"It's okay, dear," she chuckled. "We've had a few laughs over that whole misunderstanding. Anyway, it was good that you got the ball rolling; we all cleared the air that day.

"You know, Blair has changed where his father is concerned," she added. "This may not matter to you anymore, but he has tried to tell his father about you many times. They've gone back and forth on it, but Carter still refuses to listen. Blair has broken off all contact with him. He refuses to get pulled back into that cycle again. He loves you very much, you know."

"He'll find someone new," Robbie said.

"I don't think so, not while he's still in love with you. And what about you?"

"I'll be fine," he said. "A relationship is the last thing I'm interested in now."

"What are your plans after graduation?"

"I've sent out a few dozen resumes," Robbie said. "I haven't heard anything back yet."

"Well, good luck, and if you have any problems with Carter, kick him out."

An Admission of Weakness

CHAPTER FORTY-ONE

Carter awoke around eleven that evening.
"Ow," he groaned and sat up. He held his aching head in his hands. "What the hell happened?"
"You went on a bender," Robbie said wryly.
"Who are you?" Carter scowled.
"Your worst nightmare?" Robbie chuckled.
Carter studied him more closely.
"Oh god, you're Robbie. What are you doing here?"
"The question is, what are *you* doing here?" Robbie asked.
Carter glanced around uneasily.
"Where am I?"
"In an undisclosed location," Robbie grinned. "And I want you to know that I will never be able to settle for just any guy now that I've had a real man."
Carter glared at him and then glanced down to make sure he was still dressed.
"Don't worry, you were a complete gentleman the whole time," Robbie said.
"You better not have tried anything," Carter growled.
"Your virtue is safe," Robbie said. "I'm not into daddies."
"I don't know what that means, but I don't like the sound of it," Carter said. "Anyway, what am I doing here?"

An Admission of Weakness

"You apparently drove to Urbana looking for your son. My brother Rhett brought you here when he saw that you were drunk off your ass. You passed out and have been asleep for the last seven hours."

"How did I get to Urbana?"

"It looks like you drove. I called your wife and told her where you were."

"Oh god, now they all know," Carter said. "Although I guess it doesn't matter; none of them will care anyway."

"I'm sorry about your family," Robbie said.

"No, you're not."

"I'm not?" Robbie said. "Gee, I would have sworn I was sorry."

"You're the one who started all the problems."

"I think you had them well underway long before I showed up," Robbie said dryly.

"You said all those things to me without knowing the first thing about me or my family."

"I knew enough," Robbie said. "Tell me the rest."

"I need to go home," Carter stood up and immediately sat back down when his head started swimming. "Whoa, the room is spinning."

"Lay back down," Robbie said. "You might as well plan to stay here for now. Maybe you'll feel like driving in the morning."

An Admission of Weakness

"I feel sick," Carter covered his mouth and sat up.
Robbie quickly dumped the contents of a waste basket onto the floor and held it under Carter's face just in time for the man to throw up. When he was done, Robbie emptied it and fetched a cool cloth for Carter's forehead.
"That feels nice," Carter sighed. "Thank you."
He drifted off to sleep again, and Robbie returned to his studying. Around one in the morning, he turned when Carter spoke.
"This is your dorm room?"
"Yes.
"I thought you lived across the hall from Blair."
"I moved after I was at your house. I didn't want to see him anymore after that."
"Why did you try to convince him he was in love with you when you knew he was straight? If you'd stayed away from him to begin with, none of this would have happened."
"First of all, he came to me, not the other way around. Secondly, he was gay before he met me, and I never tried to convince him of anything."
"What makes you think he's gay?"
"The fact that we've slept together about a hundred times kinda helped me piece things together," Robbie said.
"But he was having sex with Danielle from the time he was sixteen," Carter frowned.

An Admission of Weakness

"At sixteen, a boy can sleep with anyone," Robbie said dryly. "But he was always confused about his sexuality. Figuring it out doesn't come so easily to everyone."

"Did it come easily to you?"

"I knew I was gay when I was five years old," Robbie chuckled. "I may not have been able to identify it in those terms, but I always knew I was different."

"When did you actually realize you preferred men?"

"I guess when I was about twelve," Robbie said.

"Blair began dating Danielle when they were fourteen. Why didn't he realize then that he preferred men?"

"I think he wanted so desperately to be straight so as not to disappoint you that he probably repressed his feelings until they couldn't be held back anymore."

"I had nothing to do with it," Carter frowned.

"With all due respect, you had everything to do with it."

"How?"

"Blair loves you very much, and he wanted to be what you wanted him to be: straight, married to Danielle, and a businessman of some sort. He took what you told him about homosexuality to heart, and he struggled between that and his true nature, and it led him to some very dark paths. One side would win

An Admission of Weakness

for a while, and then the other, and it just about tore him apart."

"So which is he, gay or straight?"

"He's gay, but he worked so hard to convince himself that he was straight that he was able to perform with a woman. But he never enjoyed it, and he didn't understand why at first. He's figured it out now."

"How do you know all this?"

"I talked to him," Robbie said. "I listened to him."

"I listened," Carter said defensively.

"You talked to him, but I don't think you really listened."

"I only wanted him to be the best he could be," Carter said.

"You wanted him to be what you considered to be the best," Robbie corrected him.

"You've been talking to my family."

"No, it's just what I've observed since I've known Blair."

"You're not a father, and you never will be, and you're especially not a Black father," Carter said heatedly. "So don't tell me you understand whatever it is you've 'observed'."

"I don't understand everything of what it means to be Black," Robbie said. "But I understand some. I'm from a poor family in Mississippi, Dr. Butterfield. And when I say poor, I mean dirt poor. Our house was a condemned shack that wasn't fit to live in. My dad was a bigoted,

An Admission of Weakness

racist, homophobic, ignorant redneck who thought the last president was the next messiah."

"I'm not surprised."

"The area I grew up in was mostly poor and very uneducated. There were Klan rallies in our town, cross burnings, and Black families were regularly terrorized. Practically every house had a confederate flag. The cops saw what was going on and did nothing to stop it. Sometimes they were even part of it.

"I saw that every day of my life. And as a gay kid, I was just one more target for all the haters. Homophobia wasn't all that different from racism as far as I was concerned. It still felt like hate."

"It's not the same thing," Carter said. "Black people were enslaved for hundreds of years."

"I know," Robbie nodded. "And I'm not making light of Black oppression in this country. Black people have always had to struggle against whites. But gay people have been oppressed as well, as have Native Americans and every other minority. Straight white Christian men are terrified that if any minority achieves equality, they will be treated the same way they've treated everyone else. So they continue to do everything they can to keep Black people down as well as women, gay people, Latinos, Jews, and Native Americans.

An Admission of Weakness

"They've kept the truth from being taught in our schools. Take the founding fathers; at least forty-one of them owned slaves, but no one taught us that. And then there was Abraham Lincoln; he wasn't the hero we were all taught he was. He freed the slaves, but he also said that the Black man was in no way equal to the white man. What he didn't understand was that race is a social construct; there is only one race. We just have different skin tones. In fact, the modern human being originated with Black women in Africa."

"How did you know that?" Carter frowned.

"I read a lot," Robbie said. "That's how I learned about Black Wall Street and the Tulsa Massacre and a lot of other things. We were never taught any of that in school."

"But those things happened to my ancestors, not yours," Carter said.

"It's still part of my history. My ancestors were there when those things were happening."

"I appreciate what you're saying, but you still don't understand why I raised my family the way I have."

"You want them to succeed," Robbie shrugged. "I get that. You know that they have to be better than the best because we live in a country that wants them to fail. That's why you pushed so hard."

"Hmmph," Carter said noncommittally.

"I still think you made a mistake," Robbie said.

An Admission of Weakness

"Oh good," Carter said. "I was afraid you weren't going to tell me what you would have done differently."
"You didn't listen to what they wanted. Like Justin wanted to go into business for himself instead of becoming a doctor, Katie wanted to marry Dillon and be a nurse, and Blair wanted to be a teacher. Have you even really accepted that he's gay?"
"Justin could have been a fine doctor," Carter said stubbornly.
"Not if he didn't want to be one."
"Katie could have married a doctor and been very happy."
"Not if she didn't love him."
"And Blair –"
"You don't have to tell me about Blair," Robbie stopped him. "I know all about him."
"Like what?" Carter asked dubiously.
"I know he's smart, but not business smart. He's kind and patient and funny, and he'll make a fantastic teacher.
"I know he's gay, and that he only dated women to please you. He married Danielle to please you and get back at me for sleeping with Ian."
"You slept with Ian? I thought he was straight."
"He's pansexual."
"Oh my god, here we go again," Carter groaned.

An Admission of Weakness

"Blair became engaged to Melissa only because you more or less forced him into it," Robbie went on. "I know he struggled with his sexuality for years, mostly because he didn't want to be gay because he knew you wouldn't approve.

"That's why your wife took a job in secret," he went on. "She knew you'd make her quit. She also knew you thought of her as a maid and housekeeper instead of a wife. I know Camilla has self-esteem issues because she couldn't live up to what you expected. So does Blair."

"So all of their problems are my fault? You sound like Ruby."

"Their problems are your fault up to a point. Once we grow up, it's up to us to move beyond what our childhood made of us. We have to learn from our mistakes and understand why we are what we are."

"So I should just let my children settle for who they are at this moment?"

"If they're happy, then yes," Robbie said. "If you've done your job right, they'll make the most of their lives on their own without your help. But if you keep forcing your dreams on them, none of you will ever be satisfied. They'll always feel they disappointed you, and you'll probably feel the same way. Why not just support them in the lives they've chosen? That's all they want from you: your support and your unconditional love."

An Admission of Weakness

"My love is unconditional," Carter said defensively.

"It doesn't seem like it. Blair hid who he was and what he wanted to do with his life because he thought you'd stop loving him if you knew the truth. That doesn't sound unconditional to me."

"So you think my job as a dad is done? That just shows you know nothing about being a father."

"I didn't say your job as a dad was done, but the hard part is done. Now you get to sit back and enjoy the results. Maybe spoil some grandchildren."

"What grandchildren?"

"The twins," Robbie said.

"What twins?"

"Oh god, I thought you knew," Robbie gulped. "Katie's having twins."

"My daughter's pregnant with twins, and no one told me?" Carter said angrily.

"I guess –"

"I need to get some sleep," Carter said abruptly. "Where's the bathroom?"

Once the facilities were used, they returned to the dorm room.

"You can have the bed," Robbie said. "I'll sleep on the floor."

"I can't take your bed from you," Carter frowned. "You take it."

An Admission of Weakness

"I guess we could both take it," Robbie said. "But just so you know, I like to spoon, and I'm always the big spoon. Also, I sleep nude."
Carter's eyes widened until he realized Robbie was teasing him.
"Very funny," he said. "You and Ruby would get along very well."

Robbie settled on the floor beside the bed. Carter removed his suit coat and dress shirt, but he left his slacks and tee shirt on.
"Does your brother speak with a speech impediment, or did I imagine that?"
"He's always had trouble pronouncing his 'r's," Robbie said.
"Has anyone worked with him?"
"The school tried when he was little, but they said he couldn't be helped."
"Nonsense," Carter said. "I believe any qualified speech therapist could help him."
"I'll look into it," Robbie said. "Thanks."
There was a minute or two of silence.
"Do you still have feelings for Blair after all that happened?" Carter asked curiously.
"I'd rather not –"
"I won't say anything to Blair, I promise," Carter said. "He's not speaking to me anyway. I'm merely curious."
"There are so many things that happened," Robbie said hesitantly.

An Admission of Weakness

"So what you're saying is that your love is conditional," Carter said dryly. "I thought so."
"It's not that. He was straight and then gay and then straight again."
"Which you said is my fault," Carter said.
"You also said he's worked through that."
"He says he has, but I don't know if I can trust him."
"If he's no longer confused, why wouldn't you trust him? Did he ever cheat on you while you were together?"
"Not that I know of."
"So you don't think he truly loves you, is that it?"
"He says he does," Robbie said.
"You know, the first time Blair really stood up to me – truly made his feelings known – was at Christmas when I hit you. He ran to your defense immediately, and he physically fought me. He tried to tell me he was gay at Thanksgiving, but according to you, I wasn't listening.
"At Katie's wedding reception, he broke down in tears because he had lost you. He believed his life to be ruined, and he blamed me for it." He thought for a moment and sighed. "And quite possibly, he was right."
"What's your point?" Robbie frowned.
"He felt his life only had meaning when you were part of it. I was key in keeping you two apart when I forced him to marry Danielle, and

An Admission of Weakness

he has not forgiven me for it. I lied to you when I said marrying her was his idea, or when I said I didn't know he was gay."

"I know."

"That means he loves you very much. Now I can't say I understand the whole gay lifestyle, but I'm beginning to realize it's much less a choice than I believed."

"It's not a lifestyle, and it's not a choice at all," Robbie said.

"I'll have to take your word for it," Carter said. "So if he loves you, and you love him, why can't you work it out?"

"There are too many problems."

"It seems to me now that I'm out of the picture, most of the problems have resolved themselves. Am I wrong?"

"I don't know," Robbie sighed. "It just seems like the universe kept putting obstacles in our way to try to tell us to give it up."

"As I just said, the obstacles are no longer in the way," Carter said. He rolled over and sighed heavily. "Anyway, good night."

The next morning, Carter treated Robbie to breakfast at a restaurant he and Naomi frequented when they attended Blair's games. "What the devil happened to my car?!" he exclaimed angrily when he saw the damaged fender.

An Admission of Weakness

"Rhett said it was like that when he brought you to my room."
"Oh god," Carter groaned. "I remember trying to drive between some safety pylons."

"Robbie, thank you for your hospitality," Carter said after paying the check. "This has been an educational experience for me. It brought back what it's like to sleep on a dorm room bed, for one thing."
"You're going to talk to your family?" Robbie said.
"I'm going to try," Carter said. "Are you going to talk to Blair?"
"I don't know," Robbie hesitated. "I want to, but I'm not sure if I should."
"You should if you love him," Carter said. "If you don't, then let him go. But I hope you'll talk to him and at least clear the air. If nothing else, perhaps you can be friends."
"I can't be just his friend," Robbie said.
"So you do love him," Carter smiled. "Now just say the words. He needs very much to hear them. Remember, his life is ruined without you. His words, not mine."
"I can't believe you've changed your mind about me and him and being gay."
"I think it was when you quoted Abraham Lincoln that I started hearing you."
"Why?"

An Admission of Weakness

"Because I saw that you understand me and my family more than I believed possible for a poor white Mississippi boy named Robert E. Lee," Carter said. He groaned. "Oh god, how will I ever tell our relatives my son-in-law is named after a confederate general?"

"I haven't taken Blair back yet, remember," Robbie said. He added tentatively, "But just in case I do, do we have your blessing?"

"I don't know. Maybe I should insist he find a nice gay Black doctor. What do you think?"

"I think you think you're being funny," Robbie grinned. "But I wouldn't quit your day job if I was you."

Carter called Naomi on the way home to Green Grove.

"Are you feeling better?" she asked.

"I am, as a matter of fact," he said. "I wondered if everyone could meet at the house this evening."

"Why?"

"I want to talk to you all," he said.

"I don't know, Carter," she hesitated. "The children are doing so well, I don't want you to upset them. Blair is brokenhearted after losing Robbie, and he doesn't need any problems from you."

"Naomi, please," Carter said. There was urgency in his voice. "This is very important."

An Admission of Weakness

"I'll see what I can do," she sighed. "I'll let you know."
"Thank you," he said. "And Naomi?"
"Yes?"
"I love you very much," he said. "I miss you."
"I'll let you know about this evening," Naomi said and ended the call.

An Admission of Weakness

CHAPTER FORTY-TWO

"What's this all about, Carter?" Naomi frowned.

The Butterfield family, as well as Dillon, Charles, and Ashura, were seated around the long dining room table.

Blair looked uncomfortable and wary, as if he was facing a dangerous predator, and the others had similar expressions on their faces.

"I finished my book," Carter said.

"You didn't need to call us together to tell us that," Naomi said.

"For years now, I've been doing wide-ranging research into my ancestors and their struggles just to exist in a white dominated society.

"As I was finishing it up at Christmas, I did some extensive introspection to see where I – we – fit into our history."

"Did you put in the idiot quote I asked for?" Ruby asked.

"It's all in there," Carter said. "Anyway, I'd like for you all to read it. For now, I'll go ahead and tell you how it ended.

"The final story was about a modern day Black family. A doting mother, an irascible mother-in-law, and a father determined to see that his four beautiful children excelled as doctors, lawyers, or the CEOs of some big corporation.

"You see, he learned in detail about the horrific tortures his ancestors endured, and he was

An Admission of Weakness

deeply moved. He was determined that his children would never have to go through anything like that.

"Being Black in the United States has never been an easy thing, as you know. The father in my story grew up in the idyllic town of Green Grove, so he was spared much of the pain and sorrow that others like him in this country have experienced. Here, he was treated as an equal by his white peers, but he knew out in the rest of the country, things were very different.

"So as his children grew, he developed plans for their futures that he believed were what was best for them.

"You see, he loved them so much that he couldn't bear for them to be hurt by the outside world."

"Carter, stop talking in the third person," Ruby said. "It's becoming annoying."

"Fine," he said. "What I'm trying to say is that I love you all very much, and I now realize I tried too hard to force you into lives that weren't necessarily right for you.

"Blair, when you started dating Danielle as a teenager, I pictured you as the CEO of Morgan Enterprises. So I pushed you to marry her and get a business degree. As it turned out, both of those plans were wrong for you."

"Now you tell me," Blair scowled.

"Katie, I believed what was best for you was to become a doctor, and I allowed you to feel you

An Admission of Weakness

let me down by getting your master's degree in nursing instead. I wanted you to at least marry a doctor, so I tried to keep Dillon away from you. It turns out I was wrong about all of that."

"Excuse me," Naomi frowned. "Did you just say you were wrong about something?"

"I did," Carter said. "Katie, I'm glad you're home to stay. The people of Green Grove are lucky to have you to care for them."

"Camilla, you are a truly great beauty like your mother and sister, but I allowed you to have self doubts instead of building you up the way I should have.

"You have a beautiful serenity and a kind, gentle spirit. I was afraid you weren't strong enough for what the world might throw at you, so I pushed you toward a field where you would have the tools to defend yourself. Once again, I was wrong.

"Justin, you never needed my guidance. You knew exactly the right profession for you, but because you didn't do what I planned for you, I failed to give you the support you needed. I'm sorry. Fortunately, your grandmother and Randall Price picked up the slack. I want very much to see this gym of yours, and if it's anything like you, I know it will be fantastic."

"You're kidding with all this, right?" Justin said skeptically. "As much as I'd like to believe this is really you talking, it can't be true. You

An Admission of Weakness

never admit you're wrong, and you haven't spoken to me in almost a year."

"I'm sorry for that," Carter said. "My job as your father was to be supportive of your dreams in any way I could, but I failed you."

"Did Dad just apologize to me?" Justin looked at his grandmother to see if he had misunderstood.

"That's what it sounded like," she shrugged.

"Naomi," Carter went on, "I owe you an enormous apology. I've treated this household like a dictatorship instead of a partnership. While I drove home today, I remembered the early days of our marriage, back when the children were still small. We were equals back then. We had very little money, but we didn't care because we had each other and our beautiful family.

"Somewhere along the line, I lost sight of that. I was so focused on my book and forcing my will on all of you that I forgot to enjoy our lives together. I let you think you were unimportant to me when nothing could have been further from the truth. I'm sorry.

"I realize now that you are all where you are meant to be: Katie and Dillon, Camilla and Ashura, Justin and his gym, Blair becoming a teacher.

"And Blair, I know it took me a long time, but I get it now. You're gay, and that's okay. You didn't choose to be gay because it's not a

An Admission of Weakness

choice. It's simply who you are. I'm happy that you've found your true self. You've become a fine young man.

"In fact, all of my children are the finest people I've ever known, and I'm proud of all of you. I want you to know that I support you in whatever you do, and I love you more than I can tell you.

"I hope you'll let me be part of your lives again because I miss you so much."

His eyes filled with tears, and he dried them with his handkerchief.

"I'm sorry for failing all of you. I wish I could go back and undo all the damage I caused."

"Thank you for saying all this, Dad," Katie embraced her father with tears in her eyes. "I love you. You never have to doubt that."

"I love you too," Camilla hugged the two of them.

"Justin?" Carter beckoned him to join them. "I love you, son."

"This is so gay," Justin muttered, but he grinned and hugged his sisters and father. "Blair?"

"I can't," Blair backed away. "I understand why you did what you did, but I'm not ready to put the past behind us yet."

He turned to his mother.

"I'm going to walk home," he said.

"Blair, please?" Carter said.

An Admission of Weakness

"I appreciate what you said, and I'm glad you understand that it's my life to do with as I please, but I lost the most important thing in the world to me, and I can never get him back." With that, he left the house and walked the few blocks to his mother's house.

The family spent the next few hours talking and laughing with one another as they hadn't in many years. It was a joyful time for them all.
"Carter, you made Katie very happy," Dillon said. "I hope you meant what you said."
"I did," Carter said. "And Dillon, I have never properly welcomed you to the family."
He embraced him fervently.
"You are a fine young man, and I'm proud to call you my son-in-law."
"Thank you, sir," Dillon said.
"As soon as it gets a little warmer, I want you and your parents to come for a barbecue," Carter added.
"We'd like that."
"You surprised me, Carter," Ruby said.
"Good," Carter said. "Now maybe you'll treat me with some respect."
"Oh, that will never happen," she grinned. "It's too much fun giving you a hard time."
"I guess you're right," he smiled. "You old busybody."
"Blowhard."

An Admission of Weakness

They hugged one another affectionately and then Carter stepped into the kitchen to make them all some coffee.

"That was quite a speech," Naomi followed him.

"It was sincere," he flipped the switch on the coffee maker.

"I hope so," she said grimly. "Why did you make it now?"

"I thought it was time."

"That's not an answer," she frowned.

"When I finished the book, I realized that it had been taking up all of my time and focus. Once I no longer had it to occupy my mind, I was suddenly at a loss. You were gone, and the children weren't here. I even missed your mother because I realized I was all alone, and I had no one to blame but myself.

"But what really got to me was when I learned Katie was pregnant with twins, and nobody told me."

"Who did tell you?"

"Robbie," Carter said. "He told me a lot of things, most of which I already knew but refused to acknowledge."

"Katie wanted to tell you, but I told her not to," Naomi said.

"Why? To punish me?"

"Yes, I suppose so," she said honestly.

"I had a right to know," he said heatedly, "even if you didn't want me to."

An Admission of Weakness

"I'm not disputing that," she said. "But you know now, so get over it."

He removed some cups and saucers from a nearby cabinet and placed them on a tray.

"Why did you go to Urbana?" she asked curiously.

"I wanted to tell Blair I was wrong," he said. "It was because of me that he was confused and made so many bad choices."

"They were still his choices," she said. "You weren't entirely to blame."

"But he wouldn't have had to make those choices if I had been the least bit supportive. I needed him to know I was sorry."

"So you drove drunk?"

"I wasn't drunk until I got there," he said.

"Still, it was very irresponsible of you," she scolded him. "I saw the Mercedes. You could have been seriously hurt."

"The only thing that mattered at the time was talking to Blair. I thought if I could convince him I was sorry, he might come back to me."

"Is that what this speech was about? Tricking the children into forgiving you?"

"You may not believe this, but I meant every word I said with all my heart."

"Well, whatever drove you to this epiphany, I'm glad for you," she said. "I think you'll be a much happier person."

"I already am," he said. "There's just one thing missing. You."

An Admission of Weakness

"Carter, I'm not ready to have this conversation," she said. "I like my life the way it is, and I can't go backward."
"I don't want to go backward either," he said. "Can't we try going forward together?"
"I don't know," she said hesitantly. "I'm afraid it would be too easy to slip back into old familiar patterns. I don't want to be an obedient little wife, and I don't want you or any man telling me what to do."
"I understand that," he said. "And I'm not asking you to move back in."
"You're not?"
"No. I don't believe you're ready, and I can't risk you turning me down."
"Then what are you saying?"
"What if we went out on a date?" he suggested.
"Are you serious? After thirty years?"
"You don't know me anymore, Naomi. We've drifted apart for years, which I know was entirely my fault. And you're practically a stranger to me too, so we need to get to know one another again. The best way to do that is to spend some time together."
"How do you know I haven't been seeing someone already?" she said.
"Have you?" he said.
"Maybe," she said evasively.
"I'll bet I'm better looking than he is."
"I wouldn't say that," she sniffed.

An Admission of Weakness

"One date with me, and you'll dump him faster than you can say…Robert E. Lee."
They chuckled together.
"Naomi, I love you with every fiber of my being. You are the most beautiful, loving, wonderful woman I've ever known. I want you to know the bridal show pictures of you took my breath away.
"And just for the record, this isn't my house or my bank account. These aren't my investments or my cars; everything is in both names and belongs to us equally. I'm sorry I made you feel your contribution to our lives wasn't important. You are the one who held this family together while I was selfishly pursuing my own dream. I took you for granted, and I'm sorry."
"I suppose I have some free time next weekend," she shrugged indifferently.

"Blair's stopped coming by the library," Robbie said worriedly.
"I'll bet you're relieved," Major said.
"I told him to leave you alone," Andres added.
It was a rare thing for the three friends to be together now that Andres and Major were both getting serious with their significant others. They were sitting at their favorite pizza place after spring break.
"Is he okay? Is he going to class?" Robbie asked.

An Admission of Weakness

"I don't know," Major said, and Andres shrugged his shoulders. "I never see him anymore."

"Maybe he's dating again," Andres said. "I gave up trying to fix him up, but some of the guys have set him up with a couple of people since we got back to school."

"Men or women?" Robbie frowned. "Is he dating men or women?"

"Does it matter?" Andres shrugged indifferently.

"I just...his dad said he was only into guys, so I wondered," Robbie said.

"Are you jealous?" Major frowned. "Because trust me, Robbie, you don't want to go down that road again."

"I'm not jealous," Robbie said indignantly. "I just think if he's dating women again, someone should warn them what they're in for."

"So you're only thinking of his dates," Major nodded and winked at Andres.

"That's right."

"You little white liar," Andres grinned. "You miss him."

"Is that why you helped him with his classes?" Major frowned.

"I don't miss him," Robbie said dismissively. "He was nothing but a thorn in my side."

"Should I tell him you said that?" Andres chuckled.

An Admission of Weakness

"Do what you want," Robbie sniffed. "Let's talk about something else."

Robbie knocked warily on Blair's door.
"Just leave it by the door," a voice responded.
"Blair?"
There was a commotion inside the room, and then Blair threw the door open. He was wearing only a pair of baggy shorts.
"Robbie?" he said, taken aback. "What are you doing here?"
"I, uh…I think you have a library book overdue," Robbie said. "I thought I'd return it for you."
"What's the name of it?" a feminine voice asked from behind Blair.
"You have company," Robbie's face turned red as he peered past Blair. "Of course you do. I'll go."
He turned to leave, but Blair stopped him. "Wait."
"There's no need to explain," Robbie said. "I already know how this show plays out."
He headed down the hall, but Blair wrapped his arms around him from behind and lifted him off the ground before carrying him back to the room.
"Robbie, this is Leann. Leann, this is Robbie."
"Hi, Leann," Robbie eked out breathlessly.
"Put me down, Blair."

An Admission of Weakness

"So this is Robbie," Leann pursed her lips while she walked around him and looked him up and down.
She was a pretty, brown-skinned woman with long lashes, a captivating smile, and enormous breasts.
"Now do you see what I mean?" Blair said.
"Um-hmm," she wrinkled her nose. "Cute, and very white."
"So now you understand," Blair said.
"Oh, I get what you're sayin', honey," she nodded. "And between you and me, I ain't a'hatin' it."
"Understand what?" Robbie said. "Because I didn't come here to be insulted."
"How is comparing you to a Bichon Frisé puppy an insult?" Leann frowned. "Gurl, they are some of the cutest puppies in the world."
"Bichon Frisé puppies?" Robbie looked confused.
"She was giving you a compliment," Blair said. "I said you were really handsome, and she asked if you were as cute as a Bichon Frisé puppy. I said yes, and just as white."
"I get kind of pale in the winter, but I'm not that white," Robbie said, unsure if he was being teased or not. "You're thinking of Mitch McConnell."
"Oohh, baby!" she punched his arm hard and roared with laughter. It wasn't just any laugh; it was raucous and completely infectious. "You

An Admission of Weakness

hate that mofo too? That makes you my new best friend. How 'bout you be Salt and I'll be Pepa?"
"I think we're more like cookies and cream," Robbie rubbed his sore arm.
"Ooohh, that's good," she laughed and punched him again.
"Ow," Robbie moved away from her. "Are you Blair's girlfriend?"
"You better believe it," she giggled. "Oh my god, this guy is too much."
"Leann's in my administration class," Blair said. "She's been helping me study."
"He keeps missing class," Leann pinched his face between her long, red-painted fingernails. "And that's your fault, you albino fool."
"My fault?"
"Isn't that what I just said?" Leann squeezed his face in her other hand.
"Is this why you stopped coming by the library?" Robbie moved out of range and turned to Blair.
"You said I was bothering you," Blair said.
"That ain't the reason, and you know it," Leann said before addressing Robbie. "It's 'cause he didn't want to see you."
"Leann, just let it go," Blair said warningly.
"You didn't want to see me?" Robbie frowned.
"I've got a large, double pepperoni for Butterfield," a voice said from the doorway.

An Admission of Weakness

"Thanks," Blair smiled and handed the young delivery woman some money for a tip.
"I'll, uh, come back some other time," Robbie inched toward the door. "You guys enjoy your evening."
"You're welcome to stay," Blair said. "I don't know what library book you're talking about, but I'll look for it."
"Oh, you know, maybe I was wrong about that," Robbie said. "Leann, it was nice to meet you. I'm sorry I bothered you."

"He knows you don't have an overdue library book, you idiot," Leann rolled her eyes.
The two had settled on the bed with their textbooks and the pizza between them.
"Then why did he stop by?" Blair frowned.
"He wanted to see you," she said. "Didn't you hear him ask why you stopped coming to the library?"
"He's the one who kept telling me over and over to stop bothering him."
"I saw the look in his eye when he thought we were dating," she said. "Gurl, he's still in love with you."
"I don't think so," Blair said.
"Do I look stupid?" she frowned. "I know a boy in love when I see a boy in love. He has that same goofy look on his face that you do."
"Do you think so?" Blair asked hopefully.

An Admission of Weakness

"Here's how you can tell if someone is in love with you," she said. "First, their pupils dilate. And second, if they hold your gaze for at least four seconds, they're in love."

"Who told you that?" he said dubiously.

"No one told me that," she said. "Who's been in love more than me? I'm an expert when it comes to matters of the heart. And from what you've told me about the last few years, honey, you needed my help a long time ago."

"So what do I do now, love expert?" he grinned.

"Okay, here's what you're gonna do, baby," she eagerly tossed her textbook aside.

After she concluded her thoughts with him, he shook his head.

"You are out of your ever-loving mind!" he exclaimed. "No!"

"I'm telling you, he won't be able to say no," she said.

The two argued back and forth until he held up his hands in surrender.

"Fine," he said. "I'll think about it, but only as a last resort."

An Admission of Weakness

CHAPTER FORTY-THREE

Robbie looked up from the stack of books on the counter in front of him and carefully hid his pleasure when he saw Blair sitting at a table with his texts in front of him.
"Where's your girlfriend tonight?" he asked.
"Oh, hi," Blair looked up. "I didn't know you were here."
"Oh," Robbie said, taken aback. "You're not here for me then?"
"I wanted someplace to study other than my room," Blair said. "This place has a nice vibe to it."
"Where's Leann?"
"She's out with her boyfriend," Blair said.
"I thought you were her boyfriend."
"I'm her GBF," Blair said dryly. "I told you I don't sleep with women anymore."
"I didn't realize you meant it," Robbie said. "Well, uh, I don't want to bother you."
"You're not bothering me," Blair said. "I hope I'm not distracting you."
"Of course not," Robbie shrugged.
He turned and walked away, and Blair grinned to himself.

At their next encounter, Blair walked up to the desk at the library.
"Can I talk to you about something?"

An Admission of Weakness

"Sure," Robbie glanced over at his coworker, who nodded and smiled.

He and Blair walked to an empty row of bookshelves.

"I never thanked you for taking care of my dad when he was here," Blair said.

"It wasn't any trouble," Robbie said. "We had some good talks. He's not such a bad guy."

"Anyway, thanks to whatever you said to him, he accepts me as a gay man, and he's fine with me wanting to be a teacher."

"That's great," Robbie said. He hesitated. "Did he tell you what we talked about?"

"No, but it doesn't matter," Blair said. "It worked, and that's all I care about."

"I'm glad. So everything is good with you and him?"

"It will be," Blair said. "Also, I don't remember checking out any library book. You must have been thinking of someone else."

"Oh yeah, I, uh, found it," Robbie said. "It was someone else, like you said."

"And just one more thing," Blair said.

He looked into Robbie's eyes and counted to himself. One Mississippi, two Mississippi, three Mississippi, four Mississippi, five Mississippi…

"Yes?"

"Who's that guy you work with?" Blair peered around the end of the shelves at an attractive, dark-skinned young man with round glasses.

An Admission of Weakness

"Uh, you mean Russell?" Robbie frowned.
"Yeah. Russell. Do you know if he's seeing anyone?"
"I don't think so," Robbie said.
"Cool," Blair said. "Maybe you'll introduce me to him sometime?"
"You want to date Russell?"
"I've been thinking it's time to put myself out there," Blair said. "I wouldn't mind dating someone like Russell. You should get out there and date too."
"I...I don't think I'm ready yet," Robbie said. "Besides, graduation is only a few weeks away. I don't think I want to get involved with anyone right now."
"It would probably do you good to get laid," Blair said. "I know it would make me feel better. Don't let what happened with me keep you from going out with other guys. I'm sure there's one out there who's better for you than I was."
Robbie was too gobsmacked to do anything other than nod.

"I have interviews with three companies in Chicago," Robbie said excitedly.
"That's gweat," Rhett said less than enthusiastically. "I guess I should start looking for a job back home."
"You want to go back to Toadback?" Robbie frowned. "Why?"

An Admission of Weakness

"Ma's there," Rhett shrugged. "Where else would I go?"

"I was kind of thinking we'd live together for a while yet," Robbie frowned. "I'm sorry. I should have known you'd want to be out on your own."

"You thought we'd live together after you gwaduate?"

"It was a dumb idea," Robbie said. "You might get serious with Vanessa and want to go wherever she is."

"We bwoke up," Rhett said.

"You did? Why didn't you tell me?"

"You're studying for finals," Rhett said. "I didn't want to bother you."

"You are never a bother to me," Robbie said. "Don't you know that by now? You're always going to be my best friend."

"Weally?" Rhett smiled widely.

"Of course. So what happened with Vanessa?"

"She's dating a football player."

"Not Blair, I hope," Robbie chuckled and then sobered at the look on Rhett's face. "Oh god, it's not Blair, is it?"

"No, but speaking of him, I have to tell you something."

"Okay."

"I saw him and that guy from the libwary having coffee on a bench in fwont of his building."

"I know," Robbie said. "I introduced them."

An Admission of Weakness

"Why would you do that?"
"He asked me," Robbie shrugged. "I couldn't very well tell him no. Maybe Russell will be a good match for him."
"Don't you still love him?"
"If you're really in love with someone, you never stop loving them," Robbie said.
"He said he wanted you back when he kept coming to the libwarwy to be with you. Why would he go out with someone else if he's still hung up on you?"
"Because I told him I wasn't ever going to be interested in him again."
"But you are interested," Rhett said.
"We were never a good match, even if we did love each other. He's decided to move on, and I think that's good. I don't want him to be alone."
"I don't want him to hurt you again," Rhett said. "But maybe you should tell him you want to get back together."
"The semester's almost over. We'll be going our separate ways anyway, so there's no point."

Blair opened his door and blinked with astonishment.
"Rhett?"
"Can I talk to you?"
"Sure," Blair said. He stepped forward and gingerly hugged the younger man. "It's good to see you."

An Admission of Weakness

They stepped into the room.
"Do you know Russell?" Blair introduced his guest.
"Hi, Wussell," Rhett said stiffly. "Can I talk to Blair in pwivate?"
"Uh, sure," Russell nodded uncertainly. "I have to get to the library anyway."
He stuffed his books into his backpack.
"I'll see you later," he said to Blair. "Nice to see you, Rhett."
After he was gone, Rhett closed the door and got right to the point.
"Do you love Wobbie?"
"He doesn't love me, so it doesn't matter."
"I asked if you love Wobbie," Rhett said impatiently. "Do you or not?"
"I love him with all my heart."
"Then why are you going out with Wussell?"
"He's just a friend," Blair said. "We're not dating."
"So I don't understand what you're doing."
"What do you mean?"
"Are you playing some kind of game with Wobbie? Why awen't you asking him to get back together?"
"He doesn't want me back," Blair said. "I can't make him love me."
"He alweady loves you," Rhett said.
"Then why did he tell me he has no desire to ever get back together again?"

An Admission of Weakness

"Because you hurt him, and he doesn't want to be hurt again," Rhett said. "Awe you going to hurt him again?"
"No."
"Because if you do, I'll beat your ass," Rhett said. "And I know you're bigger and stronger than me, but I'll still fight you."
"I promise I'll never hurt him again," Blair said.
"Then let him know you love him."
"He knows that already," Blair said.
"Then make sure he understands how much you love him," Rhett said. "Go big. Make a gwand gesture, something he'll never forget. That's the only way you're going to win him back."
"Are you sure he'll take me back? I don't want to –"
"If you're afwaid of making a fool of yourself, then you're too much of a pansy to be in a welationship with Wobbie," Rhett said bluntly. "I guess I was wight about you after all."
"I'm not a pansy," Blair frowned. "I'm not afraid of making a fool of myself for Robbie. I'm just afraid he'll say no. What will I do then?"
"The only way you'll find out is to try."

Robbie arranged his job interviews so that he could cover them all in three days. The first interviewer was so impressed with him that she

An Admission of Weakness

sent him to her supervisor for a second interview. The second company seemed uninterested in him, and he wasn't particularly anxious to work in their less than welcoming environment. At the third corporation, the CEO's executive assistant, David, met with him personally.

"Valedictorian of the U of I business school," David smiled as he sat down behind his desk. "Very impressive."

"Thank you," Robbie nervously glanced around.

The office was large and richly paneled, with elegant modern furniture, expensive fixtures, wool rugs, and a wall of windows that looked down on downtown Chicago.

Of the three companies he had interviewed with thus far, this was the largest and with the most opulent offices. It was simultaneously welcoming and intimidating.

He and David discussed the job for which he was applying.

"Typically, this position is held by someone with more experience, but so far that hasn't worked out very well. CJ – that's our CEO – hasn't found anyone qualified enough."

"Surely there are hundreds of more qualified people than me," Robbie said. "I'm just graduating from college."

"That's true, but you're exactly what we're looking for," David smiled again. "Someone

An Admission of Weakness

with fresh, new ideas. CJ knows most of your professors, and they, as well as your dean, all say the person we want is you. I have a copy here of your final paper for Professor Glenn. I hope you don't mind, but I presented it to the board at our monthly meeting. Everyone agreed it was brilliant. I believe that was what sold CJ on you.

"After meeting you in person, I'm even more impressed. You are articulate, personable, and confident. You're very likeable."

"Thanks," Robbie said.

"CJ relies on me to make the final decision when it comes to hiring executives, so I want to offer you the position before some other company snaps you up."

"Seriously?" Robbie looked dumbfounded. "Y-you're offering me the job?"

"I didn't get where I am by being a poor judge of character," David chuckled. "You see, not that long ago, I was you."

"Excuse me?"

"I grew up like you did, in poverty with an abusive father. However, I wasn't as lucky as you."

"How did you know –?" Robbie said with astonishment.

"I did my homework before this interview, and I know who you are: honest to a fault, generous, and kind. You took care of your

An Admission of Weakness

brother and sisters even when you were a child yourself."
"I just did what was necessary," Robbie said.
"You did more than that. Your mother told me she relied on you to keep the family together."
"You talked to my mother?"
"I needed to know who you are," David said. "And you're exactly the kind of person we're looking for.
"Just between us," he grinned, "I only hire people I would feel comfortable working for someday. I have no doubt that you'll be running the company eventually.
"So name your terms. Whatever they are, I'll do my best to meet them."
"I guess I don't have any terms," Robbie said uncertainly.
"You will start out with a six-figure salary, four week vacation, full benefits, stock options, and use of the company cars. After one year, you'll have access to the company yacht and beach house in Oahu."
"Are we still talking about the junior executive position?" Robbie gulped.
"CJ rewards talent," David chuckled. "That's why my husband and I own a house in the South of France."
He stood up and extended his right hand.
"Do we have a deal?"
"Can I have a little time to think about it?"

An Admission of Weakness

"Fine," David winked. "Fifty thousand more a year, and that's my final offer."

"I'll take it," Robbie jumped to his feet and eagerly shook David's hand.

Final arrangements for Robbie's employment were confirmed and then David sent him to the head of human resources to sign some contracts.

"Welcome aboard, Mr. Lee," she smiled and shook his hand. "You're going to enjoy working here. CJ is tough as nails, and upper management will demand your best, but they also provide a terrific environment in which to make that happen."

She told him she would make one of the company apartments available to him until he and Rhett found a place of their own.

"And don't worry about a car," she said. "One of our drivers will be available to you twenty-four hours a day."

Exhilarated at finding a job so quickly, Robbie returned to work at the library and found a vase with five roses in it for him sitting on the main desk.

"One appears every day with a note," Russell said. "A different person delivers each one without saying a word."

Before Robbie could read any of the notes, a young woman approached him.

"Are you Robbie Lee?"

An Admission of Weakness

"I'm Robbie," he nodded.
"This is for you," she handed him a single red rose and a folded piece of paper before turning abruptly.
"Wait," he said. "Who is this from?"
She ignored him and kept walking. He frowned and read the single sentence on the paper:

Which heaven to gaudy day denies.

Puzzled, he read through the other pages. Ah, he smiled, they were the first six lines from Lord Byron's poem 'She Walks in Beauty'. The pronouns had been changed from she to he. Someone was telling him that they considered him beautiful.

"That doesn't sound like Blair," Andres shook his head.
"He's not romantic," Major agreed. "Besides, isn't he dating Russell?"
"I think so," Robbie said. "So I wonder who this secret admirer is, and why did they wait until the week before graduation to make their feelings known?"
"Who knows?" Andres shrugged.
"Congratulations on the job. It's amazing you landed a position like that on your third interview."

An Admission of Weakness

"What are you working on?" Blair asked Robbie as he passed by the library's main desk.
"I'm trying to write a speech," Robbie sighed frustratedly.
"For what?"
"For graduation," Robbie said. "What are you doing here?"
"Studying with Russell," Blair said.
"How's that going?"
"It's good," Blair said. "He's almost as smart as you are."
"I'm glad it's working out for you," Robbie tried to sound sincere. "By the way, you didn't send me any –"
"Any what?" Blair frowned.
"Oh, nothing. It's just that someone sent me some flowers but didn't sign their name."
"You've got a secret admirer?" Blair grinned. "I'm not surprised."
"You're not?"
"Lots of guys probably want to go out with you," Blair shrugged. "By the way, Andres told me about the job. Congratulations."
"Thanks. What about you? Have you found a job yet?"
"One of the third grade teachers back home is retiring, and I'm her replacement," Blair said. "I'm surprised Dad let me interview for it."
"That's great. You'll be back home with family."
"What's Rhett going to do?"

An Admission of Weakness

"He's coming with me for now."
"Good. I worry about him being on his own. Not that he couldn't handle it. I just think he's better off with you."

"I heard about the roses," Leann plopped her ample bosom on the reception desk at the library and grinned.
"Blair told you?"
"Yes, he did," she grinned. "Someone has a secret admirer."
"I guess so," he admitted sheepishly. "It's funny because I thought they were from Blair at first."
"What's funny about that?"
"Because he's not the kind of guy that sends flowers. Besides, he's dating Russell. And I told him I wasn't interested anymore."
"But you are," she said. "I saw that when you stopped by his room that night."
"It doesn't matter," he shrugged. "He's got his future, I've got mine."
"Why not make it one future together?"
"He's moving back home, and I'm moving to Chicago."
"A whole hour apart," she said dryly. "Gee, how would you ever work that out?"
"Can I help you find a book, Leann?"
"Lead me to Lord Byron," she said. "That poem of his drives me wild. 'She walks in

An Admission of Weakness

beauty' and all that. It's like he was talking about me."
"Lord Byron?" he looked up sharply. "Why did you mention him?"
"I've been thinking about him ever since your secret admirer wrote you those notes."
"Blair told you about those too?" Robbie's eyes narrowed.
"Yes," she sighed wistfully. "He thought they were so romantic."
"I never told him about the notes," understanding dawned in Robbie's eyes. "Oh my god, they're from Blair."
"Of course they're not," she said.
"They have to be," he said. "Why would he do that? He just got through telling me he and Russell are doing great."
"I'm telling you, Blair didn't send them," she said.
"Then who did?"
"Um, I did," she said.
"Why would you send flowers to a gay man?"
"Well...I was planning on turning you," she said.
Abruptly, she grabbed him by his shirt front with both hands and hauled him over the counter to kiss him on the lips. She released him a few seconds later.
"Any change?"
"I'm still gay," he panted.

An Admission of Weakness

"Well, you can't blame a girl for trying," she said before hurrying out the door.

An Admission of Weakness

CHAPTER FORTY-FOUR

It was graduation day for the University of Illinois Gies College of Business. Robbie's mother, aunt, and sisters arrived in town for the occasion and took him and Rhett out for breakfast. Flora and her daughters and sister were dressed fashionably and driving a new Chevy Suburban.

"My own son a'graduatin' from college summer come loud," Flora beamed.

"It's summa cum laude, Ma," Vaneeta grinned.

"Whichever it is," Flora said. "It just means he's at the top of his class, and outa more than eight hundred people too. I'm a'tellin' ya, no mama could be prouder."

"And he's already got that fancy job lined up in the big city," Aunt Rosetta said proudly. "You watch, one of these days he's gonna be running one of those big corporations. Robbie, I always knew you'd be a huge success someday."

"Thanks, Aunt Rosetta," Robbie blushed.

"And look how handsome you've become," she said. "When you left home, you were just a little boy. But now you're all grown up."

An Admission of Weakness

"And Rhett, you're just as handsome as your brother," Flora said with motherly pride. "Look how you've filled out. I hardly recognized you."

"Ma," Rhett grinned sheepishly.

"And what about Vaneeta?" Robbie put his arm around his sister. "Graduating with honors and going to nursing school in the fall. She was just a little girl when I left home."

"Well, we could sit and talk all morning," Aunt Rosetta said. "But we've got a graduation to go to, and it won't do for the valedictorian to be late."

"Well, this is it," Blair took a deep breath.

An Admission of Weakness

He and Andres and Major were standing in the locker room in their football uniforms with several of their teammates. "The last play of my college career. What if I blow it?"
"You won't blow it," Andres said. "All you have to do is go out there and give it all you've got."
"We're going to be right there with you," Major added. "The whole team's got your back."
"That's right, man," the other guys said.
"Then let's do this," Blair said determinedly.

There were hundreds of student names to get through at Robbie's graduation, so the speeches and pomp were kept to a minimum. He was allowed five minutes for his valedictory speech, in which he thanked his family, friends, classmates, and professors. He spoke of the world's promising future due to people like his fellow classmates.
"Lastly, I want to say thank you to a special friend I made while I was here. He's not even here today to hear this, but he knows who he is. It's because of him that I am the man I am today. He showed me how important it is to be honest with myself and the people around me. I'll always be grateful to him for that, and I'll always..." his throat closed up with emotion, "...I'll always love him. Thank you."

An Admission of Weakness

He moved away from the mic but paused when he heard a shrill whistle pierce the air. He and those on the stage with him looked around, and the audience craned their necks to see where the noise was coming from.

Robbie's mouth dropped open when he saw the Marching Illini drum major march down the center aisle in full uniform with his tall baton in hand. Behind him were one hundred members of the university's marching band, and as they marched, they began playing Starship's 'Nothing's Gonna Stop Us Now'.

The crowd and people on stage whispered among themselves with disapproval and surprise at this unexpected interruption of their ceremony. A few grinned with delight and clapped along with the peppy song.

The drum major reached the front of the auditorium and turned to face the audience while the band spread out along the front of the stage. When the last band members reached the front, they stopped marching on cue. Robbie noted with astonishment at least a dozen football players standing behind them, and the man in the middle was holding a red rose.

When the music ended, Blair removed his helmet and handed it to Andres.

"Robert E. Lee, this is for you," he said so that the entire room could hear him. "I love you."

A single oboist stepped out from the ranks and gave Blair a note.

An Admission of Weakness

And we can build this dream together, standing strong forever,

Blair's voice was wobbly as he sang the tune off-key.

Nothing's gonna stop us now, and if this world runs out of lovers, we'll still have each other. Nothing's gonna stop us now.

There were titters from the audience as well as applause.
"Oh my god," the dean groaned under his breath.
"I know I can't sing, Robbie," Blair knelt on one knee and held up the rose. "But I don't mind making a fool of myself for you, because you're worth it.
"You always liked the fact that my jersey was number seven, so I'm wearing it today because it's always been lucky for me, and I need all the luck I can get right now," he pointed to the number '7' on his chest. "I'm not dating Russell. I told you that to make you jealous.
"I know that was a stupid thing to do," he went on. "But love makes you do stupid things. Like sending you roses with words from Lord Byron."

An Admission of Weakness

"This is a graduation ceremony!" the dean of the college snapped impatiently. "You and your friends get out of here."

"I will, sir, and I'm sorry for interrupting your graduation," Blair held up a hand toward him and eyed the security guards approaching from both sides. "Just give me five minutes. That's all I ask. It's a matter of life and death."

"Life and death?" the dean rolled his eyes. "You're flirting with another student."

"But I could die of a broken heart," Blair said. "You don't want that on your conscience, do you?"

"Fine. Don't let it ever be said that I stood in the way of true love," the dean sighed, and the audience laughed and cheered.

Robbie blushed at being the center of this kind of attention. He was embarrassed, intrigued, and moved by Blair's display.

"Robbie, I'm a screw-up," Blair went on hurriedly. "Everyone knows that. But I've finally grown up. I'm done lying to myself, and I like who I am now. And that's mostly due to you. I'm ready to really love you. I admit I wasn't before, but I am now.

"So what do you say? Do you still love me after all that's happened?"

He waited expectantly, and the audience unconsciously held their breath and leaned forward with anticipation.

An Admission of Weakness

"No pressure here, Robbie," Blair began to sweat, "but I really need a yes."

The audience laughed, and several people began chanting 'say yes'.

Was this really happening, Robbie wondered, or was he dreaming? Blair had gone to all this trouble, involved over a hundred people, and risked making a fool of himself, all for the love of Robbie. He heard only sincerity in Blair's voice and pure love in his eyes. He clearly was a changed man, as his father had said. He had indeed grown up, and he loved him.

"Robbie, will you please say yes so we can get on with things?" the dean said sternly but with a twinkle in his eyes.

"Yes, sir," Robbie said.

"Not to me," the dean pointed at Blair. "Say it to him."

"Please, Robbie," Blair said. "I love you, and I can't live without you."

To Robbie's surprise, Blair's entire family except for Justin walked up the center aisle to stand with him.

"Say yes, Robbie," Carter said cajolingly. "Unconditional love, remember?"

Making his decision, Robbie jumped off the stage and faced Blair and his family.

"Yes, I love you," he said just before he leaped into Blair's arms.

Blair spun him around and then set him down.

An Admission of Weakness

"He said yes!" he yelled to the throng. "He said yes!"

The crowd cheered enthusiastically while Robbie and Blair kissed. Blair's family and the football team surrounded the two of them and offered head rubs, pats on the back, and hugs.

"Yippee," the dean said dryly, but even he applauded.

Robbie and Blair ran up the aisle.

"Robbie, wait!" the dean called after them. "You still have to graduate."

"Oh right," Robbie said. He kissed Blair again. "I'll see you after the ceremony, okay?"

"Okay," Blair smiled.

He felt exhilarated, as if he could literally walk on air. For the first time in his life, he was completely and utterly happy with who he was as well as with his life. He had a loving family that was finally able to be open and honest with each other, he was going to be an uncle, he was a college graduate and had an exciting new career about to begin, and best of all, he was madly and passionately in love with the most wonderful man in the world!

Blair and Robbie introduced the Lees and the Butterfields to each other after the ceremony wrapped up.

"I'm pleased to meet ya," Flora shook Carter's hand. "You got a beautiful family."

An Admission of Weakness

"You do as well," Carter said graciously. "I'll bet you're very proud of Robbie."
"I am," she nodded. "I'll admit it took me a while to come to grips with him bein' gay. An educated man like you probably had no problem with it. But I had to do some learnin' on the subject." She nudged him with her elbow and chuckled. "I'll bet you had a hard time a'gettin' past his name: Robert E. Lee."
"I'll admit it took some getting used to," Carter admitted.
"I let his pa think we named him after the general 'cause he was a big fan. But the 'E' stands for Eustace, not Edward," she chuckled. "'Course he was an idiot, so you can't judge the rest of the Lees by him."
"I am very fond of Robbie," he assured her. "He's made a big difference in our lives."
"That Blair is somethin', ain't he, pullin' off a stunt like this? He's an amazin' young man. You done somethin' right when you raised him."
Flora turned to Naomi.
"Naomi, that is one of the purtiest dresses I ever seen. Where'd you get it?"
"It's an Abernathy original," Naomi smiled. "Your dress is lovely too."
"I never had the money for nice clothes before," Flora said. "Now I can't get enough of 'em."

An Admission of Weakness

"Why don't we all go out for lunch?" Carter suggested. "My treat."
"I never say no to a free meal," Aunt Rosetta chuckled and took Carter's arm. "Or to a good-looking man either."
"Aunt Rosetta," Robbie scolded her. "He's a married man."
"Aw, I'm just talking," she grinned and waved him away. "I'm going to find out where Naomi found him so I can get me one just like him."
"We'll go change and join you in a few minutes," Blair said. "Robbie, you're coming with me."

Blair pulled Robbie into the locker room and guided him to the shower area, set off around the corner from Andres and Major and the rest of the team.
"I can't believe you did that," Robbie grinned. "You're lucky you didn't get kicked out of school."
"I already graduated," Blair grinned. "Forget all that. I love you. I can't believe how much I love you."
"I love you too."
"Good, because I can't wait another second to fuck you."
"We can hear you," Andres called out. "If you're going to fuck, you're going to have to do it quietly."
"You guys filming it?" someone asked.

An Admission of Weakness

There were hoots and more rude comments and lots of laughter from the team. Some of the guys gathered to watch.

"I've always wondered what gay guys do," Slick said.

"They can take turns fucking each other," someone else said. "I wish my girl could do that."

The men continued to discuss the pros and cons of gay sex while Robbie stripped off his cap and gown and then doffed the rest of his clothes.

"You don't mind the guys watching?" Blair grinned and undressed.

"We've had an audience before," Robbie grinned at Blair's teammates. "Let 'em watch." He kissed him, and Blair pushed him against the wall while he tongued his way down his body.

"Holy shit," Slick said when Blair took Robbie's penis into his mouth.

"I wish my girlfriend would do that."

"If you want a good blow job, get a gay guy to do it," someone said. "They know how to do it right."

Robbie and Blair ignored them while they enjoyed each other's bodies. Finally, Blair laid Robbie on the floor and inserted himself into Robbie's ass.

"Does Ebony like anal?" another man asked Andres.

An Admission of Weakness

"She's too much of a lady," Slick frowned. "Hey, Robbie, doesn't that hurt?"

"You should try it sometime, Slick," Robbie grunted. "It's fantastic."

"Who's willing to fuck me?" Slick looked around for a show of hands. "Major, you think Simon would let you show me what it's like?"

"You seriously want a guy to fuck you?" someone said.

"It looks too painful," another guy frowned.

"I'm not letting no dude in my ass."

"It's fantastic," Robbie panted while Blair pounded him.

"It looks hot," Slick said.

"Slick, I'll introduce you to a great guy named Russell if you'll just shut up til we're done here," Blair gasped.

"What?" Slick shrugged at the astonished looks on his teammate's faces. "There's nothing wrong with being curious. Open your minds, bros."

Blair and Robbie both climaxed to cheers from their audience.

"I'm holding you to your promise, Butterfield," Slick said as he and his friends dispersed.

Blair collapsed on top of Robbie, his manhood still buried deeply in his ass. Robbie held him and wrapped his legs around his waist.

"Are you really going to introduce Russell to him?" he asked.

An Admission of Weakness

"You heard him," Blair chuckled. "He wants to take it up the ass. Who am I to stand in his way? If he decides he likes it, I can't think of anyone better for him than Russell."

"I love you," Robbie caressed his face.

"If it's half as much as I love you, then that's all I need to know," Blair grinned and kissed him.

An Admission of Weakness

THREE MONTHS LATER...

"You were the most beautiful woman I'd ever seen thirty years ago," Carter smiled. "How is it possible that you're even more beautiful now?"

The two were standing in their bedroom, and Naomi was wearing the wedding dress she made.

"Oh stop it," she put on her other sapphire and diamond dangle earring. "I shouldn't even be talking to you."

"Why not? I'm your husband, so you'll do as I say, woman," he growled and kissed her neck.

"I didn't promise to obey at our first wedding," she grinned impishly. "And I sure as hell am not going to do it for this one."

"Don't worry," he said. "My bossy days are over. You can be in charge for our second marriage."

"I think I'll take you up on that," she kissed his cheek. "Here, do as I say and put this garter on my leg."

"Yes, ma'am," he grinned and knelt in front of her. "You know, we've already broken the rules by me seeing you on the day of our wedding. Why don't we have a little premarital sex?"

"Carter," she looked scandalized. "The minister's downstairs, and I am not that kind of girl."

An Admission of Weakness

"I know," he chuckled. "That makes it all the more sinful."

"Well," she mused, "sex *is* more fun when it's sinful."

He eagerly untied the bowtie of his tuxedo.

"We don't have time, you idiot," she giggled. "Maybe during the reception."

"I'll meet you up here after the first dance," he slapped her on the ass and then retied his tie.

"Carter, behave," she scolded him.

Carter and Naomi had dated all summer while they continued to live apart. He usually picked her up at her house, and they would go to a restaurant or the Gallery or a movie. He always brought her flowers or perfume or some dainty candies. He even brought her the sapphire and diamond necklace with matching dangle earrings that she was wearing today. Sapphire was her birthstone and her favorite gem. Sometimes they would relax in her back yard or take a leisurely walk, whatever struck their fancy.

Carter proved himself to be a changed man. He realized how closely he had come to losing his entire family, and he was never going to let that happen again.

He found himself falling in love with Naomi all over again. How had he permitted himself to take for granted the most wonderful woman in

An Admission of Weakness

the world for so many years? He understood now how much she meant to him.

Now that he was different inside, the man on the outside was happier, nicer, and friendlier to everyone, especially his wife. He treated her as an equal partner in their marriage and found that being with a strong woman in the bedroom was exhilarating.

As for his children, he was everything he promised them he would be. He was attentive and supportive, and he actually listened to them and to Naomi when they spoke to him.

He understood the term 'reborn' now, because that's what he was. He had been blessed with a second chance, and he was determined to make the most of it.

An Admission of Weakness

CHAPTER FORTY-FIVE

"We should have combined all these weddings," Rhett said while he struggled with his tie.

He was standing in Blair's bathroom in the Butterfield house with Blair, Robbie, and the other men in the family.

"That might have been a little hard to pull off," Blair grinned and helped him with his tie.

It had indeed been a busy summer for the Butterfields. In June, Camilla and Ashura tied the knot in a small, private ceremony behind the Butterfield house. In attendance were only the family and a few of Camilla's and Ashura's friends. She insisted on wearing the wedding dress her mother helped design and that Katie had worn at her wedding, so Ashura agreed to wear a tuxedo. Camilla's friend Reverend Oliver Paine from the Episcopal Church performed the simple rite.

In July, Ruby and Charles married in the Episcopal Church. Their first weddings were conducted in front of a justice of the peace, and it was Ruby's dream to have a proper wedding, especially after seeing her daughter in the bridal show.

So Naomi fitted the same dress for her mother, and Carter pulled out all the stops.

An Admission of Weakness

"It's the least I can do if the poor slob's going to spend the rest of his life with a miserable old biddy like you," Carter said.
"You can afford it," Ruby said. "You have every dime you ever made, you skinflint."
"You're just lucky I invested my money," he retorted. "Otherwise I'd be hiring you out as a maid, Florence."
She chuckled and kissed him on the cheek.
"Thank you, Carter," she smiled. "I love you."
"That's because I'm so damn loveable."
"I wouldn't go that far," she said wryly.
There were thousands of flowers, a string quartet, a limousine, and a fabulous dinner for the reception at Amico's Italian restaurant.

Charles Jr. and Cheryl attended his father's wedding looking extremely devoted to one another.
As it turned out, the company Robbie worked for in Chicago was Morgan Enterprises, and the CJ that the executive assistant had referred to was none other than Cheryl Jean Morgan.
One evening in June before Robbie left the office, he knocked on Cheryl's open office door.
"What?" she barked impatiently. When she recognized Robbie, she immediately dried her reddened eyes and wiped her nose. "Hello, Robbie. What do you need?"

An Admission of Weakness

"I wanted you to have these projections before I left for the day," he said.

"Thank you," she tried to smile.

"Are you okay?" he asked. "I don't mean to pry, but I don't usually come in here and find you crying."

"I might as well tell you. Everyone's going to find out eventually," she said. "Charles wants a divorce."

"I'm sorry," he frowned. "That must be tough."

"Between that and Danielle, I think I'm going to lose my mind."

"What's wrong with Danielle?"

"She hasn't spoken to me since I cut her off," she said. "You've met Ian. What is your impression of him?"

"I don't want to get in the middle of your family problems," he said hesitantly.

"Robbie, you're doing a fantastic job here," she said dryly. "I can't afford to fire you just because you give me your honest opinion."

"Can I get that in writing?"

"Absolutely," she grinned. She tossed him a set of keys. "Here, the yacht is yours if I fire you."

"Fine," he sat down across the desk from her. "Ian is a great guy. He's smart and funny and very talented. He plans to be an orchestra leader someday."

"But does he love Danielle?"

"Very much," Robbie said. "He's a much better fit for her than Blair was."

An Admission of Weakness

"Are you saying that because you wanted Blair for yourself?"

"Hey, it only took a few months of being married to Danielle for Blair to come to his senses."

She laughed at that and then grew serious again as Robbie went on.

"Ian and Danielle are a good match. They both love music, and she has one of the most beautiful voices I've ever heard. I could see Ian leading the orchestra while she sings or plays the piano."

"But I raised her to marry a banker or doctor," Cheryl said. "What kind of life can an orchestra leader offer her?"

"He can offer her love," Robbie said. "Blair could never have given her that."

"Blair would have been a disaster in your job. God, what was I thinking hiring him?"

"Can I offer some advice?"

"Am I going to like it?"

"No," he said honestly. "But I would like to see you happy, so I think you need to hear it."

"Fine," she sighed.

"Let me just hang on to these first," he picked up the yacht keys.

"You are always the bright spot in my day," she chuckled. "Thank god David found you."

"You want the best for your family," he said. "I get that. But what you consider the best may not be what they consider the best."

An Admission of Weakness

"For example?"
"Charles isn't happy working in an office," he said. "He's a musician at heart, and he wants to own a music store."
"What kind of profit is there in that?" she snorted.
"What does it matter?" he said. "You've got more money than God."
"Let me have those keys back," she held out a hand.
"You think the two of you working together makes your marriage stronger, but it's making it weaker. You love this company, and you enjoy the work, but Charles is miserable here."
"So you think I should fire him?"
"Do not fire your own husband," he said. "He's a straight man, and their egos are way too fragile to handle that. Just talk to him and listen to him. Let him tell you what he wants instead of you telling him what to do."
"I work with a hundred straight men," she said dryly. "They're all big babies. Why do you think I hired a gay man as my assistant?"
"My point is, you can't tell Charles what's best for him because he's a grown man, and he knows his own mind. Let him be who he wants to be, and you'll both be a lot happier."
"But what if he still wants to leave me?"
"If he loves you, he won't leave. All he wants from you is love and understanding. Give him that, and he'll stay.

An Admission of Weakness

"The same with Danielle," he went on. "Accept her for who she is and what she wants and who she loves. So what if she fell in love with a musician? You did too."

"But Ian will never be rich."

"If you're worried about her doing without, let her know that you're here to offer whatever financial support she needs."

"She'd never take any money from me."

"Then you did something right in raising her," he said. "But let her know it's there if needed. Give her and Charles your unconditional love and support. If you can do that, they'll stay."

"How does one do 'unconditional' love?" she said the word distastefully.

"It's not a bad word," he laughed. "All you have to do is stop running their lives. When you feel the urge to tell them what to do, resist it and tell someone in the office what to do instead."

"I do like telling people what to do," she said thoughtfully. "Maybe I'll take my frustrations out on you."

"Do I get to keep the yacht?" he grinned.

"Yes."

"Okay then," he laughed again. "You've got a deal."

Danielle and Ian attended her grandfather's wedding and sat with her parents. The relationship between mother and daughter was

An Admission of Weakness

still working itself out, but they were at least speaking to each other civilly. Danielle saw the change in her parents' marriage, so she was willing to give her mother the benefit of the doubt.

Cheryl had relented where Ian was concerned. She had to admit that he was a genuinely nice young man who was clearly devoted to her daughter and cared nothing about her family's wealth. She saw the change in Danielle's demeanor when Ian was around; she was bubbly and cheerful instead of the morose person she had come to know for the last ten years.

"We haven't even got to your wedding yet," Rhett complained.

"Two more weeks," Charles patted Robbie and Blair on their shoulders. "It's not too late to back out, boys."

"Don't give him any ideas," Robbie said. "Do you have any idea what it took to trap him?"

"So the whole thing was a trap?" Blair frowned. "I should have known."

"Yes, it was all part of my master plan," Robbie wrapped his arms around Blair's neck and kissed him. "And you fell for it, you gullible fool."

"You got the fool part right," Justin said.

An Admission of Weakness

"You're one to talk," Blair said. "What does Isabella see in a freak like you? She could do way better."

"Of course she could," Justin said. "But fortunately, she hasn't realized it yet."

"Dillon, awe you nervous about becoming a dad?" Rhett asked.

"I'm scared shitless," Dillon said. "But I don't want Katie to know that, so don't say anything. She's counting on me to be her rock."

"You're gonna be a gweat dad," Rhett said confidently. "Anyone who is as good with horses as you awe will be good with babies."

"Thanks, Rhett," Dillon smiled. "I needed to hear that."

"Her due date's coming up, isn't it?" Charles said.

"Two more weeks," Dillon said. "But I don't want to think about it, so let's talk about something else."

"How about Blair's wedding?" Justin said. "I can't believe there were thousands of Black guys at the university, and you had to fall for a white one."

"You don't always get to choose who you fall in love with," Dillon said. "You'll learn that one of these days."

"But why did you have to go out with a white guy? Especially one named Robert E. Lee."

"I'll try not to take that personally," Robbie said dryly.

An Admission of Weakness

"You should take it personally," Justin frowned.

"Justin's just afwaid that Isabella is the only girl in town that will have him," Rhett said.

"He's slept with all the rest," Robbie added.

"They don't want him because he has a teeny weenie," Rhett grinned.

The others burst out laughing except for Justin. He started to utter a retort, but Blair stopped him.

"Don't!" he said sharply. "You say one more word, and Dad will be my best man instead of you."

"Whatever," Justin scowled and left the room.

"I thought he was on board with you and Robbie?" Charles frowned.

"Wasn't he the one who said you were a fool to let Robbie get away?"

"But now that I'm actually marrying him, he's got some sort of issue with it," Blair sighed.

"Forget him for now," Robbie said. "Let's get your parents married again."

The ceremony was held in the Butterfield's back yard as Camilla's wedding had been. Carter's brother officiated, and the Butterfield children stood up with their parents. It was a sweet and funny ceremony, and when it was over, Ruby and the other women in the family set out all the delicious food for the reception.

An Admission of Weakness

Just as Carter and Naomi headed for the stairs for their carnal rendezvous, Katie cried out in pain.

"Mama!"

"What is it, sweetheart?" Naomi returned to her side with motherly concern.

"Something's wrong."

"Is it the babies?"

"I don't know," Katie said in a frightened voice.

"Just stay calm, and Dad will call the hospital," Naomi said soothingly.

While she and Ruby settled Katie in a kitchen chair, Carter called the patient advisory nurse. Naomi held Katie's hand, and Marci fetched a cool cloth for Katie's forehead.

"They're letting Dr. Kosyak know," Carter ended the call a few minutes later. "Are you having contractions?"

"I think so," Katie began sweating. "I just know it hurts."

"I think we should take her to the hospital," Ruby said. "First time babies can be unpredictable."

"I agree," Dillon said worriedly. "Let's go."

"Let's see what the doctor says first," Carter said.

"Mama, something's happening," Katie said tremulously.

She looked down and saw a small pool of blood on the floor.

An Admission of Weakness

"Carter, call an ambulance!" Naomi cried in a panicky voice. "She's bleeding."

The three dozen or so Butterfields, along with the Talbots and Robbie and Rhett gathered in an empty waiting room at Green Grove Memorial Hospital. Dillon and Naomi stayed with Katie while the rest of them waited with trepidation. Carter paced up and down.
"When will they tell us something?" he said worriedly. "That's my baby girl in there."
"Come sit down, Dad," Camilla said.
"I can't," he paused to stroke her cheek affectionately. "I have to keep moving."
"Dr. Kosyak is an excellent obstetrician," Ashura said.
"I know," Carter said. "He delivered all of my children. But is he used to dealing with problems like this?"
"I'm sure he'll know what to do," Ashura said.
"That's easy for you to say when it's not your daughter," Carter said grimly.
"She's going to be okay, Dad," Blair said.
"Dillon will be devastated if anything happens to Katie," Justin said.
"She's going to be okay," Blair frowned.
"I'm just saying women and babies die in childbirth all the time," Justin said.
"She's not going to die or lose the babies!" Carter snapped angrily. "Everything's going to be fine!"

An Admission of Weakness

"Justin, keep your mouth shut," Camilla exclaimed.
"Don't tell me what to do," Justin glared at her and then left the room without a backward glance.

Rhett pulled some M&Ms from the vending machine in a small alcove off the main hallway and glanced over to the side. Justin was sitting in the seating area with his head in his hands.
"Your sister's gonna be alwight," he said.
"Will you talk right for once, dammit!" Justin cried impatiently. "You sound like a baby!"
Rhett sat down beside him and offered him some candy.
"People have made fun of me my whole life," he said. "The way I talk, my limp, I'm too thin, I'm dyslexic. It doesn't bother me anymore, so you can say whatever you want. Because I know why people like you make fun of other people."
He waited, but Justin ignored him.
"Fine, I'll tell you why," he said. "People that make fun awe insecure. They know that if their faults were as visible as mine, society would make fun of them too."
"I'm not insecure, so don't try to psychoanalyze me."
"You're insecure about something. That's why you act cocky, and why it makes you feel good to put other people down. You think somehow

An Admission of Weakness

it makes you better than them. But you're not better; no one is better than anyone else."
"It figures you'd be the kind of moron that spouts stupid platitudes," Justin said rudely.
"You just did it again," Rhett said. "You're pwoving it every time you talk."
"Shut up and go away," Justin glared at him.
"You shouldn't feel insecure," Rhett said. "You're smawt and good-looking and muscular."
"You're just saying that."
"Why would I say something nice to someone who keeps insulting me?" Rhett said. "You know who told me no one is better than anyone else?"
"I don't care."
"Wobbie told me," Rhett said. "He taught me and my sisters not to look down on anyone."
"Good for him," Justin said sarcastically.
"It is good because Pa taught us to hate everyone that isn't white and Chwistian and stwaight. He thweatened to kill Wobbie for being gay and shot a big hole in the side of the house. Did you know that?"
"He wasn't actually going to shoot his own son," Justin said disdainfully.
"You didn't know him. If Wobbie hadn't left wight then, Pa would have killed him."
"He wouldn't have risked going to jail for murder," Justin said.

An Admission of Weakness

"The police would have just looked the other way. They hate gay people as much as Pa. But even gwowing up with all that hate, Wobbie still believes all people deserve love."
"Why are you talking about this right now?" Justin said impatiently. "My sister may be dying, and all you can talk about is your stupid brother in your little baby voice."
"I know you're worwied about Katie. So am I," Rhett said. "But you should be glad our bwothers found each other. Wobbie is the best thing that could have happened to Blair. He was as big a jerk as you before he met Wobbie.
"At least Blair outgwew the bad person he was. I don't think you will. You'll always be a jerk."

The Butterfields kept a vigil all night at the hospital. Dillon and Naomi took turns staying with Katie. Dr. Kosyak, who was a man of few words, spoke to the family briefly.
"She's holding her own," was all he said.
"And the babies?" Carter asked tremulously.
"We'll have to wait and see," the doctor said and left the room.

At five in the morning, everyone was asleep in the waiting room wherever they could find a spot. Naomi quietly woke Carter, Clint, and Marci and beckoned them to come with her.
"She's okay," Naomi told them.
"Thank god," Clint said.

An Admission of Weakness

"And the twins?" Carter gulped.
"See for yourselves," Naomi pointed to an open door.
Katie was sitting up in bed holding a tiny figure wrapped in a pink blanket. Dillon was sitting beside her with a blue bundle in his arms. They looked up and smiled when their parents entered the room.
"Good morning, Grandpa," Katie said to Carter. She looked tired but happy.
"Oh my god," Carter whispered. "A boy and a girl?"
"Say hello to Dillon Clinton Talbot," Dillon said proudly.
"He's beautiful," Clint beamed and kissed his son's forehead. "Thank you, son."
"And this is Amelia Naomi," Katie added.
"Everything's okay?" Marci stroked the infant's little brown arm.
"They're perfect," Katie smiled.
"And Katie's fine too," Dillon grinned. "You are all officially grandparents."

An Admission of Weakness

CHAPTER FORTY-SIX

"You made fun of Rhett?!" Blair said, outraged. "How could you do that?"
"He was annoying me," Justin shrugged. "I was worried about Katie, and all he could talk about was 'Wobbie'."
"And you think that gives you permission to insult my fiancé's brother? How would you like it if I made fun of Isabella's family?"
"At least she's Black."
"If you had a problem with Robbie being white, why did you help us get together?"
"I didn't think you'd actually marry him," Justin said. "He made it pretty clear at Christmas that he was never going to take you back."
"So basically you didn't mean anything you said," Blair said.
"I guess not," Justin shrugged.
"Why are you suddenly acting this way?" Blair demanded.
"Why do you have to marry him? Why not just live together? You're just going to screw around on him anyway."
"I will not," Blair said indignantly.
"You'll meet some woman while he's in Chicago and fuck her. You know you will."
"I love him," Blair said. "I don't want anyone else but him. And I'm done with women anyway. I couldn't fuck one if I tried."

An Admission of Weakness

"You used to, and so did he," Justin said. "I saw the videos."
"That was when I was confused about who I was," Blair said. "I'm not confused anymore."
"Still, if one of those women in the videos came up to you, you'd do it with her," Justin nodded knowingly. "You know it, and I know it."
"Look, I'm not planning on cheating on Robbie with anybody."
"You should," Justin said. "Monogamy is unnatural."
"Maybe it is for you, but it's not for me and Robbie. We're in love, and we would never do anything to hurt each other. I almost lost him for good, and I won't risk that again."
"Well, I don't like him or his retarded brother, and you're a fool for getting married."
"Fine," Blair said. "If that's how you feel, then don't come to the wedding."
"Fine, I won't!"

"You mean to tell me you're not going to your own brother's wedding?" Ruby said.
"He doesn't want me there," Justin shrugged. Since her marriage to Charles, Ruby had moved into his charming cottage, leaving Justin alone in the apartment above the gym.
"Of course he does," she glanced around the apartment distastefully. "Just look at this place. It's filthy!"

An Admission of Weakness

"So?"
"So you're not usually a slob. Do you want to tell me what's wrong?"
"Nope," he continued studying his phone.
"No, you'd rather sulk and act like a child," she said disgustedly. "You're a grown man, for god's sake."
"Go away, Grandma," he said impatiently.
"I own part of this business," she reminded him. "I can be here any time I want."
"But this is my apartment now," he retorted.
"I'm going to the store to buy you some diapers. You may as well dress like a baby if you're going to be one," she said before walking away.

Robbie and Blair were married two weeks later in the Butterfield's living room. Sue Jameson, a former teacher of Blair's, officiated the ceremony.
Blair and Robbie wore matching black tuxedoes with scarlet bowties and cummerbunds, while Carter and Rhett's, as the best men, were black.
Robbie's family arrived a few days before the wedding, and Naomi and June fitted his sisters with matching scarlet dresses and heels so they could stand up with their brother. Katie and Camilla were dressed in scarlet as well.
Naomi took Flora to the showroom and picked out an original mother dress for each of them,

An Admission of Weakness

compliments of Snake and June. Flora was overjoyed to own an actual original gown and couldn't stop smiling.
"I feel like a girl again," she whirled around as she studied her reflection.
She disappeared mysteriously for a whole day before the wedding but refused to tell anyone where she had been.
The house was decorated with dozens of red and white rose garlands and bouquets, and the living room was cleared of furniture to make way for two dozen white chairs with red sashes. Many of Blair's extended family members disapproved of a same-sex wedding, so they opted to skip the event. That was hurtful to Blair, but it wasn't unexpected. Neither was he surprised by Justin's absence. But he was happy that at least Andres, Major, Ebony, and Simon were there.
Blair wished things could have been different with his brother, but at least his father was being supportive. Surprisingly, he and Robbie seemed to be fast friends, and Blair suspected it had something to do with their time together in Urbana.
The rest of his family made Flora and Aunt Rosetta and the girls feel welcome, he was glad to see. His mother and Robbie's mother were becoming quite good friends in spite of coming from two vastly different cultures.

An Admission of Weakness

The guests found their seats while Ian played a number of classical and pop selections on the piano. Finally, Danielle stood up and sang a slow, sweet version of Starship's 'Nothing's Gonna Stop us Now' while her grandfather accompanied her.

Blair had told her tentatively about the wedding, unsure how she would react. To his surprise, she was happy for him and Robbie and offered to sing at the event. Robbie was not aware that she knew how he had influenced her mother to change her ways, and she would be forever grateful to him. She was also indebted to him for setting into motion all the events that led to her reuniting with Ian.

Robbie and Blair walked down the center aisle while Danielle sang, and they stood in front of the fireplace with Sue.

Most of the ceremony was a blur to Robbie and Blair, but it didn't matter. They were too happy to care about anything except spending the rest of their lives together.

Carter dropped a garbage bag in the trash bin by the garage. The reception was still going strong in the house.

"So you decided to show up after all," he frowned when he looked up and saw his son.

"I came for the food," Justin said sullenly.

An Admission of Weakness

"You refused to come to the wedding, and now you expect food?" Carter said. "Sorry, but it doesn't work like that."
"Fine," Justin shrugged and turned away.
"If you apologize to Blair for missing his wedding, you can have some food."
"No thanks," Justin started to walk away.
"Justin, wait," his father said. "What's going on with you?"
"Nothing."
"Something's wrong," Carter said. "Why don't you tell me what it is? Maybe I can help."
"You can't help," Justin said. "I'll figure it out myself."
"Figure what out?"
"Nothing."
"Okay," Carter sighed. "I won't push you. But I'm here whenever you want to talk."
"Thanks. I'll see you later," Justin dug his hands into his pockets and walked away.
"Come on back and have some food," Carter said. "Never let it be said I turned away one of my children."
He put an arm around Justin's shoulders and guided him into the kitchen.
"Well, I'm surprised to see you," Ruby said when she saw Justin with his dad.
"Fix yourself a plate," Naomi said briskly. "We missed you."
Justin silently filled a plate with a half dozen sliders, pasta salad, and some desserts.

An Admission of Weakness

"Go on in and say hello to the family," Naomi gave him a little push. "They've been asking for you."

Justin sat down on a stair tread on the wide staircase. A few relatives stopped to talk to him, but he had little to say. He focused on his food until someone sat down beside him.

"Your brother was really hurt you didn't come," Robbie said.

"He's the one who told me not to," Justin said sourly.

"Because of what you said," Robbie said. "He wanted you here, and you know it."

"I don't need a lecture from you or your idiot baby-talking brother."

"Okay, I've had enough of you making fun of him," Robbie said angrily. "If you want to make fun of someone, make fun of me. But leave him alone. He's never done anything to you."

"I wouldn't know where to start making fun of you," Justin said.

"You think you're a big man, don't you?" Robbie said. "Well, if you're so tough, let's go outside right now, and you can prove it."

"That's a laugh," Justin snorted. "A pussy like you wants to fight me? You couldn't hurt a fly."

"Then you should have no problem coming outside with me," Robbie stood up.

"You've got to be kidding," Justin laughed.

An Admission of Weakness

"I'm not kidding," Robbie said. "I'll fight you right now unless you're afraid I'll whip your ass."

"Fine," Justin set his plate down and followed Robbie to the front door.

Before Justin could throw a punch, Robbie simultaneously shoved him and hooked a foot behind his. Justin landed on his back, and Robbie sat down on him.

Justin blinked with astonishment and then bodily lifted Robbie off himself. He tried a right cross, but Robbie ducked away and repeated his earlier move. Once again, Justin found himself flat on the ground.

"I can keep doing this all day," Robbie grinned. "You're a pretty lousy fighter."

Justin shoved him away and got to his feet. This time, his fist connected with Robbie's jaw, and Robbie lost his balance and fell. Justin was on him in an instant and pummeled him until he was abruptly tackled from the side.

Blair had seen what was happening and immediately went to his husband's defense. With a fury he had rarely felt, he repeatedly hit his brother until his father and Dillon pulled him away.

"Stop it!" Carter shouted.

Andres and Major held Justin back while Rhett ran to Robbie's side and helped him sit up.

"Awe you okay?" he asked frantically.

An Admission of Weakness

Flora rushed over and held a napkin to Robbie's bleeding nose.
"What the hell's the matter with you?" Charles slapped Justin on the back of the head.
Unexpectedly, Rhett ran at Justin and hurled himself at him. He knocked Justin off balance and started hitting him.
"No one hurts my bwother!" he yelled angrily.
Andres held him back, Major restrained Justin, and Carter and Dillon continued to keep Blair from going after his brother.
"That's enough!" Carter roared.
"He started it," Justin panted and pointed at Robbie. "I was minding my own business."
"Justin, get in the house this minute," Naomi glowered at him.
"It was his fault," Justin said defensively.
"Get in the house before you find yourself fighting me!" Naomi said sharply. "Now go!"

"Well, either Robbie or Rhett got a few blows in," Naomi placed an icepack on Justin's bruised eye.
"Leave it," he scowled and pushed her hand away.
"You leave it," she said sternly. "Now tell me what's wrong."
"Nothing's wrong."
"The only way you're leaving this house is in a body bag unless you tell me what the hell is wrong with you," she said.

An Admission of Weakness

"Mama," he grinned at her attempt at a threat. "Did you just say hell?"

"Talk, or I'll tell Grandma you're stealing from the business."

"I'm not stealing from the business!" he said indignantly.

"It won't matter after she gets through with you," Naomi said. "Now talk!"

"I can't talk about it with you," he said.

"Why not?"

"Because I...I did something kind of stupid," he said hesitantly.

"What did you do?"

"Can I tell Dad instead?" he asked.

"Fine. I'll send him in here, and you have one chance to tell him," she said. "If you don't, Mama and I will hold you down until you talk."

"So tell me about it," Carter said grimly as he sat down in a kitchen chair.

"I kind of did something I shouldn't have," Justin said.

"What?" Carter asked patiently.

"I slept with Isabella's best friend," Justin eyed his father uneasily.

"I thought you and Isabella were getting serious," Carter frowned.

"I didn't plan it," Justin said. "She came to the gym and flirted with me."

"I see," Carter nodded. "And Isabella found out about it and broke up with you."

An Admission of Weakness

"It wasn't my fault," Justin insisted. "She came on to me. What was I supposed to do? Say no?"
"Yes, that was exactly what you were supposed to do!" Carter snapped. "Don't you care about Isabella?"
"Of course I care about her," Justin said.
"Just not enough to keep from sleeping with her friend," Carter said dryly. "Don't you see what a betrayal that was to her? From not only you but her friend as well."
"I didn't do it to her."
"No, you did it to her friend," Carter said dryly. "And by screwing her friend, you screwed yourself and Isabella out of any future you might have had."
"We're not married," Justin said. "I'm free to fuck anyone I want."
"You are now that she dumped your sorry ass," Carter agreed. "I don't blame her for breaking up with you."
"I didn't think she'd find out."
"Justin, I can't believe what I'm hearing. You're trying to justify cheating on the person you care about, and then you're upset because you got caught and she ended things between you.

"That's not how a man acts, son. If you wanted to have sex with this other young woman, you should have talked to Isabella first. If she agreed that you were both free to be with other

An Admission of Weakness

people, then I suppose it would have been okay.

"Obviously, she has deep feelings for you, and you treated them as if they didn't matter to you. Do you have any idea how hurt she must be? Do you even care?"

"Of course I care," Justin said. "But Amy wanted me, and I didn't want to say no."

"Then you don't care enough," Carter said. "Isabella apparently isn't the woman for you. Or more correctly, you're not the man for her. She deserves someone who loves her and puts her above his own selfish desires."

"Monogamy is unnatural," Justin said. "Men aren't meant to be with just one woman."

"That's not a justification for cheating and lying," Carter said. "If you don't want to be monogamous, then be honest with whomever you're involved."

"But what do I do about Isabella?" Justin asked. "I don't want to lose her."

"Why? There are a thousand more like her," Carter said. "If you start now, you might be able to have sex with all of them in the next few years or so. In the meantime, Isabella will move on and find the right man for her. Clearly, that isn't you."

"But I don't want her to find someone else."

"Justin, you can't have it both ways. You think she should be faithful to you while you go out

An Admission of Weakness

and sleep with whoever you want. Why should she settle for someone like that?

"You have to make a choice here," Carter said. "Either make a commitment to Isabella, or let her move on while you sleep with every woman who comes into your gym."

"I only slept with Amy," Justin said. "I haven't been with anyone else since Isabella and I started dating."

"So why Amy? Why not a dozen others?"

"I don't know," Justin said. "It's one wedding after another around here all of a sudden, like everyone has to be married to prove something."

"You think people get married to prove something?" Carter said. "You clearly have no idea what marriage is about. You're either not ready for a commitment, or you're afraid of it. In either case, you have to let Isabella go."

"I don't want to," Justin said. "I want her back."

"So you can go out and sleep with other women while she sits at home waiting for you?"

"What was I supposed to do when Amy seduced me? Not sleep with her?"

"Justin, you have some serious growing up to do. And if I was you, I'd get on with it before you end up old and alone."

An Admission of Weakness

CHAPTER FORTY-SEVEN

Ruby and Katie tended to Blair and Robbie in the downstairs bathroom while Flora and Rhett sat on the side of the tub.

"Who started it?" Ruby asked while she held ice to Blair's knuckles.

"I guess I did," Robbie admitted. "He called Rhett a name, and I decided I wasn't going to listen to it anymore. I challenged him to a fight."

"So Justin started it," Katie said dryly. "What's with him lately? He's been in a foul mood for weeks now."

She cleaned his split lip and placed a little piece of sterile tape on the corner of it to hold it together.

"I don't know for sure," her grandmother said. "But I haven't seen Isabella around for several weeks. I think they might have broken up."

"He was probably screwing around on her," Blair said.

"What makes you say that?" Rhett asked.

"He told me I was an idiot for getting married because he thinks monogamy is unnatural," Blair said.

"It's that misogynistic, toxic masculinity," Robbie winced while Katie rubbed antiseptic on his eyebrow and forehead. "Guys like that think they can treat women any way they want."

An Admission of Weakness

"They think women are just sex objects," Blair added.

"He's slept with every woman around," Katie said. "Even a couple that are married."

"Oh my god, please tell me you're joking," Ruby groaned. "Surely even he knows better than that."

"He knows better, but he doesn't care," Blair said wryly. "Women he sleeps with are like a trophy. Married women are the ultimate prize."

"Maybe he an Isabella have an understanding," Katie said.

"Isabella's not that kind of woman," Ruby said. "Amy Sanders has been hanging around the gym lately. Of course, he gets lots of attention from all the women."

"Amy was Isabella's best friend in school," Blair said. "I wouldn't put it past him to sleep with her."

"What name did he call Rhett?" Flora asked.

"I'd rather not tell you," Robbie said uneasily.

"It doesn't bother me," Rhett said. "You can tell her."

"Tell me," she said sternly.

"Baby-talking idiot," Robbie said reluctantly.

"Retarded," Blair added.

"A stupid baby," Katie said. "But he calls everyone names. Don't take it personally, Rhett."

"I don't," Rhett shrugged. "I know he's a jerk."

An Admission of Weakness

"He's just young and stupid," Robbie said. "He thinks with his hormones instead of his brain. He'll grow out of it."
"I'm not so sure," Flora said grimly.

"Okay, you and I are going to have this out right now," Blair rolled his tuxedo shirt sleeves up and faced his brother in the back yard.
"You don't want to fight me, man," Justin said. "I've been working out a lot."
"I'll fight you," Major scowled. "We'll see how brave you are picking on someone bigger than you."
"Let him take me and Blair on," Robbie crossed his arms defiantly.
"Twy the thwee of us," Rhett added coldly. "You fight Wobbie or Blair, you're gonna have to fight me too."
"I'll gladly fight Justin," Andres grinned. "It would be a pleasure to teach him a lesson."
"Stand back, boys," Flora removed her heels and stepped in front of them on the soft grass. "Ma will handle this."
She turned to Naomi and Carter, who were standing on the verandah with the rest of the family.
"Do you mind?" she asked.
"Be my guest," Naomi grinned.
"I'll get you some boxing gloves if you can wait just a minute," Ruby offered with a wink.
"Justin, do not fight," Carter said sternly.

An Admission of Weakness

"Relax," Justin rolled his eyes and grinned. "I'm not going to fight some old woman."
"You think I'm old?" Flora said.
"Well, you're not young," Justin said.
With a sudden kick, Flora sent Justin to his knees, painfully holding his injured testicles.
"Hey!" he cried indignantly.
"What? Did an old woman just kick you in the balls?" Flora said innocently.
"Yes, you did," he grimaced.
"What are you gonna do about it?" she said.
"Nothing," he said sourly.
"Why not?"
"Because I can't hit a woman," he said.
"Sure you can," she said. "You think it's okay to sleep with us, cheat on us, lie to us, treat us like sex objects. Why can't you hit us?"
He didn't answer, so she slapped him across the face a few times.
"Why can't you hit women?" she asked again.
"Dad!" Justin implored his father.
"Don't look at me," Carter shrugged and hid his smile. "This is between you and Flora."
"Come on, Justin," Flora said. "You thought it was okay to hit my sons and your brother. I'm givin' you permission to hit me too."
"Ma, you can't let him hit you," Robbie said.
"Justin, if you hit my mother, I will kill you."
"And I'll kill you again," Rhett added.

An Admission of Weakness

"Boys, Ma's got this," Flora said sternly. She turned back to Justin. "You have permission to hit me. So let's fight."
"I'm not going to fight you," Justin got warily to his feet.
Flora acted like she was going to hit him again but kicked him in the groin instead.
"Goddammit!" Justin groaned. He doubled over and glared up at her. "Stop it!"
"I'm just gonna keep hitting you 'til you hit me back," Flora said.
Angrily, he stood up and took a swing at her. She ducked away and kicked him yet again. He went down and curled into a ball. She grasped an earlobe and twisted it firmly.
"Did you call my son names?"
"I was just joking," he protested.
"Did you call my son names?" she repeated.
"Yes."
"Did you cheat on your girlfriend?" she asked.
"Stop it!" he cried out in pain.
"Did you cheat on Isabella?" she twisted his ear harder. "Answer me!"
"I didn't mean to," he cried out and tried to pull away from her.
"Did you cheat on Isabella?" Flora repeated. She maintained her grasp on his ear.
"Yes!" he cried.
"Yes what?"
"I cheated on Isabella," he yelled.
"And you think that's okay?" she demanded.

An Admission of Weakness

"No," he said.
"Is it okay to treat women like sex objects?"
"No!" he yelled.
"Is it okay to lie to women?"
"No!"
"Do you think you're better than women just 'cause you have a dick?"
"No!"
"Don't lie to me. Do you think you're better than women just 'cause you have a dick?"
"Yes!"
"Does it make you feel like a big man to sleep with women and break their hearts?"
"No," he said.
"That's another lie, and you know it," she said. "Does it make you feel like a big man to sleep with women and break their hearts?"
She twisted his ear more.
"Yes!" he cried. "Dad! Help!"
"You're doing fine, son," Carter grinned.
"Are you gonna apologize to Isabella and Blair and Robbie and Rhett?" Flora asked.
"Yes," Justin said. He had tears in his eyes by this time.
"Yes what?"
"Yes, I'll apologize to them. Let me go."
"Are you goin' to treat women with respect from now on?"
"Yes," Justin said tearfully.
"Yes, what?"
"I'll treat women with respect from now on."

An Admission of Weakness

"Okay then," Flora released him and helped him to his feet. "I'm gonna wait right here while you apologize to these boys and call Isabella."

"That's the single greatest thing I've ever witnessed," Blair laughed.
He and Robbie were lying in Blair's bed that night with his head on Robbie's hairy chest.
"Ma would have made a great football player," Robbie laughed with him. "Poor Justin."
"Poor Justin my ass. He had it coming," Blair said.
"At least he'll never look at women quite the same way," Robbie chuckled.
"Forget Justin," Blair moved to lie on top of his husband. "This is our wedding night, baby. I think that calls for something special."
"Do you want some more champagne?"
"No," Blair said seductively. "I want to do something we've never done."
"And what would that be?"
Blair whispered into his ear and then waited for Robbie's response with a grin.
"Blair Butterfield, you are a dirty, dirty boy."
Blair rummaged in his closet and held up the leather harness from his videos as well as the padded leather ankle and wrist restraints.
"I can't believe you kept those," Robbie chuckled. "You were unbelievably sexy in that

An Admission of Weakness

harness, even though you were fucking Tina and Fred."

"I want you to wear it tonight," Blair smiled wickedly. "I'll wear the cuffs and be at your mercy."

Robbie pulled him down and kissed him fiercely, and the two men made love until the early morning hours.

An Admission of Weakness

EPILOGUE

Robbie and Blair settled into their new bedroom for the first time. It was a pleasant, airy room with a fireplace, large windows, tray ceiling, and an attached dressing room and master bath.

It had been a year to the day since their wedding. Their new house was located on Green Grove's east side, a few blocks from Carter and Naomi. They bought the modern, three-bedroom brick home from an elderly man who was moving to Minnesota to be with his children.

It featured everything they were looking for: fireplaces, an open floor plan, finished basement, front porch, and large back yard with a patio, built-in grill, and hot tub. Their neighbors were a doctor and his wife, the chief of police, and the bank president.

The two of them had admired the house for months, but unfortunately, it wasn't for sale.

"I wish Mr. Neathery would decide to sell," Blair said one day at the dinner table.

"Me too," Robbie sighed. "It's the perfect house."

"Why don't you look for something between here and Chicago?" Carter suggested. "Then it wouldn't be such a long commute for either of you."

An Admission of Weakness

"We want our kids to go to Green Grove schools," Robbie said. "Besides, our families are here."

"Perhaps you should talk to Mr. Neathery," Ruby said.

"I tried that," Blair said.

"You did?" Robbie frowned. "What did he say?"

"He said he couldn't sell the house to anyone," Blair said.

"Why not?" Naomi asked.

"Because he already sold it to Robbie and me," Blair watched Robbie's face.

Robbie merely stared at him blankly.

"Robbie, did you hear Blair?" Carter grinned.

"He sold the house to us?" Robbie said disbelievingly. "Y-you mean we bought the house?"

"We bought it," Blair grinned. "It's ours. Or it will be in a few weeks."

"He's been dying to tell you all week," Naomi chuckled.

"You all knew?" Robbie glanced around the table.

The whole family laughed and nodded.

Camilla and Ashura were in town for the weekend as usual. Since their marriage, they had worked together in his clinic to do whatever they could to help the impoverished citizens of Chicago's Southside. It was

An Admission of Weakness

rewarding work, but quite challenging, and they welcomed the weekend respites in Green Grove with the Butterfield and Lee families. Dillon and Katie and the twins had come for dinner since Camilla, her husband, and Robbie were all going to be home.

Both the ranch and the Talbot Saddler Company were thriving, and Katie was enjoying her part time nursing job at the hospital. Besides being a mother, she was actually caring for people, which suited her warm and caring nature better than a desk job in an office somewhere. The twins were doing well, and Ruby, Naomi, and Marci eagerly took turns babysitting when Katie had to work.

Ruby and Charles took most of their meals with Naomi and Carter unless one couple or the other had special plans. The pair continued to volunteer their time with the Green Grove school system, and Ruby worked part time at the gym.

Now that Charles Jr. and Cheryl's relationship had been rejuvenated, they often came to visit his father. Danielle and Ian were also frequent visitors to the cottage.

With their connections and – let's face it – their money, Charles Jr. and Cheryl were able to hire an agent for Ian and Danielle, and the talented pair began to perform concerts all around the metropolitan area. Thanks to their agent and Danielle's beautiful soprano voice, their names

An Admission of Weakness

became familiar all over the city, and requests for concerts began to pop up all over the Midwest.

Naomi was the happiest she had been since her children were small. Carter was once again the man she had fallen in love with, her children were all nearby and happy and successful, and her job at the W.H. Abernathy House of Fashion was exciting and gratifying.

Carter and Naomi insisted that Blair continue to live with them until he and Robbie figured out their living arrangements. With Robbie working fifty hours a week at Morgan Enterprises, it was all he could do to get to Green Grove on the weekends. When he couldn't make it to the Butterfield's home, Blair would go to Chicago to be with him. Fortunately, Cheryl allowed him to keep using the temporary apartment in which the company had set him up. With the money he saved the company in his first year, he had earned his salary three times over, and she wasn't about to risk him going somewhere else. She provided a company car for him to drive back and forth and gave him a raise to ensure his loyalty.

She needn't have bothered, Robbie thought, because he loved his job. The work itself, the benefits, the wonderful people, and Cheryl and Charles Jr. He had not expected to like the couple based on his experience with Danielle, but they were actually pretty terrific.

An Admission of Weakness

She even paid for a home office to be put in his new house so that he could work from home part of the time. He still had to go to the office two to three days per week, but he didn't mind. Blair started his teaching career a few weeks after their wedding, and he was enjoying it immensely. Green Grove students were taught to value each other for their differences as well as their similarities. They were also taught the un-whitewashed version of America's past, including the atrocities committed against Native Americans and the Black community. Even LGBTQIA+ studies were included, and bullying was a zero-tolerance offense.
Blair was soon offered the assistant coach position for the football team, and he eagerly accepted it. He was excited to be part of the sport again.

"No one told me you bought a house," Justin frowned.
"That's because you can't keep a secret," Camilla chuckled.
"I resent that," Justin said indignantly.
"You couldn't wait to tell me Mama was having an affair," she reminded him.
"That wasn't a secret," he said. "That was just something I thought was happening."
The whole family laughed, and he joined in sheepishly.

An Admission of Weakness

"Okay, but keeping a secret isn't always good," he said. "Look at the secrets Katie and Mama kept. And Dad's keeping a secret right now."
"What secret are you keeping?" Ruby asked.
"Justin, eat your dinner," Carter said. "My, these rolls are so soft."
"Carter?" Naomi frowned. "What have you done?"
"Fine," Carter said resignedly. "I bought you a special present for our anniversary."
"It's a trip to Hawaii," Justin said. "You're going to stay in the Morgan's beach house for two weeks."
"Hawaii?" Naomi said excitedly. "I've always wanted to go!"
"I know," Carter leaned over and kissed her. "So Justin, what was that about you being able to keep a secret?"
The whole family laughed and shouted happily at one another for the next few minutes.
Justin's business was booming, and he had hired two new personal trainers, a yoga/Zumba/Pilates instructor, and a receptionist to help with the influx of customers. The gym was now open twenty-four hours a day to handle the crowds.

"I'm sleeping 'til noon," Blair yawned.
"We can't," Robbie automatically yawned in response. "We're meeting everyone for brunch at Rhett's at eleven."

An Admission of Weakness

Three days before Robbie and Blair's wedding last year, Flora called on Brad Jameson, the leading realtor in Green Grove. Together, they met with the owners of a popular restaurant located in a mansion west of the downtown. The graceful house had once belonged to a member of the town's founding family. Its current owners turned the first floor of the huge house into an elegant steak house while maintaining the second and third floors as their residence.

They now wanted to retire and sell the establishment, so a deal was struck, and Flora was handed the keys.

A few days after Blair and Robbie's wedding, she made her announcement at the Butterfield's dinner table.

"I hate to see you leave," Robbie said unhappily.

"Me too," Vaneeta said.

"Wobbie, I've been thinking," Rhett said hesitantly. "Maybe I should go back with Ma."

"What?" Robbie quickly hid his displeasure.

"I still haven't found a job here, and you and Blair don't need me awound being a third wheel."

"You're not a third wheel," Blair said. "We love having you around."

"Actually, I've got a surprise for Rhett and Robbie and the girls," Flora said. "We ain't

An Admission of Weakness

goin' back to Mississippi 'cept to pack up our things."

"What do you mean?" Robbie frowned.

"I can't leave you with these northerners all by yourself," Flora grinned mischievously. "Rhett's always wanted to manage his own restaurant, and I know everything there is to know about runnin' one. Well, I just happen to be the new owner of a restaurant right here in town."

"How did you buy a restaurant?" Robbie looked confused. "You've only been here a week."

"It don't matter how it happened," Flora chuckled. "The point is, Rhett has a job managin' our new restaurant. And me and Rhett and the girls and Aunt Rosetta have a fancy new place to live right here."

"I'm going to manage a westauwant?" Rhett said disbelievingly.

"You shor are," Flora smiled. "And not just any restaurant, but the fanciest place in town."

"The Steak House?" Carter looked surprised.

"That's the one," Flora said. "It's right next door to June's house, the one called Rosehill Manor."

"Wow," Charles whistled. "That's one of the most popular places in town."

"Carter and I love going there," Naomi said. "It's so elegant."

An Admission of Weakness

"Wobbie, did you hear that?" Rhett smiled widely. "We're all staying in Gween Gwove!"
"I heard," Robbie said happily. "We're all going to be together."
"Families stick together," Flora smiled.

With Flora's knowledge and experience, the month long transition from the restaurant's former owners was fairly seamless. The public quickly grew very fond of Rhett and Flora and their southern charm.

As a housewarming gift for Blair and Robbie's new home, Flora invited everyone to the restaurant for brunch.

"Robbie, where does this mattress go?" Rhett hollered.
With Carter's encouragement, Rhett had worked with an excellent speech therapist for the past year. Carter helped him with his exercises, and as a result, his speech impediment had all but disappeared. With his speech and limp corrected, his self-confidence reached an all time high.
"Bedroom at the top of the stairs," Robbie yelled back.
"You heard him," Rhett said to the person on the other end of the unwieldy object. "Move your ass, loser."

An Admission of Weakness

"He works out twice a week in the gym, and suddenly he's Arnold Schwarzenegger," Justin grinned good-naturedly.
"One of these days, he'll be able to whip your butt," Isabella patted Justin's ass affectionately.
Over the past year, Rhett and Justin had become good friends. No matter what insult Justin threw at him, Rhett came back with one better. It soon became a contest to see who could come up with the best one, and Justin began to see Rhett in a new light. The young man had not had an easy road, yet he remained cheerful and undeterred. He never let anything get him down, and Justin respected that. Also, he was envious of Robbie and Rhett's close relationship, and he endeavored to have the same kinship with his own brother.
He had spent the last year working to earn Isabella's trust back. She was special to him, more so than any other woman, although he still wasn't completely sold on the whole monogamy thing. Still, he didn't want to lose Isabella, so the two of them were open and honest with one another.

Blair snuggled up against Robbie and sighed contentedly.
"It's been a wild five years, hasn't it, baby?"
"It certainly has," Robbie agreed and put an arm around him.

An Admission of Weakness

"But I think we're stronger for having gone through all the craziness."

"I'm definitely less inhibited when it comes to sex now," Robbie grinned.

"That's for sure, you wild man," Blair chuckled. "But I wasn't talking about sex. Our relationship is what it is because you made me come to terms with who I really was."

"You did that on your own," Robbie said. "You should be proud of yourself."

"I guess so," Blair said. "I see now that when you're strong, you have no reason to lie to yourself or others; the truth comes easy. Lying only comes easy when you're weak."

"That's enough philosophizing for tonight," Robbie said. "I love you. Now shut up and go to sleep."

"Did you just tell me to shut up?"

"Yes, I did," Robbie grinned. "And if you're smart, you'll do as I say."

Blair sat up and straddled his husband's naked pelvis with his bare ass.

"You think I'm afraid of you?" he said.

"Aren't you?"

"You should be afraid of me," Blair raised an eyebrow wickedly. "Because I'm going to fuck you so hard you'll be walking funny for a week."

"So stop talking already and get to it," Robbie grinned. "But put on the harness first."

An Admission of Weakness

"I love you, Robert E. Lee," Blair leaned down and kissed him. "You are the best thing that's ever happened to me."
"We're the best thing that's ever happened to us," Robbie chuckled.

And so Robbie and Blair, Rhett, Flora and her daughters, Aunt Rosetta, Carter and Naomi, Katie and Dillon, Camilla and Ashura, Justin and Isabella, Danielle and Ian, Charles Jr. and Cheryl, and Charles and Ruby all lived happily ever after.

THE END

An Admission of Weakness

ACKNOWLEDGMENTS

The characters in this book are fictional, and Green Grove is a fictional town. However, they're very real in my imagination. As I've said in my other books, I am very fond of the citizens of this wonderful community.
I wish the world was as utopian as Green Grove. Stories there always have a happy ending, the good guy always wins, and true love conquers all. I go to Green Grove whenever I need solace from an increasingly grim world.

As always, I dedicate this book to my wonderful and patient husband Eric.